0

1

JUDAH'S PROPHECY

G. AUGUSTINE

To Mom, Dad, Micah, and Gideon.

PROLOGUE

My father and mother died when I was fourteen.

"GET UP! NOW!" Father yelled into my ears. His frightened look told me that this wasn't one of our drills again. It was the first time I saw him horrified. I remembered his features so vividly— long curly hair, hazel eyes with dark circles under them, strong cheekbones, and a sharp jawline. There were so many scars on his neck and face that it was impossible to count.

The day had come. I flinched in my cot, stumbling out of my bedsheets. Omar, my younger brother, was still paralyzed by sleep. I grabbed his shoulders, shaking him awake.

"Omar," I said. His eyes fluttered open, but he quickly tried to go back to sleep. I rolled my eyes, shaking him again. "Wake up, please."

"I wanna go to sleep."

"We don't have a choice." That made him sit up. "We have to go. We're under attack."

Our living room was in shambles. Seats topped over, cupboards wide open. Father was busy trying to gather as many supplies as he could. Mother was stuffing our clothes into her large satchel. Against our front door was a wall of chairs to block anyone from the outside.

We watched our parents hypnotized in a trance. Father clenched his teeth after pulling his old sword and bowing out the pantry.

Mother cursed under her breath after toppling a vase, slicking her black hair back in annoyance. While our parents moved like worker ants, we stood still like statues. We had always wondered what it would be like if the Craleans raided us. The only solution we had was to run and never look back.

Our family lived in the poor fishing town of Jaawed. We didn't have enough money to travel to our country's capital, Pyria, where there were havens of refugee camps, offering safety for those who could survive.

Father moved to Jaawed after discharging himself from the army and meeting my mother. They then lived in a cottage on the outskirts of town, being honest farmers to provide for the ongoing war. When it was safe enough, we took camping trips or trekked along the routes of trade to explore our lavish planet.

It was called the Dragon's War, a careless battle fought between my home country, Basalia, and the country just across the Kigamouth Lake: Crale Imperium. Teachings from scholars record that the war began after Crale demanded Basalia give up their lands from the city of Pyria to the city of Shekka. Crale claimed it was righteous land for the empire, and sent an ultimatum to Basalia. If they did not comply, Crale threatened bloodshed.

Pyria was the promised land for all Basalians, and when citizens heard the news of the ultimatum, most were begging for the council to go to war. They came in thinking it would be a glorious legendary fight that would be the talk of the 14th century. What they failed to realize is that the war carried on much further than they had anticipated.

When the war's anniversary came around, Basalia held parades to remember the dead. Fathers, wives, sisters, daughters, sons, brothers, and friends died every day on both sides. Mages and witches fought as knights and squires clashed their swords in the middle of forests and fields.

It made sense why my father was so urgent. His family was on the line, and with every second that ticked, equaled how many steps left it took for the army of Crale to reach our doorstep.

Knock.

Everyone froze. My mother covered her mouth with one of her hands to shelter herself from making any sudden sound. Gripping his sword in anticipation, Father slicked his hair back with a shudder. My brother's entangled fingers vibrated against mine while I gulped in fear.

We were too late. The town guard failed. Nothing was stopping Crale from pillaging and destroying our village now. Before a tear slipped out my eye, Father caressed my face. His always valiant gaze was now filled with worry.

But other than fear, acceptance dripped out of him that day.

"Hide. Now," he whispered through clenched teeth. Mother nodded in agreement; her prying eyes begged us to stay hidden.

I dragged Omar into our pantry, left of the living room. Leaving a small crack in the door, Omar and I squished ourselves against crates and pouches of food and supplies.

With a slam, our front door exploded into pieces, shattering into hundreds of splinters and planks. Mother hid behind Father, their stares vigilant.

"Hello, peasants," a booming voice said. A dark aura filled our living room. Still, Father didn't reply to the figure who had walked inside. It was a short goblin who wore a black and yellow cloak, reminiscent of the Cralean flag. Two human soldiers entered from behind, their swords drawn.

"What the hell do you want?" Father's voice was shaky. The goblin's eyes were a glowing red, differing from everyone else in the room. His pupils were a dark crimson, the outer part of his eyes a voided black.

"I'll offer you two choices." It took a while for him to unsheath the blade from the strap on his back. "I can either split you in half or cut off your head."

The metal blade was already stained with a bloody, light hue. Omar gripped my bicep, curling against me for some warmth. I tried to stop myself from hyperventilating, only focusing on my father. He stepped back from the goblin's trifling words.

"Don't think you can kill me so easily," Father said, his fear covered with fake confidence. He gulped, raised his sword to the goblin's eyes, and shook his head. "Don't you underestimate me, you little green—"

The goblin took one step forward and grabbed Father by the throat.

He was nothing to the goblin.

Only a pile of filth.

"Let go of him!" Mother shouted in alarm. She ran up to the soldiers, only to be punched in the throat by one of the goblin's underlings. My brother and I choked out a quiet sob, doing our best to not make a sound.

"Let's cut you in half, shall we?" he growled, twisting his mouth into a demonic smile. The goblin snatched the dagger from Father's hands, stabbing him over and over in the stomach. He laughed maniacally as Father's chest erupted in a mountain of blood, leaving stains on the walls.

My mother cried and begged for the goblin to stop, only for her pleas to fall on deaf ears. Father was already dead by the time the goblin stopped, his mouth agape, eyes morphed into a gray emptiness. As he gurgled blood, the goblin twisted the dagger deeper into his stomach. I gritted my teeth in anger. My cheeks became soaked with tears, as I tried turning away to shield myself from the abhorrent view.

I didn't weep for my father, knowing I might be next. The goblin released him from his grasp, and my father fell to his knees. *DAD, GET BACK UP!* The voices in my head screamed. *PLEASE!* With a flash, the blade of the goblin swung downward, separating the man that raised me into two.

I shrieked, slamming the door shut. Thank the Dragon that I had closed it quietly, knowing that I would've been dead in a heartbeat. The sound of a thump erupted my right eardrums before a second did the same on my left. I collapsed on the floor of the pantry and buried my face into my knees, crying as Omar sobbed into my shoulder. It was hard to weep in silence.

The goblin breathed heavily as his boots boomed on the wooden planks as he walked closer to the pantry door. My mother must be lying near it, because the goblin very clearly asked my mother, "Oh? You think I'm done with you?"

Mama sacrificed herself for both of us.

"Please. Please... No," she urged as his feet scuffled against the floor.

"You seem fun," he sneered. My eyes widened.

"NO! Please..." She cried.

It sounded like she was trying to crawl away, but the goblin had pulled her back, gripping her tightly as she screamed in agony. She cried for help for thirty long minutes, while the goblin growled, screeched, and shouted curses at my mother.

I didn't block out the sound of the blood. It oozed, squelched, and bubbled outside. With my palm on my mouth, I tried to imagine myself in a safe place, but I couldn't.

Omar seemed torn. He looked empty. We tried to stay silent. The goblin huffed, like a monster that wanted to quench its thirst for blood. I stayed still for what felt like hundreds of years, before clasping onto the doorknob and swinging it open.

Blood was drenched all over the walls. My father had been split in half, and his dead body was already covered with flies and maggots. Mother was dismembered. She was left on the floor with her limbs being separated from her body. The images in my mind that formed that day were etched into my brain forever, and I would always see the screaming image of my parents in pieces within my nightmares.

Everything faded into black darkness as the horrid expression in my mother's eyes was engraved into my soul. It was as if I faded out, but this particular moment was something that I couldn't remember at all. But the beautiful memories I had with my parents were gone, and what was left were the images of their deaths.

I had only remembered walking outside my home, with my brother holding my left arm. The air was tinted with smoke and gray, and the inner town was on fire. It was set ablaze, engulfed in an ocean of inferno. When I breathed in the polluted air, the only scent I got was pure death.

Omar and I took steps through the town road as we saw bodies upon bodies, all burned with the buildings around them. It seemed like Omar and I were the ones who survived. It was a magnificent stroke of luck, or perhaps, the hand of God who saved us.

I took a deep breath while walking, trying to erase the corpses out of my mind as I focused on carrying all of our belongings, or what was left of it. My eyes rested upon limbs everywhere, as the stone road was stained with liquid crimson, seeping into the cracks. At the center point of the Jaawed was a fountain. On the top was the flag of Crale, a black flag with a yellow sun in the middle of it.

As I walked away from the burning town that I used to call home, I set two goals in my mind. One, join the Basalian Army, and two:

Protect my Omar with my life.

"God, did you give up on me? Did you give up on me and Omar? Why do I have to live in this world of pain and suffering and greed and lust? Why can't I live normally, like how a child is supposed to be?"

- A journal entry from Kedar in 1432, in Pyria.

ACT ONE:
BROTHERHOOD
7 YEARS LATER.

Alfdan Prison, Crale Imperium.
150th day of the 1438th year.

ONE

P ain scorches from my back as my eyes flash open with
anger.

Memories of torture fill my vision, as I look around in the
cage they've kept me in. I hear the splashing of someone
walking through the murky puddles, with the cracking of a
whip filling the air.

My back burns again as I push myself out the bed. The
corners of my eyes begin to fade to black already. I gather the
strength to stop looking down at my filthy, gunk-covered feet.
Raising my head, I see a prison guard giving me a stink eye.
His brown, lifeless eyes glimmer at me. He wears a black tunic,
and a yellow armband on his left sleeve.

"You. Come to the mines. Now," he tells me coldly. A
tattoo streams across his neck, helping me catch his first name:
Hassan.

The conditions get worse by the day. Mold grows on the
cage floor. Metal crumbles and rusts. *This has to be a goddamn
war crime,* I think. Comfort and peace don't exist in Crale.

My vision blurs as I lean on the metal bars and keep myself steady. All of the malnourishment that my body's been subjected to has made me rot.

After my general died whilst trying to fight against the Craleans, we surrendered, since we were outnumbered and out-geared. I was the only one who insisted on fighting, but Omar had to stop me before I could get myself killed. Before long, I was tied up, tossed onto a carriage, and brought here. Alfdan Prison.

I've been here since the new year. Fifteen weeks. 150 days have passed, all with suffering and sorrow. As I walk down the hall, waddling with chains on my feet and hands, I reminisce about… simpler times. Mother. Father. Alive.

It's been seven years. I've lied, stolen, cheated, and killed to survive. Omar has never wanted to kill, that's the last thing he wants. Omar can barely swing a sword. Yet I've forced him to fight in the army with me.

I offer him a glance as I pass by his cell. Bruises and cuts cover his face. His hazel eyes have no emotion behind them as he scrunches his overgrown curls. A couple of days ago the guards beat him for trying to steal some bread. Since then he shivers at the sight of a yellow armband.

My feet splash against the stone tiles on the floor, murky with brown and gray. Basalia and Crale have forgotten about the spoils of war. The camps and the POWs, the dead husbands and wives.

I keep quiet to myself as we finally exit outside. The loincloth I'm wearing doesn't even make the effort to protect my skin from the impending heat. Hassan and I are greeted by the sights of the prison's courtyard.

My toes curl into the burning sand. I wince in pain every time I take a step. There's a familiar smell here. It's metallic, coppery even. It's blood. I take a deep breath, inhaling the somewhat comforting scent.

There's a podium in the middle of the courtyard. It's where they hang anyone they deem as a war criminal. Plenty of my comrades have ended up tied to the noose.

Most of Alfdan is made of captured Basalian soldiers. The others consist of murderers, robbers, and extortioners of Crale. But even they get better treatment than us. A special hatred resides for Basalia in Crale's heart.

From their hate I've earned things— there's a long, light jagged scar across my nose bridge now. But it makes sense. Craleans hate Basalians as much as Basalians hate Craleans. We hate each other for how much wrongdoing we've done.

Hassan and I approach the entrance of the mines: a cave opening near one of the courtyard's walls. It leads to a black hole of nothingness. I clench my eyebrows to relieve the sweat dripping down my forehead. The mines are cold, and it's easy to catch a disease. But, it's better than rotting in my cage.

It's hard to find a reason to live. The only one I can name is to keep my promise of protecting Omar. But I've failed in the worst way possible.

"Don't just stop," Hassan growls, prodding me. I realize I've been staring at the darkness for too long. "Go inside."

Sighing, I trek down the stairs to the mineshaft. With a grunt, I blink as my eyes lay upon a beautiful, spacious cavern, almost blinding me from reality. Shouting prisoners shake my eardrums as the faint glow of lanterns spreads through the cave.

Stalactites hang from the ceiling, and a wall of stalagmites surrounds me on the path to where I mine. The rush of an underground river weaves and turns next to the path. Flowstones pour out, hanging over my head. Chattering bats mingle above me as Hassan leads me on. It doesn't take long for us to arrive at the strip mines. A mile-long mined-out hallway stretches from left to right. Prisoners scour for rubies, golden ores, diamonds, anything they can get their hands on. For every gemstone, you'll get rewarded with a meal.

Getting emerald awards one piece of bread. A ruby can get you half, while a jade can get you one loaf. Hassan and I reach a branch of the strip mine, and he hands me a worn-out pickaxe, watching from a distance as I get to work. The stone cracks and falters with my strikes. *Maybe I can get a jade.* My hands quiver as I grunt and swing over and over.

I grit my teeth, tears almost leaking out of my eyes as I try to focus on the stone. After a few minutes of finding nothing, a touch on my right shoulder makes me jump. Turning around, there's an old man with long, sprawling hair. His eyes are grim with gray, matching the color of his hair.

"D-do you have any food?" he says. He's skinny, his collarbone and rib cage prodding at his skin. I don't dare to hesitate, having nothing to offer.

"No," I reply coldly, my stomach growling. The cracks of the stone drown out his needless complaining. He sighs, bare feet splashing on the floor before fading out into the darkness.

Soon enough, my mining session gets interrupted when someone shouts in the hallways. I grumble before peeking my head out to see the needless commotion. The old man's now struggling with a different guard as he tries swinging his pickaxe at him.

"HEY! KEEP WORKING!" Gripping his dagger, the guard shoves the old man to the ground. I shake my head in disappointment, knowing that I can't stop the inevitable.

"NO!" the bony man shouts, throwing his pickaxe to the ground. "I CAN'T TAKE THIS ANYMORE, GODDAMMIT! KILL ME!"

Roaring in frustration, the soldier glares back at the man in disgust, thrusting his blade forward. I watch in horror as the soldier stabs the man in the throat. My eyes widen as the soldier gawks, holding the old man still as he gurgles blood.

"Is this what you wanted?! DEATH?!" he spits. It's brutal; his blood starts to stain the stone floor red.

The soldier recoils his arm back, swiping his dagger at the dead man. His head comes flying off, bouncing off of the wall and landing on the floor in a horrific splat. I jump back after his hair brushes against my toes, the blood from his neck flooding the floor. The guard widens his eyes at me as I put both of my arms up in submission. But he smiles.

"You," the guard says, uniform soaked in blood. "Clean that up."

I grit my teeth in disgust. With the head on my left hand, and my right dragging his limp wrist, I hurl the dead man across the floor, his body leaving a trail of blood.

Prisoners watch as I drag the corpse through the sand in the courtyard. I push him over the ledge of the pit, and he lands on a pile of rotting arms and legs. Maggots and flies eat at the decomposing limbs. I glance away fast, trying to ignore his dead eyes staring at my soul.

As I walk back to the cave, voices clamor around the podium. When I turn my head, there are maybe fifty people surrounding the stage. I try glancing over the heads blocking my view. On the stage are a couple of guards and a tied-up figure.

"N-No, NO! Please!" They shout. I blink into consciousness. *Omar?*

As much as I want to be wrong, I'm not. Omar's on the podium, on his knees, restrained with rope. One of the guards has a dark, black aura surrounding their fingertips, mouthing a spell. *Mana-users. What the hell did Omar do to deserve a punishment from a mage?*

Phasing in and out of the crowd, I try getting to the front of the podium, not even having a plan in mind. I can't watch Omar meet his demise. The prisoners are chattering, shouting, and jeering. It's wrong; they enjoy watching his suffering. The guard puts a finger in the air, signaling everyone to quiet down as his aura-stained fingertips wrap around Omar's head.

"We captured this disgusting Basalian seasons ago, near Welock Chasm," the guard explains. He's a middle-aged goblin, maybe in his early 50s with green skin that gleams in the sun. It seems like everyone is in my way, blocking me unconsciously.

Goblins are short, so when I get closer I'm stunned to see a massive goblin covered in numerous battle scars. I walk, hyperventilating as he instills fear in me with his mere presence and daunting figure. If I get to him, he'll fling me into the sky even with my six-foot frame. The low growl of his voice only enhances the stench of pure evil in the air. "He has refused to obey the commands in our prison, knowing full well the consequences."

"Because he is a Basalian, he gets a special treat from us Craleans." He continues, smirking like a madman. The goblin raises one of his fists in the air, displaying the dark magic. "As one of the commanding guards, I took it upon myself to master the darkic arts!"

Darkic arts? I freeze. It's one of the three magical techniques mana-users possess.

"With this spell, this broken boy will be made anew. Perhaps he will now obey the glorious empire after we take his mind!"

The crowd whispers among themselves, and I stare straight into Omar's eyes. We lock eyes as he grits his teeth at me. The only message that I get is a spew of words and rage as if he accepts his fate.

"Filthy Basil trash," he continues, spitting into my brother's face. Before long, I find myself pushing people out of the way and throwing them on the ground in wrath. Clenching my fists, my bloodshot eyes widen, as I try to do anything I can to get closer to the podium. *Almost there. If you die, Omar, we die together. I don't care anymore.* "This Basalian spat on our guards, stole our meals, and refused to become a slave to our gracious empire!"

I scoff as prisoners cheer, putting their fists up like we're at some sort of damn rally. *Are they sane?!* My thoughts scream. *Crale is the one they are being imprisoned by!*

"We shall shed this man anew for his sins!!" he shouts. The crowd roars in unison, as I try clawing my way through, but it's too late. My brother's eyes widen in despair as the goblin recites something under his breath.

Gray energy expels out of his hands, surrounding Omar's head like a cloud of smoke. He falls to the ground, shivering as foam bubbles form out of his mouth. Omar screams in pain as his head shakes vigorously. I scream like a primal, tears streaming down my face as I try not to sob.

But his "execution" gets interrupted.

A duo of hooded figures with a black, golden-lined cloak hops down from the fortress walls. There's a symbol on their backs, displaying a mysterious golden piece of stone. Perhaps, a gemstone.

They wield small throwing knives, and they throw them at the guards below. Their shots hit perfectly, the soldiers immediately falling to the ground as the crowd disperses, trying to run away from the hooded figures. *What the hell? As if my day can't get any worse,* I think.

I stand still waiting by the podium, but the guards don't care to notice me. They just look at those two hooded figures in pure fear. The first one steps up to the lone goblin, as Omar convulses on the ground next to him. They surround him, as the green man put both of his hands up in defeat, trying to spare his life. One of them steps forward, not even glancing at Omar as the voice that comes out of their mouth is coarse and dark.

"Ah, this might be the one."

Hang in there, Omar. I'll come and get you, I think, trying to avoid eye contact with these mysterious people. The person who steps up grabs the goblin by the throat before glancing down at Omar. Through the hood, their jade eyes narrow. The goblin chokes from their grip, and he does his best to stay alive.

The other figure stands idly, glaring at me with crimson eyes. A long strand of braided hair stuck out of their hood, and they grip the blade at their handle tightly, as if to make sure I'm not going to try anything stupid. Their faces are covered by the hood's long shadow. The sunlight casting above illuminates the shining armor they wear.

"Wha-what are you doing here? Who the hell do you think you are?" the goblin stammers, sweat trickling from his forehead. The other figure steps forward, tilting their head slightly as they stand next to the first. They seem like they're interrogating him up on the stage, but Omar, on the other hand, has completely stopped moving. I silently thank God as his stomach rises up and down, indicating he's barely alive. The figures haven't taken notice of me yet, so I try hiding at the edge of the podium.

"Why don't you just let these Basalians go, hm?" a feminine voice asks, soft like silk. The goblin growls as I take a peek up top. He struggles against the first figure's grip. My eyes widen when I notice the second figure pull out their blade and stab them in the stomach.

His mouth gurgles blood, before the first figure throws him off of the stage, landing behind me. As they both hop off, I try

28

sneaking my way to my brother. I caress Omar's head in my arms, trying to shake him awake. I glance up, realizing that both figures are standing above me.

"Hold it."

The first slowly pulls off his hood, ears sticking out from his head. He has emerald eyes, accompanied by strong cheekbones and long, streaking blond hair.

The elf narrows as the second figure pulls off their hood. She's a human with light brown skin and braids parting down the middle. But there's something off about her features. I can't tell what it is. Her eyes are blood red, and they stare through my soul. I grit in fear, trying to shield myself from her threatening gaze.

"I can explain," my voice falters, trying to not be their next target. The elf squints as the woman examines every inch of me. "I was—"

"State your name," the elf interrupts. I gulp. *Maybe he won't kill me,* my thoughts tell me. *There's got to be a chance.*

"Kedar," I stutter, looking at the scar on the woman's neck. It runs down to her collarbone, and she flinches away from me when noticing my stare. The elf widens his eyes at me, as I wait for a knife to go down my throat. *This was a mistake, I should've taken Omar and ran.*

"I can sense your mana. You can be useful to us," he says to himself. *Useful? Like a slave?* My thoughts ring. *As long as Omar was safe, I didn't care about what I had to do to keep him alive. But my mana... mine isn't awakened. What's he on about?* "So it is decided. Do you want me to free you out of this hell?"

"Escape?" I stammered. "My brother... he can't leave my side."

"Alright, fine. But your brother... it might be best to check if he's fine," he sighs as I try shaking Omar awake again, only

29

for his body to remain still. I grunt through clenched teeth as Omar slowly blinks his eyes open, gleaming at the sun.

"Omar? You okay?" I ask only to have no response. Omar's glaring into my soul, his mouth hanging wide open. I hug him tightly, hoping he's still the same man. The two people behind me watch on in silence.

We lock eyes. Not a single essence of emotion is in him. He tries opening his mouth to speak, but his voice is coarse.

"Who am I?"

"Omar. Your name is Omar."

"The Basilians are a curse to this world. What the hell do they even fight for? Some holy land? There is no real justification in their motivation for fighting against the Cralean fists. All that this country and nation sees is a chance for urbanization, exploitation, and advances in our agriculture. Do not stop marching when they cry out for Basal; rather, use it as fuel to only quench the thirst for blood."

A Perspective on Basalians, Written by Cralean Historian Nubian Juven, in 1421.

TWO

Everything was a blur after that. The prisoners weren't too happy with their entertainment being interrupted, so they started a riot. Amid the chaos, the elf offered his hand to help me up the fortress walls. Omar weighed only a hundred pounds, so lifting him up was easy.

Once my feet touched the sand of the desert, I breathed in the fresh, warm air, free of the smell of blood. The man and the woman eventually led us to a carriage, parked near an oasis.

Running up to the little pond, I started stuffing water into my mouth after letting the elf safely place Omar inside the carriage. The taste of the water was like magic; it had been seasons since I had a single drop of clear liquid. After realizing the two were waiting for me, I followed them, letting the horse they had attached to their carriage lead us onto the dirt road.

Omar passed out after trying to comprehend what his name was, closing his eyes in a deep sleep. His soft snores illuminated the ambiance of the four of us traveling down the path, and the horse neighed softly as it tried doing its best to pull the cart along.

The whispers of the two assassins invade my eardrums, so I eavesdrop on them, staying behind but close enough to hear.

"Why'd you bring him along?" she asks, taking a glance at me. The elf sighs, setting his hands on his hips as I pat the horse's head, running my fingers through its hair. The prisoners in the fort are probably rounded up about now, being scolded by the wardens.

It won't be surprising if the Cralean army is chasing us, biting their teeth at our heels. The assassins have killed one of the commanding officers, so they'll be hunting us down with everything they've got.

Those two, on the other hand, are glowing against the sunlight. Both of them seem like mana-users. The girl's stare throws daggers tipped with magic, while the elf's voice speaks through magical threads. But they aren't mages or wizards. They are using their magic to be assassins.

They seem nice enough, but that symbol on their backs... it's impossible to decipher who these two even are. But still, they've saved me. There's a level of secrecy with them. Only the sound of their hushed whispers wisp through the wind.

The cart moves slowly as I pet the horse while pulling it along. It whinnies softly, accepting my warm gesture. The soft breeze of its mane and forelock only heightened the silence. Looking ahead, the girl is the most quiet out of the two, but her combat skills are something else. Watching her sword tear through the goblin's skin is horrifying. The elf seems more open to me, happily offering some proper clothes and shoes before the long walk.

He gave me a dazclava, a white, long white robe that covers up to my ankles. The elf handed me a canza, a long, fabric wrap to cover my face and prevent sand from getting into my eyes. He finished my outfit with some brown sandals I desperately needed. My feet feel so much better now, not burning from the heated ground.

I hesitate before catching up to them. We're shoulder to shoulder, but they barely acknowledge my presence. They walk softly, masking the sounds of their steps. I take a gander at their armor. It's plated with metal, and there is a brown belt above the black pants they wear. It reminds me of a Basalian knight's armor. Along the belt are throwing knives and ropes, and on the back of their hoods is, of course, the golden gemstone symbol. Even with the armor, they are fast. They move like they're weightless.

"So, you guys got names?" I ask before they glance at one another. The girl narrows her eyes as the elf nods. He turns towards me, green eyes complimented by the rays of sunlight shining on his iris.

"I'm Lapis, and she's Ruby," he replies, motioning his hand at Ruby. His tone is swift like a cheetah running through the savannas. However, their matching names of gemstones reminded me of the symbol on their backs. These aren't just any names. They are *code* names.

I lock eyes with Ruby as she quickly turns away from me. Lapis is a little more lenient, giving me a slight shrug once I offer a questioning look.

"Fake names? Really? You know my real name but I can't know yours?" I argue, crossing my arms, and furrowing my brows.

There's a low scoff. It's from Ruby. "You don't need to know."

She grips the handle of the blade fastened on her waist, a serious look in her eyes. She won't play a single mind game with me. Her glare, though lasting for only a couple of seconds, left battle scars.

Trying to ignore the heat is even worse. My robe can barely contain my sweat. I wipe the beads from my forehead, urging myself to stand upright. Lapis and Ruby aren't even fazed, staying inside the bubble of their calm demeanors.

"The hell's that supposed to mean?" I try, glancing at the dark circles under her eyes. They must be traveling day and night to get to Alfdan. All of that is to kill a singular prison guard.

"Just stop it with the questions already." Lapis' voice shoots me down. "We'll answer your little questions later. For now, we need to focus on getting the hell out of this desert."

I'm still a bit skeptical, but he's got a point. Right now, we're in the middle of nowhere. Pinakada is a sea of sand. The only way to get around is with trade routes. One false turn and we'll end up at the Cralean capital.

I don't even know where we're going. I offer Ruby a glance. She's looking down at the ground, staring into nothingness. Even though I hesitate, I tap her shoulder anyway. Her responding glance is teetered with annoyance.

"Uh, where exactly are we going?" I say awkwardly. Her eyes twitch at my words. A blink tells me what I've said finally registers in her head.

"Saitra. It's a town north of here, maybe three more miles away." She heaves a long sigh. Ruby glances at the canteen on her belt before taking it. Then she takes off her hood, after another defensive glare. I step back a bit.

The shape of her eyes is like almonds. Her skin is made up of a blend of dark and light, while her cheekbones and nose are sharply defined. A necklace sat on her collarbone, boasting a red gemstone that sparkled under the sunlight, while the scar on the right side of her neck I've seen earlier ripples through her brown complexion. On her nose is a small piercing, and on her ears are small, hanging ruby earrings. Her lips are luscious and full. I say nothing as she takes her time to sip from her canteen. After she closes it, she puts it back on her utility belt.

"That armor's heavy, isn't it?" I ask her. Lapis is right. I ask too many damn questions.

"It's not heavy. Well, to you it is," she replies. "You get used to it after a while."

"I—" she puts her palm up to stop me.

"Since you ask so many questions, Kedar, why don't I ask you something for once?" She asks. My feet crunch against the dirt every time I take a step as I look down. *What does she want to know?* Pops into my mind. "How did you end up in that prison?"

"It's nothing special." I wheeze, wanting to collapse on the ground from the blasting heat. Ruby glances at the heat waves in front of us, and we both enjoy the god-awful view, watching the horizon wiggle. "Joined the Basalian army. My legion got captured. Then I got thrown in here."

"Basalia? I see...." she whispers, eyes narrowing before she glances back downwards. Maybe she's Basalian herself. Ruby's too hard to interpret either way. Hell, she's probably from Crale.

"Hey you two, Saitra is coming up," Lapis interrupts, taking his hood off and basking his face in the Hayian sun. His long strands of blond hair flowed down before he closed his emerald eyes.

Squinting my eyes, a small town begins to immerse itself in the distance. From here, it looks beautiful, even under the wiggles of the heat waves. An oasis is on the right side of the town, acting as the town's main water source.

Through the palm trees that surround the outskirts of town, crowds of every race line the streets, and my heart begins to flutter a bit. Even a smile plants across my face, realizing that maybe, finally, I can take a rest. The horse carrying our supplies mimics my excitement, whinnying loudly as it too, can get a bit of rest.

Soon enough, we arrive at the town, sweaty, tired, and fatigued. As we walk, nobody cares to ask if we are Basalian or if we are Cralean. Although Saitra is in the country of Crale, restrictions are light since it's a bordering town. Refugees probably come in from all sides, and most border towns usually welcome people with open arms.

Their attitude towards us doesn't quite reflect the looks of the city though. Every building is crumbling, and now and then I spot rubble scattering through the buildings. Some houses are burned beyond recognition, a product of the fire arrows from both opposing sides of the war. Luckily enough, Saitra has intact, fresh adobe houses and a huge fountain in the middle of the town square. I resist the temptation to walk over and slather myself in the water, drinking it all up.

Horse carriages pass the four of us with the dead bodies of civilians and soldiers, filling my nose with the rotting smell of death. Even with stores blocked and closed with planks, families being torn by war, and soldiers rounding every corner looking for perpetrators, the people of Saitra have bright, welcoming smiles on their faces.

Barracks line the outskirts of the town with Cralean soldiers who huff and puff as they spar with their swords, preparing for any upcoming battle coming from Basalia. I'm not too intimidated by the close proximity of Craleans with hardened looks in their eyes. The harsh reality of war has changed me.

I see no point in fighting anymore. It's all just pointless death, coming from hungry leaders desperate for power and influence. If I die, I will just become another statistic. After all of this, I'll escape from war and live with my brother in the east.

Death in my family is very common, as my father recalls it. The Dragon's War has affected my family for three generations. He's told me about the times when you can walk outside without an arrow being shot in your head. Times when wives and husbands aren't separated from each other because of war. That peace almost sounds like a myth today, because I can't even sleep in peace as a soldier. Although I love my country and its people, there's a limit when it comes to brutality. There is a point where I've come to question whether or not it is even worth fighting anymore.

Ruby nudges my shoulder slightly, knocking me out of my stir. Omar is busy slinging over Lapis' shoulders, still unconscious. Probably best for him to stay asleep.

I quickly follow them into a building, with a sign that said 'Gloomy Tavern and Hotel'. When Lapis opens the door, the lively music fills my eardrums as I take a gander. The floor is made of desert wood, and in front of me is a bartender with rows upon rows of alcohol behind him. Tables and chairs scatter through the tavern while goblins, humans, elves, and fariks dance and sing in the middle of the bar.

The four of us weave through the tavern, and Lapis leads us up wooden stairs. On the walls are paintings of the Pinakada desert, bright with its yellow colors and hearty sand dunes. As our boots click against the steps, a thought arises in my mind: *I've made it out. Alive.*

At the top of the stairs is a room with a receptionist desk in the back. Sitting on a chair is a lone Farik, who's browsing through some records and papers. I scrunch my sandals a little on the carpet below me, relishing the presence of shelter. For three seasons I have been confined to a rotting cell. It's fulfilling to finally be under an actual roof again. Though looking dull from the outside, the adobe buildings hold such a beautiful interior.

"Room for three," Lapis says, walking up to the receptionist. He pulls darkos out of his pocket, which are gold coins with a Cralean coat of arms in the center. In comparison to Basalian currency, lorelocks are copper coins, with our God Basal in the middle, spreading his wings wide.

The receptionist looks up. She is a farik. Fariks are dogs that walk, talk, and have eight fingers and eight toes. There are pets in our world, but fariks won the battle of natural selection with their intelligence and lengthy lifespan. Most fariks actually live up to being over two hundred years old. The farik in front of us has brown, chocolate-like fur and triangle-shaped sharp ears that point upwards. She doesn't seem that old, but you never know when it comes to fariks.

She gladly takes Lapis' darkos and leads us to the third floor, opening the door to our room before taking the trek back downstairs.

"Geez, she's ancient," Lapis whispers as I laugh.

"I'd say she's 250," Ruby proposes, bringing out a little smirk.

The room we buy is spacious, with three beds in a row, separated by a couple of feet. Lapis sets Omar down slowly on the nearby couch. Before long, he begins to snore softly after he twitches a couple of times. I give Lapis a nod of thanks as he responds with an emotionless "You're welcome."

Afterward, I quickly head to the bathroom, where I finally open the door to look at myself in the mirror. Sliding off my dazclava, I notice my face has been riddled with dirt and gunk. On my nose is a long, stretching scar, and I have heavy eyebags. My hair is all over the place while my curly hair hangs lower than my ears. I breathe a heavy sigh as my eyes trail down my skinny body, a result of seasons of malnourishment.

After going back downstairs to retrieve some bath water, I pour it into the marble tub. I undress and hop in, exhaling my breath slowly, letting my tense muscles relax into the warm liquid. A square-shaped aperture is in front of me, where sunlight shines down into my face. I groan, closing my eyes in annoyance as I toss and turn in the water.

Once I finally clean up, I put on my old clothes, since I don't have anything else. It's disgusting, but I don't have a choice. I open the door slowly, gritting my teeth at the horrid scent.

Lapis and Ruby are chattering over at the dinner table, each with a wooden cup in their hands. They didn't seem to notice me, so I only watched them speak by opening a small crack.

"We have to get out of here. And quick," Ruby says, scratching her head. "Once the Cralean soldiers start looking for us, they're going to tear this town apart."

Lapis looks down, taking a sip from his wooden cup. Both of them aren't in their armor anymore. Lapis has a broad, muscular figure under his shirt. He wears the same necklace as Ruby, which boasts a blue gemstone that sits on his collarbone. His head is square shaped, his elvish ears sticking out as if he has knives for ears. He tucks his long strands of blond hair behind his ear as his green eyes seem to glow a bright emerald. His forehead wrinkles and smile lines indicate he's probably decades older than Ruby.

"The goal is to get back to the Order." I raise an eyebrow at this. *Order?* "This is the fastest way to do it."

Ruby's braided hair is parted in the middle, slithering down to her shoulders. The nose piercing she has sparkles against the shining sunlight coming through the windows. Ruby shakes her head in denial. "I know, but what if we get caught, for the

Dragons sake? We're holding fugitives. I still don't know why we brought them along, Lapis. It doesn't make sense to me."

"I see something in Kedar and Omar, Ruby. Though faint, I can sense the power of their mana…" Lapis replies, trailing off as Ruby gives him a questioning look. He pauses, taking a sip of his drink before talking again. "They would be useful companions to the Magister. Assassins is how I would put it."

"Omar is clearly out of condition, Lapis," She explains, glancing over to Omar, who's still snoring on the couch. I can only watch them in wonder. I've never awakened my mana before, and neither has Omar. *What the hell is Lapis talking about?*

"That's exactly why I'll find the solution to whatever illness he has. Once we fix him, we'll bring him back to the Order, along with Kedar. It is a vision I have in my mind. Ruby, you must understand," Lapis blinks as he motions his hands in desperation. "We recruited you in the same way —"

"Kedar, come out," Ruby injects suddenly, glancing at me through the open crack of the wooden door. I recoil back slightly, realizing that she's caught me eavesdropping on them.

Slowly but surely, I turn the knob of the door, my sandals clanking on the adobe floor below me. Lapis seems disappointed in himself as Ruby motions over to the chair on the front side of the table. I gulp as I cautiously sit down in front of them, their eyes glaring into my soul. Ruby breathes a shallow breath, breaking the silence.

"Would you like to know our plan, Kedar?" Ruby asks. Their whole conversation fills my mind with incomprehensible thoughts. Each step I take in trying to figure out who these assassins are is another foot deeper into the black hole. Lapis looks away from me as I nod slowly, trying to not feel too comfortable yet.

Ruby rolls her eyes at me before she continues. "The whole reason why we came to Alfdan prison was to kill Gargon, that goblin. We aren't supposed to rescue you."

"Why did you save my life then?" I sternly ask, tilting my head upwards before squinting my brown eyes. This would be a great opportunity to pry some answers out of them. If they see potential in me having mana to control magic, why would they act so cold and distant towards me and my brother?

"Recruitment. The order needs new initiates because it is slowly dying," Lapis blurts out as Ruby stares at him with daggers in her eyes.

She takes a sip of her drink as Lapis scratches the top of his head, gritting his teeth in nervousness. "In all honesty, when me and Ruby first came across you, I could sense a certain glow in your soul. It is faint, but I recognized it as mana. Perhaps this may be some sort of coincidence, but I see you being an assassin for the Order."

Mana users can sense how powerful people's magic is. This explains why Lapis says he 'recognized a glow.' But still, it doesn't make the slightest bit of sense. I don't have mana awakened.

"Lapis, I don't want to fight anymore. I want to run away from all of this death and war. I can't take up on your offer, 'cause I need to find a way to get my brother back to normal again," I explain. He seems slightly disappointed, but his face shifts, giving me an expression of understanding.

Ruby clicks her sharp nails on the wooden table as she rests her cheek on her palm, not even batting an eye at me.

"Well, I guess it's set then. First, we'll travel to Jiya, and then—"

The floor shakes as the sound of an explosion begins to ring out in our ears. I jump off of my chair before covering my ears. I struggle to stand up before looking outside of the window to see what's going on below me. Smoke and fire riddle the air as the sounds of screaming begin to overpower the hellfire.

"Seriously?" I hear Lapis say behind me. "I didn't even get to try the bathtub yet."

Once I look away from the window, both of them are gone. I groan in annoyance before rushing downstairs and out of the tavern, where people are scattered through the bar, each trying to get away from the explosions coming from the right side of town. People are standing along the dirt path looking towards the smoke, while others gather their children to run from the fires.

Weaving through the crowds only results in me seeing glimpses of their signature black and gold cloaks wisping through the crowd. Eventually, I catch both of them in an alleyway leaning against the wall as Ruby pokes her head out to see the commotion a bit better.

"What are you two doing out here?" I urge, narrowing my eyebrows. My heart nearly stops beating as I realize that I've forgotten Omar. He is for sure oblivious to the fact that there is chaos raining down outside. More explosions begin to flood my ears as I struggle to maintain my balance to look up at Lapis. "We should be running, Goddammit!"

Nobody answers me except Ruby. "The cleansing of Saitra has already begun, sadly enough."

The cleansing is a common method from the Cralean Empire to rid their town of any citizen from Basalia. From my own experiences, I've seen soldiers walk into towns demanding people to identify themselves as Cralean or Basalian. If they aren't Cralean, then they'll be killed on sight.

"There are about one thousand infantry and a couple hundred archers out there," sighs Lapis as he puts on his black gloves, sweat slowly beginning to drip down his forehead. "Crap. You think they're heading our way, Ruby?"

"They're coming from the west, Lapis, meaning there must be a battle in the lakes. The only thing I can imagine them doing is trying to cleanse this place instead of trying to look for us," Ruby explains, shaking her head. As Lapis and Ruby both pull their hoods up, I clench my teeth before looking back to the tavern where we just are. Buildings all around it begin to catch fire as people run with satchels, screaming in fear.

"Why the hell would they explode the town then? I've never seen that before," I say, scratching my head.

"It's a new method. So many defectors have been popping up in towns that Crale has just decided to bomb their own people," she scoffs, glancing towards me with her darkened eyes. Saitra is already broken down, and the Craleans throwing bombs only enhance the grim look of the town.

"Kedar, follow us. We need to get back to our hotel to grab our things," she urges, pointing backward with her thumb. Lapis gets up from the wall, as we all run to the Gloomy Tavern, knowing we have little time before soldiers show up on their doorstep. Rushing upstairs, I burst into the hotel room, expecting to see Omar still lying down on the couch, snoring softly.

Realizing he isn't there, I find myself looking everywhere in our room. Soon enough, my fingers lay on the door of the bathroom. Slowly, I turn the knob, expecting nothing but the smell of soap inside.

Omar's standing in front of me, a petrified look in his empty pupils.

Life is mana. Mana derives from the soul within. It lets the user manipulate magic in all sorts of ways. This practice was once made illegal hundreds of years ago because rogue mages are running rampant. After the Law of Magic was established, wizards and witches received acceptance for their magical awakenings. Now we use them in wars such as the Jezzebel. Was it right to let us mages be free, if we are to use our magic for the simple purpose of causing death?

-   A statement from a fire wizard during the Jezzebel Wars, circa 1200-1300.

THREE

My brother doesn't seem cooperative with us when trying to speak to him. Lapis has to throw him down on the wooden floor before Omar can dolphin-dive straight out of the window. The three of us try holding him down so he can stop squirming, kicking, and wailing.

"AHHHHHHH! AH!" he shouts, flailing around and struggling as Lapis quickly snags some rope ties that are lying on the table. Omar jerks his head back and forth, trying to escape from our grasp. Before Lapis holds my brother's arms behind his back to secure him down, Omar's shouting, screaming, and booting like a toddler.

"Goddamnit Omar! Stop moving! What the hell is wrong with you?!" I plead, furrowing my brows angrily. It's haunting to try and convince myself that perhaps this is all some sort of nightmare.

"AUGH!" he yells, trying to crawl out of Lapis' grasp. The elf slams him back to the floor, wrapping the rope around his wrists, while I watch in grief. We drag him downstairs, with restraints and a gag to cover his mouth. Lapis and I carry him like a table, or a hunk of meat we just got from hunting. Once we get to the first floor, it's desolate and empty, while people scream in fear outside.

Crale soldiers despise the Basalians. They treat us like animals, torturing our people because of where they are born. Hundreds are kept in cages and more are burned at the stake. Towns that are once part of Basalia are now transformed into concentration camps, forcing people to become prisoners, and churning out resources for the war.

"Damnit, Kedar!" invades Lapis, snapping me back to reality. He huffs heavily as Omar stops moving completely, passing out from exhaustion. His mouth curls into an annoyed expression. "What's up with your brother?!"

"I don't know!" I frantically reply, wiping the sweat off of my forehead. My hands shake as I swing the back door open, leading the four of us to run through the alleyway. Our boots slam against the stone pavement, as the huge bag that Ruby slings over her shoulder clanks and clunks with our supplies. I glance at the assassins. "He acted the same at the prison, all empty-like."

"Looks like the after-effects of a horrid spell," Ruby chimes in, huffing and puffing.

The goblin has torn through Omar's mind with the power of cursed magic. From what I know, some spells can traverse the magic's unruly effects. *There must be a way for me to get Omar back,* I whisper in my mind. As we turn the corner, three Crale soldiers are busy inspecting corpses on the pavement for valuables, anything that they can sell or barter.

Two of them are human, and one's a goblin. Once they notice us creeping towards them, the goblin slowly curves his green mouth into a satisfying smile. They unsheath short swords out of their belts, as we stop in our tracks completely, eyeing the three men.

"Hello, Basalians," the goblin says, as his metal-plated armor clunks while stepping towards us. Cralean soldiers wear metal helmets with a signature yellow armband, along with a shield on their backs. Heavy plates cover their shoulders and legs. Crale's coat of arms is in the middle of the chestplate— a black lion wearing a golden crown with two swords in the back.

My condition renders me incapable of fighting. I can barely pick up that pickaxe for the Dragon's sake.

For now, the only thing I can do is to hold Omar over my shoulder. Lapis and Ruby don't seem fearful at all, giving each other a bold look. But Lapis smiles like they're just your run-of-the-mill alleyway thugs. The elf looks at Ruby, nodding as she takes a small step forward, her expression dimming at the three men.

"Get out of the way," she spits, beginning to unsheath a short blade from her waist. It's majestic. The sword doesn't have a hilt, the metal blade radiating against the sun. Red and black fabric slithers around the handle while little yellow gemstones are engraved into the middle of it. One second she's standing next to me, the next she's charging at the speed of light, before planting her feet right in front of the goblin.

"Grah!" the goblin exclaims, stepping back slightly in surprise. Ruby's presence is intimidating, but the soldier never waives, pulling out a sword. "Goddammit! You—"

Ruby slashes the goblin's eye, blood exploding onto the ground. I flinch as I can only watch the soldier fall to his knees, gripping his other eye tightly. He widens the only pupil he has left, before looking back to his two comrades. "Gods! What are you two doing! Kill them!"

The two soldiers lurch forward before dashing to Ruby, who raises her sword in preparation. Swords cut through the air as the clangs ring through the alleyway. Lapis stands still as

Ruby dodges every swing with precision, sliding through one of the human's legs before stabbing him in the back. His comrade tries cutting off Ruby's wrist, only for her to counter by slicing his throat wide open.

The screams of the men echo through Saitra as they writhe in pain from Ruby's precise slicing. It takes seconds for them to go completely silent, from choking on their own blood as they fall to the ground, dead.

We run up to her, seeing Ruby wipe the blood off of her armor. She gives us a blank expression as her blade clicks on her belt. "Gods. What are you looking at? Let's just go."

Walking in silence, we stealth through the alleyways, running into more guards but leaving them as corpses to create a trail of blood.

The Cralean flag begins to rise high in the sky, where the middle of the town square is. It's a jet-black flag with a yellow sun in the center, dancing in the wind. Soldiers take a rest at the fountain, their eyes still alert with paranoia as some hoist the dead citizens from the ground.

Crale is a country that preaches how they're the "shining sun of Haya," the only country in the world providing every citizen with freedom and outright respect. But over the years, more and more corrupt leaders are atop the ranks, making the country violent and merciless to others.

Since the beginning of the Dragon's War, countries have always expressed their distaste for Crale. The Lauvee Dynasty and Sulalat Basal have both been supporters of Basalia for centuries. Dracotheism is what connects our countries together. At the start of the war, they joined Basalia's side, but it led to Sulalat and Lauvee's territories being overrun by Crale's more dominant, war-experienced forces.

After ten years, Sulalat and Lauvee both withdrew themselves from the war after millions of people died. Since then, the nations have been keeping close eyes on our country, giving us aid but not involving themselves in the conflict. It's part of the reason why our country hasn't been completely invaded yet.

But this has come with the expense of needy conscription. It's why me and Omar have joined the army. The battlefield bewilders us. My mind keeps filling with the memories I've had of every battle with Omar. Every single one, I left him alone without care, going off to fight off wave after wave of soldiers. I should've done more to protect him. Lapis coughs, interrupting my thoughts as we stream through the alleyways, not daring to look back.

"Where to, goddammit?!" asks Lapis, carrying my brother. Omar's fast asleep, not fazed by the gruesome situation that we are in. Ruby darts her eyes towards him, sighing heavily.

"Well, the first thing that we need to do is escape out of this damn hellhole," she replies, clenching her teeth tightly in frustration. "I have no idea what else to do from there, but we gotta find some way to get to Jiya."

"Jiya?" I repeated. *Jiya.* I've heard of it once before but never seen the place with my own eyes. At least it's in Basalia's borders, and anywhere that is Basalian land feels exactly like home to me.

"Yeah. I know somebody there that might be able to reverse the spell that's affecting your brother," she explains to me, the bag on her back clunking and clicking from our supplies.

"Ah, yes. Alright, well, we might as well scurry our way out of here then," Lapis chimes in, nodding forward as he calmly wipes the sweat dripping down his forehead. He seemed dedicated to carrying my brother from the lowly hands of Hex to the great lands of Jura.

We trek our way through the town, eventually finding ourselves at the front entrance, where it's completely empty. Once I look behind me to see the town square, there are piles of dead bodies littering the roads, still twitching from Crale's brutal attacks. No soldiers are in our sights, meaning they went deeper within the city to look for more civilians to "cleanse."

Ruby grunts as we begin to trek over the huge sand dunes of the Pinakada desert. A sea of yellow sand stretches from miles upon miles on end, without a single oasis in its sights. I clear my throat. My whole body is running on fumes from the heat and malnourishment in the fortress. I haven't even had the luxury to enjoy a meal.

Surprisingly enough, Ruby sits down in the sand, sighing as she grabs a broken stick. Lapis looks down at her questioningly, before gently setting Omar down on the ground as well.

"Alright, we might as well draw up a plan since we're far away enough for them to even consider looking for us," Ruby grunts. Little crunching sounds from the sand pop every time Lapis takes a step, as he begins to pace back and forth. He's huffing softly, with sweat dripping from the side of his forehead.

Ruby removes her hood, basking her face in the sun as her braided hair flows down her frame, almost reaching the surface of the ground. She rubs her forehead, gripping the stick tightly before beginning to draw out a small map in the sand. It's faint, but I can recognize a river and some trees drawn by her silky hands. Lapis bent his knees to gaze at it a bit better, before worriedly glancing over to Ruby.

"We might have to go through hell if we want to cross Kigamouth," she declares, resting her cheek on her hand before pouting a bit.

Kigamouth is the lake in the center of Basalia and Crale, separating the countries by five hundred miles, and encouraging armies to fight naval battles using wooden boats and metal cannons. Crossing over the lake will be hell if we even dare to try it, because if we are caught by Cralean patrols, then we will be shot dead with arrows in a heartbeat.

"By the Dragon! Are you serious? I thought we would take the long route to just go around Kigamouth," Lapis grits, putting both palms on his head in shock. Ruby shakes her head at the elf.

"We gotta try, Lapis. If we did go around the lake, how long would it take us? Thirty days? Forty? I'm not willing to travel through trenches and charred forests to cross the border to Basalia. It's our only choice." Her face is stern now, looking back to the drawings in the sand.

I stay silent, watching Lapis and Ruby's little debate, constantly looking over to Omar to see if he'll wake up from his damn slumber. His eyes are closed tightly, and a light snore erupts from his mouth every couple of minutes. He must be in some sort of coma, and only God knows when he'll wake up again.

"Goddammit. You're right. We might as well," He says, sighing heavily before looking at me sympathetically. "Look, Kedar. We need your cooperation if you want us to help out your brother. Are you okay with that?"

"I'm fine with it," I explain. Every passing second it feels as if Omar's losing himself in his sleep, and there's no way in hell I'm letting that happen. In fact, I'll do anything to keep Omar alive. Maybe even kill again. "I'll follow you guys."

I look up to the sky, the beautiful mixes of pink and white shaping to form a new color. The sun still shines without wavering, trekking through the day before it can have a rest at night. With each passing second, a hint of orange begins to appear on the horizon, as it starts to shine on my pale skin. Lapis and Ruby are busy preparing for our upcoming journey, gathering themselves to prepare for the long walk to the lake.

"Hell yeah. Let's get this over with then," Ruby grits, adjusting her long braids, and tucking it behind her ear. She seems content while tossing the branch to the ground. With the clunking from her sack, she begins to walk upward across the dunes, leading the rest of us to follow her.

I dust the sand off of my shoulders, stretching my arms above my head. A twang of ash begins to form a hellish scent on my nostrils, so I glance to see the entire town ablaze.

Saitra is immersed in hell itself. We are all gazing at the town now, hearing the chants of Cralean soldiers, praising the deaths of their civilians. Though we are far away enough for the soldiers to not notice us, the echoes of their chants still make it seem they're still biting at our heels, doing anything to try and kill us.

"Holy Dragons," says Ruby, stepping next to me. She's on her tippy toes to see over the town's walls. Her crimson eyes shine brighter with reflections of smoke and fire. Though her look tells me she's in shock, her face is still stern, keeping her fearlessness. "I can't believe it… they boiled those people alive. All that's left of the town is ash."

"Honestly, it's not a surprise. Crale would be the type of army to do this," urges Lapis, frustration churning in his voice. Lapis stands beside me, Ruby on the other side. She takes Lapis' words to her mind, before nodding slowly. The three of us gaze upon Saitra, set to smithereens in front of our eyes.

It's hard to not think about death. Images form in my mind of dead people all begging for their gods to help them, only for it to fall on deaf ears. I push those images in the back of my mind as we start to walk along. Those men, women, and children have lives. Lives that are now in ruins because of the

Cralean army. Lives that are now hopelessly in vain, with innocent souls at the pearly gates.

"Alrighty, how many days to Jiya?" I ask Lapis, turning my head towards his tired look. He has the same dark circles under his eyes that Ruby also has. He glances downward, before handing me a pensive look.

"Two days," he sighs, holding Omar with his arm tightly. Ruby's clinking and clanking coming from the bag is pretty loud, even though she's already far from us. "We might as well catch up to Ruby before she gets out of our sight."

Once we got close to her, she seemed all jumpy, somehow elated. She's energetic compared to how stoic she puts herself out to be. Ruby offers me a glance.

"You ready for your legs to feel like jelly, eh?" she asks as Lapis tries to measly keep up with us. We seem to be walking in an infinite circle. For a second, I can swear I've seen those sand particles before.

"Hell no," I sternly say, before glancing over to Lapis, who's deflated as he tries to carry Omar. "I can do this. Right?"

I'm wrong. My legs are doused in lava. I glance up hopelessly at the night sky, the stars shining bright. My shoulders shake from the immense night chill of Pinakada. The stars remind me of Jheanne, my father.

"Stars give people hope, son," I remembered him saying, pointing to the stars above. "Basal made the stars to give us a promise that he will never fail us, even through our darkest times. Even when darkness is all around us, the stars and the moon still shine on, Kedar. Never ever give up. Promise me."

Being the toddler that I was, I blindly replied with a happy yes, before my dad tucked me in bed. I dreamed about Basal with his outstretched blue hand, promising me peace and love in my nightmares.

Now that I'm older, it feels a bit exaggerated, but I know comrades that still believe. Stars will give you hope that the Divine Dragon is still watching over the world, doing his best to keep peace in check. But with the war I've been forced into, it's hard to apply the idea of God to everything. My perspective has changed time and time again. Basal's done something to Lapis' heart that makes him believe that I'm worth something. For the past two days, the rations that they've given me tell me that God wants me to stay alive. If he doesn't, my book would've been closed long ago.

We've been keeping our trek west to the Kigamouth Lake. Next to the Pinakada desert lies the lake, with the shores full of lush greenery, compared to the solemn dunes of the inner deserts. Over time, the two battling nations have been using the desert as a frontline for many phases of the ongoing war.

Every few hours we come across skeletons covered in sand, and an abandoned camp near them. Right across the lake is the port city of Jiya. Luckily enough, as we get closer to the shores, we're greeted by greener environments, that is the savanna biome that I'm currently traveling through with Ruby and Lapis at this moment. I might even be able to drink from the water if we get there alive, since Kigamouth is a freshwater lake, after all.

We are all walking side by side, Ruby to my right, and Lapis to my left, who seems destroyed from carrying my brother. Any amount of energy that I try to gain from breathing a bit deeper is in vain because after walking for that long, I can barely muster up the courage to breathe anyway.

I glance over at the trees in the distance, before making sure there aren't any cheetahs lurking in the tall grass we are walking across. The six hours of sleep is burning out, and fast. Only my willpower is enough to make me stand upright.

"Lapis," pouts Ruby, looking up at him with droopy eyes. "Bring a damn camel or horse next time when we travel, okay?"

"S-shut up," he stammers, gritting through his pearly white teeth. Eventually, he coughs, clearing his throat. "I've been carrying someone for three days straight. Do you know how annoying that is?"

He flashes me his furrowed eyebrows and upside-down smile, and I try to conceal my grin. Even with the dazclava covering my face, the creases of my eyes can tell anyone that I'm giggling.

I squint through the tall grass and trees to see a dark blue line on the horizon. My eyes widen as I try to not shed a tear. The glittering sparkles coming from the dark blue line confirmed it.

There's no mistaking it. We are here. Kigamouth Lake.

The lake is massive from the shores, stretching far and wide. Glitters of the moonlight dance like fairies on the surface of the water, while a serene forest resided on the other side.

Lapis' face lights up as he finally realizes that he won't carry Omar for long anymore. It's amazing compared to the lifeless deserts, filled with the grim reality of war. Ruby sighs in contempt, putting her palm over her heart. She stretched her arms as the soft clanking of our supplies invaded the sound of the soft call of the birds above. We're on our last leg, and the only thing stopping us now is—

"How are we getting across this lake?" Lapis deflates. His groans and whines are tuned out by me distracted from the mesmerizing sight of Jiya. From here, I gaze upon the stone buildings with subtle, dark wooden roofs. Each light represents the promise that the people of Jiya are alive and well, even in these hard times.

"Here. It's run-down, but it's our only choice," Ruby's voice points out, motioning her head to the left. I look at the boat which sways softly from the waves of the lake. She's right, the boat is run-down, with rotting wood covering most of it. Dens and bumps cover the left and right sides, and the oar is split in half.

"Goddammit. I'd rather take this than walking around the lake for forty days," Lapis murmurs, as the four of us walk over to the boat. Lapis hoists Omar onto the thing, and it rocks violently once he thumps onto the deck. Next, Ruby takes off her bag and plops it down to Omar, before Lapis inspects the half-broken oar.

Lapis pushes the boat into the lake, and Ruby and I sit next to each other in the back. We can tell he's running on fumes, judging by his constant shaking and shivering from the soft chill. The soft lapping of the water makes me droopy as Lapis rows slowly across Kigamouth. In the water are tiny fishes, swimming through the currents and under our boat.

"So, what's this plan to help out my brother, anyway?" I finally say, trying not to doze off. Lapis huffs and puffs, trying to row the boat faster with each stroke. Ruby grumbles as she turns to me, melting from exhaustion. She flips back her hood.

"Just sleep, Kedar. It'll be best to tell you in the morning," Ruby replies. Her hand reaches up and scratches the long scar running down the side of her neck.

The four of us silently row along, with the serene ambiance of the buzzing bugs, flowing water, and the sights of Jiya comforting me. Not to sound cheap or anything, but maybe I fit in with Lapis and Ruby.

Ruby falls asleep after setting her elbow on the edge of the boat. She snores in sync with Omar, except it is softer and quieter. Lapis must've assumed I'm asleep too, judging by his silent rowing. Ironically, I find myself unable to sleep at all.

The sound of silence hasn't invaded my ears in a long time. Because of all the battles I've been in, my hearing must be damaged after having to endure the sounds of explosions and screams. I glance at the sky again, to observe the thousands of stars. They twinkle in the night, shining through the dark blue space they are immersed in. Perhaps, my father is right about stars. Maybe they really do give us hope and peace.

But that doesn't last for long. It never does, a voice whispers.

"For the sake of god, don't enlist your children into the army! Don't believe anything they say! Don't believe the Craleans and the *Shurta,* by GOD! Save your children!"

- A screaming, wounded Cralean soldier after returning from the frontlines of the Dragon's War, 1401.

FOUR

*M*onster.

I shoot up. My vision is cloudy. My eyes dart left to right as I slowly come to my senses. The smell around me is of blood and bone. *Alfdan,* I shudder. The word *monster* keeps repeating in my head as if someone is whispering in my ear. Sweat drips down my forehead from the heat, and I look down to see my dirty hands, dripping with red blood. It's all too familiar: rust on the metal, the rotting mattress, and the gunky floor.

In the cage with me are corpses upon corpses on the ground. Each one of them has their mouths agape, their eyes pointing towards mine. I recognize the bodies, most being my comrades, some being my childhood friends. Their mouths begin to move, chanting the word *monster* over and over again. I clench my teeth before trying to cover my ears, trying to ignore their pleading voices.

"Shut up! All of you! SHUT UP! GODDAMMIT!" I cry, quivering with fear. The voices keep going, as their eyes begin to turn redder than blood. But there are two people amid the corpses that look all too familiar. "Mother? Father? No, this can't be... please..."

"You failed, Kedar," a voice says to me. My father narrows his dead stare, blood dripping down his chin as his whole jaw begins to detach from his face. It lurches downward every time he speaks. The red veins are the only thing connecting his lower front teeth. "You made a promise. Protect Omar. Guide him. And what have you done?"

The chants get louder every passing second, as I try to find the right words to speak. He's right. I've failed on my promise. Every passing night in the damn prison I've prayed for Omar to never ever become like me. As the chants got louder, memories began to flash through my mind in this horrid nightmare. Thoughts of Omar begging for me to stop the killings, beginning for us to go home.

My father begins to step towards me, his handless arms reaching for my shoulders. A horrifying grin is on his face as the soft splashes of his bare feet soak in the murky water and invade my ears. I try stepping back, only to find myself sliding against the cold, rusty bars. He comes closer, widening his mouth agape.

"PAY THE PRICE! PAY THE PRICE, YOU MONSTER!"

He's about to eat me.

"Kedar!"

I snap awake, almost tumbling out of the soft mattress I'm on. My arms are shaking, and I'm soaked with sweat. After a couple of minutes of heavy breathing, pushing that nightmare I have is a bit easier. I put my hand over my heart to try and calm myself down, before quickly shielding my eyes from the sunlight.

Ruby... wait... Ruby? My eyes blink away the blur, seeing Ruby giving me a worried look as she sits on a wooden stool. She raises her brows, blinking her red eyes.

"Are you okay?" she says, tucking her braids behind her ear. The sun seems to glow on her skin. She doesn't wait for me to answer, noticing the sweat dripping down my forehead. "Dragons. Did you have a nightmare?"

"Shut up," I reply, trying to brush her off. My hands keep shaking as I grasp the edge of the bed tightly, getting up to slide on my sandals. "Just ignore me. Please."

"Ugh. Fine," She scoffs, getting off the stool before walking out. Her boots click against the floor as I still try to recollect myself. *What's wrong with me? Gods. I shouldn't have snapped at her,* I say to myself, shaking my head measly. Easily enough, I replace the heinous nightmare with the memories of last night.

The second we arrived, Ruby tapped me awake to lead the four of us down the road and to a mansion. Lapis has a brother named Farid, who happily took us in despite us staining his floor with mud.

The room I sleep in is decorated with paintings all along the walls, showing the beautiful environment of Basalia. I dig my slippers on the soft fur carpet and tuck the fur blankets on the white mattress.

It's like I'm living in a dream. The chandelier above me radiates a subtle light mixing with the sunlight coming out the window. Every part of the mansion is so hypnotic. Part of me believes that I don't deserve this, while another part of me perplexes with joy.

I sigh as I open the bathroom door on my left, revealing the dazzling bathtub inside. As I brush my teeth, I can't help but feel so alienated. I look at my tired, brown eyes as I fix my curly hair, flailing all over the place. My hands still shake as I grab a towel, wiping sweat from my face. Thank the Dragon I look a little better than before. My skin is no longer a hellish pale. It's the golden tone I've always known. I slowly stroke my beard, before grabbing some small shears. I cut the overgrown edges, going out of the bathroom after lining it up with a slight trim.

Ruby and Lapis' voices echo through my mind as I remember them telling me about a man who can possibly help my brother. We're supposed to visit him today, and hopefully, he can heal Omar's condition.

I splash some water on my face, before walking out the room and into the hallway. Before long, I walk down the spiral marble stairs, my sandals clicking with every step. The chandelier above shines down on me, as I see Lapis, Farid, and Ruby sitting around the dining table.

The mansion is spacious. On the left is the dining room and a kitchen, and on the right is a luxurious library.

The table where Lapis and his brother sat is made of glass, and the chairs have gemstones embedded on the edges of them.

"Good morning," Lapis nods, chomping down on a piece of bread. "You ready?"

I nod back before sitting with them. My eyes glance towards the honey apples in the middle, which I don't hesitate to grab. Once I take a bite of the yellow apple, the sweet flavors immediately burst into my mouth. I sigh, loving the sugary taste as it silently crunches every time I bite into it.

I glance at Lapis' brother. Farid has a sharp jawline, with a metal piercing on his left ear. He wears a golden necklace over his black tunic while tapping his fingers on the table. Seems like he has jewelry on almost every part of his body. Farid slicks his blond hair back, revealing his pointy elf ears and blue eyes. He doesn't bother to look up at me since he is busy reading the newspaper in his hands.

On the front side, the heading reads:

DEFEAT OF THE BASALIAN NAVY IN A NAVAL BATTLE IN THE SOUTHERN KIGAMOUTH LAKE: OVER 800 DEAD, AND 8 SHIPS SUNK.

I wince, knowing how horrible the war's been going this past spring and winter.

Especially the naval battles, which are common in the Lake. Cannons and the sounds of war cries are the only things you can hear. My father has noted to me how my uncle lost his life to the depths of the sea.

Once I finish my apple, I change into a dark blue tunic, with black boots and a brown belt. Lapis and Ruby are waiting at the door, and she gives me an annoyed look when I try offering her a light smile.

The sun shines on my face as we sneak through the alleyways, yet again.

Omar being knocked out and over Lapis' shoulder draws curious looks. As we stroll through winding roads, I immerse myself in the buildings of Jiya. The buildings are beautiful. Most are made of stone with wooden-lined windows, some the color blue or red. The town hall of Jiya stands out the most, towering over most buildings.

The tall golden statue of the dragon Basal is at the front side of the building. It looks like a courthouse, with white paint, pillars, and windows with gold linings. Basalia got its name because of the Dragon Basal.

Since he's the god of Dracotheism, his presence is plastered everywhere throughout the country. On war helmets, plates, cups, clothing, you name it. Even on the flag, the blue dragon is in the middle, stretching his wings wide in the blue background.

While we walk, Ruby and Lapis aren't wearing their usual assassin attire. Instead of the signature robes, Lapis has on a blue tunic, while Ruby wears a red gown. They still have the same utility belts on their waist, each with throwing knives, bombs, and daggers.

We cross through the stone streets as markets line the sides. People crowd the markets, doing anything they can to make a living in these harsh times. Otherwise, huge hotels, neighborhoods, taverns, and stores are all that the city has to offer.

"Not to be annoying, but where can we find this guy, anyway?" I ask Lapis, who's still firmly holding on to my brother. He's still in his coma. His eyes are tightly closed as he snores softly into Lapis' shoulder.

"Don't worry, Kedar. Once we get to his shop, everything's gonna make sense. Trust me." He throws up a thumb, affirming me. Once he sees the questioning look on my face, he scratches the back of his head while looking down at the ground. "Just wait."

I pout as we walk near the decks and shores, enjoying the view of Kigamouth. The temperature is perfect compared to the heat of Pinakada. Luckily, there isn't a single Naval battle, which will deafen the sounds of seagulls. Soon enough, Lapis and Ruby both lead me to a dark, winding alleyway.

"Dragons. We've been winding down these paths a little too much lately," I say out loud, we twist and turn our way through pathways.

"Well, we assassins are secretive. We try hiding anything from the public eye. Very few know about the existence of the Order," Ruby explains, squinting her eyes at me. A couple of twists and turns later, we arrive at a shop at the end of the alleyway. Ruby scoffs. "We're here, Kedar. Once we heal your brother, we'll be out of your hair."

It's a small building, extremely run down. The windows have bright lights, though, so maybe this place is still in business. Ruby and Lapis don't even bat an eye at me as they walk to the front door, opening it with ease as the sound of a bell invades my ears. Once I step onto the wooden planks inside, a man looks up from a desk.

He has soft wrinkles on his face, indicating his somewhat old age. On his head, there's no hair, and his skin is the color of sand. A snaking tattoo slithers across his right arm, and his eyes are a dark, deep brown. On the other hand, the shop is filled with rows upon rows of potions, liquids, and other amenities. Ruby and Lapis have led me to a brewery.

"I haven't seen you two in years," The man says, nodding at my two assassin companions. On his neck is a jet-black piece of stone, solidifying his association with Ruby and Lapis. I assume he's about to get out of his seat, but he rolls his chair out of the desk to reveal that he doesn't have legs. He sits on a wooden wheelchair with metal wheels. A bracelet made out of black, obsidian beads is fastened on his left wrist. Ruby lets out a smile, holding her hand out to the man.

"It's been quite a while, Obby," she says, as the both of them shake hands. Lapis sighs before shaking his hand as well.

"Oi. Who's this youngster you've brought into my shop, eh?" Obby asks, glancing over Ruby's shoulder to catch a sight of me. I nervously back away, scratching the back of my head.

"This is Kedar. On my shoulder is his brother Omar," Lapis explains to me, responding to Obby's questionable look. As

Lapis recounts how he found the both of us, I scour around the shop, poking around blue potions with smoke and a glass bottle with black liquid. "His brother's got some problems, and it'd be best if you try helping us out."

"Eh. They're a bunch of strange fellows indeed, but I won't do this for just anybody. The four of you should follow me into the back room," he suggests, raising his eyebrow as he begins to weave through the rows of products, leading us to a wooden door in the back.

"Are we paying this guy? I mean, he doesn't really know me, and yet he seems so willing to help," I whisper to Ruby, leaning into her ear. She rolls her eyes, putting her hands on her hips. I glance at the rotting wooden planks on the floor.

"Obby's been our friend for over a while," She explains. "He's helping us because we Order members help each other. Besides, he's the only one that has the potential to reverse the effects of any sort of magic, as far as I know."

Obby grunts as he twists open a doorknob, leading us into the backroom. Inside is a long table in the middle, where Lapis decides to lay out Omar. Dark circles are under his eyes, and his skin is a harsh, pale gray. But a soft snore escapes from his lips, letting us know that he's still alive.

"Alright, young lad. Why don't you start from the beginning? Explain exactly what happened," Obby sighs, going over to a side table to shove some leather gloves on his hands. He pulls on the brown and gray goggles over his head to shield his eyes, before giving me a questioning look, awaiting my answer.

"Omar was supposed to be executed," I try to recall, replaying the instances of Omar being on the podium in my mind. Each second of my memory horrifies me, reminding me of the incomprehensible conditions of the prison. It all went flashing through my head at once. "One of the Craleans— a goblin, had a dark aura that surrounded his hands. After pressing fingertips into the side of Omar's head, he can't remember a single thing. Not even his name."

Obby strokes the underside of his chin, covered in gray and black stubble. He rubs both of his hands roughly, clenching his teeth as he looks at Omar through his brown, glass goggles. "Alrighty then. Perhaps this might work, by the grace of the Dragon."

He gathers a long sigh, rolling himself to the side of the table. Omar still has his eyes closed shut, his head slightly vibrating. My eyes widen as he cautiously grips tightly at both sides of Omar's head, before closing his eyes tightly. I turn to Lapis, who's crossing his arms, leaning against the stone wall. "What's he doing, exactly?"

"It's a memory spell. Designed to recall the memories lost up to four weeks ago. Luckily enough, your brother fits that period, it being only two weeks since we found the both of you at Alfdan."

I watch in wonder as a purple aura rises from Obby's hands, as Omar begins to shake vigorously. Ruby walks up to the table, holding Omar's wrists down as Obby works his magic.

Sweat pours down his forehead as he tries to hone in more on Omar's memories, fishing them out of the sea to return them back to him. Ruby grunts, as the gloomy light of the lantern above us completely burns out, the room darkening. Her eyes widen at Omar. "Obby! I think this is too much!"

"Gods! What's going on!" I shout, rushing to Omar's side. Omar starts trying to release himself from Obby's grip, only for Obby to try and hold him down harder. I take the initiative to press down on Omar's chest, trying to glue him to the table.

"Shut up! Everyone just shut up and hold him down!" Obby replies, his voice muffling from the glowing presence of his mana. Lapis proceeds to hold down Omar's wiggling feet, further enhancing our effort to keep him fastened.

"Dragons, Obby! What's happening with 'em?" Lapis urges, clenching his teeth. Omar opens his mouth and begins to shriek, filling the room with his ear-wrenching screams. I recoil back a bit as my eardrums vibrate with the sounds of his wailing. Obby and Ruby seem completely unbothered, fighting through the unholy noise.

"I'm trying, but there's nothing there!" Obby explains before a resounding explosion invades the room, muting Omar's screams completely.

A huge shockwave rams me to the wall, my back wrenching in pain. The same goes for the rest of us as Obby groans at himself on the floor. Omar stops vibrating completely, now frozen like a statue. I grasp at the side of my hip as I walk over to Obby, lending him my hand.

"You good?" I cough, blinking away the pain. Obby's unaffected, but his goggles are shattered. I wrap my arms around the underside of his shoulders, hoisting him back to his wheelchair as he lets out a heavy sigh.

"That doesn't matter, lad. What matters is your brother." he glances over to Omar, who is just a few feet away from us, completely still. Lapis and Ruby are banged up quite a bit from the purple explosion, with Ruby wiping away the blood dripping down her nostrils. "It's bad, Kedar. I have no idea how to describe it to you."

Ruby and Lapis' eyes widen, as Obby coughs violently, covering his mouth with the leather gloves on his hands. He scratches his bare head, with an eerie look in his dark eyes.

I clench my teeth. "Did the memory spell—"

"It isn't exactly a memory spell," he cuts me off, trying to recollect himself. Ruby scoffs, setting her hands at the edges of the table trying to take a closer look at my brother. Obby's mood darkens. "I tried exploring his mind, but something kicked me out. Something dark."

My eyes widen. "What's that supposed to mean?"

"Needless to say, those soldiers cursed him. It's called Njuperoxia. It's designed to completely erase one's mind, clouding it with confusion and utter emptiness."

He shudders in his wheelchair, looking down at the wooden floor with a blank stare. "I've known this spell for 20 years. And one thing I know is that there's no way to crack it. No possible way to fix it. In the end, your brother will be a shell of himself, Kedar. No recollections of you, no nothing. It is a punishment that I'd never wish upon my gravest enemies."

I clench my teeth and furrow my eyebrows in utter anger. "No. There must be a way to fix this. Come on, Obby. You must be bluffing. Joking." My voice urges, contorting my face into a mix of rage, anger, and grief. Ruby shakes her head slowly, as Lapis has an appalled look on his face. Obby shakes his head in denial.

"There's simply nothing that I can do, Kedar. I can't cure your brother. I may be able to reverse a couple of spells, but I do not have the skills to reverse a curse like this," he sighs, covering his forehead with his palm. His words go into one ear and out the other. But I know that what he's saying has to be the truth. My brother is gone. "The curse will ravage him for the next ten hours, and once he wakes up, he'll no longer recognize who he is. So I suggest that you spend as much time with him as you can."

My eyes droop, my body melting into a puddle of black goo. Lapis coughs, reaching for Omar to hoist him up on his shoulders once again. After Obby offers his deepest condolences to me, we walk out of his shop and into the city, with empty looks on our faces. There's little point in coming to

Jiya because my brother is gone. My nightmares are right all along. Without my brother, I am nothing.

"Kedar, are you alright?" Ruby asks, invading my thoughts. She sighs, scratching the back of her head as the sun begins to set on the city. Wisps of pink and orange fill the air as I try not to explode in tears in front of them. In ten hours, Omar will have woken up without knowing anything.

"No," I coldly reply. "How the hell do you think I am? My brother's gone, Ruby. But I'm happy that he's not dead. If he's dead… I wouldn't have known what to do with myself."

I glance at the children playing on the streets, without a care in the world. We were so innocent back then, not knowing war. If only I can turn back time and right my wrongs, maybe I can be happy again. But even though Omar isn't dead, his soul is gone, and I can't do anything to get it back.

"Kedar…." a voice whispers beside me, leading me to snap out of my trance. Ruby sighs, walking beside me as we trail Lapis. We watch him effortlessly carry Omar back to Farid's mansion with ease. Before long, she locks eyes with me, squinting. "I want to talk to you. Let's go to the dock."

I hesitate, but nod. After telling Lapis we are traveling to the docks, we strut alongside the shore, relishing ourselves in the dimming sunlight. A couple of minutes of silence goes by before I open my mouth to speak. "What did you want to talk about, Ruby?"

Our boots thump on the dock as we hear the calls of seagulls above our heads. She doesn't say a word while I find myself leaning on the wooden railing, glancing at the fish below. I hear her hands clasp together as she leans her back against the railings, looking down at the blue water with me. "Look. I'm not exactly on the best terms with you, but I'm honestly kind of worried."

I maintain a stern look on my face, clogging every emotion that tries to ooze out of me. The best thing that I can do is listen to her speak. "I just wanted to make sure you are fine."

There's a pause. "Didn't you say you had plans if Omar got cured?"

"Yeah, I did," I reply, gazing up at her. "I just wanted the both of us to live the life that he would've wanted. Just peace, no war. But I failed. The Omar that I'll know from now on will be just a hollow shell, an empty heart."

I ruffle my hair with my hands, pushing the curls out of my face. Ruby looks ahead towards the falling sun. The colors reflect off of the waters, showcasing its light, orange glow. Nothing obscures the beautiful view, and nothing is deafening the soft calls of the birds in the sky.

"Well, if you want to leave us, do so as you please. Me and Lapis won't stop you," she promises me, brushing her braids behind her ear.

"Yeah, but life will be harder," I explain, looking down at my boots.

"You have a nightmare, right?" she asks after we both stand in silence for a few minutes. I nod.

She stares deep into my brown pupils. "When I was young, I had nightmares every single day. Maybe they aren't as brutal and violent as yours—" Ruby gives me a small smile— "But I adapted. I moved on, which was hard, but I did move on. From all of my pain and suffering."

Perhaps Ruby and I are more similar than I thought. We stand there in silence, simply immersing ourselves in the sunset. I wonder what her life is like. *Is she broken?*

"This isn't your fault, Kedar. I can tell that you blame yourself. And it's not good. Learn to forgive. Learn to fix your mistakes rather than drown in them," She reassures me, a tone matching my mother's. It reminds me of how she constantly warned me, advising me to never do wrong in the world. But I broke her promise too. "Just think about it for me. Alright?"

I nod and think about our conversation as we walk back to the mansion in silence. Ruby's definitely experienced the same type of hardships that I have, judging from her advice. It might be a stretch, but it's safe enough to assume.

A couple of minutes later, we arrive at Farid's mansion, gazing upon the glass windows and the small garden in the back. The size almost replicates the Pyrian castle in the capital of Basalia, only being a couple of sizes smaller. We walk inside and head to our rooms, and I find myself staring out of the window, clenching at the bed sheets tightly.

I sigh on the edge of the bed, looking at the marble fountain outside. Mixes of pink, yellow, and purple flowers blend in with the soft green color of the garden, providing it with the smell of pure arnithian lavender. The talk with Ruby has cleared my mind. It calms me, and her advice keeps echoing in my head over and over again. *Forgive yourself.*

I might as well visit my brother, I say after a couple of more minutes in silence. My hands are shaking as I slowly lurch the door open, walking through the hallways as I glance at Farid reading in his library down below. Before I open Omar's door, I stop to hesitate.

He won't remember who he is, but I can make him remember. I grunt before swinging the door wide open, expecting to see my brother in the bed.

But he's gone.

Arnithian lavender is a plant, bred from lavender and Arnithia. Arnithia is quite an expensive, luscious spice indeed, only growing northwards in Hexia. When powdered and seasoned into food, it gives the product a mix of umami and salty taste. When bred with lavender, the flower's smell is quite pleasurable, only to be described by Queen Lauvee X: "Lovely and inspiring."

-   *A Hayan's Guide to Botany: Volume 3*

FIVE

*N*o. *This can't be happening,* I shout before frantically looking outside the window. My eyes scan the garden. I clench my fist to throw a punch at the wall, stopping myself to glance towards the bed. The blankets are tidy as if nobody's ever there. But on top of the blue blankets lies a small note, with dark burns along the edges.

I grind my teeth together as I throw out the idea of him escaping. No—Omar's gone. Kidnapped by people who want him... *but why?* I calm myself down, sighing as I glaze my fingers over the rough paper. Every single possible thought runs through my mind. The Cralean soldiers from Alfdan probably took him back to make him rot in his cell. Sweat runs down my cheek as I try to resist having a panic attack. I open the half-folded note, noticing the writings in the middle of it. There are only four words that I can make out.

This is his destiny.

This is his destiny?! I repeat in my mind, reading the words over and over. They're indecipherable, and they can mean almost anything. I hyperventilate as I put a hand over my chest. My hands are shaking again, and I can barely compose myself. After I slip the note into my pocket, I take one last look at the room. Everything is untouched. Omar must still be in his coma.

I close the door softly, beginning to walk downstairs in a panic. Ruby and Lapis are sitting on the dining table side by side, speaking in low whispers. As soon as Lapis glances up at me, he knows something is wrong. *It's my fault*, I repeat in my mind.

I slam my hands on the table and they both jump. Lapis gives me a questioning look as my voice churns. "Goddammit... they took him. They took Omar. He's gone."

Ruby's eyes widen. "The hell are you talking about? You're joking, right?" She frantically asks, putting the cup of tea in her hands back onto the surface of the table. Lapis sighs as he takes a long sip, before shaking his head solemnly.

"Kedar, Kedar," Lapis coughs, tucking strands of his long hair behind his ear. He fidgets with his earrings in deep thought. "What the hell happened?"

"I went into Omar's room to check up on him, and he's gone. Nowhere to be found," I reply, tensing. "All that's left is this note."

I place the note on the table as Lapis and Ruby deeply examine the paper, checking every side, edge, and stroke of it. Lapis' eyes widen as he flips the small piece of paper to the back, revealing the symbol of an obsidian lion being worshiped by a monk.

"Dragons. This is bad. Very bad. This... this symbol," Lapis says to himself, as Ruby heightens her eyebrows slightly in shock. He turns to Ruby before whispering in her ear, talking amongst themselves again as they leave me standing there in confusion.

76

"What? What is it?" I question, wiping the sweat coming down my forehead. Each passing second can be Omar rotting in a place he doesn't recognize. We have to find him.

"This symbol reigns from some of the most dangerous people on this planet. You *do not* want to mess with these people, Kedar," Ruby whispers, a look of horror on her face. The paper appalls them. A dubious tone sets on their faces.

"That doesn't matter at all. I just want my brother back. Whoever these guys may be, I'll get my brother back no matter what," I urge, gripping the edges of the table tightly. Lapis scoffs while Ruby shakes her head.

"Kedar, don't you dare mess with these people. We don't want you getting killed," She admits, glancing at the lion on the note. The harsh reality begins to set in my mind. I can't do anything in my condition. Some of the wounds on my chest haven't even healed, and they open when I stretch my arms. I don't even know who this mysterious group is, much less where they may be.

"Look, tomorrow, we can part ways. But if you want, we can train you enough to be able to handle these guys. After that, we'll track your brother down, one step at a time," Ruby offers, before I roll my eyes in annoyance. This is the worst time to try and recruit me into their group of assassins. But they do have a point. If I try going after them myself, who knows where my corpse might end up.

"Goddammit! I can't do anything!" I yell, looking at the chandelier hanging from the ceiling. My eyes glance back down at Lapis and Ruby, who are awaiting my response. If I choose to go with them, there is a slim chance that I can find my brother.

After a couple of minutes of thinking, running through all of the possible combinations of events that can happen within the span of my joining their assassin group, I cave in. "Alright. Fine. Let's do this. I'm coming with you."

Ruby and Lapis go back upstairs while I decide to take a stroll through the city in search of one thing: a pack of cigars. I haven't had a smoke in so long, and one puff can really get all of the worry out of my mind. It takes me a bit to get into the night market, but I find it at the end of an alleyway, hidden from the rest of Jiya.

I browse the stands. After killing Cralean soldiers, I'll get a cigar and light it up to smoke over the dead bodies. It erases my anger.

A farik sits at a stand with trinkets and gimmicks, and on the side is a pack of dark brown cigars. I walk up to her, fumbling around in my pockets for a single coin.

I pay her two hundred lorelocks, walking away from the stall with a happy smile on my face. Soon enough, I quickly lit it up with a match, sticking it in my mouth to relish the smoke. The flavor is bitter, yet it's fulfilling.

As I lean in the darkness of an alleyway, a memory forms to remind me of the last time I've smoked a blunt.

"Dragons," Omar said, invading my thoughts. I breathed heavily, looking at the burning hole filled with charred bodies. Another battle in the books, it seemed. The clouds of smoke that arose from the pit were the perfect mix of blood and bone.

"Omar, shut up. Can't you see I'm enjoying the view?" I snapped, taking out a cigar from my pocket. My lungs breathed in the hexian tobacco as I exhaled slowly, mixing it with the smoke from the pit. I took off the metal helmet on my head, smearing the blood on it with my two fingers. Each death seemed to quench my thirst more and more. Each soul that I

took reminded me why I joined the army, to take as many lives as I could.

"Oh. Sorry," He whispered, the sound of his boots crunching on the soil fading away as he left me alone to watch the pit. I chuckled to myself, clutching the pendant that sat on my neck. It was the same necklace my father wore, a red gemstone complete with golden lining.

"Can't you see, father? Do you not see me avenging your death?" I whispered, rubbing the red stone of the pendant tightly. The ground all around me was riddled with bodies from both sides, the only feature differentiating them being Crale having a black and yellow uniform, and Basalia having a gold and navy blue uniform. I sighed as my eyes glanced over to my brother, who was busy inspecting his short sword. That bastard. If only he was more useful in battle. Then maybe he would understand.

I exhaled the smoke out of my mouth yet again, looking up to the moon above. The more I kill, the more I feed. Perhaps it is my destiny. It's my fate to be a killer. Whatever Omar blabbered about all the time is nonsense.

Peace doesn't exist for people like us.

I woke up the next morning with a cold shiver. Once I collect myself, I head downstairs to see Ruby with the huge bag of supplies over her back, while Lapis has his arms crossed.

They're back to their assassin-like attire, with the golden-lined cloaks. I walk up to them in confusion. "Wait. What are you two doing?

"I'll have to be honest with you, Kedar. I feel like we're being followed, meaning that we have to leave Jiya at this very moment," Lapis explains, pulling his hood up. Ruby nods in agreement, as I give Lapis a skeptical look.

"Well, where are we going, then?" I reply, narrowing my eyebrows.

"We gotta get back to the order's headquarters in Ardon. It'll take us quite a while to get there, but it'll be worth it once we get to safety," Ruby explains, gripping the strings of the bag as our supplies clank and clink.

I'm about to reply to Ruby before we hear a blood-curdling scream. Looking up, Farid is wailing, while a dark figure behind him snatches him by the throat, dragging him up the steps. Our eyes widen in shock, as Lapis dashes at the speed of light. Before he can make it to the front of the steps, the figure stabs him through the stomach, blood spurting all over the marble. The figure throws him off the steps, and Farid lands in front of Lapis with a hard crack.

"Brother! No!" Lapis shouts, before me, and Ruby springs into action, trying to catch the dark figure. I catch a glimpse of them, only to reveal the assailant wearing a red demonic mask with white horns. They have a jet-black cloak, and wield a short sword that looks sharp enough to cut through steel. Lapis is blinded by anger as he swings at the figure on the top, but they endlessly dodge his attacks. Me and Ruby dash up the steps as they jump down to the first floor, attempting to run out the front door to escape.

Ruby quickly pulls a throwing knife wrapped in red cloth at the handle out of her belt. She throws it with precision, stabbing the figure's back, and making him immediately collapse to his knees on the marble tiles.

Lapis jumps down from the stairs as we follow him to confront the dark figure. He tries limping to the doorknob, but Lapis attacks him with a swift kick at his wrist, letting him writhe in pain. I watch as Ruby uppercuts his chin, making the mask explode into hundreds of pieces. Under that mask is an elf with a huge smirk on their face. Their chin soaks with blood as they spit out a tooth on the floor.

"That was easy enough," He musters to say before Lapis punches him in the nose. The elf whimpers before his body thumps to the ground, and Lapis clenches his hand around his neck, lifting him up in the air with a vengeful look in his eyes. He narrows his eyebrows at the elf, still smirking even though most of his face is swollen with black and blue.

"Who the hell sent you here," Lapis says, calmly at first. But veins on his neck pop as he grits his teeth harshly. "WHO THE HELL SENT YOU HERE?! HUH?!"

The elf chuckles, as Lapis tightens his grip against his neck. He coughs out blood, before tapping on Lapis to convince him to stop. "You know who. Sworn enemies of this little order you have. I've been ordered to kill any Disturbed member I see."

Lapis curses and yells, before thrusting the man's head deep into the marble tiles, making his face explode. The man quickly puts his hand up at Lapis in fear. "Wait. I can tell you where He is. Wait—"

Lapis doesn't bother hearing him out, using his leather boots to stomp on his face over and over again. I watch in horror as Lapis grunts with each stomp, screaming in agony. Pink matter splatters all over me and Ruby.

Before long, Ruby steps up to hold Lapis' biceps, pulling him back from the corpse. Lapis hyperventilates, his bloodshot eyes darting from right to left from the shock. A resounding cough fills the air, as we realize that Farid is still alive.

Me, Lapis, and Ruby run to Farid, wheezing on the cold tiles of his mansion. Blood slowly streams out from his mouth, as he clutches on his wound tightly. Lapis grits, kneeling to his brother as tears well up in his eyes. "Farid…"

Farid can barely muster up an answer, his blood flooding the floor. He slowly lifts up his hand, trying to caress his brother's face. Dark circles from under his eyes as death creeps upon him. The glitters of the chandelier above are sparkling in his pupils, as his breath slows.

"Ruby!" Lapis exclaims, turning to her with an urgent stare. "Please, there's gotta be something you can do. Use your magic."

Ruby only provides him with a solemn gaze, her head lowering at the black and white checkered floor. I never knew Ruby could use her mana, but the thought of her being able to use magic intimidates me. Ruby's clearly deep in thought. She eventually raises her hands over the wound.

I gaze upon the open, red gash that Farid has on his stomach. The blade must've tipped with poison. There's a flowing black liquid coursing through Farid's veins.

"Lapis, it's impossible. Farid's been poisoned, and it's too late. It's already gotten to his heart. Even if I did try to stop the poison, it's already attacking his whole body," she admits, lowering her eyelids. Lapis is in denial, grasping onto his brother's wrist, shaking it in desperation. Farid is luckily still alive, but all he can do is breathe his last breaths.

"Just try, Ruby. Please," Lapis begs before she surrenders a deep sigh. I squint at Ruby's hands as a light blue aura begins to arise from the fingertips of her black gloves. My eyes widen as Ruby concentrates on stopping the poison but to no avail.

Farid begins to convulse, just like Omar in Obby's backroom. He spits out blood as Ruby tries to squeeze out the poison from his wound. Lapis clenches his eyes tightly, praying for her mana to work. I can only watch in anticipation as Ruby struggles to heal Lapis' brother. Farid's hand springs up from the floor, clutching at Lapis' arm.

82

"Brother. Let me go. Let me die. I'm not worth your time, all of you need to run," He coughs, blood running through the crevices of his teeth. His blond hair is stained with red.

"No, we have to save you. We have to try," Lapis urges, grasping at his wrist even tighter.

"No... just... go..." he says as a gray glaze sets over his blue eyes, and his breathing slows to a halt. Ruby regretfully removes her hands from the corpse, the harsh reality that Farid is dead setting in our minds. Lapis is the first to react, gripping his brother's shoulders.

"NO! Farid... PLEASE! ANSWER ME!" he urges, shaking his shoulders lightly. All that Farid provides him is a dark stare, as drops of blood flow from his mouth, staining the dark blue cloak that he has on. Lapis begs for his brother to come back for a couple more minutes, before eventually letting him rest on the floor. I scratch the back of my head, backing away from Farid's dead body as his veins begin to glow slightly black, the poison eating each of his organs.

Lapis returns to the dark look on his face. The elf looks blank. He immediately walks past Ruby, before clutching the front door to pull it wide open. I notice he turns his head one last time to take a glance at me, his tears drying on his cheeks.

"L-Let's go. I don't want to be here anymore," Lapis whispers, going outside to the front garden. Me and Ruby gave each other a skeptical look as we followed our elf companion, not making a single sound. I don't know how to console someone with death, but I know Omar can. He has once consoled our comrades after losing their friends and families. If he is here, Lapis will be in a better mindset instead of the dark place he is in as of now.

"Lapis...I'm sorry," I stammer, springing into action. He doesn't answer me. We walk down the side of the road, none of the citizens knowing what we have been through. It's like a

83

switch went on in Lapis, signaling him to return back to his normal state.

"Don't try to speak to him. He's grieving," Ruby suggests, grunting as she hunches the bag over her shoulder. She messes with her cloak, barely gathering any attention from the crowds of people we pass. We find ourselves following Lapis as he twists and winds through the streets, never looking back.

"We'll be traveling to Ardon over the next few days," Ruby continues, glancing up at the shining sun. "You should prepare. The man we're about to meet should train you up. By then, we'll investigate Omar's whereabouts."

I stay in silence as we find ourselves outside of Jiya's inner city, miles away from Farid's mansion. Lapis still hasn't turned around to look at us, as the only thing that comes out of his mouth is a couple of grunts and sighs. As me and Ruby trail behind the grieving elf, I can't help but wonder.

As we begin to hoist ourselves on the docks, my mind keeps flourishing. With all of these deaths and horrible predicaments we encounter, Ruby and Lapis establish themselves as part of a mysterious group.

Who are these people?

Civilians have witnessed the assassination of Crale's famous general Maruce Halverman. During his speech after the Battle of Cantai, a figure from the crowd killed him in cold blood— stabbing him in the neck and leading him to bleed out on the stage's floor. Healers close by tried to revive him, but it was too late. The assassin was gone, and the people were devastated. If anyone has any sort of information about a black cloaked figure, then please, go to the *Shurta* station to report it to the authorities, and give justice to our great general.

- An excerpt from a Cralean newspaper, printed in around 1434.

SIX

As we walked, Ruby proceeded to explain to me what to expect from Ardon. She described it as a prosperous town along the Eden River, separating from Kigamouth Lake. Every single step we took prompted me to glance behind to make sure we weren't being followed. My mind had still been on high alert ever since Lapis' brother died, and the same went for those two.

We crossed the Lake using one of Farid's boats at the docks. Once we got off, a merchant outpost was near shore, and we gladly purchased horses to be on our way.

We slept once our entire trip, and that was when Ruby declared herself exhausted. It was only six hours, but it fueled me enough to keep walking down the river, to seek Ardon. Luckily enough, since we rode horseback, it trimmed the time it took to get there by around one day.

Now, as the wind blows across my face, I blink my way through the air. By now, The *Shurta* are probably investigating Farid's house.

We're already fugitives for Crale, so I pray that the Basalian *Shurta* won't see us as enemies, too. It's hard to keep my body on guard and manage my sanity at the same time since we're a long way to Ardon.

The dark brown horse that Lapis has bought for me has a dark brown mane. Every time I urge it to go forward, it neighs softly in exhaustion from our long trek. The animal's as tired as I am, looking like it'll collapse at any minute. Ruby has a drop of sweat running down her cheek as she rides with me. We follow Lapis, riding on a bright white horse. He keeps silent, never daring to speak to me.

Ruby maneuvers the horse while all wobbly-like. It's obvious she's never ridden a horse before. She's a pretty serious girl until she falls off a horse. It's funny but not worth laughing at. I don't wanna risk getting slapped into oblivion.

I'm still hurt by the fact that Omar is gone but Lapis' situation is far worse. His brother lost his life. From the looks and glimpses I catch from Lapis every now and then, it seems like he blames himself, completely torn. It's really my fault. Ever since they've brought me along, death has been following me around everywhere.

We ride our horses along the Eden River, my horse whinnying softly as its hooves crackle on the green grass below. The rushing streams of the river made small glimmering sparkles as the sun above completely blinds us.

Ruby tells me how the river runs straight through Ardon, splitting the city in two.

The weather is cooler than usual. Only the soft sounds of saltless water entertain me, and the slight hum of Ruby soothes the silence that radiates from Lapis.

87

Ruby has gotten me a black cloak to wear to blend with our surroundings and under it,. But the constant blow of the wind reminds me that not bringing my dazclava is a mistake.

After a couple of minutes of silent walking, the dark outline of a city becomes clearer in the distance. It's hard to see since the sun's rays distort my view. Perhaps once I arrive, I can finally get some answers about who Ruby and Lapis really are.

Three hundred feet in the air lies a beaming tower, far higher than all the other buildings in the city. What's revealed is a large golden spire, with a pyramid on top. Along it are patterns of ancient dragons and mythical creatures surrounding Dracothesim. It's a Draconic Beacon, a common place of worship for Basalians.

Stone walls surround Ardon as the River Eden flows through it, with both sides of the town connecting with a wooden bridge. Small sailboats flow along the wide river, as some civilians fish in the lush streams. A story that my father once told me darts in my mind, one that spoke of a Divine Dragon that once came down to Haya.

"Kedar, you must listen," he said, clasping his hands together. I cautiously looked up at my father, busy with the novel I was reading. My dad took the initiative to pull out a book from under the dining table, as the soft chirp of crickets invaded the windows to my left. In the middle of the wooden dining table was a candle that was almost about to go out. It shined in my face, giving me minimal warmth as my dad flipped through white pages.

"Listen to what?" I replied, slightly annoyed by his disturbance.

88

"I haven't read you this story yet, and I might as well do it now since your brother and mother are sound asleep," he explained, slicking his long curly back a bit. My father cleared his throat as I agonizingly set my novel down to hear him out. I could spell out the letters on the front cover of the book: The Codex of Basal.

"What the hell is that?" I asked before my father slapped my hand. It strung as he proceeded to narrow his eyebrows at me with a disappointed look. I shrugged, looking down at the table in pity.

"Language. Anyway, this is The Codex of Basal, words spoken from the man above," He continued, clearing his throat as I peered to take a glance at the words on the paper.

"What's the story about?"

"It's better when we just read it together," My dad said, sitting next to me to offer the book. He flipped to the near end of the book, before reading the lines to me.

"'And the Divine Dragon said, For all the land you see, hill to hill, is what I have presented to you. And each generation that comes after you lay down and die, belongs to them. For the children of Basal are destined to rule the land which is deemed holy, until they may hold their last breath.'"

Even though it seemed pretty straightforward, it felt like each word that my father said streamed out from ear to the next. I raised my eyebrow, not sure what to interpret from this scripture. "It doesn't make sense to me. What's it supposed to mean, Dad?"

"God promised for us to have this holy land. It where once the prophets walked and spoke of Basal, preaching his word. This is why we fight this war, Kedar. To keep it safe. Protected. If you do go to war when you're older, my son... just know that your mother and I are with you. And know that when you put on that armor, you're putting on the armor of God," He replied.

Still, it confused me out of my mind, but I decided that it wasn't worth mentioning.

But it makes sense to me now.

I've never picked up The Codex of Basal myself. My father has read me many stories from it. One of them is the Day of Judgement when Basal sends down his angels in a time where the people of Basalia are attacked. Even though it's been fifty years, nothing has yet to happen, even though millions have been killed on both sides. Even the people of Crale are suffering, not just the country of Basalia. They too hope for an end to this petty war.

I glance back at the tower. Basalians use it mainly for prayer. From what I know, Dracotheists kneel in front of the tower before saying their prayers, presenting them to speak to the divine being. The only other time I recall looking at one is when Craleans struck it down, forcing the large golden towers to crash to the ground.

Ardon seems exceptionally more sacred than other towns because of the towering pillar of gold. Even though Dracotheism is the most popular region across the continent, denominations reject some ideas about it. One of them claims that the prophet Elian is the son of Basal. Some say that he's god, and Basal is merely the one who prospered. Though there are three divisions of Dracotheism, they are all united because of one thing: The Dragon War.

"Praise Basal, we're finally here," says Ruby, interrupting my thoughts. There's a subtle smile on her face. Archers on the walls look down at us from below, examining our presence. We inch towards the stone walls, as guards at the metal gate check each and every person who dares to come inside.

We find ourselves glancing at the two Basalian soldiers waiting for us to step up to them. They're both wearing the same uniform I once wore as a soldier. It's heavy metallic armor, with a helmet that covers and masks their faces. On top of their heads is a long, slithering white colored fabric, indicating that they're low-ranking soldiers. In the middle of their shields, they hold the iconic colors of Basalia: Blue, yellow, and white.

Both soldiers hold an intimidating long spear, before they step in front of us, blocking our way inside. They practically pounce on Lapis and Ruby as they glare at me from my boots to my curly hair. One of the steps towards Lapis. "Hey. What's your business here, you three?"

"Relax, Levi," Lapis says in a sultry tone, taking off his hood. "It's me."

"Eh. Just makin' sure, if that makes sense to ya," the second soldier says in a coarse goblin accent. "Who's the new lad behind ya?"

For the first time in days, Lapis glances back at me, his eyes narrowing. He sighs, turning back at the goblin soldier. "He's nobody you should worry about."

The two soldiers give each other a look. One of them shrugs. Soon enough, they pull up the metal gates, letting us into the blooming town. Even the soldiers are intimidated by Lapis' sheer presence. As we pass along, Ruby scratches the back of her hood before giving the soldier a sympathetic sigh.

Once we get inside, we're greeted with marketplaces, shops, restaurants, and inns. The buildings mimic the ones that are in Saitra and Jiya, having adobe houses with wood supports, along with stone structures with wooden roofs. Hints of other religions surround us. There are Farrikkian shrines, Juran chapels, and Elf temples.

The city is diverse, with all races living together in peace. Most civilians look full of themselves, while some are skinny and malnourished. Refugee camps are right at the entrance with people who've separated from their friends and families. Children run through the streets while some try snatching anything off of Ruby's belt, only to fail helplessly.

As we ride our horses through the streets, we find ourselves coming closer and closer to the Golden Tower. People are in a circular formation as some wait in lines, seeking to pray at the Dracotheistic pillar. Up close, it blinds me with the majestic sight. We walk past the towering piece of gold in awe.

The three of us strut across the bridge to the south side, and I glance at the river below. Fishes of all kinds swim through the fast-streaming water.

"Alright Kedar," Ruby begins, taking off her hood. "We're heading to the Onyx District. Once we get to the headquarters, just let us do the talking. Trust me, you don't want to leave a horrible impression on him."

Him? I repeat in my mind. As we cross the sign marking that we are stepping into this "Onyx District," I scour over the seafood stands that goblins owned, the humans selling their jewelry, and fariks with their tarot card reading posts.

"Who's *him?*" I inquire, prompting Ruby to raise an eyebrow.

"You'll find out soon enough. He'll explain everything."

The district is small but bustling. We can't trek through everyone since most of them are standing in our way. We head down a dark path. *Great.* Another instance of assassins gathering in dark alleys. We unmount our horses, following Lapis down the winding walkway. After a couple minutes of turning left to right, we find ourselves in front of a wooden trapdoor.

92

On it is a gemstone that resembles an onyx. Lapis grunts as he clasps his hand on the handle, clenching his teeth as he swings it open. I look down at the elf. "Hey Lapis... about your brother..."

"Kedar. I know you're about to apologize, but it's not your fault," he starts, heading down the stairs that lead into the dark underground. Ruby and I follow suit, as the trap door closes with a winding thunk. "It's mine. I should've known that taking you guys to Farid's mansion was a mistake. Of course, those damn rats will figure out where we are eventually."

"Don't be like that," I reply, using one hand to clasp his broad shoulders. He glances down at me, blinking with his emerald eyes. The soft glow of the lanterns on the wall reflects off the sides of his cheek, creating an orange and yellow tan. "It was nobody's fault. I couldn't stop what was happening, you couldn't stop what was happening, and Ruby couldn't either."

"Farid is dead, Kedar. I should've done something," he explains, our boots echoing in the desolate tunnel. At the end is a wooden door on the right side, with a huge metal keylock. I kick off a piece of cobweb on my boots before giving Lapis a heavy sigh while Ruby walks with me.

"I know, but don't put it on yourself. It'll only make everything worse for you," I propose, sniffing my nose from the dust inside. We find ourselves at the door as if waiting for someone to unlock it from the inside. Lapis gives me an appreciative look.

"You're right, Kedar. If I cannot save my brother, then I'll save yours," he says. The elf turns his head. "I swear on my life."

I nod. "Sounds good. What are we waiting for, then?"

"Ruby, did you bring the key?" Lapis asks, his attention turning towards her. Ruby's already setting the bag down, trying to look inside. Her expression turns solemn as her hand digs through the bag.

"Damn. I must've forgotten it in Saitra, too..." She drifts off, a soft blush rising to her face. Lapis shakes his head before lifting his fist to the door.

He bangs the door a couple of times, the sound echoing across the tunnel. "Amber? Topaz? Bixbite?"

Lapis clenches his right fist and bangs on the door harder. After a couple of minutes of this with nobody seeming to answer the door, Lapis stops with his obnoxious knocking, noticing Ruby giving him a stink eye.

"Um, Lapis?" says Ruby, shaking her head slightly. "Stop being so loud before Onyx comes and kills us."

Lapis ignores her before giving her a stink eye back, banging his fists on the wooden door like a maniac. I recoil back, standing next to Ruby as Lapis continues his relentless assault on the door.

"Please, tell me there is someone in here!" Lapis yells, his fists turning blood red. I nervously wait behind Lapis as Ruby heaves a sigh, crossing her arms in disappointment.

She rubs her eyes and yawns as Lapis continues to knock, never wavering. Eventually, he stops, prompting me to take a peek at the little window in the door. A dark figure stands in front of us before Lapis smiles awkwardly. They swing the door wide open as Lapis chuckles, trying to hide that he just left dents in the door.

"Gods and Dragons, Lapis," a masculine voice says, stepping out to peak at all of us. He is a tall man, with skin slightly tanner than Lapis. We lock eyes with each other as I notice the slim glimmer in his light brown eyes, the same color of the hair that he has flowing down the sides of his head. He wears a leather brown vest on top of his long-sleeved white shirt, while he sports brown boots and gray pants.

"Canya knock just once, mate? You're really killing me over 'ere," he declares, giving Lapis an annoyed look. The man reaches up to scratch the wing tattoo on the back of his neck before slipping a quick nod to Ruby. We lock eye contact again before he looks at me from top to bottom.

"Just let us in, Bix," Lapis groans. The man hesitates, sighs, and steps back into the entrance. Ruby and I follow Lapis as he walks right in, revealing us to the interior of their headquarters.

The circular room inside splits off into three hallways. In the middle is a large circular wooden table, with ten chairs all around it. The roof is small. In the middle is a huge, yellow gemstone. I realize who Lapis and Ruby have both taken me to.

Onyx.

"Alright, let's get the elephant out of the room, eh? Who's this bloke you've brought with ya?" the man says, narrowing his eyes at me. I spot a dangling red gemstone hanging from his neck, replicating the same style that both Ruby and Lapis have. His ears are slightly pointy, implying that he might be a half-elf. The wrinkles on his forehead and cheeks tell me that he's around the same age as Lapis, if not, younger.

"I decided to bring him here because I can see the potential, Bix," Lapis chimes in, the man maintaining his questionable look at me. Bix scratches the back of his head, rolling his eyes.

"That's what ya always say Lapis, and most of the people you bring here end up dying before the first damn trial," he slurs, his deep Basalian accent affecting his voice harshly. Bix leans against the stone bricks of the wall, putting his leg up and sealing his eyes shut. "I highly doubt this soft bloke can survive three seconds."

The elf shrugs at Bix's remarks. Bix squints at me. "But if fate wills it, ya should find the old man in his chambers. He's been there all day, and aye have null idea what he's up to."

"Alright. Follow me, both of you," Lapis sighs, as we circle around the table and walk to the middle hallway. On the floor are red and gold carpets, and the walls are lined with hundreds of candles. Bix gives me a harsh stare as the soft clunk of Ruby's bag echoes behind me. Before the room can fade out of sight, Bix motions his hand toward me.

I stop in my tracks, letting Lapis and Ruby walk ahead, not knowing I've left them behind. "What? What is it?"

"What's ya name, lad? You look pretty banged up, scars everywhere. I know you must be a war veteran," he says as my boots ruffle softly on the carpet. Bix meets me at the edge of the hallway.

I chuckle at his remark. "Yeah, I've been in some battles. My name is Kedar, by the way."

"Well, Kedar... good luck, mate. You're going to need it," the half-elf says, giving me a slight nod of approval.

I catch up with both of my assassin companions, Ruby and Lapis, not batting an eye to question what I'm doing back there. A slight tingle rises from my spine, because of how eerie this whole place is. The air is scentless. Soon enough, we see a solemn door at the end of the hallway lined with gold.

An onyx is embedded in the middle, not a single lock in sight. A slight drop of sweat drips down the left side of my cheek, as I can feel the gloomy heat of the candles on the wall warming up my skin. Before Lapis can knock, Ruby steps in front of him, giving the wood's surface a slight tap as she makes out a sigh.

As the door opens, Lapis turns to me and puts his pointer finger to his lips, to let them do the talking. Ruby clears her throat, her voice is soft and elegant. "Sir? There's someone that Lapis brought that I think you should see."

I hear the shuffling of feet against the red carpet and out steps a dog, old as the beginning of time. His furry ears drip slightly downwards, and I still see the wrinkles through his brown fur. The old dog's eyes are a golden yellow.

Even with him being shoulder height beside Lapis, intimidation is omitted from him.

"Boy. Tell me your name," he rasps, his voice old and fragile. He raises his hand, reaching out for mine to shake it. I don't hesitate to clasp my hand with his, realizing how bony his fingers feel.

"K-Kedar," my voice stutters. "My name is Kedar, sir."

"Teaching magic is difficult. Every student that I come across is different, their power on many different scales. Some may be more powerful than others when starting out on their journey as a witch or mage, but others can find their mana weaker when responding to their commands. But a certain student of mine, named Onyx, indeed shows promise. I wish to nurture, and make sure he does not become another wilted flower."

- A journal entry from ▮▮▮▮▮▮▮▮, date unknown.

SEVEN

Onyx relieves me with a soft smile to relieve my nervousness. "Interesting name Kedar. It means darkness, straying from the light."

My hands tremble in his, so I shake it a bit harder and straighten my posture. "Yeah. Odd name, I guess you can say."

He shuts the door behind him after leading me inside. On the right is a mirror-lined with gold and a bed with white and gold patterns. On the left is a bookshelf and a desk full of papers with a pen on the side.

"Well, how'd you get that name?" he questions, clasping his hands together. Fariks are known for their lengthy lifespans. No wonder why most are political leaders. Onyx seems to have been here since the beginning of time, his ancient age gleaming. His tail wags under his white and gold robe, awaiting my response.

"My parents named me Kedar because I was born on the same day that Frudith died. The townsfolk called me his reincarnate," I force out, stuttering slightly as Onyx is busy shuffling through papers at his desk. A small trickle of sweat happens to drop down the back of my neck. This is the man who can possibly lead me to save my brother. Onyx may look old, but I sense the secrecy radiating from his being. He must be powerful.

After a couple seconds of tense silence, the dog replies. "I sensed your presence the second you came inside the city of Ardon, Kedar."

I question the possibility of him noticing me in my head as he struts toward me, looking up at my face while squinting. "What brings you here? I know most of the people that Lapis sent me are... underwhelming, to say the least, but I can already sense something different within you."

Onyx must be a mana user, just like Lapis and Ruby. There's no way that he can detect me without the presence of his magic. The fact that he can detect my soul... it's frightening. I can tell that he must be some sort of powerful mage.

"It's a lengthy story," I chuckle. "I have no idea how to explain the whole thing to you."

"Well, perhaps the both of us can sit down at the entrance," He proposes, smiling as he licks his sharp canines. "It'll enlighten you more, hopefully."

Mere minutes later, I find myself scrunching at the seats of the table. Lapis and Ruby are both leaning against the wall, chatting amongst themselves as I prepare to explain myself to the old dog. Bix is nowhere to be found once we get back, and I assume he's out there in Ardon, up to some assassin antics.

I clear my throat and spill everything that's happened so far— from the horrors at Alfdan to our travels to Ardon. The whole time, Onyx has his fingers resting on his chin, his eyes deep in thought. Once I finish my story, there is a long pause in the room, while Onyx takes in every word.

"You're in an interesting predicament here, to say the least," he sighs, tapping a finger on the desk before slicking his dog ears back. "I imagine you assume I can explain everything to you?"

"It's why I decided to come here when I really should be chasing after my brother right now," I admit, bouncing my leg under the table. Onyx gives me a heavy sigh, pulling out a scroll from the robe.

"I'll have to be frank with you, son. You've gotten yourself into a dark rabbit hole, and there is no going back," he begins, before sliding the paper across the table and over to me. Once I pick it up, I realize in the middle is the same symbol that is on the piece of paper in Omar's room.

"This is the symbol that you told me about earlier, yes?" Onyx questions, raising his brow a bit. There's no questioning it: the familiar lion and monk matched it exactly. Even though I know we aren't being followed anymore, it still sends tingles up my spine. I look up at Onyx and give him a reassuring nod.

"This is the Veils of Judah. Or Judah's Veils, if you want to call it that. They're the sworn enemies of this order," he explains, before noticing that I'm holding my hand up to stop him.

"What order are we talking about, exactly? I mean, who the hell are you guys?" I urge, Onyx's ears perking up. His yellow eyes shine further with the glowing light of the onyx gemstone shining down on him, forming sparkles in his pupils. His expression shifts; the tone is more calm.

"You are in the headquarters of the Onyx Order, Kedar. Operating under me, we're the most notorious underground group that exists on the planet of Haya. Transcending across over twenty nations, we've been keeping everything afloat

101

before you are even born," he replies, boldly. I'm unimpressed but skeptical. Sure, Onyx may have the answers to where my brother is— but that doesn't mean he's completely trustworthy.

"How can people like you defend our planet when you've let the Dragon's war go on for generations, Onyx? It doesn't make sense in the slightest, old man," I shoot back, letting Onyx rapidly tap on the table's wooden surface.

"You see Kedar, I've been trying to stop it for years," he answers, his tone softening more. "The Veils of Judah are behind this horrible war, which is exactly why it is of utmost importance for me to stop it all completely."

"Tell me," I offer, trying to give him a little bit of grace. "How'd it all go down?"

"Fifty years before the Dragon's War even began, my brother, Judah, brought one of his left-handed men, Shay, into Cralean power. Judah is the leader of the Veils." He pauses, resuming after Ruby brings him a mug filled with tea. The scent doesn't deafen the tension of the room, even with its flowery and rosemary scent. "From what I've uncovered for the past two hundred years I've been trying to kill him, he created the association to take over the world in the shadows. It's been difficult— he always escapes from my grasp right when I think that I've caught the bastard in the act."

"What exactly has your brother been behind, anyway?" I inquire, making Onyx chuckle. He scratches the back of his head, narrowing both of his brows to create a serious look.

"The Basity Massacre, The First Jezzebel War, The Second Jezzebel War, The Farikkian Genocide, The Cleansing, Omma, and now, The Dragon's War. And that's just to name a few," he says, waving his hands in gestures as he lists out the horrible acts that his brother's indulged himself in. Each event comes to my mind in an instant. It cements his brother as one of the worst people to ever walk on the planet.

"Judah will do anything to achieve world domination, Kedar," Onyx continues, sipping his tea. "I've heard of all of the abhorrent acts he's done to people: executions, torture, killings, you name it. It sounds like I'm the biggest failure of the millennia, but I've finally found the formula for his actions. If you join us, then excellent. The Order's been losing too many members lately, and manpower is the one thing we lack when it comes to his army and ours."

I tilt my head to the right a bit, not trusting him at all. For the past two hundred years he's failed to slow down his brother from causing every single world-damaging event in history. But Onyx has a hopeful look on his face, and it is also a pitiful one. The words that he's told me before ring out in my mind: *I can sense something different in you.*

Perhaps the old man can help me get my brother back. It's a slim chance, but it's worth trying. "So how does this place work? Is there anything I must do to get into your Order, Onyx?"

He chuckles, a smile encrusting on his face while his canines blind me with a white shine. Onyx grips the mug on the table, gladly taking another sip. "Are you sure, Kedar? You want to join us?"

I award a glance to Ruby, who's squinting at me while expectedly leaning on the side of the wall. My face turns back to Onyx, giving him a slight nod. "If it means getting my brother back, then by all means. I'll do anything."

"Alright, well, the first thing that I'll admit is that you need some training," the old man says, crossing both of his arms. I recoil back in surprise.

"That's insulting, Onyx. No way you think I need training. I think I'll do fine, even against you," I try as he awards me with another chuckle. He lurches out of his seat, while I do the same.

My voice stutters when trying to grab his attention. "Hey… Onyx? What the hell are we doing?"

"If you really think you can join us without the handicap of training, then prove it to me," he says, standing across from me. I tremble in my boots as Onyx raises both of his hands in preparation to fight. He gives me a fearless gaze, as I hold up my fists.

"Look, I don't think we really have to do this. I mean, you're an old man. I don't want to have to fight you—"

He zips like lighting, streaking across the stone floor while Lapis and Ruby watch, snorting at my predicament. I dive out of my way onto the wooden table and try crawling across to get to the other side. Onyx immediately appears in front of me, throwing a punch towards me at inhumane speeds.

A piercing *thud* runs through my stomach as the surface of his bony knuckles touches my skin. I see the corners of my eyes fading into black as my head erupts in pain after I fall to the floor. My hand grips the bruised wound as I wince and groan.

"I'm at the prime age of two hundred and forty-seven, Kedar. And yet I find myself beating people who are light years younger than me," he admits, clasping his hands together in satisfaction. I squint my eyes, realizing he's standing over me, while Ruby and Lapis are to my right, making sure I'm not dead. "If that was Ruby, she would've lasted around 6.38 seconds before being hit by one of my punches. But you lasted around 0.97. Now do you believe that you need a slight bit of training before even considering completing the trials required to join us?"

I roll my eyes at his remark, spitting out blood onto the stone floor. He sighs, turning to Ruby. "Heal him. He's slow but bold. I can use that."

I cough as Ruby kneels at my side, putting her hands over my wound, never making contact with my skin. "Dragons. He really isn't kidding."

"He's being overdramatic. Trust me," she chuckles, a blue aura enveloping her hands as she patches me up. The black mark on my skin slowly fades away as she pumps her mana out to heal me the best she can.

"Ugh. Well, safe to say that he's right," I tell her, sitting up when the pain from the middle of my body subsides. "I really need to train myself up, especially because I haven't really fought or killed anyone in a while…"

Ruby lends out a hand and after hesitating for a couple of seconds, I reach out and clasp my hand against hers, letting her pull me up from the cold stone floor. Onyx is standing in front of us, his arms crossed while giving me a sly smile. I look down in embarrassment.

"Ruby, it would be best if you trained him since your camp isn't too far away from here," he offers, while Ruby scrunches her face up in shock.

"Seriously, Onyx? You think I can train… him?" she asks, looking back at me. I give her a questioning look as she sighs, holding her forehead with the tips of her fingers while gazing at the floor. Onyx doesn't flinch a bit, only giving Ruby a slight shrug.

"Well, I'll have to be honest. I think you should have the abilities to at least ready him for the Beast," he replies, giving me a solid wink with his golden eyes. I flinch at the word. *Beast?!* My mind repeats, my fingers trembling. He's right. I'm rusty from being in that fortress.

Before long, I find myself tipping my hat to Lapis, wishing him farewell. Ruby grunts when opening the door to the outside tunnel, and we both walk in silence.

I awkwardly clear my throat, trying to ease her up a little bit. "So, where are we going, exactly?"

"Well, you'll see, Kedar," she snorts while gripping the trapdoor, hoisting it up by herself. Ruby takes off her hood to bask her face in the resting sun.

Then she sprints off at a blazing speed. "Just try to keep up!"

We twist and turn through alleyways. My breath hitches once I realize how fast this girl is. Her boots stomp the little rocks on the pavement with every step she takes like she's in a hurry.

"Dragons! Ruby, wait up!" I cry out to her, right before she stops abruptly at a dead end, jumping up to insert her fingers into the cracks of the building. She relentlessly hoists herself up, never turning back to look at me.

"Here! This should be the first thing you'll learn from me! Just keep up, and don't lose me! Don't think I'll be coming back for you!" Ruby shouts, jumping from ledge to ledge, grasping at the wooden handholds flawlessly, scaling the adobe buildings without mistake. I try following her, only to realize that the wall is completely smooth— and I have to jump up to fit my fingers between the minuscule cracks. My mouth heaves a sigh before I buckle my knees with all of my might, launching myself off of the stone pavement.

I feel my two fingers slide right inside the ledge, and I find myself hanging by a thread. By now, Ruby's long gone, and the only chance I have to catch up to her is scaling the roofs with her as fast as I can. If I can't get through such a simple task like this, how can I spare the chance to save my brother?

After a few seconds of struggling, I hoist myself up to the next, before scaling the side of the building, finding myself on the roof. I see the little speck of Ruby in the distance, never wavering.

To catch up, I need to jump from building to building without slipping or falling to my death. Even though I'm only twenty feet in the air, I can still die if I'm stupid. My eyes dart at the ledge to the end of the roof, then over to the ledge at the next. I shuffle my feet onto the floor, clenching my teeth as I try mustering up the courage to jump.

It's like a switch turns on inside of me, and I sprint towards the ledge. My legs buckle and I leap across the ledge. It looks impossible, but once I hoist myself from the floor, I realize I made it.

My eyebrows narrow, my new confidence filling me up as I flawlessly jump from brick buildings to adobe buildings, never slipping, never falling. With each jump, Ruby seems to become closer and closer, the distance between us decreasing every time. My sweat soaks me from head to toe, but as long as I pass the stupid tests that Ruby hands off to me, I can't care less.

Every part in the lower half of my body hurts like hell— but it doesn't matter. Ruby's doing exactly what she promised not to do, which is to wait for me to catch up with her. She might be an odd girl at most, but at least she can sympathize with me a bit. The bottom surface of my feet burst in pain as I hop on one of the ledges before launching myself nine feet to the next, the slam of my boots with the harsh surface of the adobe building ensuing pain in me like no other.

"Well, well, well. What a surprise. I actually thought you wouldn't even make it up the first wall," she chuckles, her hands on her waist. It's alarming how easily Ruby can do all of this with how heavy her armor is. Every jump she makes seems automated like it's just a casual thing for her.

"Shut up," I huff, heaving over to rest my hands on my knees. "That was scary. Really scary. I hate high places."

"Well, all of that hard work has got to be worth the view, am I right?" she tells me before pointing out the beautiful view.

Ruby isn't wrong. It's almost worth risking my life for. I can see everything the city has to offer.

The flashing lights of the city blind me, hundreds upon hundreds of buildings lining every street. I see the bridge connecting the east side and the west side, along with the huge golden tower in the middle, splitting the sky apart.

The sunset highlights each part, the mix of adobe buildings and brick buildings creating the reflection of an orange and red haze. It's mesmerizing me, and once I turn to Ruby, I see her smiling, noticing how much I admire the view.

"Well, Kedar, I have some bad news for you. The next jump might be a little bit too scary for someone like you," she teases while I pout. Ruby turns to her left, revealing a huge, one-hundred-foot-tall building next to us. It's made out of brick and stone, with windows upon windows on each side.

"Basal. Don't tell me you're gonna—"

"Hell yeah, I will. Just watch and learn," Ruby says, giving me a salute before planting her feet deep into the ground below her. The boots she wears dig deeper into the wooden roof that we're standing on. I realize we're only seventy feet high, and the gap to the other building is fifteen feet, miles longer than the distance that I've jumped from earlier.

"Ruby... if you die—"

"I won't die. I've done this hundreds of times, and plus, I wouldn't want to die in such a stupid way like this," Ruby responds, dashing at the speed of light, reaching the ledge of the building in an instant.

I try reaching for her to stop, but my fingers barely graze her armor. She buckles her feet before diving across the gap, her right foot in front of the other. My fingers tremble in fear as she splits the air in two, chopping oxygen like hot butter. She grunts as I see her insert her fingers into the brick's crevices holding onto the ledge by an inch.

"Ruby! This is bad! Get down before you hurt yourself!" I propose, seeing her scale the high-rise building with a certain gleam in her eyes that tells me that she isn't going to stop at all. Before long, I see her disappear over the ledge, a bright smile on her face as I know exactly what she's about to yell out next.

"Your turn! Get up here!" she yells out. A drop of sweat trickles down the backside of my neck. I have to do this. For my brother. For the sake of his life.

I grit my teeth, calculating the percentage of how likely I'll survive. It takes me a couple of minutes to stop myself from hyperventilating into oblivion. I squint, trying to remember what handhold Ruby gripped onto to assure her safety. Narrowing my pupils, I see the crevice that she grabbed— a small crack in the bricks of the skyscraper, enough to support her hands.

An instant injection of fear seeps through my spine. I really don't have a single choice but to jump. "Goddamnit. Let's just get this over with."

When my feet charge up as I leap for the wall, everything seems to slow. I flail my legs and arms through the air like a fish on land. My fingers come in contact with the crevice, injecting me with pain. I glance at my fingertips. The skin's been peeled off. I bleed, the red liquid seeping into the bricks.

The blood trails down my arms, my sleeves dripping with crimson. My muscles tighten, and every nerve of my body feels like it's being lit on fire. I try hard to hold in the scream that's about to come from my vocal cords.

"GOD! GODDAMNIT!" I wail, reaching for the next handhold to grab onto. My fingers are drenched in blood, some of it falling to the ground below.

My eyes make the mistake of looking down. The pavement only enhances my fear, the thought of me turning into bits crossing my mind. My whole body is shaking.

I reach for the ledge, and with a grunt, my hand clasps on it. Small rocks seep into my cuts as I wince. Hoisting myself would be complete suicide. I try grabbing the ledge with my other hand, only to slip.

My hand— my left hand— falters, leaving my right hand to hold me up.

"OH CRAP! DAMMIT!"

The thought of me dying is really invading my mind, but there's no way I'm about to give up like this. But with every passing second, every single finger begins to tear off. Ruby saving me isn't something that'll happen in my lifetime. But I might as well try.

"RUBY?! RUBY, PLEASE ARE YOU THERE?"

Nobody answers as my heart begins to pump harder and faster. A hand reaches over the ledge, wearing a jet-black glove. I feel the hard grip come in contact with my wrist before it completely pulls me over the ledge like I'm a feather. A shade of red covers my eyesight as I plant into the pavement with blood spurting out of my nose. Ruby. Holy Dragons, it's Ruby.

Ruby's looking down at me, ruffling her braids. "Kedar, are you alright?"

"Fight and fight and fight, and you will find yourself stacked against kindness and Hayanity.

Ignore and ignore and ignore, and you will find yourself stacked against your own emotions.

Lust and lust and lust, and you will find yourself stacked against false love."

- A Lauvee Dynasty Proverb

EIGHT

Ruby gets on one knee, offering her hand. I glance at her

black gloves, her fingertips poking out of the ends. My hand clasps with hers as I pull myself off the stone floor. There are red stains on my palm and cuts on my fingers.

"Dragons, Ruby. I almost died back there," I wheeze, sitting down on the ledge. My eyes glance up, making contact with hers. Her arms are crossed together as she gives me an expecting look.

I plant my hands onto my knees, huffing and puffing. "Give me a second. I need a break…"

She shrugs, nodding before sitting next to me. We're close, but pretty far away too. My blood and sweat mix into a disgusting solution, creating a light reddish color that stings like salt. This isn't the first time this has happened, so I'm thrilled. I haven't bled from the fear of death in a while. Ruby scoots over, her eyes widening.

"Let me see, Kedar. I can heal you up," she begins, grasping her fingers around my wrist. I glance up, my heart still thumping from the climb. Her hand hovers on top of my palms as a low, blue aura omits from her fingertips.

The silence makes me a bit flustered. Ruby doesn't seem to care much, because her face is stern, hyper focused on closing my cuts. One by one, the slits on my fingers stitch up itself without pain. Ruby reaches to the back of her belt, pulling out a white wrap.

"Alright, that should be enough for now," she sighs, narrowing her crimson eyes as she slowly wraps the gauze around my fingers. Once she finishes, she glances up to my face as I turn away to clear my throat. She raises a brow. "Um… you alright?"

"I'm fine," I reply, recollecting myself. "Do you have water on you? My mouth is dry."

She nods, pulling out a canteen. Soon enough I find myself gulping down gallons of water, desperate for hydration. It takes Ruby's crossed arms for me to realize that I've finished the bottle.

"Oh, sorry—"

"It's whatever. I don't care much," Ruby snorts, tucking her braids behind her ear. "We might as well kill a little bit of time here."

"What do you mean by that?" I ask as she scratches her arms out before yawning. The dimming sunlight beams on her face, making her skin glow.

"Well, I don't know you much. How'd you end up in that jail cell?" she questions. Ruby wanting to know me has been out of the question because of how distant she seems to be. With a bit of hesitation in my mind, I stroke my beard with a gulp.

"Well, after both of my parents died, me and my brother both decided to join the army," I reply. Looking back, I regret it all. "Years later, we lost a battle to the Craleans. Winter and spring passed before you and Lapis found us, and I have the scars to prove it."

"Dragons, that's horrifying," she replies, her voice muffled. Her arms are wrapped around her knees as she keeps eye contact with the concrete.

"I've never been close to my siblings like that," Ruby explains, tilting her head to the side as she stares through me with those red eyes. A breeze blasts through ruffling my hair in all kinds of directions. Maybe she's telling the truth— her life may be worse than mine. "You love him. That'll be something I'll never have."

"You have siblings?" I blink, trying to lighten the dim mood that suddenly riddles her face. "Um… How many do you have?"

"Well, I have a lot. Seven, actually. Five older brothers and two sisters," she answers, her face a bit sunken. Ruby glances over to the city, her eyes immersing in its presence as she observes the heavenly view before sighing solemnly.

I stare at her blankly, taking it all in. Maybe one of her siblings is an assassin working for the Order. It isn't out of the question. But it confuses me how Ruby doesn't feel loved because she has so many people to connect with. My father's been dead for a decade, and I still love my brother the same.

"We're all half-siblings. None of us have the same father," she explains, breaking our silence as she blinks away her emotions. Only confusion spreads on my face, and once she realizes my twisted expression, she chuckles to herself.

"I was born in a brothel, and…" Ruby pauses, glancing at her golden tone before drifting her eyes to mine. "I don't even want to remember."

114

"Oh. Well, what happened to your family?" I ask.

"Well, my mother died..." she freezes again, clearing her throat.

"After that, I unlocked the use of my magic, and Lapis found me in an alleyway, cold and freezing from shock. He took me to Onyx, who talked some sense into me. Later I learned most of my brothers died in battle, captured and hanged by the ropes. Eventually, I joined the Order to use my mana for the better. It's how I got my code name, Ruby. 'Shaped rough and intimidating, but red like the color of hearts and love' is how the old dog describes it. But if you ask me, he's just being dramatic."

"Is that why you all use code names? To erase your old lives?"

She nods. "Yeah, that's basically it. My old name was Laila—"

Ruby stops abruptly, clearing her throat before awkwardly looking away from me. A smile encrusts on my face. Ruby brings herself back to her more serious self to cover up her little mistake.

"I won't spoil it for you. Besides, I'm only supposed to help you train anyway," Ruby snorts, leaning back and resting her head on the ledge. In her pupils isn't a single ounce of fear as she practically dangles off of the edge. I can tell she watches the sunset here a lot.

"Ugh," I can hear her whisper, focused on the sparkles of the stars encrusted in the night sky. "I am not supposed to tell you my damned name."

"Well, that's fine, Laila I mean, Ruby."

Ruby and I burst out laughing. The faint glow of the streetlights and buildings illuminates the smile on Ruby's face further, and the sounds of the chatter below enhance the soft ambiance.

"Come on, Kedar. We wasted a bit too much time up there. If we hurry, we can get to the training grounds by dawn," she interrupts, hopping off of the ledge before yawing. *Training grounds...* I repeat, smiling. *I haven't heard that word since I was a soldier.*

Ruby leaps off of the hotel roof like a maniac, landing on the next building like a feather. I do the same, my feet hitting the ground as adrenaline begins to pump through my veins. After resting for a bit on the rooftop, there's nothing that can stop me from keeping up with Ruby. Every ledge I leap over feels like nothing.

My mind fades in between the lines, as I automate my movements, only focused on the task at hand. With all of this running and jumping comes the harsh silence I have to endure between the both of us and another memory arises. It's the first battle I've ever participated in.

"MOVE MOVE MOVE! RAISE YOUR DAMN SWORDS, HATCHLINGS!" the general yelled as the fifty of us looked at him with pure bewilderment. I was the only one who glanced up at the old man with pure excitement. My first taste of bloodshed seemed to only be at a moment's grasp.

The soft and low shivering of my brother riding his horse next to me could only be described as an annoyance. He, in fact, was an obstacle himself. Omar couldn't even use his sword right, swinging it from side to side like a damned animal. It was obvious he was scared.

"Brother... Please think about what you're doing! What we're doing! This isn't what Mama and Papa would've wanted!" Omar urged, holding the reins of his white horse

116

tightly as a single drop of sweat dripped down from the side of his forehead.

"It is, dammit!" I talked back, immediately placing my hand on the pendant. My hands caressed the necklace, rubbing it back and forth as I exhaled softly, breathing in the humid air. Some of our comrades drew curious looks— probably wondering why I was being so obnoxious.

We're blazing through the Zaidus Plains— the staple grasslands of the continent. We geared up to charge at the enemy fortress just across the river. The slow whinnies of the horse soothed me a bit, almost making me forget about the battle that was about to ensue.

"Almost there, hatchlings," the general said to us in a low whisper, the golden ribbon on his helmet streaking through the air as he turned around to look at our lonesome squad.

"On my command, we blaze across the river. Mages, you have the task of blowing up the walls as much as you can. Infantry units and knights, storm that damn fortress with all the might you got. We've talked over this hundreds of times, and now is the time and place where we lose everything or win it all for ourselves. Does that sound clear, hatchlings?!"

"SIR, YES SIR!" the crowd shouted, the fortress beginning to fade into view. All that I could remember was that it was made out of stone, looking impenetrable judging by the large watch towers and high walls, lined with archers. They all looked oblivious.

The men and women, mages and knights, all have subtle, scared looks on their faces. My brother has the worst expression out of all of them— he had his right hand clamped over his breastplate, trying to calm his breath. I snorted as the general screamed a war cry, signaling for the battle to begin.

Our horses streaked across the rivers at an unholy pace, ending up in front of the walls in mere seconds. Mages thrust their hands forward as their mana began to crumble the left wall, creating a hole big enough for most of us to fit into. The archers on the walls could barely react as they noticed us sneaking past all of their walls and defenses, with no time to alert the other troops of their demise.

My brother was nowhere to be found. Pfft, *I thought to myself.* I'll find his corpse sooner or later.

I clenched my teeth before pulling the short sword out of its sheath flawlessly, swinging it downward to the first person I laid my eyes upon. A Cralean soldier wearing black and yellow, now reduced to blood. In mere milliseconds their head was on the ground, trying to blink away the pain that came over their nerves.

I hopped off of my horse, red filling the corners of my eyes. Another one. Another soldier to cleanse their sins. My sword streaked through the masses. Mages and knights began to watch me transform the soldiers into piles of dust. Their screeches and cries weren't something that was going to stop me from disconnecting all of the limbs from their bodies. The ground was blood red. There wasn't anything that was going to hold me back anymore, with another soldier dropping down with his face hanging from his jaw.

Yes. Yes. This is exactly what I'd imagined the battle to be. The chokes and the screams meant something to me. Every soul I sent to hell fueled the revenge I taste for my father and mother. They would want me to kill every last person on this planet to make sure their lives were not in vain. This was what they would've wanted. This was what I wanted—

"DRAGONS! KEDAR, QUIT IT!" a voice urged as I felt two arms wrap around my waist, constricting my movements completely. The adrenaline in my head began to flow a little slower, as I gazed at the battlefield. Everyone around me was

completely converted into blood, their bodies the only thing that remained. I huffed and puffed, trying to calm myself down.

"That's enough, Kedar. They're all dead. No more fighting, please..." Omar's voice urged as I felt his head rest on my back. I looked down at my hands, which were doused in crimson.

Maybe I'll stop. For now. Just a bit.

"Hah!" You're keeping up!" Ruby invades, snapping me back to reality. The smile on her face lightens my mood a little.

I sprint like a cheetah, hopping from one building to the next, the moonlight beginning to gleam on my tanned skin. Every step and breath I take fuels my energy to keep going. Eventually, me and Ruby are both running together, calculating each step to mimic our movements. Sweat drips down my back and my forehead, and my heart races.

The girl next to me seems unfazed by all this constant running. Her eyes are filled with determination, caring about nothing except surviving the next jump.

"Dragons, Ruby," I cough, trying to blink the shine of the moonlight out of my eyes. "How far is this base you've been rambling on about? It seems to be hundreds of miles away...."

She simply rolls her eyes at my struggles. "We're almost there, Kedar. Calm yourself down. Like I said, we'll be there at dawn, maybe. We've been messing around out here for so long it seems the sun's about to rise up again."

I'm silent the rest of the way. She leads me onto the outskirts of the city. The gleaming, golden tower is out of eyeshot, disappearing into the night sky. Soon enough, the towering walls that surround the city get closer and closer.

My knees feel so close to shattering as I slam myself down to the next rooftop. But I continue anyway. We find ourselves in front of walls. Ruby doesn't hesitate as she leaps upwards, disappearing over the edge in seconds. I grumble in frustration.

The gap between the building and the wall seems closer than the huge structure she made me climb earlier, so I confidently jump across the long gap, grunting as I plant my feet onto the edges of the wall without bleeding this time.

There isn't much of anything waiting for me up top, but there are cross patterns that line the railings, along with a couple of watchtowers with benches. On the left are bushes against the railings, giving the bland wall a bit of greenery. *The air is a bit thin.* I take a deep breath to try and calm myself down from all of the constant sweating from the climbing, jumping, and running.

Footsteps descend from the tower to the right. Ruby glares.

"Kedar, the bushes! Hide, you idiot!" She whispers through her teeth, diving into the plants without any hesitation. I gulp before nudging myself inside next to her as we watch through the tiny gaps.

The branches pierce the tips of my skin, making me writhe in pain a bit. Ruby shushes me from making any noise, so I only focus on trying to look at the figures that are walking just a couple of feet away from us. There are two guards, wearing higher-ranking uniforms than the ones we saw at the gate. The only difference that distinguishes them from one another is the red ribbon instead of the white ribbon on top of their helmets.

"Delilah, have you heard about the leader of the Veils? He's begun to make some serious moves," one of them says, as they both take a seat on the wooden benches against the railings. It confuses me as to why we are even hiding in the first place — mostly because the soldiers seem to know about the Onyx Order. They won't even bat an eye at us from the looks of it. But either way, Ruby decides to stow both of us away in a bunch of green bushes.

"Seriously? Big moves? Judah? I doubt it," the other says, sitting on the bench like a slacker, clutching her spear tightly as she deflates.

"I'm not kidding," he continues, taking off his helmet before sipping his canteen. "The spies in the West have been killed. It's gotta mean something, am I right? None of Onyx's agents have died for about ten years. Now, all of a sudden, they're dying? There's no fathomable way that the Veils will go for us next."

"Hm. I mean, that's only one incident. Is there anything else that we should worry about?" the woman asks, raising one of her eyebrows.

"Have you heard the hellfire that's been going down in Saitra? For days there's been cleansing, with the Cralean army searching for any Basalian they can get their hands on. They're looking for something. I know it," the other soldier says, gritting his teeth together. My eyes lighten up at the name.

Maybe I need to ask them if they've seen him. I lurch forward before I feel a tuck on my shoulder, looking back to see Ruby shaking her head, knowing exactly what I want to do. Frustration runs through my mind. She clutches onto me harder, and I finally give up trying to resist. Ultimately, she is right. We need to just listen for now.

"Have you told Onyx about this yet? This info seems worthy enough for his old dog ears," Delilah says as the man takes another swing of his water bottle. Sweat drips down my forehead as I try to slow my breathing to conceal my presence. It seems me and Ruby are a couple of seconds away from getting any potential information about my brother.

121

"You're right," the man replies, closing the cap on his canteen before putting it back onto his belt. "We should go back already."

Ruby still has her hand on my shoulder as I finally pull her off, rustling the bushes as my pupils are hit with the shining light of the moon.

Before I step out to greet them, a dark figure hops down from the watchtower where the soldiers come from, immediately stabbing the man. Delilah screams, seeing her comrade's throat get slit.

I don't have a weapon, so Ruby is the one who charges the dark figure, pulling a dagger out. They turn around, wearing the exact same mask as the assassin that killed Farid. She dashes back, and the Veil continues his assault, struggling to stab the woman in the stomach.

The lady soldier holds her ground for long enough, but she eventually falls to the stone floor gurgling blood, seeping into her metal armor. Ruby and I immediately chase the figure, who's trying to climb back up to the watchtower.

"Augh!" they scream, their mask exploding into pieces. Behind that mask is an elf with bloodshot eyes, and a hellish smile on their face. It's hard to keep eye contact. His gaze is from hell.

Ruby tries to stab him with her dagger, only to be blocked by his blade. My veins begin to pump with adrenaline as I dash forward, punching the side of his left arm. In mere milliseconds, the blade he's holding drops to the ground from my sudden intrusion, giving Ruby time to unleash an attack.

She tries thrusting the blade through his cloak, but he seems to recognize it coming from miles away. He dashes forward, huffing and puffing to recollect himself.

"You really have to ruin my damn day," the Veil yells, mimicking a living demon. I bury the bottom of my feet deeper into the ground as I try to ignore his remark. A sneer escapes from their lips as we hear him gripping the handle of his knife harder.

"I had to travel tens of miles away from Saitra just to chase down these Basils," he slurs, licking the bottom of his lips. The absence of wrinkles on his face only tells me that he's about as young as me and Ruby. It's horrifying; what's someone like him doing working with a group like the Veils? "I guess it isn't worth it, eh? Since you know a little about what's truly going on."

"Maybe it's a good time for you to tell us the rest of what's going on with you Veils," Ruby rasps, her eyes deadset on the elf. However, he barely seems threatened by her at all, putting the blade in front of his lips. His tongue wraps around the metal as he licks the red liquid off, narrowing his eyebrows hungrily.

The whole time the elf stares menacingly at the both of us. My fists curl up, eager to turn his face into a living, breathing pulp. Ruby nudges me at my shoulder, making a motion with her head that tells me: *charge at this bastard.*

I don't hesitate in obeying her orders, my legs churning as I bolt forward, my hand outstretching. Ruby throws the dagger, slicing through the air as I feel the tips of my fingers graze through the metal. I snag the handle, sending the elf into a panic. It takes milliseconds for me to thrust the weapon through his black cloak. My fingers start shaking under the pressure. *Blood.*

The constant cries of pain from the elf seem to stream from one ear to the other, as memories flash before my eyes, his expression mimicking the same faces those Cralean soldiers had. It's harsh seeing his eyes filling to the brim with fear. As his lips curl and sweat drips down his forehead, I get sent into a frenzy of guilt. But there's pleasure too. *No.* I urge. I can't succumb to this. Not now.

"Grah! Hell! Get off of me, filthy Basil scum!" he swears as I clench my eyes tight trying to shove him deeper to the ground. The footsteps of Ruby running toward me deafen out and I only stop trying to keep him in place when realizing she's already constricted him with her arm, choking him out.

"Let's have a real talk before I snap your neck and leave you on the walls to rot," Ruby growls, leading me to stand back up, still in shock from what I've just done. If it's Ruby killing him, she'll slit his throat in a heartbeat. It's necessary. *It's either life or death*, I try explaining to myself, hitching my throat as the elf struggles against her grasp.

"You idiot! You think I'm going to tell you anything?!" he says, blood dripping down his chin. The elf keeps wriggling around like a fish on land, his hair disheveled and cloak soaking in his own blood as the knife sticks out of his stomach. Spit from him lands on Ruby's face, making her grab the handle and thrust it deeper into his abdomen. She twists it, forcing out a scream from the intruder.

"AHHH! OH GOD! FINE! FINE!"

Ruby notices the expression of stress on my face and tries giving me a sly smile before wiping the blood splatter from her chin.

"Your days are numbered. The world will be cleansed soon. Oh so very soon..." he invades, huffing and puffing as his brows narrow. "You'll regret this. All of you. You'll be begging for mercy."

"You're the one begging for your own life here, Veil," I jump in angrily. The elf's eyes light up as it generates a curved smile on his face.

"It doesn't matter, now that I think about it. I know none of you can stop it from happening," he replies, dodgier than ever. Ruby glares at him, but I widen my eyes at her threatening glance. We might as well keep him alive for now, just in case he has anything else to spill to us. "The prophecy must be fulfilled. It must be. Don't come running to Judah asking for any sort of su—"

"I'd never ask that dog for anything," Ruby interrupts, trying to control her anger. "Whatever you're talking about, it's all bullcrap. We'll just kill you here, right now, so say your last words."

"Last words? Poetic, isn't it, basil?" the elf's teeth chatter, his body shivering under the chill of the night. His cheeks begin to match the color of the moon, pale and lifeless. "Then so be it. MADH YUDHA!"

And he rips his cloak—

Only to reveal dozens of grenades on his bare chest. Once we hear the soft sizzle erupt in our eardrums, we both widen our eyes in shock.

I dash forward, Ruby grabbing my wrist as she tries catching up to me. The elf shrieks out the phrase over and over again as I curse in my head.

It's like an instinct. I glance back to see the elf smiling as I wrap my arms around Ruby's waist, diving to the ground as my shoulder slams into the hard floor with a crack. My nerves immediately burst in pain before a resounding explosion invades our ears, sending us tumbling across the ground before slamming into the wall of the watchtower.

The silence kills me. Ruby's body feels lifeless in my arms as my eyes widen in fear. Her eyes are closed shut, blood dripping from the side of her lip. "Ruby? Goddamnit! Wake up!"

"Shut up. Shut up…" she whispers, shaking her head as she blinks her eyes open, looking down to see the piece of shrapnel attached to her stomach. Without hesitating, Ruby reaches down, her hand wrapping around the piece of metal, soaked in blood. I watch as she grunts, pulling it out and releasing a sigh as she begins healing herself. "Don't yell. I'm fine, I think I just hit my head."

"Well, as long as you didn't die," I breathe out, pushing away my worries. "I still need a teacher, ya know."

"I totally forgot about that. I'm not very used to traveling with other people anyway. I only went with Lapis because Onyx was too worried I would die," she explains, wiping the sweat off of her forehead Once she lays her eyes on me, her pupils dilate as I give her a confused look. "Look at yourself, Kedar! Don't you realize you're bleeding everywhere?"

A sudden pinch of pain erupts at my back, and I collapse to the ground, shivering as the adrenaline wears off immediately. Pieces of metal are embedded in my skin, all broken shards from the elf's dagger and Ruby's knife. I try blinking the pain away like Ruby, but I can't. Once I glance up at her...

Everything turns black.

Do not underestimate a healer. While indeed, healers do heal the sick, the wounded, and the insane, they can kill and hurt as well. It's almost unexplainable, but what I can declare is this: your outside nature does not reflect one's mind and soul. What you have done well does not reflect what you intended. Take heed of a healer on the battlefield.

- Excerpt from *Magic's Innuendo: a pleasant guide to all known magic,* Written By Frudith, the Golden Mage of Basalia, 1407

NINE

"Kedar...Dragons. Wake up, goddammit!" A voice splits through my eardrums as I blink my eyes open. Ruby looks stressed as she holds her hands out over me, her palms glowing blue.

I take in my surroundings. With the tapestries and wooden pillars, I'm guessing that I'm in a tent. I'm lying on my back, my head resting softly on a pillow. Pain inflames my abdomen when I flinch.

"Don't move... You... idiot," she whispers, gritting through her teeth. I grumble, letting her work her magic. The pain subsides, but my heart keeps ringing in my ears. I cough blood on the blankets and mutter curses.

"What... What the hell happened?" I muster out, craning my head towards her. This generates a sigh from Ruby, scratching her nape.

"You passed out from shock. I had to drag you all the way here. You've been out since yesterday night," she explains, rubbing her temples. I get up, fighting through the pain of lying flat on the wounds from my back. A groan erupts from my mouth as I hold my stomach steady, trying to focus on staying awake.

Before I can apologize for her having to carry me all the way down here, she puts her hands over my abdomen again. I squint my eyes in confusion.

My stomach bursts in agony, as my vessels begin to rip and tear apart from whatever she is doing. Trying to open my mouth to tell her to stop is meaningless because she's dead set on healing me.

"Stop struggling! I'm trying to reconnect your blood vessels to help it flow better!" Ruby attests, keeping me in place. It's hard resisting to scream, so I attempt to not move at all.

After a couple of more minutes, with sweat rolling down the side of her forehead, Ruby finally stops messing around with the insides of my body, setting her arms down as she blinks away her stress. I'm still sore, but I breathe a sigh of relief, just happy that it's over.

"What did you do to me?" I huff, gritting my teeth. Whatever Ruby did to my body— it must've saved my life.

"Don't worry. I just used my mana to manipulate your body to return back to its normal state," she replies, trying to lighten the mood with a smile. Her armor's gone, all she wears is a lengthy black robe that covers her entire body and goes to her ankles. I grumble again, shaking my head a bit.

"Sounds complicated," I say, yawning as the pain dims away. Ruby's luckier than me— having the ability to use mana in the first place is rare. Most mages and wizards are hard to find since awakening mana usually involves emotional trauma and turmoil. "But I'm just glad it worked. The pain seems completely seamless."

129

"Well, sometimes it doesn't work," she jokes, as I recoil back in surprise. "Some people can't undergo the process, and their body gives out when I try putting their organs back in place."

"Damn. Can you... hurt people with your magic?" I question, wondering whether or not Ruby has the power to possess such abilities.

"Yeah," she admits, looking down with a solemn look. "I can kill people on accident, though. It's why I travel alone. Lapis just needed help with that stupid mission."

A moment of silence follows before Ruby grabs a steaming cup on my bedside table. The tea omits the scent of honey and rose. Ruby gulps it all down before spreading the tent wide open.

I block the sunlight with my hands, but it still blurs my vision with black spots. With a groan, I stand up as she slips away from my grasp again, disappearing into the light. From outside, I can hear metal clanking, like she's setting something up. "Kedar! Get outside! Rest time is over!"

I sigh, slipping on a tunic and my boots before heading out. Once my eyes finally adjust to the light, I realize that we're in a secluded camp in the middle of nowhere, surrounded by tall oak trees.

Blue tents surround a campfire in the middle, still smoking from being used from last night. Ruby hobbles with a huge satchel in her hand, huffing and puffing as she carries it across the camp to set it down at the logs in front. Once she puts it down, she starts to take out pots, pans, fruits, and vegetables.

"Wait. Are you seriously planning to train me while I'm injured?" I ask, coming up behind her. She glances back as she realizes I'm pointing to the gauze wrapping around my arms and torso. "Isn't that overkill?"

130

"Well, how do you feel? Perfectly fine, right?" Ruby asks, grinning. I try moving around, stretching my arms out. I don't feel any sort of pain. I stare into her eyes, nodding my head.

"That's exactly what I thought," she chuckles, pouring a canteen full of water into the pot before lighting the campfire. Ruby has a clammy expression on her face as she quickly tosses in carrots with potatoes and pieces of meat. "Well, once we come back from training, my soup should be all boiled up. I hunted for some turkey in the forests while you are sleeping, so we can at least have something to eat while we're out here."

My feet crunch in the grass as I take a seat next to her to watch her mix it all with a wooden spoon. The reflection of the bubbling water is tinted red from the color of her pupils. I dig my fingers against my thighs, sniffling as I try to look away from the sun that's trying to blind me. "Man, how are you even going to help me train for Onyx? The old dog doesn't seem to trust me a single bit."

"It ain't easy, that's for sure. Onyx will explain it to you once we get back. But honestly—" she takes a deep breath before sighing— "I have no idea how I'm supposed to do this. I've never trained anyone in my life."

A stressful look falls upon my face as I realize the grim reality of our situation. After a couple of minutes of thinking, a spark erupts in my mind as I rest my two fingers on my chin. "Well, you should train me to prepare for the trials that Onyx is going to put me under, right?

"Hm… you have a point," Ruby answers, gritting her teeth as one of the boiling, sizzling bubbles pops and lands on her wrist. Her hand hovers over the burn, healing it instantly. "I didn't train since Onyx deemed me worthy enough to undergo his 'tests'. But I have a couple ideas. Follow me."

Ruby jumps up, before shuffling through her brown bag again, pulling out a sword and three throwing knives. We walk in silence as she begins to lead me outside of the barracks. My arms and legs nick at the feeling of sharp bushes pressing up against it, as Ruby tries dodging the flies that try to land on her.

After a couple of minutes of trekking through the covers of greenery, a beam of sunlight strikes my face as I cover myself to give me some shade. What's revealed is a huge, yellow and green field fading in and out with the forest. As we walk through, my toes clank at something metal on the ground. I look down to see a skeleton grasping at his weapon, his hollow eye sockets staring into my soul.

"Aw, dammit. You brought us to an old battlefield?" I grumble, beginning to spot the hundreds of skeletons around the field, their shields and armor a mixture of black, yellow, blue, and white.

"It's the only field that's nearest to my camp," she proposes, resting her long sword against her left shoulder. Ruby takes a moment, smelling earthy scent omitting from the bodies around us. Luckily the smell doesn't affect me too much, but the undertone of corpses littering the field reawakes memories of war from my mind.

"Um— where should we start?" I stammer. Ruby seems to be reminiscing on some sort of memory as well, but maybe it's more sadder than mine. She's been here before.

"First, it would be nice to see how you act in battle without a weapon to defend yourself," she lectures, dashing away from me until we're both glaring at each other from a long distance. Sunlight gleams on her golden face, mimicking the blinding shine coming from her blade. It's a straight, long but thin sword that has a black and red wrap around the handle, gold stones embedding into it. I recognize it's the same sword she used during our stints in Alfdan and Saitra.

"Wait. You're kidding. You're not about to attack me with... *that.*" I point to her blade, scrunching my eyebrows as Ruby glances down at it, a smile beginning to encrust her face.

"Just try not to die."

Ruby digs her feet into the grass, preparing to charge at me. I step back to try and get some distance between us, failing when I see a flash of dark red hair. My instincts lead me to shift my body to the right, making Ruby miss her initial swing.

"Not bad. Where was that when Onyx was 'testing' you?" Ruby huffs, laughing from the thrill. I have to find a way to get that damn thing out of her hands, or else she'll tire me out. As she continues to spew out words of nonsense, I try to find a weak point that she may have, but none comes to mind. Her stance signals she doesn't have any injuries from the explosion a couple days ago, but the way she swings that sword...

To her surprise, I lunge for the handle, making her swipe the sword away, her eyes widening when realizing it's just a distraction. My shins connect with her feet, sweeping her off as she tumbles to the ground, landing on her back. Before I can try getting on top of her, Ruby kicks me in the stomach, prompting me to spit out blood as I land on the grass.

Ruby's already preparing to split me in half as she stands up. I curl my fist into the dirt, throwing it on her face. A scream erupts from her mouth as Ruby tries wiping it away, while I use the opportunity to pull back my arm to punch her stomach. I grit my teeth, going a little easy on her, punching with minimal, lethal force.

She stumbles back, regaining her balance before widening her eyes with rage. Her voice darkens. "Don't pull your punches on me just because I'm a woman."

I spot a dagger from one of the skeletons. I pick it up as Ruby starts charging at me again, moving faster than Onyx. My hands react fast enough as our blades clash together to block Ruby's jabs.

"I'm not, I swear," I try explaining, gritting my teeth as I dodge her attacks. "You— I'm not even..."

"Why the hell are you holding back?" Ruby irks, pushing against me as the sharpness of the sword chips away at the rusty dagger. "I'm not your comrade right now. I'm your damn enemy."

"I know. I know, goddammit, I KNOW!"

A growl escapes from my lips as I knee Ruby in the stomach, stunning her for enough time for me to wrap my arm around her neck and choke her. She grasps for air as she drops her sword. Red dots riddle my vision as I tune out her struggles.

"Okay, Okay, Ow! I give up!" Ruby coughs, immediately bringing me back to reality as I release her onto the ground, making her drop on one knee. I look down at my shaking fingers, trying to step away, my boots crunching on the bits and pieces of bones. *I almost killed her.*

"Dragons, Ruby...," my mouth stutters as I see her right hand grasping against her neck, wiping the sweat trickling down her nape.

"Don't start with that. That felt nice. You know, battle and stuff," she coughs, tucking her braids behind one of her ears. Once she gets up, she tries catching her breath by resting both of her palms behind the back of her head. My eyes dart to her neck again, noticing the faint red mark along with her long scar.

"I could've killed you," I urge, curving my lips downward as she rolls her eyes at my remark.

"I would kill *you* first before you could finish the job." She picks the sword from the ground, hoisting it against her shoulder again.

134

"You're pretty damn good at fighting. But you gotta stop holding back —"

"Are you really okay?" I interrupt.

I take my thumb and smear the dark brown dirt marks off the sides of her face. She's surprised by my touch, but she doesn't shy away. She stares back at me. Only a little bit comes up against my finger, so I grab the handkerchief out of the pockets of my trousers, wiping it a little harder this time. "You seemed... out of it."

Ruby doesn't answer initially, but she keeps eye contact as I smear the dirt from her cheek.

"Do I have to say it again? I'm fine," she replies, smacking my arm off of her as she shakes her head slightly. "Let's go back. That soup is probably done by now."

I smile at her carelessness as we clean up, walking through the forest to get back. Once we enter, Ruby scurries off to the sizzling pot. I sit down on the log, glancing up at the sunset as the day seems to go by fast once again.

"Aw crap! Dragons, it's all burned!" Ruby exclaims, the scent of overcooked vegetables invading my nose. I try not to give a reaction, only clenching my teeth tightly together to maintain normality for her. "We don't have food to eat... this is bad. Very bad."

"I'll be fine. I can survive without food," I joke, trying to lighten the mood as she pours out the sloppy concoction on the ground. She buries her face in her hands in embarrassment.

"Gods. God no," Ruby groans, looking up at the pink-tinted sky in disbelief. I snort, hiding it with a cough as Ruby flashes me a glare of anger. My hands immediately jump up to protect my innocence.

"Look, I can go to the market tomorrow. I'll wake up early and get everything. Sounds good?" I say.

"Do you even know where the market is?

135

"Uh…"

"Exactly, Kedar," she grumbles, pressing the tips of her fingers on the edges of her forehead. "Exactly. Exactly…"

Our night ends with Ruby stomping to her tent after ordering me to sleep in the one the farthest from her. It doesn't take me long to realize that she's sleeping in the exact tent I woke up in. I open the tapestry to see a small bedside table, along with a pillow and blanket in the middle of the makeshift floor. I collapse into the blanket, and I close my eyes expecting myself to wake up with Ruby hollering at me to come with her to the market.

Sizzling and the sounds of bubbling shoot me awake. *Ruby went without me?!* I think, stumbling out of my tent after slipping on my boots. The rising sunlight is easy to ignore when seeing Ruby on one knee tending to a pot hanging over the fire.

"Kedar… you're awake…" Ruby nervously chuckles, scratching the side of her cheek as she flattens out her long skirt, robe tight at the waist. "I went without you. Luckily, they're up to stock in ingredients, so I gladly brought them back here to boil it all up."

"Well, what's on the menu today, chef?" I muse, trying to play into her formal tone, sitting down on the log before trying to peer into the pot.

Ruby only responds by rolling her eyes. "Well, it's the soup that I always cook for myself. Chicken, carrots, and potatoes," Ruby explains, opening the lid. Her face douses with steam. She coughs it off as I finally get the opportunity to see what she has in store.

The chicken I spot floating around is somehow overcooked and undercooked at the same time. Ruby stirs it up with a wooden ladle as I begin to look at the damage. I cringe when seeing the carrots falling apart from their softness. She probably just put in the potatoes since it's still hard.

To tie it all up, the stew has a sour smell, making me realize she just used spring onion, salt, and pepper. The water looks unseasoned.

"Does it *look* good, at least?" Ruby interrupts, as I see the expecting look on her face when I glance up. She barely seems to notice that the soup is from hell. *Be nice, Kedar. Be thankful she cooked for you.*

"Yeah, I guess you can say that," I reply, stammering. I do not want to see what Ruby looks like when she's pissed.

"I've been cooking this ever since Onyx decided to let me live here," she happily explains, her golden skin radiating in the sunlight. Ruby looks like a proud mother seeing her child go off to war, never realizing they may die at any moment. "Do you know how to cook, Kedar?"

"Uh, yeah," I answer as Ruby sits next to me. We both watch the pot's bubbles rise up and down over and over again, and I sigh with sadness. There's no way to fix that concoction anymore. "My brother and I are living on the streets, so I had to cook."

"I had to run away from home kind of like you guys," Ruby explains, mentioning her mom's death. "Teaching myself isn't too easy."

I grumble. Ruby definitely needs to teach herself a little bit more. "Well, I can teach you to cook something... better than this."

"Yeah. It can get pretty old sometimes," Ruby shrugs, opening the pot before smelling it once again. "Enough with talking. We should eat."

I shake my head to hide my fear as Ruby rummages through the brown bag set against the log, pulling out two bowls. I gaze in horror as she hums, opening the lid to the pot, and using the ladle to scoop up the soup.

Oh god. Here we go, I think to myself as she hands it over to me. The smile on my face isn't going to last forever. I keep repeating the phrase *'just be thankful'* over and over again in my mind to try and ignore the fact that the scent mimics the rotten apples I used to have for breakfast on the streets.

"What happened to those soldiers was unbelievable. Once we get back, we have to tell Onyx what happened," Ruby tells me, scooping some carrots and potatoes from her soup and gladly chomping them down against the spoon.

"You're right," I reply, trying to keep the conversation normal. My stomach churns at the sight of carrots, so I slip some cut-up pieces into my mouth. It's mushy and soft, mixing with the sour water. I'm so close to gagging and spitting the rest of it out, but I shove it down my throat anyway. "Onyx needs that information. Maybe it's the key to finding my brother."

"You're right," she remarks, taking a long sip as I breathe out my exhaustion. Thankfully enough, Ruby hasn't noticed that I've barely eaten anything."Well, he'll know one way or another. He's the magister, after all."

I raise my eyebrows at the word. Calling a mage or wizard "Magister" is the same as naming someone as King or Queen.

"Don't you think it's necessary to inform Onyx about the dangers of the Veils?" I ask seriously. Everyone can be at risk if another one of their men steps inside the city.

"Onyx knows well about the Veils, Kedar," she states, setting her bowl aside as I realize that it's licked clean. It's hard to believe the girl can endure the taste, but maybe I'm being a little harsh. "Onyx knows every guard in the city, which is why those two knew who he was."

I trust Onyx when it comes to finding my brother, but I've only known the old dog for maybe two days, and everyone treats him like some sort of saint. Even a wise man has flaws, and I might as well be the one who can crack it.

"You ready? We should get to training, since we're all filled up," Ruby says, standing up with her bowl in hand, not even batting a glance at mine. I put it aside while she washes it off at the pond near her tent.

I meet Ruby at the entrance to the barracks, a brown satchel against her chest. A look of determination sets on her face as we trek through the forest again, finding ourselves in the same field as yesterday.

"Tell me: have you shot an arrow before?" she asks as I see two figures in the distance. I wave at them, thinking they're people, only to realize it's two dummies against a wooden stake.

"Never. I've always used a sword, not a bow. Wait. Did you set this up?" I question, as she nods gladly. One dummy is only thirty feet away from us, while the other is one hundred feet away. Both are made of hay, tied up with pieces of rope. On their heads is a red cross posing as a target. Ruby sets her satchel on the ground, pulling out three throwing knives and a red apple.

"Alright Kedar, hopefully you see where this is going already," she explains, offering me the blades. Ruby can come up with a way to train me for Onyx's little initiation but doesn't have the skills to cook some simple soup. "Here, hold these."

The knives are short, twelve to fifteen inches long. On the handle is a red wrap, and on the side of the blade are four letters: *R-U-B-Y.* I smile at the sight of her name.

"We call it a razqatar. It's one of the prime weapons that a member of the order uses for anything, including stealth, assaulting enemies, or assassinating targets. This should be an easy thing for you to learn, since shooting a bow and arrow is much harder," Ruby instructs. "Go ahead, try hitting the dummy."

I nod, grasping the blade tightly before looking at the one closest to us. The slight breeze and the shining beams of the sun are small things that can throw me off. I take a deep breath, locking both of my hazel eyes on the X mark of the figure. Ruby has her arms crossed, waiting for me to make a move. My arms coil back as I glance back at my target before I jerk forward and throw it as hard as I can.

I stumble as Ruby snorts. Throwing or shooting things isn't one of my strong suits. It's more *slash, clash, and dash*. Once I finally recollect myself, I squint my eyes at the dummy to look at the damage. I've missed it.

"Oh God," I hear Ruby laugh, surprised at my abhorrent aim. Embarrassment begins to swell inside of me as Ruby clears her throat to brighten the mood. "You'll be fine, Kedar. I didn't get it on my first try either."

Ruby walks up to the blade embedded in one of the skeletons lying on the ground, and she pulls it back hard enough to shatter its bones. She tosses the blade at me.

"Just do it again," Ruby commands, walking behind me to observe. I coil my arm back again, trying to launch the knife straight into the dummy's face. A smile curves on my lips as I keep myself upright this time but to no avail. I miss the head completely, the knife landing on its foot instead. Ruby walks back to pick up the knife again, handing it over to me with a sigh.

"We might be here for a while," she admits as I give her a look of defeat. I clench my fist on the razqatar, trying to gather the strength and motivation to get through this.

"Alright. I'll do it again," I reply with determination. There's no way I'm letting some knife-throwing stop me.

"We'll see about that," she coldly replies, not amused.

My arm coils back a little bit slower this time, just like the string of a bow. I close one eye, ignoring all sense of sound and scent— purely focusing on the target.

I clench my teeth, throwing the knife as hard as I can. The knife sails off course, not even hitting the dummy and instead going into the bushes of the forest. I groan. Everything really comes back in a circle.

"Yeah. We need to work on this," I hear her say behind me. Ruby's right. I glance at her as she takes out an apple from her satchel and begins munching on it innocently.

My stomach grumbles. *Maybe I'll just finish the soup.*

Ruby's Soup Recipe!
1. A dose of water, any amount.
2. Squeeze a whole lemon in there, or more if you want!
3. Chop off fresh carrots from the marketplace, and make sure to get some potatoes and chicken.
4. Bring the water to a boil and add everything in!
5. When it looks cooked, it probably is cooked.
6. Its best when the carrots are completely mushy just like the potatoes! It'll be perfect, I swear.
7. As for the chicken... just make sure it doesn't look completely destroyed... heh.

- Written on a sheet of paper from Ruby.

TEN

Ruby and I train for days with no success. Luckily, she's

persistent enough to give me as much advice as possible, which I need desperately. We travel through the greenery again, but this time, Ruby has an exhausted look on her face.

"Four days, and not a single throw on target," she sighs, fiddling with the throwing knives in her hands. I don't answer her remark, but she's right. My progress is slow, and it doesn't seem like I'll be able to hit it anytime soon.

"Well, fourth time's the charm, right?" I stutter, picking at the scar in the middle of my nose. We spend four hours every morning in the fields. I've thrown the knives hundreds of times, but each throw seems worse than the next. Sometimes it lands in bushes, and sometimes I'll throw it backward, almost hitting Ruby.

She's been cheering me on from the sidelines while also cracking plenty of jokes. Usually, I find myself debating whether or not Ruby prays for my downfall or hopes for my success.

My mouth is ripe from the taste of Ruby's soup from earlier; my tongue's tinted with a horrible smell. Maybe I'm getting used to the taste, it's hell to finish the whole bowl. If Ruby catches me trying to throw out the food, she might kill me. So I stuff the whole concoction down my throat instead.

Once the dashing sunlight hits my face again, I stare with a mix of determination and loss. One side of me is ready to face another day, while the other is ready for everything to be over with. My arm's sore from all the throwing, so I rotate it back and forth a couple of times to free myself up a little.

"Geez, you're melting, Kedar. You alright?" Ruby asks, giving me a hopeful look. Her feet crunch on the sticks we walk on, then she hops over a skeleton. The dummies fade into view, and I take a deep breath to prepare myself for another training session.

"I should be fine," I huff, reassuring her. The chirps from grasshoppers harmonize my impending failure, but I tune out the noise the best I can. "I'll hit one of the dummies today. Hopefully."

I'm standing thirty feet from it, the other in the distance. Ruby hands me the knives as I silently pray.

If I can't complete any of this training, then there's no point in trying to decode my brother's whereabouts. My thumb grinds against the little grooves on the razqatar's handle, as I look at the reflection of my hazel eyes in the metal.

"You look confident, *friend*," Ruby says, crossing her arms together. I roll my eyes and nod to assure her. The knife's grip has gotten familiar for the past couple of days. It must be a sign. I have to get this done. For Omar.

"Friend?" I repeat, my mind registering. Ruby isn't bothered, but she gives me a questioning look. "I didn't know you considered me a friend."

144

"Why not? I mean, we've been hanging out a lot recently. Isn't that what you call a friend?" There's annoyance in her tone. I put my hands up in innocence, making her shake her head in disappointment. I nervously chuckle. Either way, Ruby's different from when I first met her. She's not the emotionless woman I met in Alfdan.

"Oh. Well, I never considered myself having any friends, except for my brother," I explain, looking down at her.

"W—Whatever!" she stutters, turning away from me as I grit. *Oh, Dragons. I ruined it,* a voice whispers in my mind. I've never had anyone to really talk to. Most of my late teenage years have been on the battlefields. There's never time for social interaction. "Just forget what I said. Throw the damn knives!"

Yes, ma'am, I joke to myself, turning away and taking a few steps closer to the dummy. My pupils keep in contact with the X on their foreheads. I try aligning the target to coordinate it with the razqatar I have in my left hand.

My thumb rubs against the handle again for a bit of luck. Ruby has a blank look on her face, waiting in silence.

I pull my arm back as my shoulder starts to sore. *I'm gonna hit this,* I urge, leaning forward and snapping my arm in a flash, launching the knife at light speed.

The razqatar spins in slow motion, splitting through the air. It curves as my eyes widen in disappointment, expecting it to sail off the mark again.

Those thoughts are replaced with undying joy as the blade penetrates the X. Everything's perfect. Complete. My lips curve into a smile as I pump one of my arms into the air in triumph.

The sound of clapping invades my ears, a bright smile on Ruby's face compared to mine. "Dragons. Finally," Ruby sighs in relief, resting a hand on her heart. "Don't stop now. Might as well try hitting the second target, right?

I coil my arm back, concentrating on the little target on the dummy. The knife wisps through the air and penetrates the X. I sigh in relief as Ruby gives me a nod.

"That was fast. I guess that's what practice does to you, huh?" she jokes, putting her hands on her hips. "We're not done yet, though. I have one little thing up my sleeve."

"Seriously?" I say after grabbing the knives off the dummies. Ruby has to put another obstacle in my way. Of course. She has a sinister smile on her face.

"Since you know how to do ranged attacks, you might as well try using it on me," she declares, unsheathing the same sword she used a couple of days ago. This time, Ruby seems more serious than last time— she's not going to hold back in any of her assaults.

I stagger back as she swings the sword, gripping it tightly with one hand. The blade's length is intimidating; Ruby can stab me from where she stands. In one swift swing, the blades of the tall grass slice up, shooting into the air.

"Ruby, what are you planning this time?" I ask, gulping as I grab two knives, putting one in each hand. These measly razqatars can barely withstand one slash.

"Why don't we spar again. Just this last time," she explains to me, using a cloth to clean the grass off the blade, using it like it's an extension of her arm. Ruby held back during our last battle. Now, she seems dead set on killing me. "Steal the sword, and you win. That's a promise."

"How?!" I question, scrunching my eyebrows. My eyes stare at the piece of metal she's holding, imagining the pain if it cuts me in half. "You'll kill me! I only have a couple of throwing knives!"

146

"Well, you won the last time, right?" she scoffs, squinting her red eyes with bloodlust. Ruby puts one foot in front of the other in a fighting stance. Her experience shows. "Just adapt."

Ruby charges while gritting her teeth against her other manically, her sword pointing at my heart. I dodge her attacks by diving to the left, but even that is useless. The feeling of the blade grazing my waist almost makes me fall to my knees. My blood's already soaking my tunic as I clasp one of my hands over it to try and stop the bleeding.

I dash backward, huffing as I pull out one of my knives. Ruby notices my plan, waving the blade in front of her chest to protect herself. I throw the knives at her ankles instead, and she falls to the ground.

A single sweat droplet drips from Ruby's forehead as she begins healing her wound. Her golden skin stitches up her blood from overflowing, and she pulls the dagger out easily, tossing it to the side. "Come on, Kedar. You never know what the enemy can do."

I grumble at her taking advantage of her magic. Before I can process my next attack, she flashes in front of me again, this time aiming for my already bleeding wound. My mouth widens as our blades spark together. I block her assault, and she grits her teeth in frustration.

Ruby leaps back, hoisting her sword over her shoulder before wiping my blood off with her cloth.

"Stop charging at me... goddammit!" I urge, having no regard for my injuries, as I rush towards her, growling in anger. Ruby isn't going to win. I won't let her.

She doesn't answer, raising the sword above her head to split me in two. I dodge again when she swings down, piercing the dirt below. Ruby's eyes widen when realizing it's stuck, allowing me to stab her left arm.

But before I can get my blade close to my skin, Ruby headbutts me, stunning me long enough to let her dash away and recover. I curse in annoyance as she begins to chuckle at herself.

"Don't try that again," she smirks before shifting behind me with inhumane speed. Ruby's using mana again, this time to enhance her physicality. I've killed plenty of mages and witches before— but Ruby might be the first to survive for this long. Each attack is aimed at my organs, and I dodge every one of them.

I block a few, letting my throwing knives get in the action as the yellow sparkles almost land on my pupils. These blades are easier to master since double-wielding weapons are more lenient to control.

After a couple of minutes of constant clashing, she leaps backward again, letting her blade pierce through the ground before leaning against it, trying to catch her breath. *I should keep tiring her out*, I think to myself. *There's no way I'll lose if we keep fighting like this.*

"You haven't tried to grab the grip of my blade yet, Kedar," Ruby shouts at me across from the field. We rotate in circles, walking slowly but steadily, waiting to make a move. "Why?"

"Can't you see me tiring you out?" I tease, my feet crunching against the long blades of grass as I step over a skeleton. The adrenaline keeps my wounds painless— but it won't last for long. I have to end this battle, and fast. "I'm just waiting for the right moment."

"Right moment, eh?" she laughs, twisting her sword around like a spear. Her hands grip the handle. All morals have been erased from her gaze— the only thing she's focused on doing is ending my life. "I'll show you the 'right moment.'"

Using one hand to hold her sword, she lifts a hand towards me before clenching her fist. My body breaks down, sweating in a fit of fear. I'm unable to move as she starts inching towards me, smiling in amusement. My hand resists my brain's command to hold up my sword to protect myself.

"Ruby?!" I say through gritted teeth as she grins, her red eyes reflecting off the sunlight. My whole body feels like jelly. "What... what have you done..."

"I told you. Adapt," I hear her say before she punches me in the stomach. I convulse, spitting out blood as I feel whatever magic she has on my release, and I collapse to my knees in front of her. My hand grips the razqatar, trying to dodge her fist, but I'm too slow. She punches me in the neck this time. I jerk back, holding my wounds in pain as I try to back away. *I'm rusty at this whole fighting thing. Dragons.*

"What the hell, Ruby?" I shout, her death-defying punches still imprinted on my stomach. Fountains of blood spurt out of my nose and my mouth, soaking my tunic again.

I come to my senses, realizing she has her back turned, completely ignoring the fact that I'm still armed. My arm sores as I get up, dashing over to stab her back. Ruby realizes her mistake, screaming in pain and dashing away. She puts her fingers over her wounds, closing them up with her magic.

The blade that she's been risking her life to protect is sprawled out on the ground. She gives me a look of anticipation like she's waiting. I make a break for it, but something holds me back. Ruby slowly gets up, walking over to her sword while giving me a heavy sigh.

Ruby easily takes it, wiping the blood streaming from her mouth as I'm still paralyzed by her pesky magic.

"Nice try," she says, leaping back to gather herself. She releases me from her grasp by spreading out her palm. I barely did any damage to her body with the stabs. The adrenaline begins wearing off slowly as pain overtakes me. My hands shudder as I slick my curly hair back.

"What the hell... did you do... " I cough, trying to fight through the agony.

"It's simple," she begins, pointing her sword at me. My mouth and nose leak gallons of blood as I cough again, spitting the red liquid on the ground. "I used my mana to paralyze you. Didn't you ask if I could harm people? Well, that's your answer."

I clench my teeth. *She did use her magic on me.* I stare back with anger in my eyes. My heart's aching, pumping loudly in my ears while my tongue tastes like rotten copper. It's familiar, yet exciting. Having blood leak from every part of my body reminds me of how thrilling battles were back then.

Ruby charges again, and I don't even try dodging as I accept defeat. I await my death as she holds her sword above her head, ready to slice my head off. *Don't give up now,* the voice in my mind rejects. *Who would remember you?*

I open my eyes as everything slows. Ruby shouts a battle cry, swinging her blade down, and aiming at my arm. My eyes dart to the blade, but I roll back, chuckling as I lick blood off my lips.

"Using magic seems a lot like cheating, Ruby," I propose. The blade hits the ground with a hard thunk as she misses her mark. Her pupils flash with frustration, with a hint of surprise and... sympathy?

"Using magic, huh?" she repeats, lifting the blade off the ground as she huffs and puffs. Already, it seems like she's preparing to use another spell. "Come on, Kedar. Battles have zero rules. Even you must know."

"If I had magic, then you would be dead already," I scoff. My heart's beating out of my chest. Ruby responds by throwing up the middle finger.

Before I can interpret her gibberish, her mouth freezes.

Hm. That would be an interesting predicament, wouldn't it? The voice asks. I pause in shock, realizing everything has stopped moving. Ruby isn't even breathing. She's frozen in time.

Everything is. Birds seem like statues in the sky, and the chirping from the grasshoppers is gone. I look around. The voice appears again.

So, would you like me to hand you our magic, Kedar? It asks. I shudder. The worst part of it is that it sounds like me, mimicking my tone and mood.

"Our magic…?" I say it out loud.

Yes. Our magic. I'm disappointed in you. She should be dead already. But here we are.... it says as sweat droplets pour down the side of my cheek. Each passing second only increases my fear. My teeth chatter as I try to stabilize, to no avail.

If you release your mana, all of your terrors will cease to exist, they explain, as I glance over at Ruby, still frozen. There's a determined look on her face, her blade high in the air.

"Mana?" I stutter. "My mana is dormant."

And who told you that was true? The voice deeply replies. There isn't a place where I can pinpoint it, because the voice consumes the sky and the ground, coming from all directions. After a couple of seconds of long silence, it speaks up again, this time urgently.

I will give you a taste of our power, it tells me. *Just let your emotions run rampant. And give me control.*

The world resumes as Ruby's war cry splits through the air, almost making me deaf. Perhaps Ruby is playing a prank on me. Another one of her illusions of magic distracts me from her true attacks. But the expression on her face tells me otherwise. She isn't smiling as if she knows what's going on. The grin she has stems from our battle. I glance down at my waist as the wound from the sword grazing me starts to close in on itself, making me widen my eyes in surprise.

Ruby doesn't seem to notice, coming closer. My hand twitches as I feel a sudden surge of energy run through my veins. I don't even bother to acknowledge Ruby's assault because I'm too immersed in the glowing, dark red color beneath my skin. *It can't be. No.*

I dash back in retreat. Ruby keeps running as I try to keep my hand steady, but it bursts with pain. My teeth clench together as a little black sphere begins to manifest in the middle of my palm. It sparkles and cracks with ferocity as Ruby's eyes notice the ball of magic, trying to dive out of the way—

Only to run straight into it.

An explosion rings through my ears as I'm swept off my feet by the shockwave. My shoulder explodes into agony, and I lie on my back to catch my breath. Resounding silence fills my ears.

"R-RUBY!" I shout, coughing before wiping the dirt off the top of my forehead. Agony rings through every corner of my body. I try moving my left wrist back and forth, but a white, sharp object sticks out as blood drips on the ground. *My bone. My damn bone.*

"Answer me! Ruby! Goddamnit!"

Silence follows as panic floods my mind. I stumble as I try getting up, holding my left arm steady while trying to ignore the pain. The wounds make me limp forward, my boots crunching on the grass. Foggy smoke's in the air, so I squint my eyes. *It must be that voice.*

The smoke clears from the battlefield, revealing Ruby lying against a tree, her eyes closed, limbs outstretched. Something inside of me makes me move faster— it's the satisfaction to see her okay. Blood drips from her mouth, heightening my fears.

I huff as I get on one knee. My free hand slowly creeps up on her as I press two fingers against her neck. A small thump radiates from her, and I sigh in relief. Ruby's alive, but just barely. "Ruby... wake up. Please."

She's mangled— her ankle sprained, her abdomen covered in blood, soaking her cloak. It's the same place where that sphere hit her. The power of my magic... It's deadly. *Our magic,* A voice rings, before I shake it off. Ruby doesn't respond to my pleadings as I mutter curses.

"Goddamnit," I grit through my teeth, before clasping my hand onto her shoulder. Trying to wake her up by shaking her shoulder seemed to be the only solution. I shook her lightly. "Ruby?! Talk to me!"

A resounding cough interrupts my shouts and pleas, as Ruby blinks her eyes wide open.

"S-Shut up..." I hear her whisper, her voice cracking. Ruby covers the wound on her stomach with one of her arms, huffing through the pain. It's like I put a dent in her. She notices my hand on her shoulder and immediately swipes my hand away.

"Don't touch me. I'm fine," she snorts, breathing heavily. A sigh escapes from my mouth before Ruby begins omitting the blue aura from her hand. My other wrist still vibrates in agony with my bone sticking out of me, but seeing her fine is everything I need.

"Dragons..." Ruby whimpers, fighting through the pain. I sit next to her, looking at the sun as she tends to her wounds. We both sit in silence, trying to catch our breaths. I'm sore in every part of my body. I wipe the blood dripping down my nose.

Her aura sounds divine, glowing and radiating brightly. It assists her body, mending her skin back together. I recoil when seeing her try to reconnect her blood vessels. It's amazing how she can manipulate her powers for good and evil.

153

"Look at you, Kedar, you shouldn't be the one asking if I'm okay," she sighs, glancing at the bone protruding out of my skin. I try chuckling through the pain, only to cough in agony.

"Well, I guess that battle was fair enough, right?" I tell her, wiping the sweat from my forehead. She rolls her eyes at my remark, before raising her hands to my shoulder to mend it back to place. I move away, covering my forehead with my other arm. "Don't heal me. I'll be fine—"

"Shut the hell up. Just let me help you with your wrist and shoulder," she interrupts, her wound sealed off. Most healing magic is temporary, but Ruby's magic is regenerative. A strong variant of healing magic. "Give me your wrist."

I offer her my arm, and she steadies it with the other to heal me. Ruby's magic moves the bone inwards to connect to my wrist, making me grit my teeth. The pain's overbearing, but my bone clicks back into place. I'm half expecting her to be mad at me, but Ruby only has a look of shock.

"That black thing... that's your mana, right?" she asks before I reward her with a slight nod.

The wounds make her robe tear apart. There's a black, charred mark that seems to already look like a scar. *If she died—* I think, erasing my imagination quickly. What matters is that she's okay. Still alive and breathing.

"I've never seen that type of magic before," she explains. With a sigh, she sits on the grass, breathing heavily as I realize how much sweat is dripping down her forehead. The healing process must be draining.

"Y-Yeah. You're right," I mutter, glancing into her red pupils. She doesn't seem too fazed about anything, really. There's carelessness in her eyes. "But I could've killed you."

"You know what, I don't mind all that much," she replies, curling herself up to hold her knees to her chest. I put my hand on my shoulder to see if it's still painful, but I feel nothing at all. "We were both trying to kill each other, and we both went a little far."

I muster a smile, glancing at the shiny sword Ruby has at her side. Though we've clashed like barbarians, there are no scratches or anything. I glance at the throwing knives, noticing the wear and tear on the razqatars. There are chips of metal on both sides.

"Well, does this count as passing your training?" I ask after a couple of minutes of us staring at the sun's pass. She gives me a quick glance, covering her mouth to slightly chuckle at my question. Her red-highlighted braids weave through the wind as she smiles.

"You're kidding, right?" she responds. "You beat me. I can't keep my hands on this damn sword. And you have mana, apparently, which was completely unexpected. Honestly—"

Her hands delicately pick up the blade from the grass, dusting it off. I widen my eyes as she offers me the sword, looking down gracefully.

"I think you've earned this."

The sword slides into my hands. It's a light, feathered blade. My brown eyes gleam back in the reflection as I rub my finger on the pointy tip. It's like a sword a warrior will want— strong, swift, and sharp.

"Ruby... are you sure about this?" I inquire, my brows narrowing as I blink at the shine and sparkles on the *sayf*. It's been so long since I've held a sword. I envision myself slicing through enemies, even though I've vowed to never touch a soul again. It's necessary. We have to save my brother one way or another.

"Yup, I'm sure of it," she explains, scratching the back of her neck. "I've been using it for five years, Kedar. I don't need it anymore, since Bix is already making me a new blade."

"Ruby... thank you," I stutter, still in shock. A light shade of pink covers my cheeks.

"Alright, might as well go back to Onyx," she tells me, sighing before getting up from the ground. We've been gone for nearly five days. I nod in agreement as we both trek back through the woods and reach our camp without delay.

Ruby leaves to change her clothes and put back on her metal armor, so I wait while looking at the fireless, charred campfire. *I'm gonna miss that soup,* I mutter in my mind, my hands brushing over the leather sheath of the blade, dark as ash.

A metal, flowery design sits at the opening of the sheath, complementing the dark and gray colors. It gives it a little shine. I smile, immediately slipping the sword into it before wrapping it around the belt of my pants.

Why didn't you kill her? You imbecile, a voice rings into my ear. I stagger back, yelping as I fall off the log, soaking in sweat. It's happening again. All over again.

Imbecile? I explode. *Who the hell are you?*

Silence follows as I wait for the voice to respond, only to hear no answer. My worries disappear when Ruby comes out of her tent, dusting off her shiny armor while throwing her black cloak around her arms.

She doesn't seem to realize the look of horror on my face, giving me a nod in the direction of the exit. "Come on. Let's go."

I sigh, following her while looking at the ground, only glancing back at the barracks once we leave. Maybe Ruby and I are friends now.

My eyes widen as a dark figure flashes through the barracks. Ruby simply walks on, oblivious to the horrified emotions on my face. I stop completely once I lay my eyes on—

Me.

Its eyes are red with violence, vile, unlike Ruby's. We both lock eyes.

And their mouth twists into a malicious smile.

"Malice, Malice, Malice. The Hayan mind only frets when it sees an array of evil directed at them. Farik, goblin, human, elf, they will react the same. The stench of fear can destroy an individual in seconds, and it is almost delectable to me."

-

ELEVEN

Ruby bangs her fist against the door to the hideout, sighing
as I try to keep my breath stable. That figure looks exactly like
me. A complete reflection, the only thing differentiating us
being the red, sullen eyes. Shaking the image off my mind
seems impossible. I soothe a little once the thought of Onyx
having answers for me arises.

The door opens as Ruby recoils in surprise. I take a peek,
seeing Onyx. The old dog grips his walking stick tightly,
blinking his eyes to fixate on Ruby's face. His tail wags as he
tilts his head upward.

"Goodness. A bit early for all this obnoxious knocking,
isn't it?" he groans, palms sliding against the smooth surface of
his staff. His white cloak blinds me with its glamorous golden
outline. The shine from his gemstone necklace makes him look
like an angel.

"Excuse my distastefulness, but it has been quite a while
since our last encounter, Kedar," he coughs, clearing his throat

as his yellow eyes lock on mine. Ruby scratches the back of her neck with an apologetic look, making Onyx sigh.

"Well, I've been training him up, magister," Ruby replies, glancing at me. Over the past week, I've changed. I'm nothing less than ready. No more doubt is in me at all. Killing seems easy now, and I can't envision myself hesitating anymore. I'll save my brother doused with the blood of the Veils.

"Hm, well, the look on his face has certainly changed since I've last laid my eyes upon him," the old dog slurs, scratching fur from his chin as he squints. "What type of training are we talking about, Ruby?"

"It's hard to explain," she sighs, batting her eyes towards the center of my palm. Pictures run through my mind— our fight, my encounter with my clone, even Ruby's not-so appetizing soup. "Kedar... he..."

"I can already clearly sense it. Awakened mana. Not from you or me. From Kedar," Onyx finishes, chuckling to himself. The old dog knows everything, his magic mysterious in every way.

He raises an eyebrow, placing a hand on my shoulder. The dog squints again, before widening his eyes in shock. He staggers backwards. Before, he had a proud smile on his face, but now he's on the floor, shaking, his sharp white teeth gleaming against the dim lights.

"I—" Onyx stutters, a horrified expression on his face. He turns away from us, walking inside the hideout. I shrug it off to Ruby, following him inside before seeing Bix and Lapis, both standing in one of the hallways to guard the entrance.

"Your mana is powerful, Kedar," Onyx continues, placing both hands at the edges of the table, then glancing up to the onyx gemstone in the ceiling. Onyx hangs his head, his tail wagging against the floor in deep thought. "But that's not everything that I saw. Not even I can explain it. But the

160

feeling... was malice, hatred, and greed. Something I've never seen in years."

Malice... My mind repeats, recalling the dark figure at the barracks. We look the same. The curly hair, the goatee, and the mustache, there's no doubt that it's me. But its eyes are red, much redder than Ruby's. I glance at my palm, envisioning the dark sphere all over again. It's happened once; it can happen again. And this time, somebody might die.

"Perhaps I'm simply exaggerating. I am certainly intrigued to observe you use this in the battle that will occur later," Onyx explains, his walking stick clicking on the wooden floorboards. The worried look on his face hasn't disappeared. *Is my magic that threatening?* A voice rings through my head.

"Battle?" I ask as I finally register what he says. "What type of battle are we talking about?"

"That will have to wait, my friend. Once you're ready, meet me in the far right hallway. I will be waiting for you to arrive," he says, dodging the question. The old man sighs, walking towards the long hall, fading into the darkness as he leaves me at the table. Lapis and Bix trot to me, both smiling.

"Well, I'm surprised. Didn't think you'd come back after training with Ruby," Lapis chuckles, the wrinkles on his aging face showing. He's wearing a blue tunic that covers his knees along with a brown belt. Ruby snorts, crossing her arms as Bix slicks back his brown hair.

"Ya, not wrong for my lad here to assume, mate. Blokes like you usually look like they can't last a single wound, but you... You're a tad bit different, mate. Different from when I last saw you," Bix explains, narrowing his light hazel eyes. I scoff at his remark as Ruby awards me with an approving look.

"These next stages won't be so easy, Kedar," Lapis begins to explain, clearing his throat as he glances in Onyx's direction. Bix nods in agreement.

"It's hard to explain what Onyx is about to put you through, mate," Bix adds in an urgent tone. "'Ere's three stayges to it, all equally horreffying. I hope that once you come back, you're one of us."

The more pressing Bix seems to be, the more his accent comes out, slurring his words into a jumble of letters that makes me pause to translate his sentences.

"Look, what I mean is," Bix sighs, noticing my struggle. He clasps his hand onto my shoulder, narrowing his brows. "I wish you luck, lad. I'm serious."

"Well, what are the three of you going to do once I'm gone?" I ask, looking at Ruby, her arms still crossed. Lapis' eyes gaze at my belt, noticing Ruby's blade sitting on it. He smirks.

"Bix and I are both going to take a long mission to Hexia, a country east of here. Apparently, the commonwealth is going under a coup d'etat. We'll come back once we stop it," Lapis proceeds to explain, tucking his strands of blond hair behind his elf ears. "Ruby's going to take over guard duty, so don't worry too much about her."

"Kedar! Are you coming, or do I have to change my mind?!" a voice rings out. Onyx is clearly annoyed. I sigh, scratching the back of my head.

"Is this farewell, Lapis and Bix?" I calmly ask, scrunching up my eyebrows. Though I haven't interacted with Bix and Lapis that much, they're both good men.

"For now, yes. I won't doubt that we'll see each other again, Kedar," Lapis beams, his white skin reflecting off the gemstone on the ceiling. He offers his hand out to shake, and I oblige, shaking Bix's hand also. I say my final goodbyes as the two of them exit out of the doorway, leaving me and Ruby in silence.

"Well, I might as well get to work, then," she sighs, sliding a chair out and sitting down before resting her head on her palms. Ruby shifts her gaze to her sword on my belt. "Now that I think of it, I've never told you the name of my blade."

"Does it have a name?" I stammer, as she scoffs.

"You didn't name your sword?" she asks, her eyes widening as I shake my head.

"Well, the name of my sword is... the *Kathi*. That's what I've called it ever since Bix forged it for me in the caverns," Ruby explains, her pupils dimming as her eyes fill with memories.

"Wait, where's your new weapon? I say, my mind drawing back to the time she told me about the axes that Bix is apparently making for her to substitute her sword. *The Kathi.* It rings in my head. *Kathi.*

She laughs, tilting her head as she stares into me. "Bix left it in the caverns. I'll show you once I go get it."

"The caverns? There's caverns down here?" I stutter.

"You'll see, Kedar. Now, hurry along. Don't keep Onyx waiting," she promises, nodding her head towards the right hallway. I sigh, gripping the *Kathi* tightly as I take my first steps into the walkway. Whatever Onyx is about to throw at me, I'll take it with ease.

A couple of minutes pass as I walk down the long, winding path. Onyx's old, frail frame fades into view. He calmly waits for me in the dimly lit path of torches. His fingers softly rub the onyx necklace sitting on his collarbone.

"Hey old man," I say, as he begins to trek into the dark abyss. My feet catch up to his soft shuffling, and we walk further into the compound. The hallway slants down like makeshift stairs. Something like this takes decades to dig out.

"Are you ready, child? This process will certainly not be the easiest," he explains, clearing his throat as he wafts away clouds of dust. Cobwebs cover the corners of the walls, while the stone bricks making up the wall already have cracks from wear and tear.

"Well, I want to save my brother, Onyx. You guys apparently have the power to help me out, and I'm not wasting any time on this opportunity," I respond, trying to keep my composure.

"You aren't wrong about that. But even if we do save your brother, what will you do after this whole ordeal? Will you continue to be with our organization, to help us stop the ongoing war?" the old man questions, tilting his head upwards. Even with his height, Onyx intimidates Bix, Ruby, Lapis, and even me. His essence is more powerful than any other mage that I've met. Trying to imagine his magic creates an image of pure, glowing light.

"Onyx, I promised before to live an honest life. To atone for my sins in the army," I begin. Omar doesn't deserve to suffer from *me*, from the reality of what I've done. It's too late to forgive and forget now. The best thing that I can do is save him. "The only reason why I've agreed to start killing again is to save Omar."

"You're right. But repentance, repentance, Kedar," Onyx offers, his walking stick clacking against the floor as we weave through the labyrinth. He's right— repentance is the only way that I can give myself any closure. "Every military man has taken a soul. Every knight has killed a brother or sister. Every mage has destroyed families. I agree with what you said. To atone for your sins. But what sins do you speak of?"

I clear my throat. It was only a year ago, but the memory is fresh in my mind.

The blazing fires of the Cralean town tickled my nostrils. Soot covered my face from the explosions, mixed with the dry blood from our enemies. We cleared another military outpost for Basalia. Most of our allies were cleaning up after themselves, dumping bodies into piles like trash before mercilessly burning them into ashes.

I breathed in another puff of my cigar, leaning against an oak tree as my finger glazed over the red stain on my blade. The number of knights and bards I killed was too many to count. Each had the same look on their face— their eyes widened, mouth agape in shock, their expression completely filled with regret.

No wonder death seemed so fulfilling to me. Their expressions. Their fear. It reminds me of the type of child I used to be. My brother's boots scrunched up against the dirt as he walked up to me. Such an annoyance. I'm surprised the generals didn't kick him out of the ranks just yet. He looked like he shouldn't even be here.

"Brother, the general requested you to clear out any of the Craleans hiding out in their homes," he stuttered, his voice timid. Omar gulped, eyeing the bloodstains on my sword. I scoffed.

"Why? What does he want to do with them?" I questioned, narrowing my eyes as the smell of smoke began to fill my lungs. The burning bodies of our enemies illuminated the atmosphere. Omar didn't seem too fond of it, covering his nose with the brown cloak he was wearing over his metal armor.

"He only asks you to bring them out, nothing more," Omar explained, the sun glistening on the sweat coming down his forehead. I looked down at the ground, processing his request. Perhaps I could make this boring mission a little bit more fun.

I sighed. "Consider it done."

My eyes scoured the town just at the bottom of the hill. Most of the houses were burning, and townsfolk were already being rounded up. The army wouldn't kill the innocent people; rather, they built refugee camps along the borders of Basalia. But these people weren't innocent. They all contributed to this bloody war in one way or another. Nobody could answer or try to redeem their sins. Not even God would forgive these monsters. The women were raising up the next generation of knights and soldiers— a prophecy for chaos. This never-ending cycle only had one, singular solution.

Finally reaching the edges of the town, I looked everywhere for any signs of remaining Craleans. There was no way I would let them get away with this. My parents died for nothing. All the Craleans should do is die. Die by my goddamn blade.

I barged into the first door that I saw. In the corner was the man, no older than thirty. A sneer escaped from my lips as their whimpers immediately filled the emptiness of the room. Their house was completely disheveled from top to bottom — dishes everywhere, furniture scattered. Bodies were decked on the wooden planks.

"Cralean trash," I gritted through my teeth, frustrated. The man's eyes dimmed, dilating from the horrors that they'd seen. "Your country is the root of all evil on this damn planet."

"P-Please..." they sobbed, covering their face with their palms. An irk ran through my veins as the soft sounds of their begging only soothed my ears. Perhaps I should toy with my prey while I'm at it.

"Don't hurt me..." the man continued, looking up with despair. If I let him live, there was no doubt that he'd be a metal worker, a farmer, a supplier, a prophet to the Cralean Empire. It wasn't a stretch. What I was doing was necessary. Solely my right. "I've seen enough. Please..."

166

I growled in anger, walking up to their curled-up body against the wall, picking up the man by the collar. Wavy hair covered his fearful eyes. A soft smile twisted across my face.

"I should be the one who is responsible for ending your suffering, correct?" I questioned, sneering through my teeth as a single tear dripped down onto my armor. My face contorted in disgust, smearing off the liquid with my wrist. "You Craleans barely have the right to be alive. Be thankful that God breathed a soul into your body."

I plunged my blade into the man's stomach as they wailed in pain. They sobbed and kicked. I gritted my teeth as I looked away from their eyes. After a couple of minutes of wailing, their cries and screams abruptly came to a stop. I closed my eyes, trying to escape the horrid view. What the hell did I just do? *My mind rang out as I loosened my grip on the cold, dead skin.*

Blood completely covered my fingers, doused in the blood that I spilled. Something felt different about this kill. Guilt was the only thing that could describe it. I killed an innocent man.

My eyes didn't even dare to look at the corpse on the floor. Knocking came from the front door as shadows appeared in front of the cracks.

"Kedar? Are you there? Find any Craleans?" the general's voice shouted, his tone tamed. I wiped the sweat dripping down my forehead as I slowly walked up to the door, opened it.

"No. I killed them."

"Kedar... that's... grotesque, to say the least," Onyx remarks, his eyes dimming when trying to envision the scene in his mind. I stare at the floor, trying to forget the feeling of the blood dripping in between my fingers. Nothing can redeem me from that. The best thing to do is to never do something like that ever again. Never.

"It was hell, Onyx. I have no idea what to do with myself," I answer. "Realization only came to me when I was sitting in that prison, and the idea of never going into battle again came to form."

"I have no words," Onyx declares, a shining beam of light beginning to poke out of the exit of the long, winding hallway. "Just... repent. Confess your sins to Basal, in hopes he may lay mercy on your soul. If your intentions are true, then you will strive to be a better person. After this ordeal, you can leave as you please. Killing shouldn't be in your daily routine anymore."

I take every word the old dog says to me, nodding in agreement. He's right about repentance. It's essential for gaining back my sanity. The guilt of being the person who has slaughtered an innocent man should never be something that anybody would have to carry on their shoulders. That reflection of myself must mimic the exact same personality back then. A wraith. An apparition. Something made to kill.

"Are you leading me to the cavern? Ruby spoke to me about it earlier," I say, trying to shift our conversation.

"Yes. The cavern of Ghunna is up ahead. Two centuries ago, I used my mana to mine out the tunnel we just walked through. It led all the way to a huge cavern, and I decided to renovate it to fit the Onyx Order," he explains, before we both step out to the limelight. I gasp as a spacious cave is revealed, stretching on for miles upon miles.

At the bottom is a large lake, where some Order members take the opportunity to fish. We're standing on a tall pillar of black stone, and a hanging bridge is the only thing that can carry us to the main section of the cave.

Lights gleam through the darkness. Shops are set up along with some houses if we're in an underground city. Onyx walks across the drawbridge before I cautiously step on its fragile surface, trying to ignore the fact that it shakes with every step I take.

Onyx chuckles as he notices my struggles. I hold on to the rope for some support as I finally reach the end. It isn't the only rotten bridge that Onyx makes me cross, as we proceed to navigate through an entire network of them. My feet squeak against the wet rock as we pass by plenty of other assassins, all busy with their own quests.

"There's a lot of Order members here," I note, nodding at some of the hard-looking men and women. They barely bat an eye at us. All of them have the same cloak that Ruby has, the color black and gold.

"There are only two hundred Order members," Onyx scoffs, as I observe at the stores and houses. Most of them are embedded into the cavern walls.

The ambiance of the compound is promising, only enhancing my wonder. Onyx is pleased with my reactions, smiling with me. A hole from the top of the cave exposes the outside world as clear water rushes in, dumping itself down on the lake below. The stone is split and cracked from years of water splashing on its sides, the edges smoother than the rest. Shades of colors emerge from the waterfall as I take a gander. It's been years since I saw one of those.

"Onyx, what do I have to do to get into this Order of yours?" I ask.

"I require everyone to complete a different set of three trials," he begins to explain. My eyes widen at the realization, remembering that Ruby never told me about the tasks Onyx made her do.

"Well, what tasks did you give Ruby?" my voice urges, as Onyx's eyebrows relax. We keep walking along the cavern, occasionally stopping to take in the sights of the underground city. It boggles me how this place is hidden from the public above.

"I told her to break her wrist and try and heal it using her magic, and so on and so forth. It doesn't really apply to you. Each task relates to your struggles, and what I think is the best solution for it. A task that I handed over to Lapis would be tying him up to a wooden post for hours, even days. It was made to control his emotions. He was a madman back then," Onyx elaborates, as the shock within me increases further.

"So, what do you have to offer me? What kind of tasks will I have to complete on your behalf?" I ask the old man, as we both stop at the edges of the stone ledge.

"The first thing that comes to mind is something I've never asked anyone to do before," Onyx begins, eyeing the waterfall. I squint my eyes, seeing the pathway to get to the top. My mind immediately pictures it. *No… he can't be serious.*

"That ledge. Jump off of it, and consider yourself one third of the way in becoming a member of the Order," he offers, realizing the horrified look on my face. A sigh escapes from his lips as he backs away. "Come. Follow me. It's time to become a daredevil."

I grit my teeth. Nothing that Ruby taught me over that past week can relate to this. My swimming skills are absent, to say the least, because most of my time at sea has been spent on a boat. I try to recollect myself as I follow Onyx closer and closer to the waterfall, as the long, winding stairs fade into view. The hair at the back of my neck tingles, my spine shaking underneath my skin.

"Hold this for me," Onyx says, offering his staff. The stairs are soaked. One wrong move and I might slip.

I sigh, nodding as I grip the wooden stick tightly. Onyx grabs onto one of the handles and hoists his frail body up the stairs slowly. The sound of pure running water filters out Onyx's voice.

"Kedar! Prepare! You will gain the wings of the Dragon today," he urges over the hard rain. Most of his white and gold cloak is soaked from the streams of water streaming towards him as we trek upwards, the shining light trickling through the roof. My eyes gleam at the reflection of the blue sky.

"What good will come from this, Onyx?! If I die, then my death must be blamed on you and you solely," I argue, slicking my curly hair back in resistance.

"Trust in the Dragon! Fear is for the ones who do not believe, and fearlessness is for the ones who invest their faith!" he quotes, yelling at the top of his lungs. We reach the top of the waterfall, and I almost slip from how wet the surface of the ledge is. Onyx and I are standing behind the flow of rushing water, the bottom of the lake below. Jumping off is a death sentence.

"How? How can I jump off without the fear of death?" I wonder as I hand Onyx his walking stick. He taps it softly against the wet cave floor as my boots squelch from the water. I let myself step closer and closer to the ledge, my breathing laboring as I clench my teeth. Nothing can prepare me for this. Not even Ruby's soup.

"Do it without question!" he preaches, waving his other arm old like some sort of mad man. Only a smile is plastered on his face. Hope is what can save me in this grim situation.

"Onyx, if I die..." I urge, turning my head towards him with a glare. He doesn't care at all, his yellow pupils widening with pure joy. This might be the first time he's headed up here.

"Did you not hear me, Kedar? TRUST IN THE DRAGON!" Onyx booms, his voice echoing off the walls of the cave.

The rushing sounds of the water bring me back to reality. If I turn back, there's no doubt that everyone will shame me. Omar will still be imprisoned, and I'll have to go through my search on my own. That's the last thing that I want. *I'm doing this for them to help me,* I remind myself. A cold exhale of my breath escapes out of my mouth as I close my eyes, trying to forget that I'm at the mouth of a waterfall.

In my head, I count to three— a little countdown for my demise. *Three.* I step closer to the ledge, feeling my boots almost slip off the slope.

Two.

Onyx cheers me on. It's underwhelming, but the thought of God keeping me alive is something that I can't erase from my thoughts. Perhaps Basal sees this as my path to redemption.

One.

I jump.

"Trust in the Dragon, for his ego is untamed
Trust in the Dragon, only fear the devil
Rest at night knowing his scales protect you
Demons and ghouls shall fret you
And peace shall be seeketh upon you
So trust in the Dragon, knowing you are not in
vain."

- A Basalian poem written by Elian, the
 fabled Son of Basal.

TWELVE

My body splits through the air like a knife as I scream in

horror. A floor of water interrupts me as I gurgle the dark cave water, and I blink my eyes open before pushing the seagrass against my face. The sliver of sunlight coming from above marks the surface, and I push my arms against the lake floor before kicking my feet to the top. Relief floods through me as my mind processes what I've just done.

I'm alive. My God, I'm alive, a voice rings out through my head. The harsh shine from above blinds me as I gulp deep breaths, paddling my feet to keep myself upright. A fishy smell hits my nostrils as I cough and slick my hair back. I begin to slowly swim my way over to the shore, where Onyx awaits me.

With his arms crossed and a smile on his face, I assume I've passed his little test. I drag my feet across the dark sand, hoisting myself up. A burning sensation tears through my scalp as I rub my pointer finger on it. Blood drips down my forehead.

I must've hit my head on the bottom floor, I think. It doesn't hurt much either way, so you might as well ignore it. Onyx clears his throat, tapping his fingers against the top of his walking stick. With an exhausted look on my face, I glance over to the old man.

"Well? Still scared, Kedar?" Onyx asks, pulling out an unlit torch. He puts it up to his lips before blowing on it lightly. A blaze of fire erupts in front of us as the torch crackles and smokes, the light glowing against his eyes. "I expected you to give up."

"I thought I was gonna die," I admit, sliding my hands against my knees before taking a deep breath. Onyx pats my back, chuckling at my response. There's fun in being so close to death. It's fulfilling. "But... It was fun."

"Ah hah. I'm not surprised in the slightest," Onyx affirms, before offering me his walking stick. I cautiously grab it, not expecting him to lift his other hand, curling his fingers into a ball. "I might as well dry you out. You're soaked."

Before I can question his intentions, a gust of wind blows the surface of my skin while Onyx outstretches his palm towards me. My arms cover my face in protest. I squint my eyes, realizing I'm dry from head to toe.

"Onyx... how do you have this much power?" I ask, handing the stick back. He already has his back turned, walking towards the mined-out tunnel on the left side of the lake. My feet crunch against the stone floor as I rush past a wooden dock. We meet at the entrance of the winding hall as he clears his throat, sighing.

"I've learned many forms of magic over the past two centuries," Onyx explains, as we both stroll down the path. Torches line the walls as the soft glow coming from the light radiates on my skin, making my golden tone glow in the darkness.

"Are you... A Triage?" I stutter.

"No. I have only mastered Astral and Elemental magic," Onyx rasps. Though he's over ten times older than me, he doesn't seem like he's rotting from his old age like before. There's a certain amount of enthusiasm within him that makes me glad he's the one leading the Order. "I learned it all from one man."

"One man?" I mirror. Someone more powerful than Onyx isn't something I expect. The dog seems all-knowing and powerful, so having a teacher is surprising.

"Yes, and he is much more ancient than I am," he confirms, licking his sharp teeth as his voice echoes through the cave. "I am not the oldest man you will ever meet. Fariks are made to be older than most of the races, but alas. The Dragon does make exceptions..."

I leave it at that. But questions arise in my mind, since Onyx has been keeping quiet about my next trial. I have no idea what to expect. "So, what's next? I know this isn't the only trial. There's more, right?"

Onyx chuckles. "Correct. I'm currently leading you to the Faqquerroblin. Subdue the beast, and we will move on to your next test."

"The Faqquerroblin?" my voice stutters, stunned by his statement. Most beasts have been killed in The Cleansing, a war against the monsters of the planet. There's no way that Onyx has a Faqquerroblin.

"Ah. Do you think that I am bluffing, child?" he asks, his voice firm. A loud, resounding growl erupts in front of us as a wooden door fades into view. Sweat rolls down my nape as I take a step back. He's bluffing. *Right?*

"You will succeed, Kedar," Onyx continues in reassurance as the light coming from the torch flickers and crackles against his fur.

"That blade Ruby gifted you... It's special, forged in fire and blood. You are different. You convinced the girl that you are the person appropriate to wield her sword. The *Kathi* was not made to be passed down so simply. She said to me that she'll keep it locked away in her living compound until the end of time, but you came along. Call it fate, but without that sword, the chances of you defeating the Faqquerroblin are simply... slim. We use the Faqquerroblin to execute any... criminals, so to speak."

"What about my magic, Onyx?" I ask, a bit relieved. Ruby seeing something in me is a bit of a stretch. Maybe the old dog is telling the truth, maybe he isn't.

"It's peculiar, different from the rest. The mana that you possess was complete with hatred, malice, and suffering," Onyx implies. "The phenomenon is familiar to—"

A chilling scream erupts behind the wooden door again when Onyx grunts, the doorknob clicking as he slides it open. He maintains his silence as the Faqquerroblin's groans and moans deafen our voices. "Perhaps this is a conversation for later, Kedar."

I grit my teeth before Onyx leads me inside the dimly lit room. Hundreds of weapons line the walls, and there are chairs around a small table. It's an armory.

"Onyx, you know I can't let it go just like that," my voice stutters before I slowly unsheath the *Kathi*. Onyx brushes his fingers against his chin, his golden eyes darting across the room. A door lies on the other side of the armory, leading to the Faqquerroblin. "You must tell me. This magic I have... it's... scary."

"The Faqquerroblin is hungry, and it seems only you can quench its thirst, Kedar." His expression dims before he places the torch against a handle on the wall. A sigh escapes from his lips. "Do not fret. It has been on my mind as well, and it will be the first topic we'll speak about as soon as we finish this trial."

Before I can detest, he grunts, narrowing his pupils. "Your task is to put down the Faqquerroblin. Once the beast is knocked onto the ground, we will move onwards. Do not kill the Faqquerroblin, Kedar. Simply induce it into a state of unconsciousness."

I shake my head, accepting defeat. There's another roadblock in front of me, and the only way I can work around it is by fighting a damn beast. With no hesitation, Onyx unlocks the door by hovering his arm over the knob, turning it with his magic. As it swings open, a glaring pit of darkness lies below, and only a ladder leads me down to my demise.

Onyx gives me a look, encouraging me to climb downwards. I clench my fist, sliding the *Kathi* back into its sheath to grip on the long, wooden ladder. My feet tremble every time I step to the next piece of wood. A low groan erupts from the darkness, meaning the Faquerroblin must know that I'm here. *Stupid trials,* I think. *I just have to get through with this.*

"Prove your worth, Kedar. Do not be intimidated by this *thing*," he echoes, his voice bouncing off the walls as the faint glow of the Faqquerroblin's white eyes blinds me. Another growl only makes me more terrified, but I trek on, stepping forward as my heart pounds through my chest.

"Remember, Kedar," Onyx hums, as I try to filter out the hungry moans. With a gulp, my boots click against the tiles of the circular dome as I spot the dragon patterns lining the floor. "Tis' now or never, child. Subdue the beast. Though it hasn't been done not once before, I believe you dare to succeed."

Shockwaves run through my being as I glance up to Onyx. He's busy standing at the doorway, crossing his arms while staring back at me. His pointer finger taps lightly against his walking stick.

My fingers intertwine with the *Kathi's* before my veins explode with a certain surge of power, draining my soul. It's like the mana is preparing itself for the monster that I'm about to face. The Faqquerroblin takes a long sniff, taking in my appetizing scent.

He knows I'm here, I think, before the beast executes a roar that explodes my eardrums. I put my arm above my face to block the sound of his groaning, peering over myself to see the man that I'm supposed to 'subdue.'

The Faqquerroblin stands ten feet tall. The long, winding nails attaching to his fingers scrape against the stone tiles as he slowly stands up to acknowledge my presence. Both of his cheeks are covered with scars cutting deep into his skin, and the glow coming from his empty, white eyes hypnotizes me. The beast has muscles that mimic the strength of over one hundred men.

He has two, twisting, maniacal horns. My hands twitch against the handle of my blade. His skin is rough, scarred from sword slashes and ax swings. A skull sits in the middle of his palms as he blinks, looking down at me. The Faqquerroblin sneers as the skull gets crushed into tiny bits when he clenches his fist. He's hungry, and the only thing that looks edible is me. The gleam coming from his white, sharp fangs only makes his stature much larger than it is.

"Listen to me, you beast," I stutter, trying to straighten my posture and keep my sword steady. My hand slicks back the coils in front of my face, giving me a wider view of the monster in front of me. A sigh escapes from my lips as I try to keep myself calm. "I swear on this blade. I will cut you down."

"You call me... a beast?" it replies, as I recoil back, keeping some distance between us as he slowly leans forward, our foreheads almost touching. The sound of his voice contains the wrath of over a thousand souls. I keep myself on guard, not letting the beast take advantage of my fear.

"Human. You mimic the words of the goblins, elves, and Fariks. Calling me a beast," he continues, grunting from the chains hanging from his neck, which hold him down against the stone tiles. The restraints are rusty and old, and it looks like the beast has been waiting for the perfect opportunity to escape and embark on a rampage far worse than mine.

"But yet, are thoust not the ones who chaineth me to this dark pit? My body has been here for over five hundred years… but my soul has been gone before the Cleansing. Are those the ones who enslaved me? Are those the ones who forced me to fight to my demise? Are those the ones who force me to kill and consume these corpses?" he cries, covering his face with his hands as he tries stepping forward.

"You are a monster," I reply, staring into the deathly gaze he hands me in response. With a gulp, I clear my throat. *Stay strong,* I echo. "Us Hayans have won the cleansing generations ago. You deserve to be locked up, staying here for the rest of your life and pleading your soul to the ones that have lost to you."

"A monster… A MONSTER?!" he bellows, screeching before tearing off his rusting collar. I glance at Onyx, trying to decipher his blank face, fearing the worst as I step back in dread. "You will truly witness a monster, human. This is your last day on HAYA!"

The flash of his horns gleams against my eyes as he charges towards me, his white nails outstretched, his mouth widening as I grip the handle of my blade tightly. *Goddammit,* I think.

The tips of the beast's nails almost graze against my nose and whizz past my ear as I leap to the side, staggering back before he growls, clenching his teeth. I glance at the *Kathi* before staring back into the beast's white eyes. Saliva drips down his chin as he hisses, getting on all fours like a lion on a hunt.

He dashes at my chest. I counter by sliding in between his legs, my small size working as an advantage for the first time in a while. He bangs his fists against his chest like an ape, screeching with frustration.

"Damn, just let me hit the back of your neck, and this will all be over with," I explain, going into a fighting stance. I turn my waist towards my enemy as I put my left foot forward. I can't waste time. I just have to get this trial over with.

"Damn humans, assuming we are thy property," he babbles on, licking the saliva dripping down his chin. He spits out a skull, the decaying object splitting on the floor with an echoing crack. "You would understand if they knew how much souls Onyx had forced me to fight."

I dwell a bit on what he says, but the Faqquerroblin interrupts my thoughts by swiping at my legs. By shifting to the side, I avoid him, but not before he plunges his sharp nails deep into my left leg, right arm, chest, and collarbone. I drop to my feet and seethe in pain. Luckily, the cuts aren't too deep to fatally injure my body. Blood soaks my tunic and falls to the floor.

Go on the offensive, I think, trying to ignore the beast lurching towards me, ready to release another assault of deadly attacks. *He'll take me out if I try to keep dodging every single one of his swipes.*

Numbness makes the pain easier to go through, along with the adrenaline coursing through my veins. Blood loss gives me a time limit. I have to knock him out now, before he rips my heart out of my chest. With a scoff, I lick the crimson red

181

dripping down my chin, before charging. Surprise riddles on his face, shocked at my fearlessness.

I leap, planting my foot onto his swiping arms. Before he can snap at my legs, I blaze up, feeling the rough skin under my boots, before slashing my sword right at him.

The beast flings me off of his arm, and I fly through the air before landing on the floor on my back with a thud. Blinking my eyes, I glance up.

One of his horns is cut in half, the missing piece lying next to me. The monster doesn't seem to wince in pain, only feeling out the new stub on his head. I clench my teeth in panic.

Pain scorches through my body as I grab the horn. A trail of blood is the only thing that separates me and the beast, but it isn't his blood. It's mine.

There's no way I'm about to fail the old dog, not after I jumped off a one-hundred-foot ledge just to land in the dark waters of the cave lake.

The beast is feral as his eyes glow white again. He puts his nails to his mouth before slowly licking off the blood that stains the tips of them. I grasp the white horn against my fingertips, wielding the *Kathi* in the other hand. A growl escapes from my lips as I try my best to fight through the pain, charging at the Faqquerroblin as a last resort.

I use the *Kathi* as a regular shortsword in one hand, while the other uses the bone like a dagger. The beast puts his arms up in preparation, and I counter by slicing the dagger upwards, cutting his hand off. A smile encrusts my face as his purple blood splatters against my cheeks.

The beast bellows, using his other hand to grip his bleeding stub. With him distracted, I use the bone dagger to slice through his legs, forcing the monster to fall onto its knees.

He drops to the ground, sinking his head in defeat. Satisfaction runs through my veins. Onyx wants me to subdue the beast, but this is good enough for him to approve. At least I keep the beast alive.

"You..." the beast winces, glancing at his twitching, bleeding hand on the floor, splurging with blood. He slowly raises his head to glare into my brown eyes, licking his fangs in fear. "A demon lies in your being, human. No wonder you've beaten me."

"W-What?!" I stutter, as purple blood from the bone dagger drips on the tip of my shoe. With a sigh, I place my blade back into the sheath, still on guard just in case he tries doing anything stupid.

"Purging it is the only answer..." he whispers, staring at the stone tiles before coughing out purple blood. A feeling of rage tickles my spine as voices begin to cloud my thoughts. *You? Calling me a demon? Do you understand who you're talking to? Are you so stricken by my blade that you have to resort to calling me such disgusting things?* "I'll kill you. I'll kill you. I'll kill YOU!"

He lunges forward, but I simply step back. Sweat soaks his forehead as he succumbs to blood loss. Part of me wants to let him live. I've proven to Onyx that I've won. Besides, it looks like he's about to pass out anyway. Another part of me wants to behead him and walk to Onyx with his head, since the beast keeps on blabbering on and on about wanting to be released. It's the only way to stop his pain.

Kill him, a voice says, piercing through the air.

What? I ask, my eyes darting around the dome room. The voice comes from my mind. *You heard me. Kill him.*

Why would I do that? I answer, my emotion shifting from triumph to unease. The world around me is frozen. The Faqquerroblin no longer shudders and glances at the absence of his hand. Onyx isn't occasionally coughing into his fist anymore. This isn't a fluke.

I only assume you must not know who I may be, someone behind me says. My eyes widen, noticing a dark figure walk up to the Faqquerroblin. They chuckle before patting the beast's head. The figure trots in front of me, and each time they step closer, I shout curses in my mind.

No, NO. This isn't real. It can't be.

It's me.

Same clothes, same hair, same everything. It's like looking into a mirror. He even has my wounds. I start to back away while breathing heavily and shaking my head in denial.

Indeed, I am you, the clone of me, says. Their arms rest on their back, and he gleams at me with a malicious smile as his red eyes glow with satisfaction.

You aren't dreaming, Kedar. In fact, I might as well introduce myself, they reassure me, reaching out their hand in greeting. The clone of me pouts once I swat their hand away. *I assume we two aren't on good terms, then?*

Hell no. We are not on good terms… You motherf— I cut myself off, raising the horn as a thought arises in my mind. Ending this man right now might be the answer to all my problems.

Go ahead. Try and hit me. I dare you, he says. I don't hesitate to swing the dagger down to cut him in half. But the horn goes through his skin without spilling a drop of blood.

Good try, he laughs, chuckling like we're best friends. *I'm not even here right now. I've simply appeared as an apparition in the physical plane.*

Plane? What plane? I ask, eyeing him up and down.

Do you not know the two planes? The spiritual and the physical plane? Interesting, he murmurs, putting the tips of his fingers to his chin, before a smirk encrusts his lips. *I am the parasite that's been lurking inside of you for the past seven years.*

184

Parasite... I whisper, glaring.

I was born from your mana. Have you ever thought about why you feel blinded during those times on the battlefield? The clone explains, crossing his arms as he shakes his head disappointedly, as if I'm supposed to know.

Explaining it now would be inappropriate, wouldn't it be? he continues, glancing at the Faqquerroblin, still frozen in time. My expression dims, realizing that trying to kill him is pointless. I am powerless in his presence. *The old dog looks so confused. How comical.*

How'd you freeze time? Is this going to be a recurring experience? I lash out, gritting my teeth together while keeping my hands tightly gripped against my blade and dagger.

I have paused time for your human brain. Our conversation, my appearance, and everything else that happens during my little visit are all conjured into a millisecond in the real world. Our mana allows me to compress this event.

My name is Munir, by the way, the parasite, or Munir, replies. He tries offering his hand out again, but I spit on his brown boots. A sigh escapes from his lips as he shakes his head again. *I want to take control, Kedar. This is the simplest way that I can put it.*

Give me one good reason I should listen to you in the slightest, my voice quivers, my hands shaking with fear. I try my luck again by swinging the dagger downwards, only to be met with his ugly, demonic grin.

Don't fret, Kedar. I won't be taking over your soul. I'll be... lending you my abilities, in the best way, of course, Munir explains, raising his palm before a black ball immediately emerges from the cold, dense air. A ring surrounds the sphere of death, sporting the same color as his pupils. It's the same exact power that almost killed Ruby.

185

Ruby is... useless to me. She is a distraction to our goals, Kedar Munir admits, grinning. *Is that not what you wanted? To kill her?*

Then our goals must not be the same, then. I only seek to save my brother. You seem to only seek some satisfaction for your bloodlust, my voice stutters, as I tap my feet against the stone tiles. Munir's face contorts with disgust. Whatever he is, he's dangerous. It gives me all the more motivation to stop him. *How can I trust you, Munir? After almost killing Ruby, anything that comes out of your mouth seems like a lie.*

I will convince you in one way or the other, Munir scoffs in a grumpy tone. The soft hum from the sphere illuminates everything around us. Before I can detest, his arms thrust the dark matter into my face as the whole world resumes.

The sound of the Faqquerroblin whimpering in pain and the soft taps coming from Onyx's walking stick invade my eardrums, as blood drips down my forehead. Munir's nowhere to be seen. Those planes he talks about... he must be hiding in one of them, waiting for the next time he can pounce.

MUNIR! I scream in my mind. *That bastard. What did he even do to me?* Nothing about me feels different. I'm still bleeding, my hands are still shaking, and the dagger is still dripping purple blood on the floor. The Faqquerroblin inches forward, forcing himself to stand even though his legs are slashed into bits and pieces. "If thou kill me, then thou hasteth the soul of a demon. If you let my soul live another day, perhaps there is some sort of human that dwelleth within you."

He charges, growling in anger as his blood creates a trail. The only thing I can do to counter his barrage of slashes and cuts is to curl my hand into a fist, my eyes locking onto his nape, recoiling my arm back enough to knock out the beast.

I thrust my hand forward, gritting my teeth before inhaling as much air as possible. *Don't kill him,* my mind tells me, trying to push Munir's thoughts out of my head. I don't need any more purple blood to be spilled on my hands.

My vision blurs with blood splatter as I stumble back, landing onto the floor in confusion. I yelp, trying to smear the purple liquid off of my face. The Faqquerroblin's head is in mushy bits around the area. His white eyeballs are staring into my soul, rolling on the floor.

The beast's body is still frozen in shock, but it eventually tumbles to the ground with a deafening splat. His fingers twitch as his body tries to figure out where its head went. Onyx's jaw drops to the floor, a paralyzed look on his face. He's scared.

My palms are dyed with purple liquid, and the veins under my forearms glow a dark red. It's surging like I just satisfied my carnal desires. The mana is flowing through me. I hyperventilate as my heart rings in my ears. *I didn't mean to kill him!* The voice in my mind protests. A soft cackle vibrates my eardrums, replicating the sound of Munir.

That blood, Kedar.

Demonic magic and its true purpose is still very much censored today. I seem to be the only wizard studying this fabled magic, due to the sleek cases which mention this condition. A Hayan, being possessed by a demon of sorts? The thought intrigues me, at the very least. I shall conduct more research in my studies, and hopefully discover the truth behind this cursed art.

- A lost document of the Demon Magick experiments, conducted by Fruidith, the Golden Mage, circa 1421-1425, true date unknown.

THIRTEEN

"Dragons, Kedar! What have you done?!" Onyx's voice rings out, snapping me out of my daze. Munir's cackling in the back of my head is impossible to ignore. Onyx clasps his hand over my shoulder, scrunching his eyebrows in horror.

"Wha- Onyx?" I stutter, staring into his glaring eyes. With a sigh, I try to calm my body down, hoping he won't notice the glowing veins in my arms.

"Gods. Let's just go back," he offers, as I nod in agreement. My body melts as my mind whirls in circles from the stress. I collapse into his arms, my knees buckling.

Feeling Onyx's arm wrap around my shoulder, I groan as the old man walks me back to the ladder.. Onyx hoists me up as I climb back to the surface.

I glance back at the destruction I've caused. The blood on the floors mixes to create the color magenta. Another cough makes me trip over my own shoes. Onyx grips my stomach with a grunt, keeping me upright.

"Lift your head, child. You must not pass out. Not here," Onyx urges while we walk down the dark cave path. My vision is already starting to blur. *Gods. I need to sleep.*

"Don't you dare pass out on me, initiate. I do not wish to carry you the whole way," he demands, gritting his teeth.

I chuckle. Onyx's voice vibrates against my eardrums, but I can't bring myself to take another step. With a grumpy face, I ignore his murmurs. I struggle to open my eyes. Sweat soaks every fiber of my skin. Black spots invade my vision.

"Onyx…" I mumble.

"Kedar!" he yells.

I slip.

How unfortunate. How is your body so fragile?

I open my eyes to a dark evening sky. The stars are absent, and the moon is nowhere to be seen. My feet tingle. Sediment engulfs me knee-deep. *Sand.*

The temperature is neither cold nor hot. Wisps of red air surround me as I slowly walk, hitching my breath. My toes curl against the black sand. I'm no longer tired. It's like I never walked into that arena. Maybe I'm just dreaming.

Wrong. You are not dreaming.

The ground begins to crumble into bits and pieces before a hand reaches out of the surface. Munir climbs out, his eyes shut. He shakes the sand from the coils of his hair, crossing his arms.

How the hell can you read my thoughts? I urge backing away. But I stumble and fall. My feet bury me back into the rocks as I grasp at Munir's ankles, grunting as I struggle under the pressure.

190

I'm you, Kedar. Our thoughts are completely the same. I read your thoughts like how a child reads a book, Munir explains, offering a hand. With hesitation prodding in the back of my mind, I sliver my fingers around his forearm. Earlier, I wasn't able to touch him. Now I can.

Welcome to this world.

World? Where are we, Munir? I stutter as he snorts, shaking his head as the bottom of his boots crunch against the black sand.

The spiritual plane. This is the inside of the mind of a Hayan. It is where I was born, and where I reside. He clears his throat, glancing downwards. *Seven years ago, you manifested me into this plane. I've been living off of your wrath for years. It is a shock to me that you haven't figured out about my existence yet.*

Well, I never wanted you to be here anyway. You shouldn't exist, Munir, I spit. I shove him back to make him pummel to the ground. Munir doesn't do anything in response. Rather, he maintains a blank look on his face. *Let me live my own life.*

Do I have to repeat myself, Kedar? Munir blinks, clasping both of his hands against my shoulders. Narrowing his brows, the fury in his red eyes plants daggers into my head. *I can assist you in finding Omar. All you must do is let me take control. It will all be better once you listen.*

Perhaps this isn't the right way for you to go about this, Munir, I argue, swatting his arms away. I'm not about to trust this creature with my body after what he's done. *You nearly killed Ruby, and now you've killed the Faqquerroblin. Give me one good reason I should trust you.*

I'll admit that I can't help it. Munir widens his eyes. *My job is to simply fulfill your desires, meaning your wrath, sorrow, pain, anger—*

I punch him in the throat. He coughs, grasping at his neck. Taking Munir seriously is the last thing I imagine myself doing. I charge, clawing his face over and over, and my knuckles bleed. With a grunt, I stand, noticing the blood dripping from his knuckles as well.

Just think about it, goddammit. He coughs, huffing and puffing as he forces himself to stand upright. *I might as well be patient. Either way, there are plenty more things to worry about in the real world, Kedar. I'll let you go. Perhaps you'll accept my offer after I... rile you up.*

Rile me up?! I gawk as he sighs in response. He raises two fingers, snapping before exploding into millions of particles of sand, sinking himself into the ground. I groan. *This isn't his mind. It's mine. All he did was come here and steal it from me.*

Anger contorts onto my face before I clench my fists.

There's no way I can beat someone who... is me.

Something's tugging at my foot. My eyes dart downward, glancing at the human hand that slowly pulls me to the ground. With panic setting into my mind, I stare at the creature revealing itself.

Red pupils replace the dark brown eyes I once knew. Her head creeps out of the dark sand, revealing her skinless body. Her face is replaced with bare facial muscles, but I still recognise her.

Mother.

My mother pulls me down, with a blank look on her face. I try shaking her off, but to no avail, as my knees get covered in gallons of sand.

She opens her mouth wide to display her sharp fangs. My mother doesn't respond to my pleas as I get pulled deeper and deeper, wondering if Munir will be the one to save me. I squirm like a fish on land.

"Mother, STOP!" I cry out, tears leaking out of the corners of my eyes. Everything blurs between reality and fiction—explaining why I have nightmares ever since the day my parents died. Maybe this is another one of them. Dreams of demons and devils eating me alive. "LET ME GO!"

"It's time to wake up, my son...," she trails off, pulling me waist down into the sand with her. I'm close to her skinless face, and I lean back in fear, her hands pushing me down further. Her voice mimics the low, soft groan of the Faqquerroblin, only twice as horrifying. "S-save... S-save—"

"M-Mother, what is it? Tell me, please!" I urge, closing my eyes. I gaze upon the horns that grow on her back, her legs completely missing from the lower half of her body, replaced with the slithering tail of a snake. Her skin is covered with ugly, rough scales that disgust me.

"Save Omar..." Her voice slithers as my eyes blur while we go deeper into the depths. My entire body melts as her voice flutters in my ear. "Stop the prophecy. If it is to be fulfilled, we will all die."

"MOTHER?! MOTHER, WHAT DOES THIS MEAN?!" I shout, trying to claw my way back up to the surface as she releases me from her grasp. Tears flood my face as I keep sinking.

And I go
down
down....
down...
And everything fades to red.

Nightmares and visions are too vivid when I sleep. Bringing myself to believe that Munir is real is impossible. Even seeing

Ruby in front of me isn't enough to convince me that I'm no longer stuck in the spiritual plane. *Or whatever the hell he said.*

Her legs cross together as she sits on a stool. I recognize her figure, but my eyes are watery and blurry even though I try keeping them open. The world is still a dark desert to me.

Ruby looks like a demon herself. Horns are on her head... are they? My mind has to be playing tricks on me. *Dragons, I'm on something,* I think, hyperventilating before trying to get out of the bed to soothe my harsh visions. My torso fumes in pain, as my head aches as much as my body. Thankfully, everything becomes clear.

Onyx has placed me in the underground caves of Ardon. The cavern covers the left side of my view, the sound of the running water coming from the waterfall, adding to the slow ambiance.

A table is at my side, with a glass of water and an empty cup in the middle of it. Trying to pour the liquid down my throat is meaningless since trying to lift my head is worse than having to fight a wave of over a thousand men. Onyx gave me one of his robes to wear. I glance at the golden lining on the sleeves. It catches my eye instantly. Ruby hasn't realized I woke up. Behind her is a wall with shelves full of books. In front of the bed are medicinal supplies along with a sink on the wall. Ruby's too busy with her novel. Her eyes narrow, her pupils darting from word to word.

My head sinks back into the soft pillow as I ruffle the blankets softly. I glance at Ruby's red gown— it's the same outfit she's worn when we trained a week back. A sigh escapes from her full lips as she turns the page, maintaining the serious look across her face.

I clear my throat as she looks up from her novel, staring into my eyes.

"Ruby, what happened? Where's Onyx?"

194

Ruby puts the book at my bedside before resting her chin on her knuckle. "You've been out for so long, Kedar. I almost thought that you died."

"Wait…. What do you mean?" I ask, my voice raspy. Ruby purses her lips as she takes a knee, picking up a pail of water. Silence radiates from her as she dips a towel into the liquid.

"You passed out in the middle of a dark hall. Onyx carried you back here and put you in our clinic, where we determined that you had a horrible fever," she explains, smearing the cold towel against my forehead. I wince while breathing heavily.

She shakes her head. "Dragons. Don't scare me like that."

"What the hell happened, Kedar?" she continues, her eyes glazing over my features. "Onyx seemed pretty shaken up after he told me to watch over you."

Pressing the towel further into my skin, I glance back at Ruby and sigh, barely remembering what happened. Only my mother's words repeat in my mind. "*Stop the prophecy, stop the prophecy…*"

"Ruby… I can't remember much," I admit as she sits back on the stool, raising a brow. The picture of purple blood immediately comes to mind. "But the Faqquerroblin is dead."

"Dead?!" she scoffs as she twirls one of her braids against her pointer finger. Pride sets in the back of my mind as I reject my guilty thoughts. "Dragons. You killed him?"

I nod.

"That's a surprise." She turns her chin to the right to display the ridge in her neck, marking her deep scar. I concentrate on it. I've seen it before, but sometimes I wonder who could've done that to her.

"Well. Great job, I guess. Onyx is furious," says Ruby, rewarding me with a light smile. "Honestly, the thought of you even passing the first trial was something hard to imagine."

"Oh, shut up," I grumble, glancing at the white bedsheets as she chuckles. Onyx must be out there somewhere, waiting for me to wake up. I have too many questions. Maybe he knows about Munir, and maybe he can help me out.

Standing up requires every ounce of my strength. Ruby glances over to watch, not bothering to help as I roll myself off the ledge, my body aching as I crawl on the mattress. My chest is covered in bandages from the Faqquerroblins slashes, and my arms are wrapped with a white cloth to hide the slits from the beast's white nails.

I wince as concern encrusts Ruby's face. Eventually, I land onto the stone floor with a resounding *thump*, aching in pain as every part of my body throbs in agony. Ruby kneels in front of me, gulping with a heavy sigh.

"I'm going to safely guess that you want to see Onyx," she concludes, her hair brushing against my cheek. I nod, trying to keep myself conscious.

"Get up, I'm not going to be with you every minute to help you out."

My hand reaches out, grasping at the wooden bedframe as my knees buckle and shake from the pressure. Ruby offers a sympathetic smile, pulling me up. She wraps her arm around my shoulder and hoists me upright, letting her arms hang against my neck as we shuffle out of the clinic.

Pairs of eyes stare into my soul in every direction. All the assassins mumble and murmur in my presence. Some random, scrawny kid from Jaawed has beheaded a monster.

In response, I glance down to not attract attention, looking at my toes as I walk barefoot against the cold cave floor. If Ruby isn't here to help me out, then I might've been crawling.

"Where is that old geezer?" my voice rasps as Ruby grunts, trying to carry me across the cavern. I'm inches taller and much bigger than her, but she's making sure that I don't fall to the ground like a damn idiot.

"Onyx should be in his office, just to the left of here," she explains as we turn left, shuffling ourselves down the underground city, passing by assassins, shops, and homes. Onyx is a mysterious yet amazing man. He built this community with his blood, sweat, and tears. "Just stay awake, Kedar. I got this."

We eventually reach a doorway in the stone walls. She sighs, letting go of me before leaving me leaning against the wall. With a click of a doorknob, Ruby swings the door open, revealing a dome that mimics the look of the arena from earlier. Candles line the wall to illuminate the air as gemstones shine on the ceiling, generating a kaleidoscope that reflects off Ruby's eyes. She takes my arm again, leading me to Onyx, who has a small desk in the middle of the dome, writing away at some records after dipping his quill in black ink.

"Hello, Magister. Kedar can't wait, so..." She glances at me again, snorting. "I decided to bring him here."

"ONYX," I say, huffing as I limp to his table, slamming my palms against the wooden surface. Ruby stands behind me as I confront the old man. He doesn't seem intimidated by me, simply writing away without rewarding me with a glance. The golden-feathered quill he uses blinds my eyes. After a couple of minutes, he finally acknowledges me, looking up with his yellow pupils.

"Resting should be your first priority, child. I wish to have a conversation with you when your injuries are not as prevalent as they are currently," he admits, his two-pointy ears drooping downwards to offer me sympathy. "Though I understand your urgency. What do you need?"

"Onyx, something happened, dammit. It's about my mana," my voice urges before my mind treads a bit on the unsteady side once again. Ruby shuffles out, giving me one last glance before disappearing.

I sit on the wooden chair in front of his desk.

The best thing I can do now is try my best to get answers.

"Hm. You seem to be in a dilemma, Kedar," Onyx offers, putting his quill back on the table. My breathing gets stable as my headache subsides, even though my voice mimics the sound of a dying horse. He taps his pointer finger on the table, sighing. "Yes, I know, everything right now seems so confusing, doesn't it? I'll do my best to explain every bit of it I can. Do not fret, child."

I nod as Onyx gulps, ready to not gatekeep anything anymore. He twirls his quill in his fingertips, licking his fangs like he's preparing himself to spill everything he knows. Onyx is wise. Munir must mean something to him.

"The magic that runs through your veins is the magic of a demon."

I grit.

"It explains why your veins glow dark red," Onyx nods, as I glance at my wrist, noticing the dark matter running through it. My fingers softly brush over it, feeling the soft hum of my mana. *Am I a monster?*

"Onyx, what's going to happen to me? I've never heard about this type of magic before in my life," I whisper, my fingers vibrating against the surface of my skin. Munir's powerful. The evidence is right in front of us. The mana that blazes through my veins... It's his.

"I don't know. Little is known about demonic magic," Onyx continues. "I cannot manifest this, but you do. But what I do know is that it affects a very small group of people on this planet, and it is the rarest magic that any Hayan can obtain."

Then, he reaches over with his right hand, clasping my own hand with his. A dark aura appears over my palms before it swirls into a sphere. It's the same magic ball Munir used to kill Ruby. Even looking at it makes me enraged.

"I've extracted some of the magic out of your veins, and this is the result," he elaborates. "It is the pure form of your magic."

"Why does it hurt so much?" I ask, my body aching from the sheer event of holding the sphere. My head's dizzy again, but I keep my eyes open. I can't pass out again.

"The magic is uncontrollable," he notes, crossing both of his arms. The sphere that swirls around in my hand slowly shrinks back into my palm. "It's like that tale my master told me. It infects your thoughts and your mind. Perhaps it's seeking to take control of your being at this moment."

"My being?" I mirror. Perhaps it explains Munir. He's just an imagination, an apparition of my mind. He's the vessel of my demonic magic.

He pouts, handing me a solemn look, before scratching the back of his fur-covered head. "It's hard to explain. Kedar. I'd say it's complicated—"

"Don't tell me it's complicated," I interrupt, clenching my fists in anger as pain radiates from every part of my body. It's like the magic is eating me from the inside. My brain is ticking dynamite that can blow any second. "You don't understand."

"Trust me, child, I understand very well!" he grunts, shaking his head frustratingly. Onyx glances at the paper and quill in front of him, clearing his throat to address the silence. "Perhaps I can assist you. The manifestation of your mana comes from one central core point. All we have to do is find that nodal point and destroy it. Call it the... root of all evil."

"That sounds so familiar. It was like what the voices were telling me in that nightmare," I admit, recounting Munir's words. He boasts on and on about having the ability to make me powerful, to make me some god.

"What voice do you speak of, child?" Onyx interrupts, narrowing his hunter eyes while his sharp teeth and yellow gemstone necklace gleam. "Tis' not a concept I've heard of in quite a while. But voices speaking to you? That is surely alarming."

"It's not a voice, Onyx. It's a little more complicated than that," my voice hitches, pictures of Munir's flashing red pupils coursing through my brain. "There's a parasite leeching off of my head. And he looks like me."

The expression from Onyx switches from shock to horror, clasping his palms in prayer before bowing his head in front of me. I don't give him a reaction, simply offering him a blank stare as I hear him mutter to call upon his God.

"Expel the demons within this holy man, Our Father in Heaven. Let the man put faith in your blue scales while releasing him from his sins and transgressions. Shaytan has placed a curse upon his soul, and we request that you release these horrors, O Father. We beg you, and we are weak to please you in these hard times, Basal. Ahmeen."

Hope is absent in my mind, since the concept of deities has been erased from my life when my parents died. But maybe I'll invest in his prayers. The look on his face as his mouth speaks the luscious words of a priest alleviates the pain a little bit. I almost forgot my head is throbbing in pain, and I'm still aching.

"Sorry, Kedar. You don't mind, right?" Onyx offers, before I shake my head in denial. "I've made up my mind. I'll help you. We're going to get rid of this demon of yours."

"You should simply rest, Kedar. Perhaps it will come in your sleep. And then, we will strike. I'll converse about it more later, when I prepare for the ultimate battle that is about to take place within your planes," Onyx continues, sighing heavily as he rests his chin on top of his palm. "I should be ready in about a week."

"A week?" my voice quivers, the thought of Omar crossing my mind. Summer has passed since he disappeared in Jiya. He must be locked up, cold, and shivering right now. It's puzzling, why did the Veils take my brother anyway?

"Perhaps. This process requires more amounts of magic than you can imagine," Onyx explains. "We can continue your initiation once you're healed. God, I can't believe this is happening."

I angrily glance at the dark veins in my wrist, clenching my teeth as the thought of Munir crosses my mind. *You're weak,* a voice rings. With a sigh, I look up at Onyx, trying to calm myself down. "Onyx, you seem to know so much about this. How?"

"It's because of Judah, Kedar. He possesses the same magic that you do yourself." Judah and I having the same magic is frightening. "Judah's Veils are darker than you'll ever imagine."

Both are brothers, living in different worlds. Onyx seeks to bring peace and Order to the lands of Haya by any means necessary, while it's like Judah is the one wanting to establish control and create an empire. It makes me wonder how long their rivalry has been brewing and how many people died because of it.

"Unfortunately, this is the exact reason why I made such an expression when realizing the power of your mana," explains the old man, dipping his quill into the inkwell, writing onto the paper scroll in front of him. "It simply reminded me of Judah. The man I resent the most, and the man that I wish to liberate the most."

"Onyx, what makes you fear Judah?" My voice quivers, recognizing the hint of nervousness in his tone.

"Before we separated, Judah and I fought in Pinakada two hundred years ago. At that time, I did not realize he had even manifested his magic, let alone knowing how to use it. I left that fight with hundreds of scars, and I haven't shown my face to him since. It is why I learned all of the arts, seeking to find a way to counter his ungodly power. And now, the fact that you have it too... it makes me wonder who else can conjure this magic," Onyx says, finishing his sentence off in a hushed whisper. Fear shockwaves through my body. A drop of sweat trickles down my forehead.

I'm the only person who can affect the outcomes of this ordeal. Sure, Onyx may be able to subdue Munir, but it's solely up to me when it comes to erasing Munir from existence.

"Kedar, I require you to put in full effort in this expedition," he begs, threatened by the magic coursing through my bones. With a cough, the sound of Onyx's old bones making a soft crackle bounces off my eardrums. At least I know what to expect over the coming week. Munir's going to beg for my cooperation, and I have to maintain my sanity to keep rejecting his offers.

"I will, Onyx," I rasp, coughing as I clasp my other hand with a firm grip. A sly smile encrusts my face as I get up from wobbling to the front door to open it to the fresh air of the cavern.

Ruby's standing outside, her arms crossed, and her expression blank until she notices me.

She grins. "Need help?"

She carries me across the wet cave floor as my soft breaths get defeated by the flow of water raining down to the lake. Ruby simply focuses on keeping me upright, gritting her teeth. Her voice quivers, a drop of sweat dripping from her forehead. "Are you gonna be okay?"

I glance at her, staring into her eyes filled with curiosity.

"You don't have to worry about me," I choke, blinking my pain. *Liar.*

We reach the entrance. I look up at the sign at the top of the cave. *Alkahf altibiyu,* I read in my mind. *Medicinal Cave.* The little establishment resembles a small clinic. I collapse on the white bed I'm on before, turning to my side and covering myself with the bed covers.

Ruby sits in her seat, picking up her book to watch over me. The next couple of hours are a blur of fading in and out of nightmares and waking up in a cold sweat. Ruby calms me down and she hydrates me whenever she can. It's night the next time I sit up, the moonlight reflecting off the water flowing down the waterfall outside.

I can't even tell what day it is. *The 197th? The 187th? There's no way of knowing anymore.* My fever and mana both rampage through my bones, and my teeth chatter even though I'm wrapped like a shawarma in these sheets. Ruby's leaning against the wall, snoring softly with the book on her lap.

I'm jealous. She sleeps peacefully, while I'll do anything to not fall asleep again. Nothing can describe the horrors that I see while in my slumbers. It's probably my fault that Munir's so attached to me. My rage, my wrath, my anger. Seeking revenge. I wipe the blood that starts to stream down my nose. *To hell with it. I'm ready, Munir. Come at me all you want. I'll kill you.*

Then, whispering voices begin vibrating in my head. It isn't from Ruby, and it isn't from anyone else. A shriveling voice whispers. I concentrate on it, realizing it's Munir, chanting and cackling from his plane. Soon enough, the whispers turn into growls, and the growls into screams.

Let me take control.

Let me take control.

LET ME TAKE CONTROL.

LET ME TAKE CONTROL.

There is a legend about a demon, soldiers dubbing it the "Doe Sensation." A shadow leaps from hill to hill on each battlefield, seeming to curse this whole legion with bloodlust. Certainly, this must be a sign of demonic magic. I will conduct more research, indeed. I must find the root of where this demonic energy is coming from. Perhaps the "Doe Sensation" is not a legend but a reality.

- A lost document of the Demon Magick experiments, conducted by Fruidith, the Golden Mage, circa 1411-1416, true date unknown.

FOURTEEN

Munir's been tormenting me for the past couple of days, grasping at every opportunity to bother me. Sleep has now become something that I hate. His begging voice keeps ringing in my ears for me to accept his proposal in hopes of letting him do whatever he wants. He preaches about "potential" and "the power that I have yet to trust."

His venom strikes at any time. When I try taking a little stroll around the cavern, I collapse to the floor before having nightmares of my parents dying over and over again.

My fever has disappeared for now, but Munir's voice hasn't. The little clicks of his tongue are impossible to avoid.

After telling Onyx everything I know about Munir, he advised me to stay strong in his presence. He explains Munir's trying to feed off of my fear to take advantage of me.

He sits at my bedside with a determined expression. Onyx's brows narrow. I groggily scratch my eyes to erase the blur, breathing a heavy sigh to compensate for my fatigue.

Munir's been eating away at my body, mind, and soul, eager to consume whatever confidence I have. The old man clasps his hands together in reassurance, inhaling the cold cave air slowly as he glances at the red glow in my veins.

"Good morning, child. I've finally figured out a solution for the demon which inconveniences you," he slurs, licking his fangs.

I offer him a skeptical look. Ruby told me that he's been alone in his office, his mana vibrating against the dome walls. According to her, he's training. *Surprising.*

"What? What is it this time?" I eagerly answer, pushing my doubts aside as he spreads one of his palms. A gold aura manifests on his furry fingertips. It blinds me, and I cover my face in retaliation.

"My master calls the method Astral Projection." His fingers tremble as he holds the magic in his hands. "An ability created by the man who was the first to wield astral magic. I can leap into your mind, and in return, both of us can take on Munir instead of you being alone. It takes a devastating amount of mana to execute, but I have no doubts. It will work." The glow is bright enough to make everything shine white. Describing it is impossible, but hope rushes through me.

"Pressing my fingers against your forehead leads us in your spiritual plane willingly. There's a catch to the whole process, though. Every hour I spend in your plane, my lifeforce drains a drastic amount," Onyx continues, biting the insides of his cheek. "We must be swift, Kedar."

I hastily grasp at his arm, gritting my teeth. "Onyx. Don't lie to me, goddammit! Have you ever done something like this before?!"

"No. This is my first time attempting this, and hopefully not my last."

I open my mouth in protest, but he shoves two fingers against my forehead. It sends the room into a white light, making everything fade away in an instant. I clench my eyes together before Onyx huffs, expelling all his mana into me.

It shines through the darkness, shredding through my soul.

When I awake, my toes curl up against the familiar, dark sand. Onyx is in front of me, blinking before collapsing to the ground. I rush over, grabbing his shoulders before hoisting him on his feet.

"Dragons! I've done it! I've done it!" Onyx coughs, letting me help him stand up. He breathes out a heavy sigh, taking a gander at the black sand around us, noticing the red wisps in the air. Wrapping his fingers around his necklace like a charm, Onyx grinds his canines together.

My eyes wander across the dunes to find Munir, but he's nowhere, meaning he doesn't know we're here yet. I grip Onyx's shoulders, silently thanking the Dragon that I'm not alone anymore. "We've done it, Onyx. Now all we have to do is find Munir."

We walk up the sandy hills, Onyx leading the way as his white and golden robe waves in the winds of my spiritual plane. He hastily trots to one of the red wisps, letting it disperse into his palm as he looks down with a dark gleam on his face.

"You are correct," Onyx admits. "It is a hassle to navigate one's spiritual plane, though. Have you tried walking through these endless deserts?"

"No," I admit, glancing at the empty blackness of the sky. "I don't even know how to get here. It's really Munir who drags me here."

These past few days have been so tormenting, I think.

"Now that I wonder, the answers can be found in the Codex," Onyx begins as we walk side by side. The desert doesn't end. It's like we're walking in circles. I offer him a questioning look.

"Here I thought someone like you would be religious, Kedar," Onyx offers, resting his arms on his back. The cane that he once used before is gone. He walks completely fine without it; his posture is straight. The same goes for me; my head never churns. Our injuries must not carry over here.

"The thoughts of each man are different," Onyx summarizes, speaking like a priest. The dog is a true man of Dracotheism. Even though he runs an organization to hunt and kill people, he still keeps his faith close to his heart. "The Codex speaks differently on this topic, though. 'The minds of men are molded in likeness to all.'"

"What does that mean?" I ask, letting the words repeat in my mind.

"We think in different ways, but God structured the Hayan mind the exact same way when he created us. A body has a soul, and a soul has a spiritual plane. The physical plane refers to how we interact with the elements around us in the real world, like trees, grass, air, and water," Onyx elaborates, fueling my curiosity. "According to the text, there are three parts of the plane in which we walk: The Grove of Memories, The Lair of Obscenities and Desires, and The Mind's Heart. I've been in my own spiritual plane many times by using my master's magic. Since we know each mind is built the same, we must find one of these places mentioned. Munir can be hiding in one of them."

"Well, where are we, anyway?" I wonder as we tread through the black sand.

"We've only been here for ten minutes, Kedar. It is impossible to interpret where we are exactly," Onyx replies. The old man treks up the dune of sand, putting a hand on his forehead to use as shade, scouring the scene left and right. "Ah, perhaps this place might be your Grove of Memories."

I catch up to Onyx after almost slipping on the sand. My eyes lay upon a lush pine tree forest, encased in a dark blue mist. Onyx's pupils dart around the greenery as he lets out a heavy sigh. Turning back, he smiles before softly chuckling. "Follow me. Munir might be lurking somewhere around here."

Both of us hike down the dunes, my bare feet softly beginning to crunch against the grass. The green pines and white particles falling out of the sky make me assume we're walking through a memory. Bushes with berries surround us as we trek through. I glance behind me, seeing the desert fading into the gray fog. Figures scurry through the tree line next to us before I step back in shock. Onyx maintains his stern expression as I breathe heavily, following the shadows.

A river divides the land, shrubs lining the flowing water. Onyx hastily crosses over effortlessly, his eyes full of wonder as we trot on. I clear my throat to get Onyx's attention, but he ignores me.

"Onyx... what the hell are you doing?" I finally ask, clutching my fingers against the boulders on the bank as I catch up to him. My breath shivers as I scale the cold river, my knees deep in the rapids. For an old man, he can get away pretty quick.

"Hold on, child. I believe that I may have found a memory," Onyx stammers. We've been walking for ten minutes around this maze. The old man is only focused on the figures that rush by. Catching my breath, I push the bushes past us, staring at two shadowy figures.

It's me.

And Omar.

My eyes widen. We're both playing in the woods. Images flood my mind. Onyx is right. This is a memory. My younger self happily plays with a stick, using it like a sword before swinging Omar, who blocks the swing with his own makeshift-stick-weapon.

"Perhaps... you remember something like this?" his voice intrudes, deafening the laughs coming from our kid selves.

"My mother and father took us to a camping trip when I was seven, and Omar was five. This is near Nisf Thueban," I reply. Nisf Thueban is a group of mountains that spans across Jura and some parts of Ultum. The mountains are nowhere near Basalia, and the thought that we're so far from home and safe bewilders me. I haven't thought about the trip in years.

"Interesting. The Grove must be showing this for some sort of reason. But for what?" Onyx asks himself, stroking the fur on his chin. He paces, letting his golden-lined robe glisten in the dark air. "Hm. Do you remember anything about your childhood, by any chance?"

"Only my parents' deaths," I admit, glancing at the frolicking children barely taking notice of me and Onyx. They don't even bat an eye at us. A part of me wants to wave, but I know they won't react. "Everything else is just void."

"Traversing through the forest must be our next mission, then. Northwest of here is a strange aura. Perhaps we should go there next," Onyx offers as I nod. The old dog turns left, his boots crunching against the fallen pine cones as he fades into the forest. I glance at the two boys behind me, wanting to see my younger self one last time.

He's much taller than Omar, his hair short and almost bald. Omar has puppy eyes, his hair tied into a bun. We still fight with our sticks, not having a single care in the world. We have no idea what famine is, what war is, what death is. Now we're shells.

"Wait."

Swearing under my breath, I shake my head in denial. Both of them stop moving, their pupils locking on me as I step back, pressing myself against a tree. Gray fog encases us.

"Don't fret, Kedar," Omar sighs, holding his stick up in the air with triumph. The younger me smiles brightly, missing three of his baby teeth. Even though it's weird that my younger brother is talking to me, I can't deny how triumphant his childish charm was back then. But he's scared. Scared of the future, of what's to come. His face is plastered with worry. Tears almost form in my eyes. Praying every day won't fix the amount of damage I've done.

"Find me, Kedar," Omar says before I have the chance to speak. His eyes dart down to the stick he holds before calmly handing it to me. With nervousness, I shakily take the innocent object from his frail, bony fingers. He maintains a bright, inviting smile. Maybe this is a good thing. "Once you see me, slap me in the face with this darn stick, would ya!"

Both of them burst out laughing. The younger me holds his stomach as he giggles hard. I glance at the stick, gripping it tightly. For the first time in a bit, my mouth curves into a true, wide smile. I return my gaze, nodding in agreement.

"By Basal, I will."

Omar puts both thumbs up while my younger self keeps quiet but is still lively and animated. This past spring and winter, happiness didn't exist. It's surprising to see me even feel a little slimmer of joy.

Both their faces begin to shatter like stone, their bodies slowly fading into nothing. Omar raises his hand to wave goodbye, but his limbs wisp away.

"Kedar, there's one last thing that you should know," younger me finally coughs out, his voice hoarse as a piece of his face falls off. He glances at the dirt, smiling at the ground. Omar merges into the fog of the Grove, and young me knows he probably has a couple of seconds left. But he's not scared. He knows why he's here. "Don't fear."

Tears form in his eyes before he disappears.

Catching up to the old dog, I ignore the waves of pain on my bare feet, the words of my younger self submerging in my mind.

"What delayed you?" he inquires before we continue our journey west, the sounds of running water vibrating against our eardrums. The aura that Onyx has talked about earlier comes to my mind, and I can only wonder what scene awaits next. Having a numerical advantage is something that'll help us beat Munir.

"Nothing," I lie, smiling at the ground. "Nothing at all."

Onyx shrugs, continuing the long walk. We trek for half an hour, hopping over rivers and pushing past bushes while swerving through tree lines. The old man is clearly concentrating on finding the aura's source, and he finds it when the sounds of screaming and groaning fill our ears. Howls of help vibrate my eardrums as smoke erupts above the tree canopy. The shouting is familiar. Too familiar.

Running into a yellow, tall wheat field, I jerk back as itches flourish on my knees. Onyx is at my heels, dashing as fear enters my mind while he gets on his tippy toes to see what's beyond.

Jaweed.

The shouts of fear and sounds of burning ash bring me back to that fateful day. It's the hour when both of my parents are slain in cold blood. I have nightmares about this moment every night, and nothing can make me forget.

"My God. What a sea of... hellfire," whispers Onyx, we push through the field. We flatten the plants before hopping over the stone walls to get on the dirt path.

Fire flails around me as the cries of villagers fill my mind. Bodies lie on the road, dead from stab wounds and ground into mince meat. Leading the way, I shiver at the severed heads on a pike.

Their mouths are agape, their eyeballs gouged out. Blood soaks into the wood, smearing their souls into it. More and more horrors are on the long, winding path, each worse than the last.

A man is on the side of the road, his intestines scattering across the ground like noodles. He's still breathing, looking at the sky with a hand over his heart, taking his last breaths. A chunk of his head is gone, leaving some of his brain exposed to the accursed air. It's a miracle for him to survive, but he won't survive for long.

Onyx glances away from the horrendous view as I twist my mouth in disgust. I struggle to put my feelings into words, but we walk on. It's futile, mountains of corpses on the road, their skin charring.

"Oh God," I whisper."Let's keep moving."

Onyx nods, muttering in prayer before we reach the center of the town, the fountain fading into sight. My fingers glaze over the stone, painted in the red liquid that the Craleans desperately crave.

I'm not hearing the screams of people asking and begging for help. It's the screeching sounds of the souls coming from the depths of darkness.

"Have mercy on their souls, Father," Onyx prays, squatting down at a body in front of him. It's a Basalian soldier, blood dripping from his mouth and soaking into his chainmail armor. An ax is embedded in his throat.

214

"Onyx.... This was the very first time I saw death," my voice cracks, as I kneel with him. I grasp at the blood smearing the fountain, resentment bursting through my heart as revenge comes across my nose once again."I can't live through this. Not again."

"Munir was born on this day, Kedar, rightfully so," Onyx admits, rubbing his hand against my shoulder in comfort. We both get up from the ground as distress still wisps at the back of my mind.

"That house has the smell of pure evil."

His finger points to a cottage in the distance. The smell of grain immediately comes to my mind as the shouts of my mother loom over my eardrums.

No. Not again. I can't. "Onyx... that's my house. My mother... and father—"

"Alright. We can wait," Onyx says, his face morphing in understanding. I sit against the fountain, huffing before stuffing my face into my arms.

"This is horrendous, Kedar. Going through something like this as a child...," he stammers, shaking his head before pacing around, thinking of a compromise. I don't even want to be within one hundred feet of that damn cottage. "We should go. The aura is getting stronger."

"Damnit, Onyx," I curse, trying to gather myself as I get up, wiping away the horrendous images in my mind. Placing my hands on my knees, I take deep breaths to prepare myself for whatever I'm about to see. Onyx is right. We're close. Eventually, I come to my senses, gritting my teeth together.

"To hell with it. Let's go."

The goblins are long gone as we arrive at the front door. Onyx looks fearless, keeping a stern face while I'm shaking, fiddling the doorknob.

Covering my eyes, I slowly creak the door open before taking a gander at the horrible scene. The halves of my father are lying on the floor as my mother's remains are scattered across the walls. Onyx clenches his teeth as we take some steps inside, the scent of death covering every inch of our house.

The pantry door opens, my younger self stepping out with shock. I watch as I fall to the floor screaming in agony. Searching through my memories, there's not one moment where I remember this happening. Blacking out is the only thing that fills in the gap, and the next memory I have of this frightful day is when I walk through the war-ridden town.

We watch my younger self curse and cry out of anger, his nails tearing through the wooden planks on the floor.

"Kedar...?" Omar asks, stepping out with the same look of shock. I don't answer as my eyes start to bleed blood red, like there's a demon coming out of me. My mouth drops as a dark figure appears to separate from my younger self's body. Even Onyx is bewildered, his pupils widening. The creature begins to grow like a parasite, its voice screaming and wailing in pain, just like me.

It stabilizes itself, slithering off me before manifesting into that familiar figure I've seen over the past couple of weeks. Munir, with his familiar red eyes. Omar gazes at Munir in horror. *He knows.* Questions in my mind arise to answer the ones I have for myself. My younger self collapses onto the ground, eyes closing in peace as I run up to check on him. Onyx trots towards the dark figure, still staring into Omar's eyes.

"Oh my God," I whisper, caressing his cheek as a trail of blood runs down the side of his mouth. *No.*

"Kedar, don't interfere. Let the memory run its course," warns Onyx, taking a step back as Munir explodes into a black goo. Immediately, I stagger, slamming against the wall as Omar begins wailing, covering his eyes in fear. The dark goo slowly begins to slither up my younger self's chest, inserting itself into my neck. I jump into action, grabbing my throat as I grasp at the dark goo to no avail.

"Kedar! Stop!" Onyx yells, pulling me off and throwing me to the ground. I struggle under Onyx's grip. Nothing that I've ever done has earned me a punishment like this. *Why does Munir even exist in the first place?*

"No! NO! NOO!" I scream, looking at my younger self in horror, processing the events that I've just witnessed. He fades into my skin, latching himself on me as we become one. My veins glow as Munir happily invites himself into my brain, body, and mind.

As sweat rolls down my forehead, I breathe out a grunt, swatting Onyx's arms off before getting up in a hurry. Clenching my teeth, I try to forget everything that I just saw. Munir's the complete byproduct of my rage. He exists… because of my wrath.

"Interesting. Who's your friend, Kedar?"

We spin to the voice behind us. I shudder.

It's Munir. The current Munir, not the Munir in my horrible memories. Sighing, he crosses his arms, tapping his bare feet against the wooden floor, stained with blood.

"Ah, yes. The old man that I see in our visions every now and then," Munir slurs, licking his lips while narrowing his red eyes. Stepping back, Onyx maintains his confident stance, glaring daggers. The stick is in the pockets of my robe, and I pull it out like the *Kathi.* "Have you come to kill me, Kedar and Onyx? How displeasing."

His eyes take a glance at the stick in my hands, tilting his head to the right to generate a curious look. Onyx recoils, almost tripping on my father's corpse. "*Yaleanukum.* Kedar was not bluffing."

"Quiet down, magister," Munir chuckles, putting his pointer finger to his lips. Onyx doesn't seem too offended by Munir's remarks, expecting the demon to act like this. "Let's change the environment, shall we?"

The memory grove fades into a blood red all around us. Black sand reappears at my feet as my toes curl against the ground. Looking behind me, even the corpses of my parents erode into the air. Munir has power. Dangerous power.

"Now, why are you poking through our memories, Kedar? I thought I could trust you. You know better," Munir says apologetically, walking towards us with arms spread out to offer me a hug. Without a second thought, I twist my mouth in disgust before slapping his arms away. He only exists from my parents' deaths.

"You're onto something," he interrupts. The old man beside me keeps himself stable and stretches his arm towards Munir before immersing himself in a yellow aura. Munir doesn't bat an eye, moving just inches from my face. I curl my fist, punching him in the jaw as he chuckles and looks back up from the sand while coughing to cover up the pain. "I exist because of our parents."

"Enough with you, Kedar. As for you... Onyx..." says Munir, glancing at him. Onyx thrusts his arm forward, seething as a thunderbolt of mana zips straight at him. Munir's eyes narrow, intercepting the bolt perfectly, catching the mana in between his two fingers. Onyx's eyes widen as Munir shatters the bolt into hundreds of pieces. "Your astral magic's been weakened. I heard great things about the leader of the Onyx Order from the hive mind. Where is that power I've been promised?"

"Curse you, demonspawn. Astral magic is the only thing that can counter the dark magic of Shaytan," Onyx mutters, holding his arm as he tries to recollect himself. Before the old man can react, Munir flicks his fingers upward, summoning three tentacles with reptilian eyes and open mouths. The beast has sharp, slithering thorns, as the squelching of the tentacles wrapping themselves around each other only enhances the grim, ghastly voices coming from the mouths.

"It is… ineffective here, to say the least. Astral magic has its flaws, Onyx. Even you should know that," Munir gawks, using his hands to control the tentacles like they're an extension of his body. My fingers tremble against the measly stick that younger Omar gave me.

The slithering creatures wrap around Onyx's feeble body, pinning him up tightly as he groans in pain. Without hesitation, I sprint, putting the stick in my robe, trying to pull the tentacles off the old man. Weakness surges through my veins, but I push on as Munir watches me struggle with a smirk on his face.

Pain radiates through my fingers as one of the mouths chomp my right pointer finger. Shrieking in pain, I pull my hand from its grasp, stumbling to the ground and falling on the sand. I glance at my hand, shaking. The stub spurts fountains of blood as I convulse on the ground, holding my wrist tightly. I'm used to being cut, stabbed, and punched every day. Scars cover most of my chest and arms. But something like this— it's different. The pain is different.

The shards of bone embed in my skin. Seething, I force myself to stand up, looking at Onyx, gritting his fangs in pain. Tentacles snake every part of his body, the mouths latching on to his furry body as they drain the old man in front of me.

"MUNIRRRR!!" I growl, glancing in Munir's direction, noticing half of his pointer finger is gone too, meaning that when I get hurt, he gets hurt in the same way. Munir realizes the anger in my voice, smiling maniacally before cackling like the devil he is.

"It seems like you won't go down unless you get in a fight. How exasperating. Oh well, I can't stop someone born from Al-Jaalad blood," he taunts, his gaze flaming with malice as the thought of being under Munir's control runs through my mind.

"This'll be the last day," I reply, curling my fingers against the stick in my hand. I'll play along with Munir's games. "I'll tear you to pieces."

"Bastard," Munir replies, shaking his head. "If we are brothers, Mother wouldn't like the sight of this."

"Don't ever call yourself my brother," I seethe through my teeth, glancing at Onyx, who looks drained, void of life. Everything around me seems to fall apart, and it's because of the demon in front of me. Munir. "You treat me as if we are friends. Do you not realize that you are a devil? A being created of this world designed to hurt and kill?"

"You sound hypocritical, Kedar," Munir chuckles, shifting his feet into a fighting stance. "Your beloved Onyx will die. So you better hurry up and kill me, before I rip your soul out of your body."

Gritting my teeth in rage, he waves me over him, smirking while stroking his beard.

"NOW COME!"

Fruidith, the Golden Mage, was found dead in his alchemy lab three days ago. The famous mage was known for his acts in the Dragon's War as well as his concise research done on all sorts of magic. When Basalian soldiers examined his corpse, it was found that his veins were black, his eyes completely red. The king's coroners have claimed that Fruidith died from Imp, a psychoactive drug recently created by rogue wizards. Allegedly, he overdosed on it, but the truth about his death is yet to be found.

- An excerpt from a Basalian newspaper titled: *Fruidith, Dead In His Lab, How Many More Mages Must Die?*, written on the 330th day of the 1416th year.

FIFTEEN

"RAHHHHHH!" I yell, charging at Munir with the stick

above my head like a madman. Swinging down, I miss, allowing him to dash to the side and slam his fist against my stomach.

Stumbling to the sand, I hold my abdomen as blood spurts out of my nose. Mana's out of the question, since any magic I have belongs to Munir. Before I can get up, Munir's forearm is immersed in darkness, covering his right shoulder. Gritting his teeth, he thrusts his hand in my direction, a beam of darkness beginning to zip to me at an unholy speed.

Rolling to the side, I dodge the hell-like beam, the dark matter disintegrating the sand. As Munir charges, fire erupts in the black desert, as I realize he isn't even aiming to kill me. Hellspawn engulfs the three of us in a circle as Munir's eyes keep flashing red with pure evil.

"Tell me, Kedar," he sneers, reaching inside his robe to grab a wooden stick. My eyes widen when I see it. "How does it feel, fighting the only man that can understand an interesting creature like you?"

222

"If there was such a thing as a lesser man, you're one of them," I shoot back, huffing as Munir's stick erupts with demonic magic. As Munir swings his weapon at my side, I leap into the air, stomping my foot on his face before he stumbles to the ground.

Munir tanks my assault, getting up and licking the blood coming down his chin. My jaw jerks back into an array of pain as I fall to one knee, gritting my teeth.

"Figured it out yet?" he offers, charging another beam of darkness. Narrowing his eyes, I take a deep breath, hoisting myself up before putting my feet into a fighting stance. Onyx's life is on the line. Mistakes are something I cannot allow. "Killing me is out of the question, Kedar. Remember, we are one and the same... hitting me means hitting you."

"You might as well be right, Munir. I can't kill you," I grunt, gripping the stick tighter as a flash passes my shoulder. I dash to the side to avoid his death ray. Clenching my teeth, I launch towards him, desperately swinging the stick. "I'd rather die trying!"

During my barrage, Munir ducks under my arm, recoiling his fist back to plunge it in my abdomen. I stumble on the sand as I remind myself that making one mistake is fatal.

"Tsk, Tsk, Tsk. Tired, Kedar?" he smiles, as I shuffle my feet further to distance myself from him. Even with the grim circumstances, an idea forms in my mind.

"Face it. I'm invincible."

"I'll find a way," I spit, seeing another ray of death immersing his forearms. Resting my palms on my thighs, I catch my breath, fearless. Munir doesn't even scare me anymore. But his power... It's viable. Expendable. "You think I'm letting my friends die?"

"Is that not what you're doing right now?" Munir replies, glancing at Onyx, his soft huffs and puffs echoing off the dunes of sand. Before I can react, Munir's ray of death shoots towards my face, and I roll to the side before charging as my face contorts into anger, sadness, and rage.

Jumping into the air again, Munir's expression turns into surprise as I swing the stick down, knowing the demon isn't expecting me to try the same move as before. A resounding crack deafens my ears as Munir yelps in pain, tumbling to the ground as I stand over his body.

Fighting through the pain of the wood on my head, I grasp the clone by his throat, holding him against the black stand. Agony surges through my neck as I choke on my own grip, gasping for air as I keep him glued to the ground, not even stopping when black dots begin to litter my vision.

Munir struggles, flailing his arms as he gurgles in his pit. A sphere of darkness forms at his fingertips, as I hold on to his neck like I'm taming the beast. If I can't beat him, we might as well go down together at this point.

Using my other hand to hold him down, I crane my neck to the side as he fails to blast me with his sphere. The scent of ash and smoke is fresh against my nostrils as wisps of vapor and blazing fire surround us. Onyx is still struggling against the tentacles, his eyes puffy and body drained. We lock eyes.

No. I have to kill Munir. We can't go down together, or Omar would be left to rot. Onyx would be left to die, and this whole journey isn't even worth the risk.

My stomach howls in pain as Munir kicks me off him. Landing next to the circular fires, I jerk my head back as soon as my curly hair almost burns up to smoke. We hurl ourselves off the ground while Munir clutches his stomach, malice in his gaze.

Omar crosses my mind as I pick up the wooden stick. Everyone around me is trying to stop me from looking for him. The training with Ruby, the trials I have to do with Onyx, and now with Munir. Omar must be cold, shivering, and starving. His being safe is beginning to feel like it's out of the question.

"Kedar! I hear you! I do want to see Omar! YOU ARE THE ONE SLOWING US DOWN, BASTARD!" shouts Munir, walking towards me. Blood drips down his nose as I wipe the red liquid from my nostrils as well. We both face each other as the heat of the fire nearly burns up my skin.

"Slowing us down?" I mimic as we circle each other. The tentacles that wrap around Onyx seep into his furry skin, generating a grunt from him. A hint of faith is in his gaze now, like the old man believes in me. "Honestly, your power is the only good thing about you."

"Is that all you see me as?" Munir answers angrily, licking the blood off his lip. We wait, dying to see who decides to strike first. "An outlet for your mana?"

"Ha, you're right. Your existence doesn't even make sense," I reply. Dashing towards him, I swing the stick, my finger still bleeding. Fighting through the pain is near impossible, but I find courage when I glance at Onyx.

"Calm down, you've got it all wrong!" Munir offers, blocking my swings swiftly. Trying to stab at his neck is futile, as I miss the mark by miles. Dashing back, Munir sighs, crossing his arms together as if he wants to call a truce. "There's a fourth kind of magic."

Staying quiet, I attempt to catch my breath.

"Darkic, Astral, Elemental. They're not the only ones," he begins. *Clearly.* "Demonic magic has been kept quiet from the outside world. Very few know, like the old man."

"Demonic magic is uncontrollable without my assistance. Without it, you'll die on the battlefields trying to save Omar," he continues as sweat runs down my forehead. The amount of blood I've lost from my finger makes me melt.

I struggle to keep myself upright to face him.

225

"Your parents' deaths birthed my existence. From then on, your hurts, worries, pain, anger, and vengeance are things that made me grow. Your malice stunts my growth."

"Every time you kill, it feeds me. The souls you take are the source of my power. I awakened from my seven-year-long slumber when I realized you've begun to starve me, not a single soul since last winter. I thought that if I gave you my power, it would motivate you to kill and feed me again. I cannot satisfy my hunger with Ruby, but..." He pauses. "Now, I'm satisfying my hunger... with Onyx."

He points to him, who's stopped moving. His eyes are shut, but I see his chest rise and fall. He's alive but unconscious. I realize Onyx is slowly losing his soul to the mouth of Munir. Munir's veins are dark red, and I see them bulging out of his arms. He's eating.

I run to Onyx. Munir looks back with a smile. He knows I can't do anything to save him.

"Onyx, answer me, please!" I beg. His eyes are open as he looks at me solemnly. He seems half dead, blood dripping down his mouth as tentacles keep sucking out his lifeforce.

"K-Kedar?" he says, coughing and spitting out blood. "What are you doing? Munir can come and kill us any moment—"

"No. I promise I'll kill him. But right now, I need help, please," I beg. His eyes widen a bit like he's realized something. Maybe there's some hope I can rely on.

"Mana drain. Yes. Yes. Mana drain, of course!" he exclaims. He starts to wiggle his right arm out of the tentacle. Onyx grunts as the thorns cut his muscles open and destroy most of his bones. Once he gets his arm out, half is bitten off. He's bleeding like crazy, but he isn't fazed at all.

"Touch him once, and all the mana he will drain. It'll be yours. That's how you kill Munir."

226

He then grabs my hand, and a white aura surrounds us. I feel the mana running through my veins. Onyx narrows, concentrating. But the tentacles snatch him again, slithering around his arm and cracking all of his bones. He wails in pain as one of the thorn-covered tentacles throws me off him.

"What do you think you're doing, Kedar?" I hear Munir say. I look and see him standing right over my body. I jerk back and move away through the dark sand, hearing the crackling flames in both ears.

"I'm still here, you know. Kill me if you please. I dare you," he says. I stand, glancing at my right hand. It's encased in a white aura. I gaze at Munir's right hand and realize that the aura is absent. I turn at Onyx, still suffering under the tentacle's grasp. *I have to save him. I have to try.*

"I still have something up my sleeve, you know," I say, huffing and puffing. But Munir doesn't seem intimidated by the mana. "I'll kill you."

"Kedar, what if I told you I have something up my sleeve, too?" Munir asks. He growls, holding his head with both hands as he shakes around. Munir goes feral. I watch in horror as two bony horns sprout from his hair. I watch him in horror as his skin starts turning red.

His teeth turn sharp, and his muscles bulge like crazy, while his veins have dark matter running right through them. He's transforming into his true form. His eyes are reptilian, and his tongue is long and slimy.

He finally opens his eyes and widens his mouth in a gape. He roars so loudly that it makes a small sandstorm wash right at me. I cover my eyes to shield myself from the sand.

"I was playing nice before, Kedar. But I'm taking off the gloves," he booms. I stand, helpless. It seems Munir used all of the mana he drained from Onyx to fuel himself. He now stands in his true, demonic form. The manifestation of my uncontrollable, dark, twisted fantasy.

"Don't think you can kill me," I say to him, pointing to his face. It resembles a bull, but with its reptilian eyes and its long tongue, it looks half-bull, half-man, half-snake, but all demon. I gulp. I have to keep my confidence for now.

He opens his mouth. An enormous sphere manifests at the tips of his lips. It makes a low, sinister hum. My eyes widen, and I turn to run, but I'm surrounded by fire. I can only stand and watch. Watch Munir fuel up his mana. He stares down at me, curling his mouth into a smile. In an instant, a death ray gets sent right towards my chest.

I scream, putting my hand on my heart. The death ray comes close to the white mana, but right when I expect it to shred right through my skin and kill me—

The aura absorbs it.

It turns from white to black, and the mana courses through me. I gaze at my hands as Munir stares. I stole his mana. It isn't much for him, but it's a lot for me. It's pumping into my blood.

"**What?**" Munir stammers, narrowing his eyes and getting on all fours. "**No matter. There's no chance you can beat me with that little mana.**"

I grit, letting the mana overtake my body. He launches himself at me, his legs dashing at full speed. His huge body flashes at me like a rolling boulder. I squint and curl my fist. *Let's try this,* I say in my head.

Munir opens his mouth to bite my head off, but I dodge his fangs and thrust my fist upward and punch him in the stomach. I roar with fury as my fist comes into contact with his thick skin.

He launches twenty feet in the air, flailing as he coughs out blood. It splatters and splurts right into my curly hair and my forehead. I smear his blood off of me as he lands on the sand with a huge thump. He grips his stomach and groans in pain.

"I like using your magic," I say as I start walking closer. My fist envelopes in a dark aura. It's mesmerizing. It's like I'm already getting used to his mana. My feet crunch into the sand with every single step. Munir's eyes flash open, and he grits his teeth once he sees what I'm doing.

"Don't think you'll have it for so long, Kedar," he says to me as a trickle of blood runs right down his chin. **"Your body is mine. Don't you remember?"**

"Since when did I ever make a deal with the devil?" I ask, kneeling in front of his face. He has long teeth, sharper than the *Kathi*. His eyes resemble a snake. He's more terrifying up close, but I keep myself steady, confident as ever.

"I've been growing off of you since you birthed me," he says, spitting blood at my face. I tilt my head to the side to dodge it. Even in defeat, he's still an annoyance. "I should have control."

"Seriously, Munir?" I say, almost laughing. I narrow my eyes as the dark aura around my fists shines brighter. "You're a parasite. The only value you have is the mana you have."

With that, I curl my hand around his huge neck. My right arm vibrates as it gets enveloped in the mana. I drain him while he struggles against me, but I have the strength to keep him down.

Munir opens his mouth, and a dark sphere begins to envelop the tips of his lips again. I jump back, the mana running through my blood vessels. I collapse to the ground and cough out blood.

Munir's shrinking to regular me. His clothes are torn, but one of his horns still sticks out of his head. He breathes heavily, and I see his skin slowly turning back to a tan brown shade. His teeth are sharp, and he has long nails. Without a doubt, he's still dangerous.

"**Kedar**...," he starts to say, gripping his waist tightly. Munir coughs up blood into his hand. He smears it on his robe. I stand there, trying to gather myself.

"**Give me back my powers. It's not yours.**"

I smile, looking back at Onyx and realizing the tentacles slowly begin to descend. He falls out of the mouth's grasp, grasping at the sand. The old man groans, blinking his eyes open to see the commotion.

My heart almost stops beating, but I sigh when I realize he's okay.

"Munir. Give up. You've lost," I say, glancing at my palm. The blood inside my skin glows a dark color, while my pointer finger heals, the wound closing completely. I stand over Munir as he finally returns to his normal state. Without hesitation, I punch him in the face, grabbing his neck to drain all of the mana that he has.

"You don't realize what you're doing!" he resists, choking on his saliva while I feed the mana into my soul.

Gritting my teeth, I twist my lips into a smile. "I know what I'm doing, Munir." Huffing, I hold him harder as his breathing starts to relax. We aren't in sync anymore; I don't feel a single thing while I choke him. Munir isn't the threat anymore. It's me.

With that, his skin starts to crack like rocks. Munir coughs and groans, begging for my mercy. "Munir... There can only be one of me. Not two. Not three. I can't let you dwell off of me any longer." The demon beneath widens his crackling pupils, his eyelids fluttering open and closed.

It seems like Munir surrenders. I let go of his neck as I watch his arms blend into the black sand, his mouth struggling to form words. He's a torso now, his legs dust. With every passing second, I struggle to envision where the demon will go after he's gone. *Maybe hell?*

"K-Kedar….," he whispers, his teeth chattering as his chest disintegrates. It looks like he can barely put thoughts into words. Staying silent, I kneel next to him, offering an ear. "Listen to me, human."

He's scared.

"Omar… has magic. *Our magic.*"

Shattering into dust, Munir mixes with the black sand. The fire around us smokes away, and I realize that our battle is over. But his words keep repeating in my mind.

A raspy voice claws at my ears.

"Kedar?" Onyx says. Looking over, he's in a daze, clasping at his half-eaten arm. I don't hesitate to run over, putting my hands around his shoulders to hoist him.

Onyx's robe is torn, and the blood on his body drips to the sand. "Dragons, Onyx. Wake us up, we have to get back."

"Goodness, child. Rest assured, I have enough mana to get us out of here," he replies in his "wise old man" tone. Lifting his left arm, a white aura envelopes his fingers as he stifles a little grin. "Without a doubt, your demonic self failed to kill me. It would take much more than that to drain all of my mana."

Onyx reaches over to my face, putting his pointer finger on my forehead while my spiritual plane fades in white. As we step into the light, I sigh.

I have to find Omar.

I find myself sitting on the bed, while Onyx winces and holds his arm. All of the wounds inflicted on us in the plane have transferred over to the physical plane. I glance down at my

231

pointer finger, half of it gone. As I stand, Onyx lies down on the bed, his blood soaking into the mattress. My mind feels so clear. Killing Munir is the answer to everything.

"Dragons, what happened here?" says Ruby, her boots thumping on the stone floor as she sees our grim situation. Shifting her focus to me, Ruby blooms with worry. "You okay, Kedar?"

"We fought a demon," I blurt. Ruby doesn't know a single thing about Munir. I don't need her to worry about me, but all she knows is that I have mana. While she rushes over to heal Onyx, I tell her everything. From me and Onyx's ventures into my physical plane, to when I kill Munir.

"Demon magic...," Ruby whispers to herself. She's able to stop Onyx's bleeding by wrapping a white wrap around the rest of his arm, using her healing magic to patch him up. "I've never heard about it myself, but... It sounds like hell."

Scratching my curly hair, Ruby hastily caresses my face with both her hands, and she examines my golden skin. She sighs in annoyance, noticing the small nick on my cheek, pressing two fingers over it to seal my wound. I blush as she furrows her brows. Her attention shifts to my finger.

"Kedar, what the hell happened in there?" she says softly, almost forgiving. Her fingers intertwine with mine as she tries to heal my stub. I quickly wipe off the pink shade on my cheeks as we lock eyes. "You know, you're lucky to have me. Who's going to heal all your wounds if I'm gone?"

She notices my silence, only shaking her head with a smirk before we stand next to each other at Onyx's bedside. It's my fault that he lost his arm, all because of Munir.

"Onyx should be fine, in the meantime," Ruby explains, tucking her braids behind her ears. With a yawn, she glances back at me. "It's been about eight hours."

My face contorts in confusion. The journey through my mind, the battle with Munir — it has been done in an hour. Maybe time passes a little differently when stuck in the spiritual plane. "Gods, it's dark outside, isn't it?"

She nods. "I've been busy reading and napping. You were sick with fever, and it was exhausting to take care of you," Ruby blankly mentions. "It's stagnant in the cavern — only me and some night-guards are awake. Onyx kinda made a commotion over here, so I had to check to see what was going on."

Onyx interrupts Ruby and I's conversation with a sudden cough, his eyes fluttering open before he clutches his arm. With a wince, he tries getting out of bed but to no avail.

"Relax, Onyx," I sigh, holding him down lightly. Onyx quickly gives up while Ruby sits on the chair, crossing her arms in sympathy. His yellow eyes reek of exhaustion.

"Isn't this quite ironic, you two?" Onyx asks out loud. "The Great Onyx Magister, bedridden and absent of an arm."

Ruby gulps, a little nervous in her tone as she speaks. "Onyx, before we got here, we found out about Judah. Some soldiers mentioned how he was making moves in Saitra, as if using the Cralean Army to kill anyone in his way."

I nod in agreement. With my demonic sickness gone, it's best to focus on Judah now. Even with this war going on all around us, nothing's going to stop me from finding Omar. "Those soldiers got killed by a Veil. Judah clearly doesn't want people mentioning his name anywhere at all."

The old man's eyes narrow. His ego is still high, not bothered by Ruby's confession. "Frankly, I am not surprised at all. My younger brother is indeed planning something, because for the last nineteen years, he's been conspiring. Usually, the dog tries to assassinate me, but he's done absolutely nothing."

"Onyx, what does this mean?" I ask, springing into action.

233

"Action shall be taken, my fellow initiate. My other assassins haven't returned in around forty days, and that usually means that they've been executed by the Veils or the Craleans. The last place I sent them was where Judah was last seen, in a town called Lelina," Onyx explains with a poetic tone. Lelina is a prosperous, major city of trade in the Cralean Empire, known for its diverse and economically-driven society.

"Your brother, Omar, must be in the same place where Judah is," he theorizes, wincing from his wounds as his breath hitches slightly. "If I can recall, Munir stated how both of your magics are equivalent."

I nod. "He did say that..."

"Finding your brother shall be the first priority. With great fear, your brother must be going through great tribulation," he explains, as I struggle to imagine my brother's current condition. Omar is being tortured, going through hell and pain unimaginable. Ruby shakes her head in grief. I still have no idea what that note is talking about. *Destiny...*

A question quickly arises in my mind. "What about my initiation? I've only done two tasks," I mention.

"You seem different," Onyx points out, a slight smirk on his face. "You mentioned how you didn't want to commit any more deaths to repent from your sins, and yet, you seem to want to take this further."

"You guys have treated me differently than I was all those years ago," I explain, glancing at Ruby. "I don't know how to explain it. It's like I belong here. Ridding evil from the world, even through death, is necessary."

Onyx narrows his eyebrows, intrigued. "I have decided. Find Judah, and you will be part of the Brotherhood. From now, until the day that you die."

Nodding, I begin to plan out how exactly I'll find Judah. Travel to Lelina... then what next? What will I do from there?

"I'll go alone, Onyx," I declare, before Ruby quickly clasps my shoulder after standing up from her chair. Glancing into her pupils, the only thing I see is worry.

"Let me come with you," she urges, before I award her with a smile, shaking my head.

"Alright, Onyx, where do we start?"

Lelina is dubbed "the magnum opus" of Cralean trade. It is one of the most important cities when considering different trade routes within the Cralean country, being facilitated through the production of steel and iron, along with copper and other precious metals. Crale thrives off of the sales of their goods, making the country have enough money to provide for the army.

- An excerpt from *Countries Encyclopedia: Crale Edition*, written in 1435.

ACT TWO:

VANTABLACK

48 DAYS LATER.

A road to **Lelina**, part of the

Cralean Empire.

230th Day of the 1438th Year.

SIXTEEN

I t's winter in Haya.

Snow is everywhere, children frolic in the middle of the streets, and hundreds of Jurens celebrate their religious season of giving. I haven't seen snow in so long. Summer and fall have passed since Ruby and I traveled to Lelina. We have crossed dozens of rivers and lakes, twisting through paths and bridges on our horses.

The snow makes trekking through forests harsh. Without Ruby's healing, our fingers will snap off from the frozen temperatures. It's difficult to make campfires with the raging blizzards.

Onyx has lent us plenty of darkos to keep us supplied with resources on our lengthy trip, Ruby and I both spending each coin wisely on food and transportation. But since our horses died of frostbite, we've been forced to walk our way to Lelina.

Aside from that, Crale's definitely been through the path I and Ruby tread on. The ruins of villages contrast with the color of ice. Corpses in the snow rot and decay, but some bodies are completely cold to the touch, as if they're frozen in time.

240

Meanwhile, I'm scrunched up in three layers of clothing—my black tunic, the metal armor Onyx supplied me with, and the silver-lined, dark cloak that Ruby gave me. On my back are all our belongings in a large sack.

The Kathi is safely strapped to the belt of my armor. The horn cut off from the Faqquerroblin is now a dagger. Bix is a master of shaping and creating brand new weapons for the assassins back in Ardon, according to Onyx. It's been easy to cut through hay-filled dummies back at the caverns, so I've been itching to test it out in real combat.

As for my mana, nothing I try to do seems to work. Onyx recalls that not much is known about demonic magic, calling my powers "unpredictable." Since Munir's death, the veins in my wrists have started to glow a black, reminding me of my violent potential.

"Dragons, are we almost there?" I ask Ruby, as she holds a map tightly in her black leather gloves. As I glance at the sun, my boots crunch on the white snow under me. It's a bit more comforting than walking in Pinakadan heat— but damn, still so tiring.

"There's going to be a fork in the road up ahead. We just have to take a left, and we'll be at Lelina, finally," she explains, giving me an assuring nod. The chilly weather makes her nose pink, matching her crimson eyes.

Groaning, I murmur under my breath. "No way it's taken us this long to get to Lelina." Sleep is the first thing I need once we get there. Trying to take turns sleeping won't work at all, since Ruby's too tired to stay awake to guard me. Both of us are on high alert from Cralean armies patrolling around the Empire — we'll be killed on sight if they find out we are Basalian.

"At least we're one step closer to finding your brother, right?" Ruby offers her brown skin, radiating against the sunlight. Over her braids is a black bonnet, her parted hair flowing down the side of her head and chest. I offer her a nod. She's right. Finding Judah means finding Omar.

"I know," I whisper, glancing at what's left of my right pointer finger. It's hard to grip on the Kathi sometimes or the horn dagger, but I've quickly adapted to it in battle. Either way, I still have to practice holding a teacup, since it always slips through my grasp without the support of my absent finger.

"That's the fork."

Pointing with my left hand instead, Ruby glances to spot the dirt road splitting into two paths. In the middle is a wooden pillar sprouting from the ground, a sign hanging from it. Ruby attempts to wipe the white snow covering it, but she's too short, just a couple of inches off of it. Sighing, I walk up to do it for her. Chunks of snow fall on us when I clean it off with one swipe of my hand. Ruby grumbles, dusting it off her shoulder. I fail to resist a slight laugh. "Let me do it next time, Ruby."

She doesn't reply, her eyes focused on the dark markings on the light-colored wood:

FORK OF NAHUM.
GO LEFT FOR THE TOWN OF LELINA.
GO RIGHT FOR THE TOWN OF ZAKIR.

"Phew. We went the right way," Ruby declares, looking up at me as we trek down the left side of the fork. While Crale's landscape is beautiful, it's hard to forget that they've been warring against Basalia for three generations. The snow covers pine trees, the cold, chilly breezing through us. I once battled here, in a place like this. It was three years ago.

The battle of Hylia Bridge.

Hylia bridge was a bridge that's an important staple for interregional trade. Plenty of Cralean, Juren, and merchants from many, many nations used it to travel easily to export their goods. But that was before the Dragon's War. After the declaration, it had always been a prime chokepoint for the armies. But that was about to change today.

"Hatchlings, look at the grace upon us."

Me, Omar, and the rest of the infantry units gazed at the stone bridge that crossed the frozen river in front of us. A long, stretched stone wall seemed to cover what was past the borders of Basalia, where the Craleans roamed. Hundreds of Cralean archers were on the walls, scouting out for anyone who tried to cross without a sparkle of fear.

"After around forty years, nobody has crossed the Hylia bridge. Not a single Basalian has made it alive," our goblin general, Arthur, declared. He led us brazenly through the Zaidus Plains, where I first shed blood, and now, he was leading this suicidal charge. "I know that most of us will not make it out of this battle alive. There are around 500 of us, clearly not enough to push through their wall. But trust in the dragon, shall we?"

Silence followed as I glanced at the soldiers behind me, who all seemed too stressed to respond to the general. Excitement filled me again. More blood to shed, it seems.

"Brother... don't do anything rash, please," Omar said, invading my thoughts. Growling, I ripped the pendant that my father gave me and shoved it into his chest.

"Goddamit, just take it, you bastard! Do you think I have anything to live for anymore?!" I asked in hushed anger, as the general began to command us to march forth, striding through the trees like wolves chasing down a rabbit. "I wish you had just died with Mother and Father. You're a damn nuisance. We joined the army to fight, not to scurry like cowards!"

243

Not even letting Omar respond, I reamed down with the infantry, blazing out the forest as the mages behind us used elemental magic to pull the trees out of the ground, blasting them towards the walls. Arrows quickly plummeted on our men as they dashed towards the bridge, meeting the Cralean guards that awaited them.

"Why the hell does everything seem to be in my way?" I gritted as I cut down a soldier, splitting him in two with my sword.

Fighting violence with violence was the only way anyone survived in this cursed war.

The resounding steps of an army irk my ears as I look at Ruby to make sure she hears it too. Responding with a slow nod, Ruby seems expectant of the Cralean forces rumbling around soon enough. To be honest, I'm a bit nervous.

"Ruby, what are we going to do? Hide, right?"

The familiar yellow sun rises above their legions as the bustling Cralean army begins fading through the foggy, cold air. It's been a while since my last encounter with a Cralean soldier... maybe sixty days? I have no idea anymore. I'm scared, not of their presence, but of what they'll do if they recognize me as a prisoner from Alfdan.

In Basalia's ranks, I've seen these soldiers daily, cutting them down in a stream of battles in jungles and grasslands. Now I'm an initiate for the Onyx Order, sworn enemies of the Veils. With my new, clear view of the world, the Craleans are menacing, intimidating with each step they take.

Ruby only answers after a short minute of thinking. "We don't hide. Act normal."

After I nod, she pulls up her hood, with me following suit. A faint chant begins to vibrate the trees around us, the Craleans pumping their weapons into the air with anger.

"HAIL THE MAN OF THE CROWN
WHO LETS US ATTACK EVERY TOWN
LET THE HORRORS WE'VE DONE BE SOUND
BASALIA WILL FALL!
BASALIA WILL FALL!
MASSACRE THEIR FRIENDS AND FAMILIES
SO THAT THEIR FAITH WILL DISAPPEAR
LET THEM LOSE THEIR SANITY
AS THEIR BASAL EYES GET FILLED WITH FEAR!"

Slowing my heartbeat, I tap Ruby's shoulder. "This chant, I recognize it. When I used to spy on their forces, they recited this chant daily."

"Crude, isn't it?" she replies, stifling a laugh, as if ignoring the impending army marching toward us. "The Cralean armies don't hesitate to share the things they've done to our people. Innocent Hayans killed in the name of glory."

My mind flashes back to when I did the same as them, going from house to house to murder any Craleans left. Quickly pushing the horrendous memory of that child out of my mind, I focus on the soldiers. Men and women of all races line the front, swordsmen staying diligent on their backline. While most wear light-weight metal armor, they also carry shields which boast the official Cralean colors— black and yellow.

Three generals are in the middle, riding their horses. It's easy to tell who the leading commanders are with their red capes over their shoulder armor. Maintaining our subtly, I heave out a sigh, stealing a glance at the elf general, a stern look plastering their face. Eventually, they pass by, not batting an eye or recognizing our presence.

"They're pretty different in battle," I blurt out once they completely fade away into the snowy fog. "Most of those soldiers believe in this false sense of glory. They think that doing this would bring honor to their families, but they'll just end up as another corpse on the battlefield. Those men will know true fear soon enough in their first battle."

Ruby doesn't respond, only nodding as we turn a corner, Lelina beginning to immerse into view. Glancing at the cottage buildings towering over the stone walls, I manage a smile.

"Dragons, we're here," I say, content.

"It took us long enough," Ruby smirks, removing her black hood to scratch the brandishing scar on her neck.

Little white flakes of snow glide to the ground around us as we spot numerous tents in front of the gate to the city. Merchants and traders offer their exotic goods from Sulalat Basal to the Vanian Islands. The Dragon's War has subsequently made the Cralean economy boom, but on the other hand, it hasn't been looking too good for Basalia's trade markets.

We browse through the merchandise. Goblins sell exotic stones that resemble the one safely pressing against Ruby's neck, while elves offer their intricate textiles and clothing. A young farik strums a lyre on a wooden podium, his singing voice swaying the crowd.

"Have you been inside Crale's cities before?" I ask Ruby, her attention clearly taken by the views. Sure, I've been in Cralean territories, fortresses, and rural towns before, but I've never had the chance to visit the urban areas of their violent empire. Ruby glances over, her red eyes filled with wonder.

"Well, once —"

Before she can finish, we hear a crazed shout behind us. The farik child from earlier is getting robbed in the middle of the market. He's trying to fight back, but to no avail as three men surround him, digging into his pockets for money. A twang of anger irks my mind, and I clasp at the Kathi on my belt to slice those thieves, but Ruby quickly grabs my wrist.

"Don't," she says in a hushed whisper. "We don't need the Shurta to be stalking us already. We should be subtle, remember?"

I grit, struggling to resist. They're toying with the boy, tossing around his hard-earned money like it's some sort of game. "Ruby... you don't get it. I have to do something."

"I'll take care of it," she interrupts, her red eyes narrowing before letting me. Watching in curiosity, Ruby's fingers on her right arm convulse, vibrating violently. Mana, the word chimes in my mind, as she clenches her fist.

The three thieves stop in a sense of confusion, before one of them begins to choke, hurling out a string of intestines from their mouth. Soon enough, the others do the same, collapsing on the wooden podium in a pool of their blood, dying the snow red.

The crowd panics in confusion as Ruby heaves a sigh, wiping a drop of sweat rolling down the side of her cheek. Without giving me a glance, she grabs my wrist, dragging me through the market in a hurry.

I gulp as I nearly trip over a branch. "Ruby, what did you do to them?

"I pulled their intestines upwards to their mouths," she grimly explains, letting go of me as soon as she notices what she's doing. Glancing away, she coughs into her arm, before staring back, clearing her throat. "They puked out their guts, basically."

"Damn," I whisper, noting how harmful and harmless her magic is. Ruby can break my bones instead of mending them together. I shrug off those thoughts as we tread through the crowd. Eventually, we find ourselves in front of the twenty-foot-tall, metal gate to Lelina.

Four guards cautiously keep watch over anyone who tries to get in. They hurl off peasants and swindlers from every nation. Now that I think of it, it's easy to smuggle me and Ruby in Crale. Frankly enough, we've trespassed here effortlessly by playing the look of "refugees."

"Lelina awaits, Kedar," Ruby declares, going through the gates.

As we both walk through, the guards ignore us. I gaze at each building that graces Lelina. Streets split the city into four different parts, with each street having stores and dark wooden houses with white snow on their roofs.

Light hints of smoke contrast with the freezing air coming from the chimneys sticking out of each house. We tread across a stone bridge as a frozen river chills beneath it. I smile as I see my reflection in the ice.

Above a hill is a castle forged out of smooth stone, its spires towering over the city. It looks mythical, surrounded by walls that are taller than the ones outside. On the other hand, there are gallows at every corner, citizens being executed for their crimes. The homeless litter each dark alleyway, their hands outstretched and pleading for money.

The guards patrolling the city, the Shurta, wear black tunics under metal armor, with a red cloth to cover the lower half of their faces. Even though Ruby and I maintain a "subtle" presence, there are hundreds of eyes gazing at us from every direction. A goblin child tries greeting a Shurta, only to be backhanded to the ground with force. Their intimidation curls and squeezes at the civilians, warning them if they disobey Cralean laws.

"Remind me, what did Onyx tell us to do here again?" I ask, shivering from the cold, ruffling the snow out of my curly hair. Ruby clears her throat, pulling out the map the old dog handed us.

"Onyx told us to kill all Veil members stationed here in Lelina," she replies, reading off of the notes on the back. "They probably have information regarding where Judah is. Finding Judah means finding Omar. Remember that." Ruby offers me a bold look.

Narrowing my eyes in worry, I realize one important thing: "Wait. Are there no Order members here to help us out?"

"It seems like Onyx wanted us to go to some place called… 'Polluck's Inn.' Nothing about other Order members," she says, rolling it up before safely securing it on her belt. I take a mental note to look out for any building that perhaps signifies this "Inn" that Onyx mentions. As we pass by antique shops, textile mills, a brewery, barracks, and markets, the bustling crowd of Lelina almost makes me forget that Ruby is next to me. It seems so easy to lose her in a crowd like this.

"Ruby—" I urge, before we both see a man dividing the crowd of people into two. He's being humiliated, walking in the merciless cold naked. Cralean Farikkians, goblins, elves, and humans degrade him, throwing stones as they shout slurs in their tribal languages.

The Crale Empire is solely derived from twenty tribes, all having their own languages aside from Angloian. Scholars call this the "Cralean Dialect," because while Angloian is a universalizing, worldly language that most people speak, there are still ancient languages that differentiate one nation from another."

"I know a little Cralean," Ruby scoffs, looking at the man with sympathy. "They're shouting, 'Shame the man! For he is a Dracotheist!'"

"Dragons, what a world we live in," I whisper, as the man collapses onto the snow-covered stone road, coughing blood as the people continue to shout. Gritting my teeth, we walk past the grim scene, noting that we have to stay ignorant for the sake of not attracting any Shurta.

Ruby shakes her head. "I knew that there were some Craleans who believed in Basal, but I didn't know how much regular Craleans hated the people who practiced Dracotheism."

She's right. Dracotheists in Crale are rumored to be persecuted daily, according to the Basalian newspapers. In fact, I've seen it myself — hundreds of Dracotheists being discriminated against by Cralean soldiers. Craleans believe that if you are one of them, then you support Basalia, which makes you a traitor, deemed as committing treason against the emperor.

Gripping the string of the large satchel on my back tightly, I remember that Onyx handed me a copy of the Codex of Basal before we left for Lelina. He recommends that I read it a bit every day for wisdom. According to the book, Basal has created this world and has left it to do the same for other planets. It's a little hard to believe, but I'll admit that it holds poise that I can't explain. It's as if every word is written by a holy quill.

"Here we are," Ruby whispers, stopping in front of a small building compressing together with other houses on the street. She hastily opens the door, as I glance up at the sign hanging from the wall, an engraving confirming our whereabouts — Polluck's Inn.

With a ring, we enter, engulfed in a gloomy atmosphere. It's dark inside, a few tables and chairs around the room, while the receptionist in front of us rests their head on their hand as they sit in front of a desk, reading a book.

"Um, excuse me...," Ruby begins, walking up to the elf. With small dark circles under his eyes, he glances up at her, clearing his throat.

"Goddamnit, did I forget to put out the sign? We're closed," he replies, as Ruby rewards me with a look of confusion. It makes no sense why an inn in all places is closed for the Juren holidays. I glance behind him, noticing the stairs which lead up to the second floor.

"How the hell can you be closed? Don't you realize that..."

I drown out Ruby's hushed anger as she argues with the elf. Looking around, a dim chandelier hangs from the ceiling. Squinting my eyes, I realize a familiar pattern on the walls. Little golden gemstones in between a soft, black line. It mimics the gemstone that Onyx has in his headquarters.

Quickly turning my attention to the elf, I recognize a purple, garnet gemstone on his neck. Tapping Ruby's shoulder, I sigh.

"Calm down, you two. What's your name, elf?"

"My name is Garnett," Garnett coldly replies, adjusting his black vest over his white undershirt. He looks like a waiter with his red bowtie, his jade eyes reminding me of Lapis. Garnett's blond hair reaches his ears, unlike Lapis, and he's a tad bit shorter than me and Ruby. In fact, Garnett didn't look a day over sixteen with his crystal clear skin.

"Perhaps you happen to know a man named Onyx?" I ask as the elf's eyes widen. He quickly reaches for the back of his belt, pulling out a shiny dagger. Furrowing his eyebrows in anger, he has a hint of fear in his eyes.

"Who the hell are you guys?!" Garnett grits, hopping over the counter after tugging a string, pulling down the window blinds. People from the outside aren't about to see what's about to go down in this old, run-down inn next.

"Whoa, whoa, whoa!" I say, putting both my hands up. "We're not here to kill you, Garnett. Both of us, or all of us, are on the same team here. You're part of the Onyx order, aren't you?"

I examine his dagger. It has a leather strap and reflects the light of the gloomy lobby. Squinting, Garnett sniffs his nose. "Prove it, for the Dragon's sake. Prove that you're from the Order."

Glancing at Ruby with a confident look, she steps forward to take something out of her cloak. The Coin of Power. A way of verifying your authority with the Order, according to that old dog. Every assassin holds one in their possession— a magical, gold coin that disintegrates when its owner passes away.

Onyx says that the coin being in another coin's presence makes both shine brightly. Garnett's eyes sparkle as he realizes what Ruby's holding.

The elf pulls a golden coin out of his pocket, and both coins glow for a couple of seconds, fading out back to normal. Garnett scoffs, putting his dagger back where it belongs. He glances at me.

"To answer your question, I know a man named Onyx."

"We have something in common then," I chuckle as Garnett sits back behind his desk with a cough. All of that coughing Garnett's been doing has reddened his nose.

"Dragons, I apologize for how aggressive I was," he declares. "Because I'm sick, we're supposed to be closed for the rest of the week. I've just been here reading my novel all day."

Ruby awards Garnett a small chuckle. "I didn't think that there were any more Order members left in Crale."

"We're barely surviving here," he whispers, as if the Shurta are listening outside. "Onyx still has plenty of assassins in different nations, all trying to interpret what the Veils are trying to do next."

He glances at a clean stack of letters and quills, rummaging through the documents before taking a letter out of the stack. Ruby and I exchange looks. After clearing his throat again, he places paper on the tabletop. "A few days ago, we got a letter. Mind if I read it aloud?"

I nod, as he holds it up to start reading:

"Dearest Council of Crale:

I've sent this letter to the members operating in the region of Lelina. Due to the lack of messages from Jade and Amber, I've assumed that both of them have been executed. I've contemplated going myself, but my injuries have completely robbed me of my movements. So, I've sent out a rookie and one of my most trusted assassins.

Their names are Ruby and Kedar. When you greet them, assist them in their journey to cleanse the city of Lelina. I fear there's about to be a great rift in the War of the Dragon. We must find Judah's whereabouts as soon as God wills it.

With best regards,

Onyx, Head Magister of the Onyx Order."

With that, Garnett closes the letter and sets it down. "So, you're the ones that Onyx mentioned, huh?"

Ruby nods. "Yeah, I'm Ruby. Next to me is Kedar."

"Peace be upon you," I add, offering my left hand. Garnett clasps our hands together, giving me a firm handshake.

"Peace be upon you as well, Kedar," Garnett replies, giving me a smirk. Squinting at the lock on the door, he uses his mana to turn the lock so nobody can enter the Inn. Standing up and turning around, he walks up the stairs behind him, before realizing we aren't following him. "I apologize. We shouldn't waste any time. Follow me, if you will."

On the first floor, Garnett leads us to a study, aisles of bookshelves dividing the room into fourths. Walking up to one of the shelves on the wall, he pulls a red book towards him. With a click, the shelf unlocks like a door, and Garnett grunts as he effortlessly shifts it to the side, revealing a huge, rectangular hole in the wall.

"Alright, this is where our Theorum is," he tells us, motioning us to move inside. Theorums, as Onyx describes, are safe places for the Order. Assassins will group up and meet in places like this, from a hidden cave or even the catacombs under Pyria. Onyx has told us Polluck's Inn will be a Theorum before our trip, and he explained how to verify ourselves using The Coin of Power.

"Hurry. Opal's been waiting for you guys for quite a bit."

"Who's Opal?" I question, as we walk down a dark, dimly lit hallway lined with stone bricks and torches. Once Garnett safely closes the door— or the bookshelf— he leads the way, breathing heavily.

"Opal is the magister of all operations in Crale," he elaborates, glancing at us. "And also my stepmother."

Ruby says that each country on Haya has a magister, one that manages all the missions that assassins in the country do. We reach the door, and Garnett doesn't waste any time, pulling it open.

"Garnett?" I hear someone say. Looking over Garnett's shoulder, I spot a goblin sitting at a desk, writing away at reports. Her hair and eyes are a dark brown, as her wrinkles

254

suggest she's forty or fifty. She glances up at us. "Ah, I see. You've brought the ones that Onyx was speaking of, yes?"

"Yes, mother," Garnett nods, smiling as we walk up to her desk. "This is Ruby and Kedar. They've already shown me their Coin of Power."

"Excellent," Opal declares, motioning for us to take a seat at the two chairs in front of her desk. Setting my satchel in front of me, I plant myself on the seat. "We can finally get down to business."

"We're here to find Judah's," Ruby offers, taking off her bonnet before ruffling her hair. Opal shuffles through some reports, looking for something.

"For the past season, everything's been quite detrimental, to say the least," Opal grunts.

The Hayan years are split into four seasons, each being ninety days. In total, there are 360 days. Rubbing her fingers on her green forehead, Opal skims through some notes after pulling a piece of paper out of the stack. "Veils have been running rampant all over the city, and the *Shurta's* been compromised. Apparently, they seek to completely exterminate all Dracotheists in the city, since Lelina is the Cralean city where most Cralean Dracotheists reside. Around 5,000 people have already died from their genocide."

I, Ruby, and we exchange worried looks. It seems like the hate for Basalians makes Crale a hotspot for Veils, because both groups share similar dislikes.

"After Amber and Jade died, Garnett and I have been doing small, but useful research," she explains. "According to my findings, there are three Veil members that have been behind this whole plot to exterminate the Dracotheists: Al-Jukar, Al-Watawat, and Al-Barsim."

I scoff. "The Joker, The Bat, and The Clover? What's up with these nicknames?"

255

"The Veils conceal themselves behind these titles to obscure their identities," she elaborates, before narrowing her eyes with fury and a twang of desperation. "You two need to find and exterminate all three of them. After that, Garnett and I plan to help the current governor take over the emperor's throne, ending this war."

Nodding, I note how Crale's government operates. Each province has a governor, who reigns over its lands. The current governor of the Lelinian province, taking over the Emperor's throne, will be essential to ending the war. If the governor is in support of ending the war, then ridding the city of Veil presence is of utmost importance. According to Onyx, the current Emperor is a Veil member, Shay.

"Dragons, how are we even going to start with something like this?" Ruby replies.

The genocide of the Dracotheists not only shocks us, but also disappoints us. If anything, it makes impending hate for Crale bigger than usual.

"Well, to start, I suggest the two of you begin with finding Al-Jukar. According to my notes, he's usually found in the slave market. He sorta has a thing for concubines," Opal shamefully explains.

Not a day has passed where I've been in Lelina, and yet, its dark secrets have already been spilled by the horrific sights around us. Glancing at my wrist, I spot the dark, demonic magic flowing through my veins.

I'll get through this, Omar, I tell myself. *I'll find you.*

And kill anyone who gets in my way.

Shay Vaughn is the Supreme Emperor of Crale Imperium. Elected in the year 1338, he is rudimentarily known for starting the Dragon's War in 1388, 50 years after his election. He is a Farik, like most other rulers of independent countries and republics. Farikkians have the highest life span across all of the four races, which is why they primarily win governmental elections easily. It is exactly why Shay has been in power for 100 years, facilitating the ongoing war with the goal of fully conquering Basalia.

- An excerpt from the Cralean Historical Scrolls in the city of Janna. Last updated in 1438.

SEVENTEEN

Slavery isn't new in Haya. Warring tribes capture their defeated enemies, forcing them to work in exchange for not being executed. Even Basalia conducted the practice before banning it in 1332. Children have been put under harsh labor in the mines, and women are executed or toyed with by the Craleans.

When Ruby and I reach the slave district, I expect the worst. Opal has given us directions to the market, and with her guidance, we start exploring Lelina to find it.

We've arrived at a dark, wide, and long alleyway on the north side of the city. Garnett has mentioned how the market is exclusively open during nighttime, so we spend the day preparing ourselves to find this "Al-Jukar."

Plenty of Cralean elites associated with the governor strut in and out of the entrance, while two *Shurta* stand in the way, identifying each person who tries to gain access to their dark catalog.

"It's so cold up here."

"Well, duh."

She slaps my arm.

We're both at the edge of a rooftop, overseeing the market below. Slaves are put on display in metal cages, some even hanging in the air like they're captured owls. Lanterns mangle over the gloomy district, illuminating the slaves and their horrified expressions. I sigh. There isn't a clear way to get into the market without forcing ourselves through the main entrance.

"Ruby, how should we go about with this?" I ask, rubbing my gloves to generate warmth. The night skies don't stop snow from falling in the crowds, and more annoyingly, in my hair. Ruby narrows her eyes, dangling her legs off the roof.

"Well, I'd say we should go in disguise. You know, act as rich people? I've always wanted to try that," she replies, managing a laugh. Boxed in by a wall of houses, the market is filled with *Shurtas* everywhere. They're on the roofs, inside the buildings, walking through the market, scanning for anything. Thankfully, the building me and Ruby are in is high enough to make us blend in with the gray environment. Stroking my beard, I blow a stream of hot air out of my mouth, generating a smoke-like vapor.

"I don't want to risk getting caught. Besides, I'm not the best actor," I offer, as she pouts. Spotting a wagon on top of the flat rooftops, I realize it's filled with dark yellow hay. On the other hand, there are four guards on the roof, all oblivious to the plan I'm beginning to form in my head.

Ruby cranes her head to stare at me. "Please tell me you got something up your sleeve."

Snorting, I lock eyes with her. "I do, actually. Watch."

Huffing, I back away from the ledge, as Ruby only observes me curiously. That's gotta be at least twenty feet, I think to myself, eyeing the distance. Now that I look at it…

that wagon will probably give me the best resistance from a fall from this height without dying.

"Ked—"

"Ah ah ah," I interrupt.

"I said watch."

Gritting, I run full speed towards the ledge, Ruby's face contorting in shock while my metal armor clinks and clanks with each step I take. Jumping with all my might, I resist letting out a deathly scream. I remember that leap off the cave waterfall.

Dragons. I had water. But this? I got hay. Goddamn hay.

Diving through the air with my arms pressing against the sides of my chest, I split through the freeze like molten lava. *The wagon. It's right there. Like, inches away—*

Making a muffled oof sound once I slam into the hay, I grunt as my body vibrates with a hounding ache. I turn around, seeing Ruby watching silently like she witnessed a miracle, her mouth wide with shock.

The resounding steps of the *Shurta* catch my attention. There are two of them walking towards the wagon with no suspicion of what I've just done. Gulping, I roll myself out, sitting behind the wagon before huffing a quiet sigh. Ruby's overseeing the whole thing, gritting her teeth with worry.

"Have you heard? Al-Jukar bought more slaves. It's ten this time," a guard says, as both lean their backs against the wagon. While his voice is a little bit hushed, it's loud enough for me to eavesdrop. The second guard offers the first a light chuckle.

"Fat old bastard," he jokes. "If I had his money, I wouldn't be spending it all on women. You know, most of the slaves are Dracotheists, captured young girls being sold to almost any place on Haya. What a world we live in, hm?"

"Don't lie to me," the first one replies, his voice not serious. "You'd do the exact same as him."

"Aw, shut up, you!" the one next to him cackles. Rolling my eyes, I drown out their conversation, learning three things about Al-Jukar— apparently, he's a fat old man. Secondly, they reference that he's sick, sicker than they are. Lastly, he's bought ten concubines.

I've heard enough, goddamnit, I think, peering my way around the wagon, them having a smoke. Pouting, I remind myself to maybe buy some cigars from the city later. For now, I'll pull out the dagger Bix has made for me from my belt, and... clear this place out.

Pouncing from behind the wagon like a cheetah, the *Shurta* has zero time to react, not even getting to pull out their swords before I plunge my dagger into the first one's throat. For Omar, I whisper to myself. The second *Shurta* stumbles to the ground, putting his arms up in fear.

"Please! Wait! Somebody hel—"

Gritting, I stab him through the forehead, letting the guard drop dead to the ground in a pool of blood. Both of them erupt like fountains. I glance up, seeing Ruby still watching, waiting for a sign to jump off the roof as I did. I reward her with a slight nod.

With a *thump*, she effortlessly lands into the pile of hay like it's nothing. Ruby coughs out dust, hopping out with a grunt as she kneels at the dead men.

"Did you get anything out of these two?" Ruby questions, pulling her bonnet tight on her head. Sifting through their red and black uniforms, she comes up with nothing that can be of any use to us. I try to resist gazing into their glazed-over, gray eyes, but I can't stop doing it. It takes Ruby tapping my shoulder to snap me out of my limbo.

As I mimic what the dead guards say, I analyze the rooftops. It's covered with large wooden crates filled with cargo and weapons— perfect for hiding behind in case we need to sneak around. Plenty of *Shurta* members are in the distance, but luckily, they're too indulged in their small talk to notice what we're doing. Realizing the blood stains on the bone dagger, I don't hesitate to wipe the stain against my light armor, trying to remove any trace of red liquid from its surface.

"Well, that's a little underwhelming, don't ya think?" she says as we both slither through the terrace, hiding behind the crates to conceal ourselves.

Ruby doesn't wait for me to reply. "When it comes to trading, Crale's got a place to keep records of everything that they barter, sell, or exchange: fruits, slaves, clothes, weapons, books, you name it."

"It seems we gotta find a way down there after all," I reply stiffly. "What should we do?"

"Might as well describe ourselves anyway," whispers Ruby, shifting her gaze at the two guards in the distance. Looking over the glowing markets below, they're oblivious to our presence, having a chatter.

Giving her a nod, we sneak and bring ourselves as close as we can to the two. If the *Shurta* spots us, we'll have many chances at successfully retreating and hiding from them. There's coverage everywhere.

Ruby's eyes glare into my soul as she nods, her pupils trailing down my jawline. Quickly shivering that sight out of my mind, she looks down at her palm, her fingers facing upwards and outstretched, manifesting mana. I gulp as she clenches her fist, as I hear the two guards grasping at their throats, trying to get out a couple of words before they asphyxiate.

Once we pull their bodies out from the other *Shurta's* impending views, we crouch behind a heavy and large stone chest. Ruby smirks, a bead of sweat rolling down her cheek even though we're in below-zero weather.

"Alright. That was... easy," she huffs. Using mana severely drains anyone's energy, rendering them exhausted or out of breath. Ruby doesn't seem too tired, though; she is definitely a little riled up from using her magic.

Swapping our clothes, Ruby throws on the black and red robe over her tank top and pants before freezing to death, while I do the same. Dragging their corpses to another wagon with hay, we place them and our armor inside, keeping our weapons. Before we leave, I make a mental note to retrieve our stuff later.

Ruby looks like a Vujike, an old Basalian warrior from some folktales, except her robe and mask are red and black instead of blue and white. Snorting as I pull the mask over my mouth, I place the Kathi and dagger on the red, long cloth being used as a belt to fasten the robe on my waist. Ruby's red necklace matches their uniform, as well as her earrings and nose ring.

"Don't look at me like that. I look like an idiot, don't I?" she innocently asks, her voice muffled.

I smile, before realizing she doesn't even know if I'm smiling or not under this damn thing.

"You look fine, Ruby. Trust me, you'll blend in."

"You know that's not what I meant," she huffs. Before I reply, she begins to climb down a wooden ladder hanging from the ledge, leading to the market below. Frustrated, I follow her, as none of the other guards bat an eye. We descend next to a tavern, where the rich of Crale gladly drink away their problems and happily eat their gluttonous meals, as if there aren't cages upon cages of people in front of them.

"Dragons, would you look at that?" I whisper as we wisp our way through the crowds. On a podium at the center of the market is a Cralean goblin wearing a suit and a hat with a pointed front brim, supplying the man with a dark yet jolly look. He's gladly putting a human and farik on auction. At my left are women and men suffering from the cold, shivering in their cages as their eyes beg for mercy.

"It's what happens when you become a part of the slave market," I point out, our boots crunching against the snow below us. I glance at the prices— 40,000 darkos for a female elf to become your property. "You're no longer Hayan. You're merchandise, just another product on the shelf."

This is darkly familiar. Men crying out for their wives as they're being taken away to be put with their new masters, wives crying out for their husbands as they're being taken away to be put into the mines. Families are being torn apart in front of my eyes. It isn't anything new. Victims of the Dragon's War are from different nations, but the same. Trauma that's never healed, only more salt poured into the wound.

"You alright?" I ask Ruby, spotting her swallow a gulp. She's disturbed, from the look on her face. I hear her process a heavy sigh, her expression relaxing, before responding with a nod. It's difficult to turn a blind eye to the horrors we've been subjected to here. Elites and royals strutting and throwing their money everywhere, their manic minds scouring all of the "fresh product."

"I'm fine, goddamnit. Take your hand off my shoulder," she manages. Shaking my head on the ground, Ruby begins to scan our surroundings. "Gods... we are looking for something, right? I can't put my finger on it..."

"Remember? A place for records..." I trail off, trying to jog her memory. She nods in agreement, as her eyes fall on a wooden house at the right side of the market. I pause, trying to make out the language. It's in the Cralean dialect.

"That's it. 'Namukladin.' Records," she smirks, translating it for me. I sigh as I read the sign on the wide doorway leading inside. Quickly making our way towards the building, we notice a receptionist inside, with shelves of scrolls surrounding us and two floors stacked with the same thing.

A green goblin is busy looking over today's sales, scribbling them on paper while squinting through their spectacles. Ruby walks up to the man and taps her long nails lightly on the desk. The goblin's so deep in their work that they don't notice Ruby until she forces herself to tap him on the shoulder.

"Anxa janneud idnia?" Ruby slurs. A bit northern, I think in my head. Ruby doesn't seem to be the type of girl to be bilingual, but here we are. Never once do I think she'll speak in the languages of Crale — but here she is, murmuring every word.

"Bahdi naidnopia nuzum," the goblin awkwardly says, dusting off the surface of his dark vest. "Naxidus crisum moxus, moalp."

I gulp. I can't understand a single word they're saying.

Her ego not faltering, Ruby scoffs, giving me a glance. "He said we can look at the records."

"Yes, I can indeed," the goblin says in angloian, offering a nod. The green man's voice is grainy and brittle, his wrinkles showing his dire age. "But alas, you'll lose yourself in all of this. Let me hand over anything that you need, dear *Shurta*."

Stepping up, I clasp Ruby's shoulder, peering down to the goblin's eye level with determination in my eyes. "Dragons. Have you got anyone who's purchased ten slaves? Maybe last week or yesterday?"

The receptionist doesn't seem suspicious... yet. Getting up from his desk, he leads us through the shelves, heaving a sigh.

"Well, if we're talking about last week... There were about two people who purchased ten slaves. Should fit your description, right?" he nervously jokes, stopping before pulling out two scrolls from a bottom shelf. They're wrapped with a red band— signifying that it's been recently written by the goblin. He hands over the scrolls — one to Ruby, and one to me.

"Once you're done, give them back to me at my desk. I'll put it back for you."

Awarding him a nod, I unravel the document, Ruby following suit. He begins to walk back to his desk, but stops abruptly, turning around with a questioning expression.

"What do you need this for, anyway? I can't really see a reason why—"

"The general instructed us to look through these," Ruby interrupts, her voice stern.

"Do you want to question the *Shurta*, dear goblin? If you do, I can't help but assume that you've... betrayed the emperor's flag."

"Ah. I see, very well then," he squeaks, hobbling away defeatedly. Ruby eyes crinkle — I can tell that she is smiling under that mask of hers. We both lean on the shelves, careful to not make them fully collapse to make the rest tumble like dominoes— to read the two scrolls.

"I thought you said you only knew a little bit of Cralean," I say to Ruby as my eyes scan over the paper.

"Well, it's in my genes, Kedar. My mother told me that my father was this Cralean, dark-skinned elf that was 'charming' and a 'nuisance,'" she replies expressionlessly. "I guess speaking dialect is in my blood. Not only that, though. I learned Cralean when I used to do missions here, back when I was nineteen. It made it easier to, ya know, blend in?"

A full minute of silence follows, Ruby glancing down at her boots, while I don't even have a response to give to her.

"Never mind that," Ruby snaps, peering to look at my paper. "Whatcha got?"

266

"Nahum Ahmed," I read. The scroll separates into columns. It has the buyer's name, the amount that they spent, and what they purchased. For instance, there's a man who bought a few jester mangos, a woman who traded jewels for florians, but for Nahum Ahmed—

"He bought ten slaves. Three farik children, four male elves, three female goblins."

Ruby shakes her head. "Can't be him. You told me something about concubines, right?"

Her fingers scour the piece of paper she has in hand. "This man, right here — Eliaan Qasim. Purchased ten female slaves from the market. Sounds like an Al-Jukar to me."

"He's gotta be stupid," I say in denial.

This man, Eliaan, is clearly rich. Perhaps he's the one providing all the monetary needs for the Veil trio, supplying resources to seek out Dracotheists for extermination. On the other hand, this seems too easy. "I don't know, Ruby. Don't you think this is a trap? I mean, he made a mistake not getting rid of his records."

Scanning his address, I realize he's on the south side of the city, near the agricultural district. He's probably living the life of his dreams in a manor, watching his war-torn slaves work for him like servants and maids. Ruby isn't intimidated, staring into my eyes.

"Let's find out if it's a trap then."

After noting Eliaan's address on a blank sheet of paper using a quill, I put the paper in the back of my uniform.

"You look so worried, Kedar. You never know, maybe he let his guard down after those Order members died," she offers, offering a look of pity. I hand her the scrolls as we walk back to the goblin's desk to return them. After getting outside the slave market, I open my mouth to speak.

267

"Let's just report this all to Opal," I say with confidence, ignoring my thoughts.

"She should know about our findings. One step closer to finding this bastard, you know?"

It's easy getting back to the theorum. I bring the notes I've taken in my cloak after our expedition. Ruby and I hike up to the rooftop, where we hastily switch out our guard uniforms for our normal clothing again. Parkouring in the dead of night, we eventually arrive, safe and sound.

"Look at that. Ruby and Kedar, back already?" Garnett scoffs, and we open the door to the inn. The bell tingles with a hint of excitement. Moonlight shines through the windows, and Garnett uses it to read his novel at a table.

"I got good news," I begin, as Garnett raises an eyebrow. He looks cured of his cold from yesterday. Ruby, on the other hand, isn't doing too well. Her nose is red, and she's coughing like hell. Looks like her magic can't heal everything. "We found out who Al-Jukar is."

"For an initiate, you work fast," he teases. After I place my notes on the desk, he examines them deeply, squinting to read in between the lines.

"Interesting, indeed. I'll tell my mother about this later. But, this is really good work, you two."

"We have two people in mind," Ruby says before sneezing a fireball into her arm. Realizing that I'm staring at her, she blushes a little. "Oh, uhm, sorry. Anyways, Eliaan Qasim and Nahum Ahmeed are the only ones who bought ten slaves, but Eliaan purchased women."

"Eliaan? I've heard that name before," Garnett replies, slicking back his middle-parted, spiky blond hair.

Now that I think of it, how does such a young kid like him end up in the Onyx Order? Ruby, too— she has mentioned how she was seventeen when she learned Cralean for her missions, which means she was already a full-fledged assassin by then.

"He's the richest man in Lelina. Apparently, the War made his family boom in economic growth, because the Qasims are the ones controlling most of the trade in the city. He's also pretty notorious for working his slaves to death during the summer, being merciless."

"Well, that makes killing him more pleasant," I duly note. "Using slaves, the idea never sat right with me. Using people. It's not… right."

"Well, sorry to ruin the vibe, but I got some bad news," Garnett declares, handing my notes back to me before I slip them into my pocket. The elf's expression mutates into a slate of worry.

"Gods, are you alright? It can't be that bad," I ask, as he gazes into my eyes, his emerald pupils solemn. Slowly exhaling, he grabs a letter off the huge stack at the edge of his desk.

Slipping the letter into my hands, he stays silent, while Ruby peers over my shoulder so I can unseal it. Slowly taking out the piece of paper, I see the symbol of a lion and a monk praying to it at the top. My spine tingles while Ruby's eyes widen before I furrow my brows at the words on the paper.

Slowly, I read out the letter:

"Greetings, fellow Order members. I have sent this letter to every theorum across Haya. You cannot hide from my eyes. Do what you want with this letter, burn it, examine it, I simply do not care. My message is constant. This is a warning. Heed this carefully.

269

For the past decades, I've received a prophecy, one that postulates the end of the world as we mortals know it. In fact, it's not going to destroy the world. If I fulfill this Prophecy I've received, this world will be birthed anew, the king as our God and Master. You mortals have failed to find me. I declare myself a prophet for my God, my King. Yet, I've been searching for many, many years for my God.

Find me, but you will not find Judah. You will find my God."

Dropping the paper in shock, I realize how impossible it is to interpret his words. A god? No, he must be bluffing. This has to be a joke, a prank to play to make fun of how the Order has yet to figure out where he is. I wonder what Onyx's reaction to this is. What's he thinking? Is he worried? Is he surprised? Glancing at Garnett with worry, I speak in desperation.

"When the hell did you get this?"

"After you two left," he shudders. He's just a kid, I think. By looking into people's eyes, it's easy to tell whether or not they've seen the horrors of the Dragon's War, but Garnett is innocent. He might know how to wield a sword or a dagger, but he doesn't know what fear feels like.

"Another assassin I know, Staal, told me that Judah isn't lying. All twenty-two theorums across Haya received this letter. The ten magisters are in a horrible panic, urging for someone to find Judah as soon as possible."

"Sounds like another reason we need to kill Al-Jukar, Al-Watawat, and Al-Barsim," I reply. Ruby nods. "Well, at least one of them knows where Judah is, right?"

"You're not wrong. But there's more bad news— the *Shurta's* gotten more aggressive after your trip to the slave market. To note, they've been becoming more and more

270

aggressive ever since Jade and Amber died." His voice lowers to a hushed whisper. "They're my sisters. Opal kept me in the theorum for days; she didn't want me to witness their executions..."

Shaking his head in grief, I pat his shoulder as Garnett stares into our souls.

"Please, be careful. Don't end up like them."

"I can promise you that, Garnett," I reply, yawning slightly. My body's still aching a bit from earlier. I'm already drained. "Ruby and I will go to Al-Jukar tomorrow. We'll finish the job, right, Ruby?"

Offering Ruby a glance, her eyes are tired, her nose red, and she occasionally sneezes from her cold. Stretching, she rewards me with a slight nod. "Yeah. I just need some sleep..."

"I'll put you two on the second floor," decides Garnett, reverting to his calm demeanor. Getting up from his stool, he leads us up the stairs again. It creaks a bit while we walk to the top, where there's a long hall of rooms. I hear Ruby gulp behind me as Garnett reaches for the back of his vest, pulling out a bunch of keys. Glancing up, I read the room number: *21*. With a sigh, Garnett unlocks the door and swings it open.

"My mother and I have been debating whether or not we should close up for the rest of the year," he snorts, motioning to follow him inside. "People still visit the country every now and then, but with all the huge battles that's been going on, I don't think people are going to risk their lives to get here just to see the Nisf Thueban."

The elf is right— since last summer, been very aggressive. Basalians have been trying to push their army across the Kigamouth lake to invade Crale's capital for a decade, and they've decided to make another desperate charge. Naval battles and landings have been occurring on the beaches, but

271

we aren't even close to the coast. Basalian generals are on the offensive this year; Crale is playing a defensive card.

As I walk into the room, I look around. There are two twin beds spaced out from each other at the back, a bedside table acting as a wall between them. On the left, there's a dining table with a pair of wooden chairs, sparkling clean. Lastly, there's a bathroom on the right side, while the walls contain patterns which have onyx gemstones along dark, golden lines. Setting down my bag, Garnett gives us a nod.

"I'll see you two in the morning. Enjoy your stay," he smiles, stepping out and closing the door. Ruby sighs, sitting on the edge of the bed on the right side, coughing. Setting our bag on the dining table, I take out all our clothes and belongings, setting them aside for later use. But I'm searching for the Codex.

Pulling out the thick, large, and heavy book, I grunt as I set it down, my fingers glazing over the golden linings of the black leather. Reading out the gold letters, it spells out: "CODEX BASAL: ANGLO TRANSLATION."

In 668, most manuscripts of the Codex were destroyed. Nobody knows what the version of the Codex was like before it was burned in a fire in the Pyrian libraries. Only a couple of hundred pages were retrieved, but scholars haven't rewritten the parts that are missing, only gluing them all together to create one big document. It's still long, but it doesn't have some parts which are "vital" to Dracotheism. Onyx tells me this is one of the earliest manuscripts translated into Angloian since he received it in the 1250s.

Turning to Ruby, I point to all of her clothes.

"Everything you need is here," I say as she nods, sniffling. I find myself in the mirror of the bathroom, examining every inch of my skin. It seems like it's... glowing? Either way, I've

272

charged myself up— no more malnourished, exhausted, and dehydrated Kedar. No. I'm a revived flower.

Taking off my clothes and putting on a white robe, I open the door to see Ruby's armor and cloak leaning against the wall. She's shivering in the bed, coughing in her hands, while snuggling with the wool blanket.

Going to her side, I ask, "Are you sure you're okay?" before she responds by nodding.

Denial.

Subtly smiling, I chuckle at the irony.

"Remember when I was like this? Suffering from Munir..."

"Yeah, yeah, I remember," she responds, avoiding eye contact. A satin scarf covers her braids, the ruby necklace on her collarbone reflecting a soft, red light from the candles at our bedside.

"You know what? You should trust me. I'll go alone tomorrow, while you can stay and... I don't know. Get to know Garnett and Opal. You should really rest, Ruby," I propose, tucking her in as she sighs deeply. Her cheeks are bright red— is she blushing? No, probably red from her cold.

"Kedar," she growls suddenly, her arm grabbing my collar and pulling me close. Anger is embedded in her expression as she furrows her brows. Dark circles are forming under her eyes— it's a side effect of all of our traveling and her ever-growing sickness. Now that I think of it, why the hell are we so close? I'm going to get sick, goddamnit. She might cough on me.

"I'm not letting you go alone."

"Uh... Why?"

"Didn't you hear me before? I'm not letting you do anything stupid."

In a teasing voice, I reply, "No need to be so protective. You really think I'll die?"

"Ugh," she retorts, her lips inches away. Her eyes avert to my right pointer finger— or what's left of it. With her scarf, she has on a black gown, contrasting with the bedsheet's white.

"Don't even think I'm implying anything. Look, if you're going to die, I'm going to be the one killing you. Not Al-Jukar. Not anyone else. Only me."

She shoves me off of her as I breathe heavily, trying to recollect myself as I gulp.

"Alright, alright. You can come. Let's try beating your cold, at least."

"You're not wrong," Ruby agrees.

"Just get me a warm, soaked towel. Dragons, I have a headache."

Obeying her, I come back upstairs with exactly what she asked for— a towel warm to the touch, not too hot, not too cold. I'm only gone for a little bit, but she's already asleep, softly snoring. Her golden brown skin complements her red-highlighted braids that run down her neck and shoulders. Smiling at myself, I scoot a chair to be by her side, placing the towel on her forehead. She winces, murmuring curses, but she surprisingly doesn't wake up to beat the hell out of me.

I press the towel a bit harder to make sure it feels more relieving. As I recoil my arm, I feel her fingers wrap around my forearm, as if she's trying to hug me. Thinking she's awake, my eyes avert to hers, but they're. I feel a small squeeze as she lets go, letting her arm fall beside her. Breathing heavily, I calm myself before getting up to grab the Codex. I sit back down, opening it up without hesitation. Dragons, am I dreaming?

Quickly shuffling those thoughts out of my mind, I open up to where I left off. The seventh chapter of the Codex.

"5: Prophet Emmanuel did speaketh on bended knees, declaring thus:

6: 'O Basal, Divine Dragon. We do implore thee to attend to our entreaties. What doth constitute true adoration with a fellow being?

7: And the Dragon didst respondeth,

Harken, O steadfast servants. I have attended their supplications. When both man and woman tend to each other's needs, forsake not the other in times of adversity, hold each other in high regard, and render worship unto their one and only true LORD, it is only then that it is faithful, true adoration amongst one another."

The Pyrian Fire is an event which occurred in the year 668. According to officials, the fire broke out after five hooded individuals showed up in the libraries at around midnight, throwing oil on every shelf. The monks tried to stop this, only to be engulfed into the flames. Thus, there is only a minute amount of chapters of the Basalian Codex which have been saved from the tragedy. If passages do not intertwine or make sense, then it has likely been burned.

- *Excerpt of the Basalian Codex: Commentary by Jard Opa.*

EIGHTEEN

Ruby's definitely not in the condition to come with me.

Even though I've done my best to take care of her, she's still sneezing and coughing all over the bedsheets, and her eyes are poisoned with fatigue. Nevertheless, there isn't any time to waste. Time to give Al-Jukar a visit.

Ruby's shut eyes and stern expression only amplify her condition as her chest rises and sinks softly. Going without her means failing to fulfill her wishes. *It's safer for her to be here, alone,* I think. Trekking downstairs, I spot Garnett sitting on one of the tables, sipping tea.

"It's like the crack of dawn. Going already?" He takes another sip before coughing. In front of him is a huge book of spells. My eyes wander, skimming through the wonderful descriptions of earthly magic.

"Well, Ruby's sick. I have to leave her behind," I declare, darting my attention away once Garnett realizes I'm staring. As a response, he sighs, glancing at the mahogany table.

"Now that I think of it, you two are pretty close," Garnett duly notes, smirking before crossing his arms. "Is there something going on?"

Rolling my eyes, I head for the front door, spotting the sun rising from the east, switching places with its dark yet glowing counterpart. The streets are littered with pounds of snow. I give Garnett a glare.

"No, so don't even start."

Garnett's smirk only gets wider. "That's what they always say."

I swing the door open, tuning him out. Exhaling slowly, I think of how many ways I can kill Al-Jukar. I strum through the crowds with my hood, getting my map.

Unrolling the damn thing, it has each territory of the city, even the shantytowns and some of its outskirts— displaying the fields where Lelina's citizens grow their crops for harvest. One of these fields is named the "Qasim Vineyard." It's genius how anyone can be a Veil, even the rich and the poor. What baffles me is how public Al-Jukar is— apparently, he's a celebrity seen dining in luxurious locations and enjoying meals with the governor. The vineyard is on the south side, near a river that splits Basalia's and Crale's territories.

Winding through the crowds, all huffing and puffing from the impending cold, I pass by the slave market we visited yesterday, now transformed into a farmer's market to mask the carnage that happens during the night. Soldiers are on the roofs, examining the corpses that they've found in the wagons of hay. I stifle a laugh— they're never going to find out who did it, even if they try.

But Garnett isn't bluffing. There's way more *Shurta* lurking around. Sporting their red masks and robes, they remind me of cockroaches crawling all over a pantry, doing anything to give their little mandibles something to chew. Hundreds of pairs of

278

eyes are on me with every step I take, but it's apparent none of them are suspicious of me. To them, I'm just another man trying to live through these dark times.

Rubbing my gloves to generate some warmth, I reach the outer gates, where dirt roads split into pathways that lead to fields outside the city. Obviously, they aren't growing anything with this winter season, but there are plenty of ways for farmers to make money, like bartering... or slave trading, which Al-Jukar does. Crale's armies freely use the dirt roads to give way, marching with power. My boots crunch with the dirty, mushy snow underneath, while I lock eyes with the war prisoners being hauled around like lost sheep.

I'm close to the vineyard now, around a quarter of a mile away. To be honest, I have no idea how I'll go about this, but the first thing that comes to mind is to snoop around as much as I can. Maybe I'll find a hint of where Judah is in the manor. Following numerous pathways and signs, I find myself gazing upon Al-Jukar's household, fading into view.

Towering forty feet high, it's sculpted out of stone bricks and white wood, blending in with the snow. On the other hand, the roof complements the place with a dark brown color. A metal gate blocks the way in, and there are stone walls with *Shurtas* on every corner, making sure nobody is dumb enough to trespass.

A crowd of people bangs the metal gates, guards shouting at the people to get back with their curved swords. I cautiously eye the commotion coming from citizens while keeping my eyes subtly averted. But, just in case, I keep my hand against the *Kathi*. Most of them shout curses at the guards, their words jumbling into words and phrases that I can barely make out, because some of them are speaking in different dialects. A recurring pattern is obvious in their appearances— most are poorly clothed. They must be from the slums.

"Give me back my money, you fat bastard!" a man shouts, pumping his fist into the air while the crowd continues their assault on the gate. My height gives me a small advantage in looking over everyone else— some guards look down from the stone walls with confusion. They clearly didn't know what to do with these shouting, angry people.

"Free our women! Our wives!" another one shouts.

Maybe Eliaan doesn't have the best reputation amongst all civilians, I note.

With a *clang,* the metal gate falls to the snow, and everyone spills in. The guards who stand vigilantly in front of the gate draw their swords. Before I can contemplate taking out my dagger, the guards swing their weapons without hesitation, blood splattering everywhere.

Shaking in horror, arrows rain from the sky, people screaming in pain while their fellow town members die all around them. Avoiding the horrid, impending attacks, I see women with arrows sticking out of their heads, and men that have tens of arrows poking out of their backs. Their blood floods the snow red.

Hyperventilating, my hand twitches against the *Kathi's* handle. *Goddamnit, what the hell are you doing! Kill the guards!* A voice in my mind says.

No, no! For the Dragon's Sake, it'll expose my identity! I can't let myself be involved in such a heinous event like this! I shoot back. People crawl back in fear as families who just want their brothers and sisters back from Al-Jukar have been sliced in two. Nearly getting grazed by the metal head of an arrow, I almost trip over a man's decapitated head. The *Shurta* aren't showing a single ounce of mercy, intestines being spilled out on the ground as hearts are pulled out and thrown to the snow.

I run and never look back, only stopping once I realize I'm in front of the gates to Lelina. It's impossible to erase what I've seen— innocent people dropping to the floor while crying out for help, the guards using their blades to cut down the people with anger. There's no *goddamn* way I'm getting into that manor. If I'm caught, who knows what they'll do to me? Opal isn't wrong.

The *Shurta* are definitely manipulated by the Veils.

I sit on a wooden bench near the side of the dirt road, merchants walking past me while traders set their tents in front of the gate to fish for some customers. It takes me a couple of minutes, but I let my heart rate soothe. Filtering out what's happened is out of the question.

Al-Jukar..., I whisper in my mind. *You bastard.*

My veins are glowing now, as I glance into the distance, seeing the *Shurta* pile up the corpses to serve as a warning for those passing by.

Those people died because of me, didn't they? It was my fault, my fault again. I sit there for what seems like hours. Coming back to my senses, the glow in my veins fades as I spot two merchants carrying chunky, hefty backpacks. A cap is tightly secured over their heads to fight the cold, while they also sport red and blue robes.

"Heya."

I get up. The merchants are pretty short, and my suspicions are confirmed once I realize they're both children, the first being maybe eleven, while the second is no older than thirteen. The older one gives me a childish smirk as their brown skin glows against the winter sun.

"Well, hello there, mister!" he begins, eyes gleaming with profit. I'm not going to buy anything, though. Al-Jukar must be a businessman, which means he likely conducts his services in his mansion. These kid merchants have to know at least *something* about the place.

"Have you two been to that mansion over there?" I ask, pointing to Al-Jukar's manor. The kid squints, nodding once he turns to me. His face vibrates with liveliness.

"Well, yeah, obviously. That's where Mister Eliaan is! My sister and I always trade stuff with him. He usually buys exotic fruits from Ultum for us, no biggie," he replies, glancing at his sister. It must be hard, hoisting these bags every day filled with products to sell to wandering customers.

"I guess you've been inside, right?"

The little boy nods, but his expression shifts, like he's trying to read me. I clear my throat.

"Tell me, what's the way in?"

"I thought we're here to talk business, bucko," he huffs, crossing his arms. His sister steps up, a little shy, but she looks up with confidence.

"Uh... There's a tunnel at the back of the manor!" she exclaims, blinking as she realizes people stare as they walk by. Clearing her throat, she gathers herself as her brother gives her a surprised expression. "

That's where Mista Eliaan brings all of his produce." Her voice drops to a whisper. "*His slaves.*"

"Hey! Lia! What the hell!" the boy pouts, shushing her. I chuckle, sifting through my pockets to grab my pouch of darkos.

"Since you told me, I guess I owe you something, huh?" I begin, trickling five thousand darkos into the little boy's hands. His jaw drops, but he smiles erratically.

"Oh, jeez! Thanks a lot, mister! This cold weather seems to discourage people from buying anything," he replies, shoving the coins into a pouch, tightly securing it with a leather string. His expression shifts, though, as he seems unfulfilled.

"Mister... why do you wanna know about something like this?"

I sigh at his question, trying to come up with a lie. But now that I think of it, maybe it's worth telling the truth.

I reach into my pocket and pull out the Coin of Power. Both of them look at it like it's the most valuable thing in the world.

"Huh. Well, best of luck to ya," the little boy says, offering a salute. I'm a tad bit surprised, since he isn't oblivious to the Coin's meaning. He rummages through his pockets before shoving a thing in my face. It's a Coin of Power, no doubt about it. I realize both of our Coins begin to glow, only further confirming my suspicions.

"Our mama is an Order member, too. She said that anyone else who has this coin was a good person."

The boy slips the Coin back into his trousers, glancing at me with seriousness. "I guess you're gonna kill Mista Eliaan, huh? Welp, we'll lose one of our only customers, but like what mama said— 'less evil in the world is good.'"

I nod in thanks. "You're not wrong, little one. Run off now, there's *Shurta* everywhere."

They go off on their little adventures, leaving me standing near the wooden bench. The two children seep into the crowd, offering me bright, wide smiles.

Unlike needles in a haystack, they wander the world like prey walking into a lion's den.

It's better if I come back at night. Less crowds, more time to assassinate that monster once and for all. To pass the time, I explore Lelina rather than returning to the inn, since going back means getting a slap on the face from Ruby.

Cralean theaters are a bore. Most are filled with subliminal hints of propaganda, while some try to depict a sense of superiority over dracotheists. *Another reason to stop the Veils from corrupting this city,* I note. Public executions take place on every street, victims being used as a warning for the people: Crale doesn't take much mercy on traitors.

I look at the dimming sun, splitting the sky into wisps of orange and pink. Night's quickly coming, and it's almost time. Time to kill Al-Jukar.

Someone bumps into my shoulder roughly as I strut back to the manor. I'm half-expecting it to be some random civilian, but it's Ruby, glancing up at me distastefully.

She's still sick, judging by her still sick red nose and pink-tinted cheeks. Ruby wears her bonnet over her braids along with her signature golden-lined cloak to dim the cold.

Her eyebrows narrow. *Damn. She's pissed.*

"So, are you doing a little exploring without me?" she strickenly asks as she follows me to the gates. It takes a while for me to come up with an answer. She can kill me by lifting a finger. That's just how Ruby is.

"Well, uh, yeah, " I cautiously reply, scratching the back of my hair. Ruby's facial expression contorts, and I expect a slap, a kick, a pinch, *something,* but she doesn't do anything.

"I've been doing some research on Al-Jukar, nothing too serious."

"Kedar, I had to sneak out of that damn inn. I tried limping out of the room, but Garnett didn't let me go. He said it would be 'best' if I 'rested' for now."

She scoffs, crossing her arms. "I had to use my magic to knock out that kid. I've been looking for you for three hours."

I try imagining the state of Garnett. Probably dozing off on that wooden table, his drool soaking into the pages of his encyclopedia. I laugh, only stopping once I realize Ruby's seriousness.

284

"Ahem, well, while you are resting, I went to Al-Jukar," I say awkwardly, while we cross back on the path to Eliaan's mansion. It's almost nighttime now. "You should prepare yourself. I figured you'd follow me, sickness and all."

"Kedar, I fight best when I'm sick, trust me," she snorts, as I roll my eyes. Resting her arms at the back of her head, her cloak blows up from the wind, her bearded axes gleaming in the moonlight. Maybe she's prepared.

"And plus, I'm wiser than you. I have the brains to prove it."

Not taking her words seriously, I reluctantly offer her a hopeful look. "Wiser? What the hell makes you say that?" Ruby is a rolling dice— she can be childish, serious, jealous, and shy. She's unpredictable.

Ruby stares menacingly while we come closer and closer to the manor. Breathing a sigh, I see the building fade into view from the chilling fog, the bodies still rotting on the side of the road.

Ruby doesn't hesitate to invade my thoughts of remembering those screaming, pained faces— "Kedar, I've been in the Order since I was sixteen. It's been seven years. I've gone through plenty of nicknames— The Red Flash, The Scarlet Maiden, The Ruby Snake. I've killed maybe two hundred people. I'm used to killing and getting away with it."

Shivering a bit from the cold, I take heed of what Ruby says. *Two hundred?* I repeat. *And she got away with every single one of them...*

I've never counted the number of people I've killed during my time in the army, but all I know is that I've killed maybe five hundred, but those are from the battlefield. It's different than killing political members and Veil members in secret. Ruby's a mastermind.

"Time to make it 201, huh?" I joke, as she stifles a small laugh. My tone turns serious. "I've been thinking about freeing Al-Jukar's slaves after we kill him."

"I'll bite. Whatcha got in mind?"

"A fire. Under the cover of night, we can kill the guards and Al-Jukar. After that, we can hide it all with this brutal and manic fire. The royals will assume this was a tragic and horrible accident, while we walk away freely and out of the *Shurta's* hands."

Ruby responds by squinting her eyes.

"Hm... that's what I was thinking, too," she replies, nodding her head in agreement.

But there's an aching thought in the back of my mind.

Why does she always have to follow me around like I'm some lost cat? My veins glow. *I can do all of this by myself, I traveled to Lelina by myself, saved my brother by myself, took care of all of this by myself—*

"Kedar? You okay?" Ruby's voice invades.

"Yes, yes, I'm fine, I'm *fine*. Let's just go."

We walk to the back of the manor in silence. Breathing in and out slowly, thinking of all of those dead, innocent people makes my blood boil to an extent that I'm familiar with. *Cralean soldiers. Dead. Everywhere.* I gather myself together. No time to be thinking about the past. Unblurring my eyes, I gaze through the metal gates. There's a tunnel seeping deep into the white-colored ground, a door at the end. At the top, five guards stand diligently, though some are clearly tired from the constant security they have to supply.

Ruby and I find ourselves standing at the top of a hill behind a wide pine tree wide enough for us to lean against. I glance down, Ruby busy fiddling with one of her axes while sitting on the snow.

"Ruby. Are you coming with me, or what?"

As I lock eyes with the guards, my hand grips tightly against the *Kathi*. *They killed them, didn't they?* A voice says in the back of my mind. Bloodlust is the only thing that can describe the reason my heart is beating so fast.

"Kedar," Ruby softly replies, standing up and putting her hands on my shoulders.

Why the hell are my fingers shaking?

"Dragons. Is something bothering you? Your veins, they're glowing, and you look like—"

"I'm fine, Ruby."

I'm not fine.

"Just let me go. Let me deal with this alone. Go back. You're sick, aren't you?"

"No. I already told you, you're not going without *me*," she urges, letting me go from her grasp, only to press her palm against my chest.

Her voice deepens. "I'm not going to let you *die*."

Worry riddles through her expression. She's nervous, maybe even scared for me.

Just focus, my mind tells me as I feel my bloodlust die.

Ruby puts her hands on her hips, making sure her bonnet is safely fastened on her head. It's like she's completely unfazed by what she's done. "Kedar, follow me. Let's just go."

Dragons, what is she doing to me?

We stealthily go downhill. There aren't any watchtowers for the manor, but there's plenty of *Shurta* on the stone walls. Ruby and I find ourselves leaping from bush to bush outside the manor. Ruby swiftly assassinates the guards on top, leaving them drowning in their own blood. We climb over the walls, collapsing to the ground with an *oof.*

Hiding behind a boulder, we peek at the guards standing outside the tunnel. Ruby's at my side, trying to recover from her mana usage as quickly as possible. Using her magic means sacrificing her stamina— each spell translates into fatigue.

Four of the *Shurta* sport the regular uniform that Ruby and I used the other day to sneak ourselves into the slave market— while one of them wears a red robe under their black armor and shiny shoulder pads. A familiar mask is plastered on their face. The same one that the Veil in Ardon and the Veil in Jiya wear. They're a Veil. With Ruby's nod, I rise from our hiding spot, walking in front of the *Shurta.*

The guards seem slightly surprised once realizing our presence, but their egos don't falter. As for the Veil, they barely react, crossing their arms as their demonic gaze scans every inch of us.

"What the hell are you two doing?" a guard says, swinging their blade at me. Without responding, I unsheath my *Kathi* and bone dagger, like a knife belongs with a fork. Both guards slash at me, displaying their horrible, but desperate swordsmanship.

Dodging under their blades, I shift the *Kathi*, the first guard's arm severing like cut-up sausage. It drops to the ground, and he screams like a newborn. The second guard, with an obvious glare of fear in his eyes, tries to intimidate me with another swing.

Blocking it with the bone dagger, I use the opportunity to slice the *Kathi* at his waist, attempting to chop him in half. He dashes back, avoiding my lethal blow.

Let your anger control you, a voice rings in my mind. *You wanted this once you stole my magic.* Furrowing my brows in anger, I realize the first guard is standing up and helplessly trying to hack their blade while sniffing tears.

"You must *want* to die," I growl, dodging his attacks with precision. He stumbles, getting back up as his blood continues to stain the snow. The first guard's face brims with anger, and he charges to stab my chest.

Swinging the *Kathi*, I block, sending his blade on the ground. His wrist twists at a horrible angle, the bones under his skin splitting into hundreds of fragments. I grab the guard by the collar as he wheezes and moans in pain. The second guard tries to whip his sword, but I use the first guard as a human shield.

I wince as the first guard's head splits in half, his brain splattering against my armor. The second guard screams in horror as I drop his comrade's corpse and wipe the pink matter on my woolly coat.

The soldier tries to speak, but no words come out. His eyes keep darting to his dead friend, seeing the glaze setting over his pupils. Wiping off blood from my gloves, I muster a smirk.

"How does it feel? Seeing your comrade's bodies making the snow red?"

"Look, if we offended you, hurt you in any way, shape, or form," he begins. "Mr. Qasim can pay you. How many darkos do you want? A million? Ten million?" No amount of money can repay this *Shurta's* sins. *Might as well put him out of his misery.*

Before he can say another word, I thrust the *Kathi* forward, stabbing his abdomen, feeling the sharp metal pierce his liver. He coughs out a gallon of blood, dropping to his knees as he looks down in defeat. *They deserved this.*

Pulling my blade out, he collapses, breathing out his dying breaths, his soul draining quickly. I breathe a sigh of exhaustion, putting the *Kathi* where it belongs. Glancing to Ruby, she's finished her battle too— two guards are sprawled out on the ground, a pool of blood surrounding them. She wields her dual axes made of Dragon's Horn metal. There are specks of soft, reflective blue that blend in with the shiny blades. The blood on the edges glistens in the moonlight.

"I'm not surprised," the Veil says, clearing his throat as he gives us an almost proud glance. "Al-Jukar has been expecting people like you to show up."

Ruby snorts, her tone feisty. "Who the hell are you?"

"Does it matter?" he replies, pacing in front of the dark entrance to the tunnel. Under his armor, he's slim, the threatening long sword on his back glowing in the moonlight.

"Yes, actually. It does." Ruby taps the edges of her axes together to sharpen them. Narrowing her eyes, she stares into the Veil's lifeless glare. "Your eyes. They're—"

"Yes. I am a Veil, sworn to Judah. I must protect Al-Jukar, so this city's cleansing can continue," he monotonically interrupts.

"You talk about this 'Cleansing' like it's a good thing," I jump in. "These innocent Dracotheists, they've done nothing to you. Zilch. And yet you still kill them?"

He musters out a low chuckle. "They're pests. Bugs. The High One wants them dead— every one of their disgusting ideals reminds him of his brother." *Onyx,* I think. "The two of you must be part of his problematic Order."

I don't have the confidence to say anything to him. Ruby gives me a worried glance, gulping. The Veil maniacally laughs, chuckling into the Cralean night sky like a madman. Wrapping my fingers tightly around the *Kathi,* I squint. *We need to kill him. He's wasting our time.*

"What makes the two of you think you can interfere with The High One's Prophecy?" he questions, his voice psychotic. Ruby's about as confused as I am— *what the hell is this Veil talking about?* Then my mind refers back to the letter from the Theorum. *A prophecy?* It seems like a bluff, but this Veil speaks of it like it's set in stone, destined to happen.

"If you're so confident about this *Prophecy,*" begins Ruby, reading my mind. "Tell us all about it."

"*Our God shall be tethered unto one of his liking. The Prophet shall shape the vessel, tune him into the ways God likes...* That is all I remember," he replies, as I feel his glaring smile through his mask. I gulp. *Tethered?* All demons must be born in this way, but what does the Veil mean by *tethered?*

"Enough with the small talk." He unsheathes his blade as Ruby and I stand on guard, vigilant.

If what this man says is true, then who's this god that he's speaking of?

Judah's God. His master. His king, my mind answers for me. Omar must know what horrors Judah's up to. Dragons, I can't even imagine what he's seen, being kidnapped by the Veils... for what?

I still can't figure out why.

My thoughts are gravely interrupted with the realization of the Veil charging towards us with an uncapped rage. "Come on! Let's stop standing around and kill each other already!"

He swings his large sword towards my waist, but I raise my sword to block his attack. My eyes widen once I see him dodge my block. *A distraction.* His blade slashes up to my wrist.

"The cleansing of the Dracotheists shall not be stopped!"

General Lanix,

There is a swordsman on Basalia's Fifth Regiment which I think you should be particularly worried about. Those who survived the battles where they encountered him call him "The Executioner." Based on their descriptions, he wields a long, thin sword that swipes and divides fast. His eyes are an emotionless, hazel brown, and his hair is short and curly. Do proceed to the next raid with caution. This "Executioner" is deadly. Rumors have it that he killed two hundred men with a small little dagger. Send James and Valerie to scout him out. Find his weaknesses to promise your victory for our glorious Empire.

- A letter from Commander Kao to General Lanix of the Cralean Empire, written on the 321th day of the 1436th year.

NINETEEN

When I first shed blood, I was sixteen. It was two years
after my parents' deaths. Omar was fourteen, feisty, and out of
control. In a way, it was comforting— his stubbornness and
immaturity almost made me feel like a father to him, except I
taught him more unconventional things. Like stealing, lying,
robbing, and betraying, for instance. Anything to stay alive.

In Alfdan, I thought about the homeless people I killed in
Pyria. Justifying it was near impossible. I had a couple of
reasons come to mind, like *it was a matter of survival,* and *it
was either me or them.* But I realized one thing.

We didn't need to kill, fight, or steal. There's no reason to
hurt each other— we're all in the same, grim situation.

It was a sunny day when Omar and I were stealing as many
apples from a market stand. During our robbery, the
shopkeeper caught us in the act, his eyes widening in anger as
he chased after us.

We were both terrified, eventually running to a dark
alleyway. When I looked back at the middle-aged man, it was

with a flicker of hate. Blame it on Munir for my bloodlust, or my desperation for survival— but I wanted to kill him. Badly.

He had a knife. All I had was my anger and pent-up rage as a weapon. I envisioned him as the goblin who killed my parents, replicating the depravity I felt toward those monsters.

Without any other thought, I was pinning him to the ground, his knife in my other hand. I looked up and saw Omar, holding four apples while his face contorted in fear. It was like he didn't see his older brother in front of him.

I slit the shopkeeper's throat, and I felt satisfied. Like I fulfilled an urge. Omar kept silent as I took his hand to drag him deeper into the slums, making sure nobody saw us at the scene.

Without Munir, I finally began to see that all the things that I claimed were good and justified were actually demented and wrong.

Revenge blurred the lines.

Alfdan transformed me. In that dark, horrid cage, I had many hours to ponder my life decisions, trying to envision a reason to live.

There was none.

All those years ago, when I promised to protect Omar with my life, I broke that promise. I never thought of him when I was trying to survive in Pyria, and when I was a killing machine in the army.

I thought of survival.

But now, here I am, thinking about saving my brother.

Maybe the *Shurta* in front of me and Ruby are the same. There's only one difference between us— he's surrendered to his demonic magic, and now it looks like it's taken control over his body. Not a sliver of hurt for his comrades is in his eyes. In fact, it's like he finds it pleasurable to see their blood soak the snow.

294

It's been half an hour, and we've barely gotten a hit on him. My wrist is slit open, while Ruby has a dent in her armor from the man's long sword. She's gripping her stomach, huffing as she tries picking up her other ax. My eyes narrow.

"Just let us pass. It'll all be over." I wipe the stream of blood running down my nose. The Veil's mask radiates with death. It's dark red, paired with two horns that curve up. Around the eye holes is a black outline, while a deathly smile that replaces the mouth hole.

"It's never over," he growls. The most we've done to injure him is slashing a piece of fabric from his tunic under his armor. "Give up. Every single assassin who tried to kill Al-Jukar has died at my hand. You cannot kill me."

"Al-Jukar is a damn monster." Ruby coughs into her fist, her sickness still showing. "You're protecting a devil."

The Veil sighs. "Al-Jukar is not a monster. Besides, if this genocide meant getting rid of women like you, then the world will become a better place."

Ruby grits her teeth before digging her boots deeper into the sand with anger.

"Whore," he sneers.

Ruby ignites.

With her axes above her head, she dashes towards him with speed, as the Veil tries to move, only to find himself coughing, holding his throat. *She's used her magic to stop his blood flow,* I think. Snapping myself out of a daze, I run up to them.

The Veil holds up his blade, blocking Ruby's initial blow. I swoop in and stab his left armpit with the *Kathi*. Screaming in pain, the Veil's blood squirts on my cloak. He wails as I drive the blade deeper, while Ruby uses her other ax to slash his right shoulder.

"Gods, how the hell did you...," the Veil stammers, as Ruby digs deeper into his flesh. He looks at Ruby with rage. "A mana-user? So we're playing those types of games, huh?"

A wave of magic thrashes through the air as Ruby blasts back, making us tumble and roll in the snow. Ruby curses as she hits the back of her head hard on a boulder. My gaze widens as she closes her eyes. She's still breathing, but she's knocked out. The Veil's mask is shattered when I look back at him.

His pupils resemble Munir's— a red glow with a dark outer rim, his cornea a hellish black. The Veil's long, straight hair runs down his shoulders, his skin darker than Ruby's. With the moonlight above, his glare omits an insidious ambience.

"Yes. This is the true me. I've let my demonic self take over my soul," he growls, saliva dripping down his chin like a beast. Then he points at me. "You. I can see the mana that flows through you, Basil. A demon's mana..."

"What?" I pause. *He knows? How the hell does he know?* My mind says. With the demonic self in full control of the Veil, he must see through me. Sensing my magic must be easy. Demons can recognize each other's presence, but Munir is dead. *How does he feel my mana?*

"Kill me. Come on, don't be shy." His voice deepens. "I want to see what you can do."

I nervously wipe the blood from the bone dagger. Averting my eyes to his arms, a dark magic rips through his veins, replicating my own. I can do the same. I'm in control of Munir's magic now. Ruby won't scold me for being 'stupid' anymore, since she's unconscious. Maybe if I can get it to activate somehow...

"I won't show mercy."

He smiles as I charge at him with vengeance. Moving inhumanly, he zips in front of me, swinging his sword to split me into bits. An unnerving energy begins to radiate with every step I take. *Am I getting faster?* I ask myself before dodging his attack.

We lock eyes, shooting daggers. Trying to dash away from me is futile— I quickly unleash a barrage of slashes to nick his cheek. Frustration seeps through my mind as he smiles, dodging every swing.

His boots slide through the snow as he finally gets far enough from me, his hair prancing through the cold winds. Gritting my teeth, I narrow my eyes, letting my rage towards him grow.

Kill him. Kill this sick bastard.

"Oh, someone's losing control. Come on, human. Let's unmask you," he chuckles, realizing my gaze of malice. My veins glow darkly. *Why the hell does he think he knows me?* The winding voices in my mind twist and twirl at unruly speeds.

I am myself. I am nobody else. I am Kedar. I am not Munir. I am doing this for justice, goddammit, not because I find pleasure in death.

"Oh, that demonic glow." He points at my wrist. "I recognize it. Although I cannot sense the demon that lurks within your plane. Nevertheless, Judah will be ever so grateful if you join our side. Be under his wing!"

I leave him no response, letting his words flow out of my other ear. My anger makes my veins glow brighter under the moonlight. These Veils, the innocents dead in the snow, even Munir— it makes my body more enhanced. My stamina is back. The muscles in my body are stronger, weightless. I fixate on the Veil— the only thing I can imagine is his corpse on the ground.

The dismembered limbs and the corpses of the innocent fill my head. Fathers and mothers are gone because they want their daughters and sons back from Al-Jukar. Vengeance. The Veils deserve worse than what they've done to those townspeople, ten times over.

Redemption doesn't exist for Hayans. Death is the punishment for all sins. Mercy gives them another opportunity to repeat their demonic actions.

The corners of my vision turn red, but there's no pain from when Munir plagued my mind. No. I'm in control.

Before I think, I charge at the Veil like a beast. I use my blades to stab him on both sides of his waist, barely giving him time to react. Roaring in rage, I drive my weapons deeper, puncturing every vital organ he has as he gasps for air.

I push him off me, and he lands in the snow with a deadly *grunt*. There isn't a sliver of confidence in his gaze. Only fear. Slowly, I walk, while he holds his wounds, groaning.

"What are you? What the hell... *are you?* You control your demon magic like it's nothing," he begins, spitting blood onto the snow. I resist the urge to laugh as he grasps at the snow, trying to crawl away from me and leave a trail of crimson.

" I've made a MISTAKE! Please... you're not blinded like the others... you're... you're..."

I step on his wrist, making him grit his teeth in pain. I kneel down until we're eye level.

"Who are the others?"

The Veil isn't wrong. I'm not blinded by a demon that possesses me. No, I possess Munir. His magic is mine until I die. And I seem to be the only one to realize that evil is defeated by evil. Showing empathy doesn't result in anything *good.* Letting him live is out of the question.

"You're not alone. There are others... who've birthed demons from their anger. It's not just you," he winces, as I edge my boot deeper into his wrist, his bones shattering as he whimpers. "Like me, they let their demon take control. It makes them into a damn cannibal. A monster. But you're not like them."

The look in his eyes tells me that the demonic counterpart is no longer there. He's in control now. His veins aren't glowing anymore. The Veil's beaten into a pulp, and now he doesn't speak in riddles anymore? It doesn't sound like a coincidence.

He realizes the anger in my gaze, his tone turning desperate.

"Look, you're different! In a good way! You're a powerful harbinger of demonic magic! Judah's prophecy will only make you stronger, into a god even! Judah's going to—"

I interrupt him by stabbing him in the throat with the *Kathi*. *Judah's Prophecy?* My mind echoes. Sounds like Judah's justification for killing all of the dracotheists. Pulling my blade out, the Veil's blood floods the snow, mixing with his comrades. What I want is to find my brother. And to do that, I have to find Judah. This Prophecy, or whatever Judah's rambling about— I won't let it happen. I'll kill anything if it means I get to save Omar.

The buzzing sound of flies makes me snap out of my daze. Those little bugs finally caught the scent of the rotting corpses in the snow.

My mind is clear. After killing the Veil, it is clear. Like I've ripped a weight from my shoulders. I run to Ruby, her eyes still sealed as she leans against the boulder. Blood drips down her forehead, and I promptly smear it off with my fingers, gulping.

"Ruby? Hello?" I lean my ear close to her lips, hearing the faint sound of her breathing. My veins aren't glowing anymore. The magic flowing through my body returns to hibernation again, but why? Now that I think of it, Ruby's an antidote— I feel *human* next to her.

I poke her soft cheeks as she flutters her eyes open. She tiredly glances at me, before her lips curve into a smile. But her expression doesn't last— her face becomes riddled with confusion.

"What the hell... Kedar... Your right eye... It's red."

I hold up the *Kathi* to check myself in its reflection. No. *No.* This can't be real. My iris is a deep dark red, while my cornea mimics the color of my pupils— a void-like black.

"Ruby... You're right... my eye..." I trail off, dropping my sword to the ground. It isn't a brown hazel anymore. *Munir's magic.* This must be a side-effect of letting it unleash without resisting it. Almost immediately, pain radiates from my eye, and I grunt as I cover it with my hand, feeling a warm liquid run down my cheek. *Blood.*

Munir told me before: "My powers feed off of the souls that you take, Kedar." The more people I kill, the stronger the demonic magic will be. Ruby uses her cloak to dab my blood, letting it soak into the fabric.

"Gods, Kedar. Are you sure you're alright?"

"Yes, yes. I'm fine," I reply, getting up as the pain from my eye fades and I stop bleeding. Offering my hand, I pull Ruby up from the boulder as she grabs the back of her head, sealing her wounds the best she can using her healing magic.

"We've wasted enough time." Ruby offers me a concerned look as the glow from her fingers wisp away. Hovering her fingers over my cuts, she heals herself and me from our battle wounds, cementing them as simple scars. I wince as my skin gets stitched together.

"Ruby. Al-Jukar's waiting for us..."

"Yes, idiot, I know. Just let me finish this."

She slides her thumb across my wrist, sealing my tendons easily.

A couple of minutes later, we find ourselves walking into the depths of the tunnel. With its gloomy interior, the soft squeaking of mice soothes the immoral ambience. Earlier, the two children told me that this tunnel is used to transport Al-Jukar's slaves. Now we're using it to sneak into his manor to kill him.

"It's dark in here," Ruby whispers.

"Are you scared of the dark or something?" I ask. Ruby replies by shoving my shoulder, almost making me tumble to the ground. We laugh as we lock eyes.

Ruby takes her thumb and smears it against my lower eyelid. Her pupils are red, but mine are different. She looks like a human. My eye makes me look like a demon.

"You have the same eyes as that Veil. But…. why is it only one eye?"

"I have no idea." I rub it. "Maybe it's my mana."

A wooden door comes into view amid our echoing boots. The wood is rotting, while a candle hangs off of it, illuminating the darkness.

Ruby breathes a deep sigh before grabbing the handle. She looks back with surprise as the door swings open.

"What the hell? There's no lock? Al-Jukar probably thought his guards were powerful enough to not let anyone near this door," Ruby declares.

Once we step inside, a horrid stench stains my nose, as Ruby and I immediately pinch our nostrils. My eyes adjust to the room's darkness as I analyze the room. There are cages on each side of the wall— maybe fifteen. In the middle, there's a stone table with knives and weapons, which suggests that Al-Jukar uses these to torture his slaves.

"God. The smell." Ruby's fingers lace around mine as she curses under her breath. Al-Jukar's slaves must live here, with little to no light or basic needs. It's impossible to pinpoint the

301

scent. Blood, sweat, tears, and rotting corpses are all combined into one.

"Just breathe, Ruby," I reply, my mind going back to Alfdan. It's just like this. My heart rate accelerates, imagining all of the deaths I saw. *The old man and those piles of corpses...* I glance at Ruby, and a surge of relief pumps through me.

Ruby stops holding my hand as a loud coughing noise makes us jump. In each cage is a slave, with over half of them being women. The rest are men, but they seem too drained to speak or acknowledge our presence. We walk to one of the metal cages to see a goblin in the corner, shivering in fear. It looks like she hasn't eaten in days, while bruises, gashes, and cuts litter her body. She wears rags, barely covering her to fight the cold. There isn't a fireplace in this room— the temperature is identical to that outside. Freezing.

The goblin's eyes are void of faith. When she locks eyes with Ruby, a horrified expression plasters against her face. *She must be one of Al-Jukar's concubines*, I think. Ruby tries to speak, but the woman responds by pressing herself harder against the corner of the cage, shrieking in fear. *So this is what it feels like to be owned. Toyed with. Treated like nothing but an animal.*

"We're not here to hurt you...we're good people. I promise," Ruby says softly. The goblin is far gone. She's lost her mind.

Ruby turns to me as I try to console her by rubbing her shoulder.

"Al-Jukar... that bastard... she's broken."

"All of these people... they need to be returned to their families. We have to save them."

She nods in agreement as we look into another cage. This time, the person inside isn't alive.

A rotting corpse of a male Farik is face down on the stone, cold floor. Maggots are chewing through his eye sockets, letting a yellow fluid flow out of his skull. *This must be the source of that god awful smell.*

Recoiling in disgust, we back away. As we walk to the exit, leading deeper into the manor, the slaves look at us in silence, too scared to speak. All of their faces are empty. It's horrible to see.

Ruby takes one last glance before opening the door out of the room. I peer through, seeing a flight of stairs which leads to a spacious room.

"Remember," Ruby begins in a hushed whisper.

"Kill Al-Jukar, save these innocent people, and burn this place down.

I nod.

We sneakily walk up the stairs, as we enter into a room of... books. *Al-Jukar's study.* There are shelves lining each wall, with an elegant chair and coffee table in the middle. Al-Jukar must read his lovely novels here before tormenting the life out of his slaves.

Ruby concentrates on her sense of sound, but she shakes her head confidently, signifying that there's nobody near us in this humongous manor. Glancing at the black, golden books, I clear my throat. "Ruby, go through these. Maybe there's something about Judah in here."

"You're right, but why does this house seem so empty? It's too quiet," she whispers, pulling a book off the wall. "*The Manifesto of Idemm Orupoa.* Huh. He reads revolutionary stuff? Interesting."

A golden chandelier is embedded on the ceiling, casting a shining, bright glow. Around us are paintings of the Dragon's War. The Battle of Ukao, The Siege of Nuka, The Massacres of Bascity— it's all there.

303

"Damnit," Ruby grunts, frustratingly as she skims through more. "There's nothing here. Just books about poetry and tales of the war since it began in 1388."

"It's fine," I tell her, waving it off. "Might as well find Al-Jukar. Lead the way?"

Snorting, she creaks open the door while I speak to check for any *Shurta*. There are seven on the second floor, while others are downstairs, standing in front of a door, likely where Al-Jukar resides.

"Goddamnit. I know nothing about being stealthy," I whisper back to Ruby. She responds with a foxy smile.

"Well, like you said. I'll lead the way." With a slight sigh, she holds up an axe, while I wipe off the blood stains on my bone dagger. Sneaking out of the library, I analyze our surroundings.

The second floor of the manor is made up of a long, winding pathway in the shape of a "U," with an entrance on each side. An even larger crystal chandelier hangs above the white marble floor below. Every guard's eyes scan each inch of the manor. Two of them look in the direction of another guard on my right. *I should wait for Ruby's command,* I note. No time to make mistakes now.

Hiding behind a cabinet against the pathway, Ruby crouches behind a brown vase, sniffling and trying to hide her impending cough. We lock eyes, and she glances at the guard. Nobody's watching him now. Pulling out my dagger, I throw it with unholy velocity. *Seems like Ruby's training worked after all,* I think, as I hear a resounding thump. Ruby heaves her ax to the other guard, who quickly dies as he's stabbed in the neck. Gulping, I crept out of my hiding spot to collect my blade.

I hit the guard in the forehead, his blood seeping through the wooden floor. Pulling it out with a grunt, I glance over the wall, the third guard panicking as he realizes his comrades are nowhere to be seen. Before I can move, Ruby's axe splits through the air, knocking the *Shurta's* head off his shoulders. *She's good at this.* I grab her ax off the ground at the far side of the hall.

Downstairs, the guards are oblivious. "Man. This must be business as usual for you, huh?"

"Well, not exactly," she replies. "Other than Lapis, I've never had anyone else help me."

I snort. "I'm probably better than you, aren't I?"

Ruby rolls her eyes, pulling something out of her utility belt.

"Not even close. You're just making this faster for me."

Ruby holds a smoke bomb— a white cloth wrapped around a gray powder in a spherical shape. She tosses it in the air, catching it with ease.

"Alright. Once I throw this, do your whole killing thing for me. Got it?"

"I won't break a sweat," I quietly reply, giving her a nod.

Ruby heaves the smoke bomb in front of the four *Shurta's* feet. It explodes into a gray, dark fog. The guards cough as they're blinded by Ruby's gadgets. Taking a deep breath, I jump off, pulling out the *Kathi.*

Within the smoke, the bloodshot eyes of a guard notice my grueling shadow. Gritting, I stab his throat, letting his blood splurt against my armor before throwing him off me. I have to move quickly — holding my breath and squinting is vital to resist the effects of the harmful fumes.

"Ammar! Where the hell are you?" I stab the guard in the stomach, as he rewards me with a deathly groan. Feeling Munir's mana swelling in my veins, I slice the guard in half, letting him wail on the marble floor.

It's like they're coming to me, I think, before stabbing the third through the throat, piercing the bone dagger through their heart. The smoke subsides, as I let myself take another deep breath with the freshening air.

A blade wisps through the air, and I quickly duck under it, swinging the *Kathi* up to slice the arm of the last guard. He whimpers in pain, clutching his stub as he drops his weapon to the ground.

"Ah! You're... you're...," the guard stutters, while Ruby slowly walks down the stairs, grasping the handle with a deathly smile.

"I see... you're part of the Order, aren't you?" The guard huffs as bags appear under his eyes, his blood streaming out of his arm like a waterfall. He wears an eyepatch on his right eye, covering the glaring scar running down his cheek.

"Correct," Ruby jumps in. "Once we kill you, Al-Jukar will be next."

"If you think Al-Jukar's going to tell ANYTHING to you bastards, you're dead wrong, you sick fu—" I stab him through the stomach, making his blood flow down his chin. Falling to the floor with a dramatic thump, I sigh. It's over.

"Gods, they're loyal to Judah like puppies..." Ruby shakes her head while I kneel to take off his eyepatch. I rub the leather, wrapping it around my head and letting it cover my eye. Better to hide my demonic magic than be executed for it.

"Kedar? Damn, you look... different." She examines me. "I like it, though. It suits you."

"I hope it does," I reply, clearing my throat as she tucks her hair behind her ear. "People will avoid me if they see me with my red eye."

"Kedar." Ruby rolls her eyes. "Stop being dramatic."

I shrug her off. "Oh, shut up."

"Enough of that," Ruby says, blinking. "Shall we?"

As I nod, Ruby grunts and kicks the door open. A fat old man sits on a desk, reading through a book with streaking, long, gray hair. On his bed lies the corpse of a female elf, her eyes rolled back with a knife embedded in the back of her neck. Ruby's eyes widen at her dry blood soaking through the mattress. It looks like the elf has been dead for hours.

Ruby charges at Al-Jukar with vengeance, snatching him by the throat. He gurgles as I spot a small lion on the left side of his monk robe, the same symbol on the letter we received at the theorum.

"You bastard," Ruby glares. She presses the fat man against the wall, making it crack under pressure. Sure, I've seen Ruby mad, but never *this* angry.

She points at the dead elf. "What the hell did you do to her?"

"L-Let me down!" he shouts through gasps. Ruby explodes, throwing him against the wall with a resounding *thud.* Al-Jukar coughs out blood while I glance at the elf. Her eyes are wide open, her skin pale, cold to the touch.

He bursts into laughter as he notices me examining his dead slave.

"Sometimes, they don't listen. I have to teach them a lesson."

Resisting the urge to slice him into pieces, I take out my bone dagger and walk to Al-Jukar, wiping the blood streaming down his nose.

"Where the hell is Judah, Al-Jukar?" I ask hastily, while Ruby stands behind me, trying to control her anger. Sweat runs down the side of his cheek while I put the dagger inches away from his neck, glaring into his soul.

Seconds that feel like hours pass, and Al-Jukar stays silent.

Before I can repeat my question, he grabs my dagger and thrusts it towards his throat.

TWENTY

"Goddamnit!" I yell, pulling my dagger out of his neck. By the time Al-Jukar hits the ground, he's already dead. Wiping the blood off my blade, I drift my attention to Ruby, her eyes glued to the woman on the bed.

"Ruby?" I stammer, realizing her frozen gaze.

Anger vibrates through her shoulder as she turns back at me.

"Kedar, we could've saved her!"

A tear streams down her left cheek. She plants her forehead into my chest, looking at the floor. I'm a bit shocked she's showing me this side of her— the only response I can come up with to comfort her is to pat her head.

"Ruby. Stop. We did what we could." She sniffs, wiping her tears away harshly.

"We didn't do enough," she grits. Her cheeks are flushed as her demeanor switches to a more serious one.

"We have to burn it all. Burn this place into the damn ground."

310

Pushing me off of her, she rubs her forehead solemnly, breathing a deep sigh. I motion towards Al-Jukar's desk. "Look, on the bright side, we have a chance to find clues on where Judah is."

She nods. "Alright. We should also find a key, Kedar. To free all of the slaves here."

The blood under my boots splatters as I greet myself to the gruesome scene outside.

But other than dead guards, I'm not alone.

A boy, his complexion darker than Ruby's brown, examines a dead soldier. Frozen in shock, he holds a metal plate filled to the brim with food. Parting in the middle, his dreadlocks are long enough to hang over his ears, while his height makes it seem like he's only two inches shorter than me, a little bit taller than Ruby. His inwardly curved nose and defined jawline align with his toned physique under his black and white thobe.

"Wha— huh?" he yelps, slipping on the blood and tumbling to the floor, spilling the food everywhere. Standing over him, I squint, examining the look in his eyes. *Is it fear?*

Clearly, he's innocent. But I don't want to take any chances. He shudders as I inch towards him. "W-Who the hell are you?! What are you doing in the master's manor?!"

"Calm down," I offer, holding out my hand. Hesitantly, he gulps before letting me pull him up, smearing the blood off of his robe.

"I'm calm." He isn't. The sweat and his constant ember eyes that keep sizing me up say it all. "Just answer me. Who are you?"

"My name is Kedar." I motion to Ruby, busy rummaging through Al-Jukar's desk.

"That is Ruby. My... partner."

His eyes peer at my hands wrapped around the *Kathi,* and he backs away, his hands up in submission. "Look, don't kill me. Please. I'm just Al-Jukar's butler. I've done no harm!"

Maybe he really is just an innocent kid, I think, removing my hand from the blade's grip.

He blinks nervously. "My name is Abubakr. Mr. Qasim— or Al-Jukar, whatever you call him— is my employer."

Abubakr waves his hands, motioning at the dead bodies on the floor with confusion. "What happened here?"

I snort. "I killed him. Well, no. He killed himself."

Ruby steps over a dismembered leg with a defeated expression as she closes the door behind her. She offers a questionable look as I shrug in response. Abubakr really does seem harmless. But nevertheless, trusting people in these times is a mistake or a reward.

"You—" his mouth drops in shock— "What?"

"We won't hurt you. Don't worry. We're here to free everyone," Ruby explains, as Abubakr's worried expression fades into nothingness.

"I've been serving him for almost a decade... I was worried I would be forced to be his butler until the end of my life." He wipes the sweat off his forehead.

"It would be great if you had a key to unlock all those cages," I say. He nods, walking into Al-Jukar's room, reappearing after a couple of minutes with a silver key in his hand.

"Damn. Al-Jukar's really gone." Abubakr hands it over gladly.

My attention shifts to Ruby as I lower my voice to a whisper. "Did you find anything?"

"No," she frustratingly replies, as we walk down the stairs to where all of the slaves are. "Nothing in that damn room.

There isn't a note, a message, not even a sign of him being a part of the Veils. It was spotless."

Shaking my head in disappointment, I breathe deeply to prepare myself for that gloomy room behind the door which Abubakr hastily opens. "You said you've been here for around a decade, right?"

"Yes." He coughs out the gray dust as we walk in darkness. "Since I was seven."

As Abubakr unlocks the cold, dark cells, I realize there's a number branded on the back of his neck. Seven. Ruby and I glance to see the shivering, cold woman we saw earlier, doused in wounds and bruises. Her expression shifts once she sees Abubakr, limping towards him while muttering gibberish. Abubakr offers a soft smile as he allows her to grasp his arm.

"They trust you," Ruby points out.

"All of the slaves do. The men, the women. I am the one who tries my best to keep them alive. I give them my food, water, anything to make their lives worth living." As the cages open with a rusty *clank,* each slave has a brand on their necks, possessing a different number. They crowd around the boy like he's their savior. We left the dead in their cages, but their lives aren't in vain — Al-Jukar is gone. Forever.

"I can lead everyone outside," Abubakr tells us over the shivering and whimpers of the ghastly crowd around him. "What will you two do?"

I smile. "Ruby and I are planning to burn this place down, so the *Shurta* will denounce this as an accident, nothing more. We'll meet you outside, Abubakr."

He snorts, nodding as he opens the door to let everyone run through the tunnel. As they leave, Ruby looks at me with a proud smirk. "I guess that was simple enough, huh?"

"We just have to burn this place down," I say as we go back inside. "Look for firewood. Anything flammable, we can use it."

Weaving through every room, I find myself standing in front of a fireplace. With couches and chairs everywhere, I assume this is some lounge for Al-Jukar. In the fireplace is dark firewood, waiting to be used.

Ruby stands next to me. "Here, help me carry these." I place it into her hands as I carry four logs, nearly breaking a sweat.

"Gods, how are we going to light this place?" Ruby wonders aloud, as I spot an oil lamp on one of the coffee tables. It's lit, providing the room with a glow.

"With this," I declare as Ruby's eyes light up. Scratching the scar running down her neck, she dips the log into the blazing inferno.

Widening my eyes, Ruby hurls the log into the shelves with books as they explode in a fire. Snorting, I do the same, throwing it against the wooden walls as they cripple into ash. Pillars dye a threatening orange-red, spreading like a plague.

Grabbing Ruby's hand, I drag her out of the room while her pupils are hypnotized by the fire. "Dummy! You should've waited for my cue!"

"Does it matter? I mean, look at this, Kedar!" she shouts over the smoke. We hustle down the stairs where Al-Jukar's room is, while the crystal chandelier falls from the ceiling and shatters into millions of pieces.

Some of the shards of glass nick my cheek, but I pay no mind.

"You're right. It's a nice sight. But it's probably better to look at it from the outside!"

"You know what, I'll agree with you on that!" she huffs, coughing into her fist. It's hot. Too hot. It almost makes me forget that we're in Crale. Running to the front door, I ram my shoulder into it, stumbling into the white snow.

Ruby slips out of my touch, her hands resting on her knees as she coughs and wipes ash from her cheeks. I laugh, almost manically. Black smoke covers the stars above, the manor falling apart amid the blend of yellow and orange.

Explosions shatter my ears, and shards of debris split through the air, landing inches away from us. Ruby smiles, fastening her bonnet. "Gods. We need to get back to Abubakr."

"And we should return all of those slaves where they belong," I add. "With their families."

Turning our backs on the manor, we notice Abubakr waiting, unlocking the metal gate to free everyone. Ruby turns to me. "What about him?"

I gaze deeply into Ruby's red eyes.

"He'd be a great assassin."

It's grueling to explain my situation with my magic to Opal—she immediately asks if my eye is okay when I got back from our trip. She's a bit skeptical, but Ruby convinces her well enough. As for Garnett, he isn't worried at all.

A week has passed since Al-Jukar's manor burned to the ground. Ruby isn't sick anymore, and we have returned all of the slaves to their families. Opal, Ruby, Abubakr, Garnett, and I are in the confines of the Theorum. Abubakr's hesitant to join us on our journeys, a little worried about his lack of combat skill, but Ruby and I agree that the kid has potential.

Garnett stands near his mother while Abubakr keeps his subtlety, leaning against the wall. It's easy to tell he's clearly intimidated, based on the worried look on his face.

According to Opal, our method is too "noticeable." A mistake on my part. Security around Lelina has become tighter, *Shurta* is on the lookout for these figures killing their comrades and pillaging Veils.

"Alright, you two. Do anything extreme again and I'll—"

"I know," I interrupt, her red and golden robe glowing against the dim candle on her desk. Unsurprisingly, there's an opal necklace resting in the middle of her collarbone. "Maybe this is a good thing— the Veils will know now that they need to watch their backs."

"Don't you see, Kedar, that's the problem!" Opal exclaims, Ruby trying to contain her smirk out of the corner of my eye. "You've made a scene. Al-Watawat and Al-Barsim will *double* their efforts to stay hidden. It'll be incredibly difficult to find out where any of them are!"

Stuttering through my response, I pout as the rustling of her notes drowns me out. Clearing her throat, her eyes narrow. "*God.* I might as well give you everything I know about The Bat."

Ruby leans in a bit, her ears perking up. Rubbing my hands to generate warmth, I realize Opal's fatigued demeanor. *Finding all of this information about the Veils must be dangerous,* I think.

"Al-Watawat is a female figure who is behind the strings of propaganda, supporting the dracotheistic genocide."

Her eyes avert towards me. "Kedar, you said you saw a play, right? What was it about?"

"It was about..." I trail off, remembering the theatre's laughable retelling of how the Dragon's War began. Apparently, it's *our* fault, not theirs. As if they didn't want Basalia's holy land in the first place. "Making a joke out of Basalians. And Dracotheists."

Opal defiantly slams her green palm to the table with urgency, as everyone in the room jumps. "With her death, the people of Lelina should hate the Dracotheists... less. Stopping hate crimes is impossible, but it would be nice if we could cut off the head of the snake."

Garnett crosses his arms.

"Mother, what about Abubakr and me? Should we send him with Ruby and Kedar?"

Abubakr cools his quiet demeanor as our eyes lock onto him. Scratching the braids on the back of his head nervously, he chuckles a bit at the awkward situation. Opal taps her sharp nails against the table's wooden surface and then nods at herself.

"Son, teach Abubakr. I can trust you, right?" Garnett pouts a bit. "Basic combat components are all he needs to know. The more allies we have on our side, the better."

Well, this is a little familiar, I think.

"I'll do it, mother. Guarding this place has been a bore, anyway," he jokes, hopping off the desk with a grunt. Streaking his hand through his silky, blond hair, he leads Abubakr out the door, closing it softly.

"Opal—" Ruby begins— "Got anything else about Al-Watawat for us?"

"Well, from what I've written, Al-Watawat likes to mingle with the rich the same way Al-Jukar does, just not... publicly. She's usually found attending masquerades in Draken Castle."

That castle is the epicenter of Lelina. Garnett has explained the history before— apparently, it's forged within the time of the Jezzebel Wars, where Fariks rose up to rebel against their home countries, even Basalia. Draken Castle has been built by the Farikkian war prisoners.

Castles are made for royals, but they don't exist in Crale. Only the governors and the emperor rule the lands, their authoritarian minds boundless. Masquerades, according to Garnett, are highly secretive. Those who are invited to the event are allowed to step foot inside and enjoy alcohol and exotics like nuju berries from Ultum and Hershore cigars from Gardon. *Damn, I need to try one of those.*

"Masquerades? Seriously?" Ruby crosses her legs. "How the hell are we going to get inside?"

Opal chuckles, rummaging through her drawers again. Onyx must have hundreds, if not thousands, of reports to read and take note of back at Ardon. It's hard to imagine how these magisters keep their sanity with this job. "Well, don't worry. I'm prepared."

My eyes peer at the papers Opal sets down on the table. Opal's tone shifts into a more excited one. "These are fake identities which I've used in the past, maybe forty years ago? I don't quite remember."

Ruby gulps as she reads the contents, before widening her eyes.

"Wait... you're telling us you want us to be husband and wife?"

Sufyan Hussein and Yasmin Hussein. Both aged twenty-six, hailing from Jura, I read, before reading it again to make sure I'm getting it right.

Ruby stammers. "You're joking, right?"

"No, not at all. You two seem to fit the role quite well, if I'm being honest," Opal says, as I feel my cheeks get hot. Sighing, I realize I can't even make eye contact with the woman next to me. Embarrassment is infecting both of us.

Standing up, I hold the paper in my hands, laughing awkwardly.

"We can do this, Ruby. For... uh... finding Judah, right?"

"You know what? Fine, let's do this," she replies, deflating. Opal clearly notices our tension, offering us a smug look. *Dragons.*

"As a suggestion, you two should buy a suit and a dress. The next masquerade is in two days," she offers.

Walking down the stairs to the lobby after saying our goodbyes to Opal, Ruby, and I notice the chattering voices of Garnett and Abubakr. Undergoing his training session already, it seems. In the lobby, all the dining tables are stacked in one corner, the blinds blocking every inch of sunlight. Only the dimly lit lantern on Garnett's desk gives the now spacious room light.

In the middle, Abubakr barely defends Garnett's assault with a wooden staff, their weapons cracking and splintering under the pressure. Garnett looks confident, not an ounce of exhaustion in his eyes— Abubakr pants, gripping his staff with a gleam of intimidation in his gaze.

We pass by the two — they don't notice us, locked in the ferocity of battle. Opening the door, I cover my eyes as a hellish blizzard erodes through my cloak. Even with all of my layers, it seems like nothing can stop the Cralean freeze.

"Man, Opal's right." I rub my hands together as my teeth chatter. Ruby does the same, cautiously stepping over the piles of snow on the side of the road. "I mean, we do need a disguise. Just like at the slave markets."

Ruby responds with silence, as if she doesn't bother to think about what I've said. Eventually, we lock eyes. "Kedar... have you been in love before?"

I blush, scratching my neck. "I... I don't know."

I'm looking for a tailor shop to get her question out of my mind. Eventually, I sigh and glance at the snow falling from above. "Maybe I fell in love with war. Maybe I fell in love with wrath. The feeling of taking someone else's life away. But that's not me anymore."

"You've told me about everything that's happened to you in the army," she begins. "That man you describe, killing and feeding on violence— it's not you. There's a soul behind those eyes of yours. Ever since I met you, you've changed every single day."

I can't even come up with a response.

She taps me on the shoulder. "Hey. You look pale."

"I— It's nothing."

"I was just asking you because I've never thought about setting down and stuff," she murmurs. "Someone's loved me before."

"Wha- huh?"

She shakes her head. "D-Don't worry about it. Doesn't matter anymore."

"Well, I... I don't really care."

My eyes trail the scar that's on her neck. It ripples her skin, giving off a lighter contrast over her brown complexion. *Stop.*

I take out the map, fumbling over my words.

"Look— there's a tailor shop near us. Maybe we can browse their wardrobe?"

Ruby and I stare at each other. *Dragons, I hope she's oblivious.* "Alright, just lead the way. Don't get us lost."

A few minutes later, we find ourselves at the entrance of "Lawrence's Tailor Extravaganza." *Extravaganza?* I snort. If anything, this building looks like a more run-down version of Garnett's inn.

"Stay sharp, Kedar."

I offer her a questioning look.

"Use our fake names."

"Why?"

She scoffs. "If we use our real names— imagine if someone found sale records of us buying from here. We'd end up like Al-Jukar."

Walking inside, rows of suits and dresses litter the store, each having a different color scheme than the rest. A human clerk is smoking a cigar at the counter, wearing a green tunic and a golden belt. *Damn. I need a smoke,* I note.

Ruby doesn't hesitate to walk up and tap the table's surface to get the clerk's attention. Yelping and dropping his cigar, he blinks as Ruby awards him with a friendly wave.

"Hi. My husband and I are looking for some dresses and some suits…"

"Imperfections do not equal beauty. Beauty is perfect, constant as all things should be. Love is what truly has imperfections, but even with these imperfections, they are still worth loving."

- Quote from philosopher, "Nadius," before being executed by the Cralean Empire for inciting a riot in 1401.

TWENTY-ONE

Ruby's question boils over for days.

I love Omar, but as for romance— the concept doesn't exist to me.

Revenge is the only thing I know.

Since Omar's been kidnapped, I've been asking the same question: *Why do I love my brother only now that he's gone?* Imagining what he's going through is otherworldly— we've escaped from our cells for him to be put in a new one. Nevertheless, my hope to find him hasn't dwindled at all. Rescuing him will only pay a small amount of the debt that I owe. Even if he's not the same person he once was, I'll still love him more than I love myself. He's the only shoulder that I have to lean on.

But Ruby's different. She makes me tumble over my words. She makes me wonder what's going on in that brain of hers. She makes me worry and get nervous even when she's gone out to buy pastries for herself. I don't deserve to feel this type of way towards her. My soul, my heart— even with her reassuring words— is still *unredeemable*.

Maybe I'm overreacting, I sometimes tell myself. *The things she does for you are purely out of pity and friendship. Just focus on finding Omar and maybe even become a defiant assassin in the Ord—*

Ruby snaps me out of it, poking my shoulder and rolling her eyes. "Dragons, Kedar. Don't tell me I have to repeat what I just said."

We're in the lobby. Outside, it's dark, the moonlight seeping through the blinds. Garnett and Abubakr are busy chatting next to each other at one of the tables. The two of them are becoming best friends lately— perhaps it's easier because they're the same age.

Ruby's scowl makes me remember what we're in the middle of— discussing our plans and strategies while in Draken Castle. Although she looks a little annoyed, the strawberry pastry she takes a bite of relaxes her expression. *Seems like sugar's the only way to calm her down.*

I awkwardly stutter, scratching the back of my head. "Uh, can you repeat what you said?

Ruby groans. "Talk to as many people as possible, Kedar. Besides, we don't even know who Al-Watawat is, much less what she looks like. With our masks, maybe it'll be a bit easier. The masquerade will make it perfect for us to stalk and kill Al-Watawat as fast as we can."

I nod in agreement. Ruby has mentioned killing Al-Watawat with her mana before. With her blood manipulation, it'll be easy to orchestrate a heart attack. Partygoers will see it as a medical emergency— as long as there aren't any healing mages on the scene, nobody can save her.

"Damn. The party starts in two hours," I note, my fingers brushing the handle of my bone dagger. Maybe I can sneak this in beneath my suit. If things get dire, so to speak, then I'll be forced to use more... conventional means of assassinating Al-Watawat.

"Dragons, I hope this goes well. We don't need Opal going ratchet again," she sighs, rummaging through her cloak. "Dammit. Do you have any spare razqatars?"

"Upstairs. I have some hooked against my armor." Ruby has a couple of gadgets and smoke bombs on her utility belt—but no razqatars. Her ax is gently placed on the table, the blood stains on the edges of the blade reflecting off the candlelight on Garnett's desk. "Why do you ask?"

"You have your bone dagger," she points out, eyeing the weapon. "I need to sneak weapons in, too, ya know. It'll get ugly in that castle if I kill the wrong person with my magic."

"Once I get the razqatars, we should get ready."

She nods.

After a bath and a light shave, I stare at my reflection in the mirror. It's hard to believe that the man who stares back is me. *Under all my scars and cuts, what do I look like? Alive? Human?* Ruby has bought us clothes that match a dark red and black scheme. Apparently, she hasn't worn a dress in a while, and she isn't about to waste this opportunity. My long suit, which runs down to my toes, lies over my black undershirt and red tie. I clear my throat before reaching for the jewelry on the counter.

Throwing the sylvanite and metal chain over my head, I put a gold ring on my other pointer finger, since the other's gone. My muscles are more toned, my skin is clear and glowing. I wrap the leather eyepatch around my head. Throwing on my silver-lined cloak to mask the cold before opening the bathroom door, I see Ruby in her nightgown while leaning against a wall.

She scoffs. "You look... nice."

"I feel rich," I grit, my boots clicking against the wooden floorboards. "Never in a century would I ever think that I'd have expensive stuff like this on my body."

"Shut up, you." Ruby shakes her head and smiles. "Just wait for me."

She wisps past me, and I strut downstairs. Abubakr and Garnett take in my presence, their eyes scanning the rugged linings on my undershirt and the patterns on my tie.

"Gods, I wish I could go with you," Abubakr sighs, standing up to shake my hand. I roll my eyes. Clearly, they're overreacting.

"Well, I would let you, but maybe after some more training," I push back, and he chuckles. Garnett fixes my tie, squinting at the gemstones on my neck.

"By Basal, you look richer than all the nobles," he begins. "I should totally be your butler or something."

He shakes my hand aggressively, and I take his words with a grain of salt.

"You guys do too much. Dragons."

Abubakr widens his eyes at the sight behind me. Turning around, I catch a glimpse of Ruby, walking down the stairs with a certain radiance beaming around her.

I'll admit. She's beautiful.

Trying not to trip over her heels, her long braids are tied into a ponytail, fastened at the back of her head. The cocktail dress she wears matches the color of her deep, rosy eyes. Her black cloak covers her shoulders, rewarding her with a bit of insulation from the freeze.

Ruby doesn't smile when we lock eyes. Instead, she grumbles while trying to fix her dress's straps. "Kedar. We're almost late, for Dragon's sake. Let's go."

Abubakr sips his tea, grasping my shoulder. "Heal this city, would you?"

"We will, Abubakr. I swear— by the time we get back, Al-Watawat will be dead."

We walk outside, fixating ourselves on the freeze. It takes me a bit to realize Ruby has her arm clamping against my bicep as she breathes out a hot stream of smoke, making sure not to slip on the ice patches on the sidewalk. "Ugh. Now I just want to get this over with."

"I mean, you said you haven't worn a dress in a while—"

"This is definitely the damn reason why I haven't."

"Well, we bought all of this," I prod, as she huffs in extinguished agreement. "Might as well get our money's worth, right?"

That makes Ruby give up and resort to silence as we trek up. Ruby shivers against my arm, breathing heavily and muttering curses. In response, I take off my cloak.

"Don't." She rejects my jacket, putting her hand up to stop me. I shrug as we walk up the stairs to the castle.

With three spires, it interconnects to form a luxurious and gothic building. The snow colors its tops white, while the yellow and black flag of Crale hangs over its walls, constantly reminding us where we are— hell in disguise.

"Alright, hand me those throwing knives," she begins. I oblige, handing over a razqatar. My bone dagger is safely tucked under the sleeves of my suit, ready for future use. Ruby does the same, tucking the razqatar under the sleeve of her cocktail dress.

A stone wall wraps around the Draken Castle, while a metal gate hastily guards its entrance. *Shurtas* are at guard, their bows drawn and ready to be fired. In front of the moat are two guards, blocking the view of the hustling masquerade amid the castle courtyard and its halls.

"Sir. Madam. What is your business here?" one asks, towering over us.

"The Winter Masquerade is commencing. We have been ordered to kindly ask citizens to leave the premises, or else they are *punished...* accordingly."

Before Ruby opens her mouth to argue, I pull out the scrolls of paper in my back pocket. With a smirk, I hand it to him with confidence.

Earlier, Opal happily forged the masquerade tickets before we left. Opal's done things like this before, saying that Onyx calls her a "magister of disguise." As the guard reads our ticket, he scratches the side of his cheek through his mask.

The Governor usually writes his signature in the middle of the paper, and the names of the individuals invited to the masquerades are written under it. Opal explained how she used replication, a type of Darkic magic. The Governor's handwriting is everywhere— on Lelinian newspapers, historical documents, and most of all, his personal diary, a prime piece of Cralean literature. It was easy to copy it over.

After a few minutes of silence, the guard huffs, handing back our papers. His voice is grainy.

"Mr. Hussein and Mrs. Hussein? That's correct, yes?"

Sliding my bone dagger down my suit a little bit, I nod. "Yes, sir."

Ruby clenches on my arm tighter as the guard clears his throat from the frozen winds.

"Enjoy the masquerade. The masks are at the entrance, for your choosing."

He turns back, waving a signal to the *Shurtas* on the walls, before we hear the metal clanking of the gate. Crossing the moat, we see a small crowd of the rich bunching together outside, waiting their turn to get in.

As the line thins, two guards in front of the doorway to the ballroom give me and Ruby a nod. *They don't even know what we're about to do.*

Ruby gasps as we gaze at the giant, crystal chandelier in the middle of the ballroom, with pillars holding up the stone roof, leading to the chair where the Governor sits. Lanterns are at every table, covered with a white cloth. All of the rich wear masks of different colors: some red, some purple, some black. Unique designs are on each of them, sending an abundance of messages.

Conversations flood into my ears about money, the war, and food. Again, it feels too easy to get into the masquerade, just like when we broke into Al-Jukar's manor.

Maybe the only difficult part about this mission is how much money we've spent on these outfits.

Over the wooden tile flooring, a long red and golden carpet glows beneath us, reflecting off Ruby's nose ring. On the far left side of the room is an old elf. At his desk are rows of masks, while behind him are cloaks, jackets, and gloves.

Handing off our accessories to the servant, our eyes wander over the mask selection. "All of these look so... fancy."

"Dammit, you're right," Ruby replies, picking up one with little cuts of black and purple gemstones around the eye holes. Without her cloak, her armor, and her weapons, Ruby looks so different. Like some sort of Royal.

Or princess.

"Just grab one that matches with our outfits," she says, picking a black mask with a red outline, covering her brows to her cheeks. I do the same, grabbing one that only covers one half of my face, leaving the right side, already concealed by my eyepatch, exposed.

Fastening the string, I look through the eyehole, examining our surroundings. Our investigation has officially begun to find Al-Watawat. But as I try tapping my shoulder to ask Ruby what we should do first, I realize—

"Ruby, did you seriously come here to eat?" I ask, walking to where the food is. There's a buffet line of containers having the most exotic and extravagant food all over Haya, free to access. Seeing it pains me. Basalians and Craleans starve every day, yet the rich bathe in gluttony.

She gulps down a bite of her pastry. Vanilla flavoring this time, from the looks of it.

"I eat nothing but pastries and my soup. The soup is your favorite, right?"

Don't you dare remind me of that abomination. Before I can protest, she grabs me by the collar, pulling me down to eye level. "And call me *Yasmin,* for Basal's sake. We're undercover."

Rolling my eyes, I nod. Servants wearing white robes put food on the guests' plates with dishonest, fake smiles. It doesn't take me long to say, "You know, maybe we should try our luck with them."

Observing the Farik in front of us, who's given Ruby her "snack," I clear my throat to grasp their attention. Clearly, it seems like this dog needs rest. Their furry ears droop down, their tail wagging slowly while they tap their fingers together.

"Ahem, excuse me."

"Oh, uh, hello there," he begins, motioning to the cakes, cookies, breads, and sweet treats that surround him. Ruby's eyes sparkle with need— a step closer and all the food will be gone in seconds.

"Would you like something?"

I shake my head as he tilts his head in confusion. "No, actually. I was here to ask if you may have heard of the name Al-Watawat."

His expression melts. Fear radiates through his stare. He stutters.

"Sir. I... I can't speak about her. You know I can't."

Sympathy reeks through my mind. He's right. Even speaking about a Veil member can get anyone killed. Besides, eyes are watching. Anyone can be eavesdropping on us. Merging into the crowd, we leave the Farik speechless. His dog eyes are void of soul.

"Well, that was a mistake," Ruby whispers as we weave through the crowd to get as far away as possible. Looks like Ruby's not getting any pastries anymore.

"He'll die if he utters a word about Al-Watawat. Best to keep him safe."

We stop near one of the wooden pillars, where fewer people are. Better to separate ourselves from the rest of the crowd.

I murmur in her ear. "Ruby... we should split up, gather information, and meet back at this spot."

"Gather information?"

"Just... listen in. Someone's going to slip up and talk about Al-Watawat eventually."

She takes another bite of her pastry before sighing. "I'll see you later, *Sufyan*."

I wisp through the crowd, getting lost in a sea of masks. Hundreds of partygoers drink liquor and eat their meals, while some dance with their partners. I breathe out, trying to hone in on their conversations.

"Yeah, my wife's being such a hassle lately..."

"I miss my son. He died in that Basil war..."

"Have you tried the pasta yet, Rohaan? It's great..."

"Well, you gotta admit, she's a pretty one."

"I'll say, I'm a bit tipsy off of this fabulous wine they're serving."

"I hear the Order's making moves."

Widening my eyes, I scour the crowd, trying to look for the source. They're talking about Onyx. But as I scan the crowd, most brightly smiling at each other, none of them seem suspicious.

There you are. Two men in black and white suits are in the right corner, away from the party. One leans against a wall, the other sipping on wine. Wearing white opera masks with dark red lining, they look like the average rich merchants. But I won't get hasty. I have no idea if they're Veils... yet.

Grabbing a glass of mead from a waiter, I concentrate on my magic. *Maybe this'll work,* I whisper before drinking my liquor. Hopefully, my magic can heighten voices from one another. With all of this background noise, it's impossible to hear what they are saying. Leaning against a pillar behind them, I close my eyes as the veins on my wrists glow. *Let me hear you,* I urge.

The rest of the crowd becomes silent.

I breathe out in shock.

Only the two men's voices remain.

By the Dragon, it worked, I huff, smirking.

"The High One wants me to deliver this to you," I hear the first man say, the sound of ruffling paper tickling my ears. "It is of utmost importance. This must be in The Bat's hands as soon as possible."

The Bat, I repeat. The two men *are* Veils. Judah's the 'High One,' after all. Peering around the pillar, I notice daggers hidden in their suits. *But damn, I need that paper.*

Walking up to them without hesitation, I notice the first man stuffing the paper in his pocket. Letting my mana subside,

332

I hear the sounds of the masquerade again. The music, the talks, the whispers. It hits me in an instant— I'm lucky enough to not trip over my feet. Pulling my sleeves further down, I hide the glow of mana in my wrists.

With the bone dagger in my left sleeve, I raise my glass of wine with the other arm to offer a kindhearted toast. "Hello, gentlemen. Fine evening, isn't it?"

Dragons, I have no idea how "royal" etiquette works.

The second man's eyes narrow, his eyes trailing up and down my outfit.

"Well, hello there, sir. How much have you had to drink, dare I say?"

What game is he playing at? "Not much, actually," I awkwardly chuckle, taking another sip. "So, where are you guys from?"

"My friend and I are from Gardon," the first man answers. Blinking, I see the second reach into his suit for something. *They're onto me, aren't they?* "What country do you hail from...?"

"Jura," I finish for him. "My name is Sufyan."

Both of them are annoyed. Pissed off is how Ruby puts it.

"Well, Mr. *Sufyan,* we're in the middle of something here. It would be best if you moved along."

The second man's dagger reflects off my ring. As much as I want to attack them, it's not wise in this crowd of unsuspecting people. *It won't be the best royal "etiquette,"* I mutter.

I offer a smile of defeat. That paper is two feet away. But the more I look into those Veil's eyes, the more I think of those Dracotheists. Corpses on the side of Al-Jukar's manor.

"Uhm, what are you...," the first man trails off, his eyes seeing the veins protruding from my wrists. *No. No.*

Take off your eyepatch, Kedar, my mind echoes.

You are concealing the most powerful magic on Haya. It wouldn't hurt to use it on these maggots.

Before I can protest, they draw their daggers, glaring at me through their masks with carnage. They're bluffing. Around all of these people?

I can imagine the headlines: *Juran royal found dead at the Governor's masquerade.*

There's a figure in the crowd. Is it me? No, no. That's—

Take off your eyepatch. Do I need to repeat myself? Munir's glaring with his demonic eyes. He wears the same clothes on the day that I killed him in my spiritual plane. A holy white robe.

He's supposed to be dead, I killed him! What the hell is he doing?

Kedar, he begins. *Trust me. Your demonic magic has potential that you are too scared to unlock.*

The Veils step forward as Munir wisps away into the air. Gone in less than a second. Stepping back, I curse my right eye surges with pain.

For the DRAGON'S SAKE!

I rip off my eyepatch as my demon eye involuntarily widens.

A horrible sting vibrates through my bones as I dart my eyes to the first man, then to the second. Their expressions turn blank before they put away their daggers. *What? What the hell did I just do?*

One takes the paper out of their pockets as red and black spots invade my vision, rendering me blind. He walks up to me, offering me the paper. "I believe you need this?"

Blood runs down my cheek. Wiping it off before anyone can see the madness, I grab the paper, putting my eyepatch on.

Munir, what did you do? I wonder aloud. The magic that I've drained from Munir— it's bizarre and unexplainable. I've

334

done little to no experimentation with my magic, mostly because I have no idea how to make my veins glow at will. But whenever my carnal emotions boil over, my mana flows.

Wiping my sweat, I stumble into the crowd, clutching the paper tightly. Partygoers give me disgusted looks as I pass by. *Gods. I must look drunk to them.*

I keep stumbling through, looking for Ruby. Eventually, I see her standing under the chandelier, her arms crossed. She blinks as she notices my drained demeanor, speed-walking towards me.

"What the— Sufyan, are you okay?" Ruby says in a hushed whisper as I huff and wheeze, holding on to my knees for support. Mustering the strength to glance up, I sigh.

"I'm fine," I cough, feeling her fingers press against the blood smeared on my cheek.

Scratching the scar on her neck, she responds by offering a look of worry.

"You're not fine. There's blood on your cheek, dummy."

"Ugh. Ignore that," I wince, fastening my eyepatch before offering the note.

Her eyes widen.

"Read this with me, will you?"

Sufyan and Yasmin Hussein.
Both lovers until death.
1250-1276

\-   A gravestone in Jura.

TWENTY-TWO

"Dearest Bat,

I appreciate your concerns. As it seems, my brother has infiltrated our operations in Lelina. While I do want to stall for a little bit longer, I will allow you to commence the utter cleansing. Instead of publicly executing our pacifist, Dracotheistic supporting governor at the winter masquerade, kill every single partygoer. I have advised your minions to store thousands of crates of bombs under the Draken Castle. When it strikes midnight, they will ignite its fumes, so escape accordingly. The Clover has sent me letters as well, expressing his distaste towards The Disturbed. My underling, Shay, the emperor of Crale, has agreed with our tactic. Not only does it send a warning to the Lelinians to reject the support of Dracotheism taking over the provincial government, but it will also kill these parasites that have undoubtedly come to assassinate you during this party.

With luck, The High One."

Bombs? I repeat. Judah's made one fatal mistake: Al-Watawat doesn't know this. We have the paper, for the Dragon's sake. The only thing we have to worry about is killing Al-Watawat before she can escape.

"We only have thirty minutes left," Ruby curses. With crowds of the Cralean rich surrounding us, there's not enough time to convince everyone to get out. It's impossible.

"Gods. We don't have a choice." I rub my chin, stroking my goatee.

"Maybe we can save everyone. But letting Al-Watawat get away…"

"Do you think that these people—" She motions to the people around us— "Are worth saving?"

The partygoers have innocent looks under their masks. They wear dresses and suits of the most expensive material—things peasants don't dare to dream about having. Now that I think of it, they probably have hundreds of slaves. *But they're still people,* my mind says.

The right to live is lost if you're drowning in a sea of sins, I push back.

"No, you're right. We shouldn't let Al-Watawat get away." Ruby nods in agreement, her eyes darting to the golden throne at the back of the ballroom. The old governor, Jakub Schinzel, chats with a woman— an elf wearing a black mask.

Ruby walks up the red and gold carpet, turning back to me and hissing, "If Al-Watawat's original plan was to execute the governor, then she's gotta be up there."

Weaving through a sea of dancing and mingling people, we find ourselves standing on the podium where the governor sits. Being protected by two *Shurta* guards, Ruby signals me by putting a pointer finger to her lips. The three women in front of him are trying to speak to the old man at the same time, rendering it futile to distinguish one word from another.

Jakub Schinzel is a withering human man. Gray hair, damning wrinkles— he has it all. Looks like he can barely even move out of his chair. He reminds me of Onyx, and it makes me sigh. *Hope that old dog's doing alright.*

Gulping, I step up fearlessly, eyeing the embroidery of the Cralean flag on the shoulder of his red and black robe. Pushing by the elf, I notice the eyes under her mask flash with a familiar blood red.

It's her, isn't it? I curse, her demonic pupils gleaming into my soul. Al-Watawat is here, on this podium, behind me. Glancing at one of the grandfather clocks against the wooden pillars, I quickly interpret the time: 11:42 PM.

Eighteen minutes, I curse again. Before I can utter a word to the governor, the two *Shurta* guards block my path while Ruby shoots daggers of death. Her brows furrow, and she grits her teeth.

"Just trust me on this," I whisper as she pushes past Al-Watawat and stands next to me. Rolling her eyes under her mask, Ruby and I turn back to the guards, who draw their short swords, leaving inches away from my throat.

The other guard clears his throat. "What business do you two have speaking with the governor?"

I slide the bone dagger up the sleeve of my suit a bit more.

"My wife and I are here to introduce ourselves. We've never been invited to the governor's masquerades before, so we felt it was necessary to personally thank him."

I'm inches away from a man who's in support of ending this horrible war— and these damn *Shurta* decide to block my way? We have to protect him from the Veil's corrupting this city. If we can kill Al-Watawat and save the governor, we'll be able to wipe out the support for the Cralean genocide by sixty-six percent.

With two key Veil members gone, who's going to support killing a bunch of Dracotheists?

The guard squints, removing his blade and tucking it into his sheath, while the other does the same. "Very well. But do it hastily." He motions to Al-Watawat. *He's in on this, isn't he?*

"The governor has more important matters to return to."

The mask almost perfectly hides her demonic eyes. A chill goes down my spine. *What the hell can she do with her demon magic?* I urge as I eye her puffy dress.

She seems oblivious, like she doesn't realize that we have already figured out her identity. If anything, she's confident. Like the job to kill the governor is already done.

Stepping in front of the governor, Ruby and I bow, offering our respects.

He nods. "Well, hello there, fellow guests."

"Hello, sir," I stammer, offering a handshake. *We have to kill Al-Watawat AND save him.* It'll be a heinous task, but might as well try it for Basal's sake. "It's my wife and I's first time being invited to one of your masquerades. We are truly and deeply grateful."

"Well, thank you as well. My vision in the future is to eventually let all people come to my masquerades— Cralean, Basalian, Dracotheist, or Juran. I'm afraid that it doesn't matter. What matters is coming together just like this, enjoying one another's company with liquor, food, and music," he hums, motioning to the piano player on the far right side of the ballroom.

Seems like Opal and Garnett aren't wrong after all. The governor isn't like the others— he seeks equality while trying to create a place of comfort for all Cralean residents. He, as an emperor, will rid the nation of its corruption and censorship. The cycle of authoritarianism will cede.

Giving the governor a hearty farewell, Ruby and I recollect ourselves as we step off the podium and stand amid the crowd. We have ten minutes to figure out a way to get the governor out of this castle while killing Al-Watawat.

I rub my fingers together. "How should we go about this, Ruby?"

"You're probably thinking what I'm thinking, right?" she asks, as I nod. "Save the governor. Kill Al-Watawat. And finally, escape."

"You think you can convince that old man?"

"I have an idea. I'll use my magic," she replies with a smirk.

I roll my eyes. "How the hell is that going to work?"

"It's simple," Ruby begins as a blue aura begins to form at her fingertips, showcasing her healing magic. "I'll lower the governor's heart rate— rendering him unconscious. While you're distracting Al-Watawat and killing the guards, I'll haul him to safety in the middle of the chaos."

I groan in agony, taking out my dagger. No point in hiding it anymore.

"Let's just get this over with."

Dashing to Al-Watawat with vengeance, I'm nearly stopped by guards, but no matter. In an instant, they're cut down, blood boiling at their slit throats. Ruby's concentrating on putting the governor to sleep. The people exclaim in horror, not noticing what Ruby's doing. Al-Watawat and I lock eyes, and I charge, stabbing her in the neck, ripping out her tendons.

Four *Shurta* guards tackle me to the ground, kicking the blade out of my grasp. Muttering curses, I see Al-Watawat bleed out on the floor, blood oozing out of her lips. *By the Dragons. I've done it—*

"Bastard," one of the guards says, pinning me down as sweat rolls down their cheek. I kick him off, only to be pulled back to the ground. Realizing I'm unarmed, the guards point their swords at me to threaten to slice into every one of my organs.

Gulping, I spit blood, realizing that the governor's no longer on his throne.

Great. Ruby should be out by now.

I cough as someone plants their heel into my stomach, sending shockwaves.

"The High One was right," Al-Watawat yawns, taking off her black mask. Her demonic eyes stare into my soul with no mercy. Her blonde hair flows like water, nearly touching the tip of my cheeks.

She leans forward, a smile forming on her face. "Cute. You thought you killed me?"

"What? No, you're supposed to be dead," I stammer, glancing at the corpse inches away from me. But it begins to fade into black ooze, seeping through the cracks of the floor and only leaving my dagger behind.

"It's called shadow magic. A demonic magic that we Veils use." She takes one of the bystander's glasses of wine and sips on it, gulping it down. The crowd looks at me with horror, hate, and confusion. *What the hell's going on?* That's what their faces tell me.

Shadow magic..., I trail off. She must've used that to clone herself to make a decoy.

Which means they knew that we were coming.

Glancing at the clock, I curse. *Two more minutes.* The crowd clamors, trying to get a gander at the commotion. Al-Watawat digs her heel deeper into my abdomen.

"Alright, everyone! Calm down!"

They go silent.

"This disgusting, heinous rat tried to kill me. These Basils will do anything for their grubby little hands to grasp at our gracious empire, isn't that right?"

Some chuckle, while some even clap. It doesn't even matter to me. We'll all be dead in a matter of seconds anyway.

"Now, what should I do with you?" Al-Watawat whispers, chuckling to herself. Before the guards stab me to death, Al-Watawat suddenly begins to choke, stumbling into the crowd. The guards ignore me, running past her as I crawl to grab my dagger.

Shoving and pushing through the crowd, I hear the *Shurta* shout after me over the gags and retches from Al-Watawat. *I'm not even going to question what just happened,* I think, as I sprint to the exit.

Grabbing my coat and throwing my mask to the floor, a squadron chases me down, as the archers on top of the walls draw their bows.

For the Dragon's sake. Why can't I just get a normal damn day—

An explosion rings through my ears as the shockwaves thrust me out of the gate. Rolling and slamming my body on the stone road, I screech in pain as my shoulder pops.

Turning back, I see the castle in flames, the dynamite already taking effect. The once-strong spires crumble to dust as guards hustle down the walls, dashing into the ruins to help the people inside. It's like the fire at Al-Jukar's manor, but much worse. The guards chasing me even stopped their efforts, running into the flames.

Where the hell is Ruby?! I curse, my eyes darting everywhere.

She has to be safe somewhere, right?

"Kedar! Up here!" a familiar voice shouts. Standing up, I glance at one of the buildings in front of the castle. On the rooftop is Ruby, her legs dangling off the ledge. Gritting my teeth, I use my other arm to climb the side of it.

"Ruby, where the hell is the Governor?" I ask as I grab her offering hand. She gives me a defeated look.

"It was either you or him. I chose you," Ruby replies as I sit next to her.

Frustration vibrates through me, mostly from the fact that my shoulder's dislocated, and I'm covered in scratches and my stomach's in pain from Al-Watawat's heel. "Ruby, you're joking, right?"

She shakes her head, her fingertips omitting a blue aura. My emotions soothe as she gets to work.

"I left him there, sprawled out on the floor. Once I saw you almost getting yourself killed, I had to step in. Save you like I always do."

"Ruby, I—"

She shushes. "Stop. Just let me put you back together again."

I look at the hellfire in front of me. Screams vibrate through the city as a crowd forms around the moat, all peering at the carnage inside. Some survivors even make their way out, covered in soot and burns. I wince as my shoulder clicks back in place. She really does put me back together.

Without her, I'd be a puzzle without its missing piece.

"There. Dragons, for some reason, this never gets old," she admits.

"What?" I say, turning to look at her.

"Healing *you*."

My eyes trail the scar on her neck, and this time she notices, taking my arm and letting my fingers rest on it. It takes me a while to notice her stare. She blinks.

"Why do you always give me that look?"

344

I fumble over my words, removing my fingers from her neck. "What look?"

"It's like I'm different from everyone else. Like I'm special to you," she smirks. Ruby's not wrong. Not a glint of fear or nervousness is in her eyes— she knows my answer.

"You are." Without Ruby, I'll be off the rails.

I don't know why, but I feel normal with her.

I… matter.

Why am I noticing things about her all of a sudden? Her rosy scent, the little nick under her right eye, the nose piercing which sparkles off the ember flames.

We lock eyes. We can't stop staring.

We can't live without each other, can we?

Ruby breathes heavily, putting her hand against my chest as I lean in. I stop, trying to interpret whether or not she's hesitating. Ruby gulps as sweat trails down my forehead.

My lips brush hers, and she kisses me back, her confidence beating mine. Her grip on me tightens as I lean deeper, cupping her face.

No, stop. I pull away, shaking my head. "I'm just not—"

Grabbing my collar, she forces another kiss, and this time I don't pull away. Her hand trails up my neck as she pecks my cheeks like she's claiming me. A smile radiates through her expression as she backs off, leaving one more kiss on my lips.

"If I wanted you to stop… I would've said something."

I have no words, heat blemishing the surface of my skin as she smears her thumb against a scratch on my cheek, healing it in an instant with her magic.

"There, that's a lot better." She dusts off her hands, admiring her handiwork. Her face contorts.

"Kedar, say something. You're frozen."

"I'm sorry—"

"Stop apologizing."

"Thanks for healing me."

Dragons. What's wrong with me?

She smiles again. "Don't even."

Ruby grabs my wrist, examining my non-existent pointer finger on my right hand. She sighs. The screams of agony and terror from bystanders watching the castle burn down are almost ironic.

They're stealing our moment.

"Kedar, you've been quiet. Too quiet. Did I do something wrong?"

"No," I immediately interject. "I'm just not used to… this."

"Me neither… but now that I've kissed you…"

Her eyes flutter, her fingers trailing up my arm.

She goes up to my neck again, but this time she resists.

I blink, shivering from the cold as she gets up from the ledge. "We should get back to Opal and Garnett. They're probably waiting for us, aren't they?"

"Yeah, we should," I reply, my heart rate now normal.

She looks back.

"I'm in love with you, Kedar. I hope you know that."

The crackling sounds of the fire below can't replicate the burning feeling in my chest.

"I do. I love you, Laila."

Opal isn't impressed.

"Kedar, Ruby, what the hell were you two thinking?"

Garnett winces at his mother's reaction, while Abubakr gives us a sorry look.

It takes us a bit to walk back to the theorum, and it's in complete silence. I've just… run out of words to say. The clock's already two past midnight.

It clearly has an effect on my eyes, and I can barely keep my lids open. I don't even have a chance to explain to Opal how it's *Judah's* plan to blow up the castle. Nevertheless, I'm getting yelled at by a goblin in the dead of night.

Comedic.

"Opal, we didn't have a choice—" Ruby starts, Opal quick to halt her.

"The castle is in flames. The people have already begun to riot and protest on the streets." She scowls, but takes a deep breath, shaking her head. "But the most important thing is — is Al-Watawat dead?"

Nodding, I jump in. "She died with the partygoers in the explosions. I'm sure of it."

There's no way she got out alive. Maybe in bits and pieces.

With a hint of anger on Opal's expression, she rubs her fingers together to generate warmth. If what's happened to Al-Jukar is an "accident," Al-Watawat is a tragedy. We're surely on the Veil's sights by now. All the more reason to stay vigilant.

"With Al-Watawat dead, two-thirds of the Veil influence has been erased from this city. In fact, there's already a smaller number of Dracotheists being executed, the number dropping from around fifty each day to around twenty-five. It doesn't sound like much, but it's progress."

The look that Opal gives makes me think that Ruby isn't even in on our plans. Ruby notices my blaming stare, and she coughs, hiding her smile.

"Trust me, Opal. Al-Barsim will be killed as quietly as possible. I can assure you that."

"If you're so excited to talk about Al-Barsim, let's start with the facts, shall we?"

All of us in the room anticipate the contents of the notes that Opal looks through on her desk.

Everyone except me. I keep staring glances at... her.

"The Clover is about as mysterious as The Bat," Opal begins, Ruby squinting. "What I do know about him is that he's the puppetmaster behind the *Shurta*. It's known that the *Shurta* operates a general commander who holds power over all of the city districts. The Clover controls the commander, essentially making him a puppet for all of his heinous crimes. Every hate crime against the Dracotheists seems to only lead back to him."

Widening my eyes, I scoff. "Sounds like he hides behind his guards like Al-Jukar. This should be easy, eh?"

Opal shoves the papers back into her drawer, responding by shaking her head. "Don't be so hasty. Never underestimate the Veils. Who knows what type of demented tricks they have up their sleeves?"

Opal dismisses us minutes later, muttering about drinking coffee and getting some sleep. She's right— the Veils have surprises, like the bombs at Draken Castle, and Al-Jukar's sadistic obsessions. It's important to think about one small mistake, and I might kill myself... or Ruby. Abubakr and Garnett split into their rooms, closing their doors with a sigh.

As Abubakr mutters a goodnight and promptly locks his room, I gulp. Al-Barsim can be the strongest warrior in all of Haya, or the most harmless, feasible man.

Opening the door to our room, Ruby's arm brushes against mine. I step inside, giving her a look once I lock it. She's still in her dress— her skin glowing under the soft shine of the candle on our nightstand.

"Ruby, what do you want?"

Her hand slides up my chest as I try to blink away my blush.

She smirks, looking up at me. "Hm. I don't know, Kedar. What do *you* want?"

Something feral, mindless ignites in my mind. I don't have to hide from her anymore. She's breaking my walls down every second. But I don't mind. I like her efforts.

My heart's taking over my mind— I can't even control myself. I must be so vulnerable to her. So new.

I kiss the scar on her neck, making her hum in satisfaction as the world around us begins to fade. She invites my touch as I grip her waist, inciting a gasp from her. "Someone's confident."

That makes me smile. She presses her thumb on my jawline, and I flutter, returning the favor by kissing her bottom lip.

We're alone.

Truly alone.

There's no more burning castle. No more shouts and screams of people suffering.

No more Veils, no more war, no more Judah.

It's just us.

Headlines: 274 Royals Dead after the bombing of the Draken Castle.

At around 12 midnight, there was an explosion rocking the middle districts of the city. Citizens wandered out of their homes to find the Governor's castle set ablaze and collapsed in pieces. Many found their loved ones in rubble dead. Benson Carter, a Farik who witnessed the whole ordeal, called the scene "horrific" and "unholy." The *Shurta* are still investigating the motive for the tragedy. On the other hand, Jakub Schinzel, the governor, was found in pieces, his head the only thing remaining from his legacy.

- Torn piece of the *Lelina Times* report which was written on the 287th day of the 1438th year.

TWENTY-THREE

T he Governor's corpse has been found dead amongst the two

hundred other bodies littering the ruins of Draken Castle. It's been a week, and the city has reached a boiling point. Many riot against the brutality of the *Shurta's* punishments, rallying for a more stable political figure to be put in place.

The whole town's in shambles now. Ruby should've left me to die there, but she hasn't. Now Lelina's streets are littered with violence at every corner, the guards trying to calm the citizens down with promises of peace. *Lies.*

We've resisted going outside the inn for three days, enjoying the safe comfort. It's a little bit boring, I'll admit— but things have been better. Ruby and I have been different since that night.

We don't have to hide from each other anymore. She's about as comfortable with me as I'm comfortable with her. It's relieving... but the feelings I have towards her are so alien. Either way, I enjoy her company. Having someone I know can understand is more refreshing than venting it out with battle after battle.

Ruby and I play a board game in the lobby called Huyin. Huyin is a game with eight columns, eight rows, checkered in black and white. Rubbing the black bead, I sigh.

Each bead moves vertically— moving it horizontally or diagonally is against the rules. To move the beads, you'll roll a die. For instance, if I roll a six, my head will pass Ruby's. If that happens, Ruby's bead gets eliminated, pronouncing me as winner.

Taking the die in my palm, I give it a good shake. My eyes widen with confidence as I toss it on the table. As it twists and turns in different directions, I grin menacingly once it lands on the number I need— six.

Ruby exclaims, digging her hands into her head in horror. "What? No, you've got to be kidding me, goddamnit!"

This marks the third time I've beaten her. In a row. With a smirk, I skip the bead six spaces, passing hers and winning the game.

"Sure, you don't want to throw in the towel?" I offer. She pouts, crossing her arms. Ruby isn't the best at Huyin... but that doesn't mean I'm putting on kiddie gloves.

Ruby suppresses herself from giving me an answer, tucking a braid behind her ear before picking up the beads again. She puts the eight white beads in the last row of the board to start another game. Her tone darkens. "I'm resilient. Don't think I'm giving up after just *three* times."

I put my beads back into place, smiling and shaking my head.

"Don't complain when I beat you again."

She rolls her eyes, grabbing the die before tossing it to the surface of the table.

Before Ruby and I can peek at the results, Garnett's boots thump against the wooden stairs as he sprints at us, sweat running down his forehead. A look of horror is on his face, like he sees a devil in front of him.

"For Basal's sake! Come quick! It's my mother—something's wrong with her!" he pleads, waving his hands around like a mad man. Abubakr— sipping tea and reading a book next to us— shoots from his seat, replicating our movements. We climb up the stairs and into the secret entrance with Garnett.

Abubakr gulps as we run down the hallway leading to her office. "Garnett, what happened?"

"I don't know, goddammit, I don't know!" Garnett huffs, blinking away tears. Abubakr is about as distressed as his mentor. "She started to shake... and then she collapsed on the floor! I can't do anything! I don't even have magic... I'd be useless if I were to help my mother."

Opening the door, we see Opal sprawled out on the stone floor. Fountains of blood flow down her chin as she coughs, blinking her eyes to stay awake. Garnett yelps, muttering curses as he caresses her cheek. Abubakr holds up his fingers to see each one shaking in fear as he can stand and watch. Ruby kneels, concentrating on bringing her magic to her fingertips.

"Opal!" grits Ruby, hovering her hands above Opal's stomach. "Don't give up on us, dammit!"

Garnett's on the verge of sobbing. *He's just a kid,* I think, as my spine tingles with horror. *He shouldn't be seeing this.* Opal convulses violently, her arms and legs jerking in every direction.

As I help Garnett hold Opal down, Ruby bites her tongue, making her blue aura shine brighter. Even though Ruby keeps her efforts, it doesn't have a single effect on Opal. Nothing's working.

Opal's screams and Ruby's muttering of curses come to a halt as the room deafens.

I hold my fingers up to my ears. *What the hell is going on?*

A horrid ring begins to vibrate as I drop to my knees. Ripping off my eyepatch, a flow of blood drips to the ground as red dots litter my vision.

Munir.

Munir.

MUNIR!

No. Munir's dead. *I saw him sink into the black sand.*

Drops of sweat form on my forehcad. I'm hallucinating, aren't I?

It'll all go away. I just have to... wait.

A crack interrupts my inner monologue as I glance at Abubakr. His neck twists three hundred sixty degrees, his mouth agape in a devilish expression. The pupils in his eyes turn blood red, and I fumble for my razqatar, stepping back.

"Relax."

The voice that comes out of Abubakr's mouth replicates his, but there's this undertone of darkness. It reminds me of how that Veil's demonic counterpart sounded at Al-Jukar's mansion— heartless, void of emotion.

Abubakr— no, not Abubakr. *Munir* stares at my blade, licking his lips in anticipation.

"Well, that's a beautifully crafted sword if I've ever seen one."

"What the *hell* do you think you're doing?" I curse, as fangs form in his smile. Abubakr's limbs bend and move in horrible directions.

Descending to the stone brick floor on all fours, Munir twists Abubakr's body up, his neck slanting clockwise. My spine rattles and my breathing heaves. Just when I think everything is going well, he has to show up.

Goddamn bastard.

"Do I not have a right to visit the man who beat me in battle?" he jokes, stifling a laugh.

Looking at my absent pointer finger, I grit my teeth and ball my hand into a fist. "You're supposed to be dead. I killed you, Munir. Why the hell are you even here?"

"Don't be so afraid, Kedar. You dissolved me into fragments. Pieces. My magic is nearly gone, and I barely have the power to manifest myself to replicate your appearance."

He chuckles, smirking wildly. **"And so, I've decided to possess your friend here. No harm is being done to him; I'm simply using him to speak to you."**

Munir is the amalgamation of the cursed, violent side of me. But we're not the same person. I've done everything to forget him, and lost my finger in the process— but yet, he lives.

"Tell me what you want, Munir. I don't need any of your lies."

"Well, to answer that question," he begins, Abubakr's hand breaking into different directions to point a finger at Opal.

"You must be wondering what's going on with your friend here."

Standing in silence, Munir uses Abubakr's body to crawl to Opal. *Might as well hear him out if it means saving her.* Ruby and Garnett are frozen in time, forbidden to move. Munir exhales, his tongue out, stretching from Abubakr's gaping mouth.

355

The snake-like tongue makes my stomach toss and turn as he swirls it around Opal's neck. A horrid smell hits my nose as I cover my mouth to hide my gag. A dark red aura begins to emanate around his long tongue. He's... examining her.

Before I can ask a question, Munir pulls back with a dragging sigh. I fumble over my words as the back of Abubakr's head starts to morph.

My eyes, mouth, and nose are outstretched from his figure, as I clench my teeth.

God. Help me.

Munir's lips curl into a smile. **"Give me a moment, if you will."**

More blood drips down my cheek from my eyelids. "Munir, at least let me ask you what you've done to my eyes."

Abubakr's front face tightens its grip on Opal while Munir's expression softens lightly. His zany tone only boils the anger inside of me more. **"I don't think I can explain it to someone as slow and incomprehensible as you."**

He begins to cackle, but abruptly stops when I throw the razqatar just inches away from his nose as it stabs the stone wall. Chuckling awkwardly, he clears his throat.

"Those red and black eyes of yours are present in every individual who possesses demonic magic. When you conjure a demon's power, the side effect is a light wave of pain, usually leading to your eye bleeding... slightly."

Munir's eyes avert to the constant flow of blood running down my cheek.

"Because you've drained all of the mana from my being... your body is completely subjected to all side effects of demonic magic.

356

You transferred all of your magic to yourself. Thus, the pain you feel when using demonic magic will be concentrated in your right eye. I assume you'll be temporarily blinded for a few minutes after using your abilities."

Without Munir, my body is vulnerable. But if I have Munir, my body won't be its own anymore. I won't have control over what I do. Munir will have that control. Even though I want to deny it, Munir's right. This magic… It's a curse. "What the hell's going to happen to me whenever I use your magic, then?"

"The more you push yourself with this magic, the more likely you are to die."

I can't believe it— everything that I've done, killing Munir, draining his magic, is it all for nothing? If he's saying the truth, demonic magic doesn't drain your stamina like regular magic. It *kills* you.

This is a damn paradox.

"But, enough with the chit-chat." Munir begins to morph Abubakr back into his human state, cracking his joints back in place, the face at the back of his head fading into his skin. Only his red eyes indicate his presence. His voice has gone back to Abubakr's, the low, demonic undertone still there.

"It seems like Opal's been attacked using demon magic."

Sighing, I wipe the blood off my cheek. *Ruby's gone through too much. She can't know that I will inevitably die.* "Who did this to her? Do you know?"

He shakes his head. "I don't," he begins, narrowing Abubakr's eyes. "But your power, *my power,* can expel the magic from Opal's body."

Munir and I lock eyes, standing in silence. There isn't a word that I can come up with to give him a response. But it looks like he's telling the truth. I might as well do as he says. But there's another thing I'm wondering—

"Ah. The demons. You must wonder how we operate, yes?" Munir inquires, as I nod.

This is entertaining to him— every second his smirk widens more and more as he notices my confusion.

"When demons are born, they are tethered to a hive mind."

My eyes narrow.

"The man—no, not a man—devil behind this is named Malik Al-Shayteen. King of the Demons. The day you *killed me,* let's call it, officially detached me from the hive mind."

A hive mind. Whoever this Malik person is, they're the true puppetmaster of all demonic magic. Judah, Al-Barsim, Al-Jukar, it doesn't matter. This man is a god. But I've never heard that name before.

"Us, the demons, are a curse to mankind. Born from the Hayan anger and rage, we are the children of Satan. Malik," Munir explains, his voice dimming. "Before everything happened between us, I saw Malik as this false prophet to all of Haya. He's someone that shouldn't be given power."

I recoil as he tries to console me by patting my shoulder. "Kedar, this is another reason I tried to take over your body. We should've worked *together.* To bring down Malik. Save the world."

"How the hell am I supposed to know that I can trust you?" I question. "This Malik guy doesn't sound real, for Basal's sake!"

"Listen to me!" he hushes, the grip on my shoulder tightening. Munir controlling Abubakr's body only makes me worry for the kid. Those dark red eyes staring at me remind me that who I'm talking to is myself.

'It exists, goddamnit! Why the hell would I lie?"

"Prove it."

358

He scoffs, pressing Abubakr's fingertips together, closing his eyes.

"My magic is limited, but I'll prove it to you."

A dark red, spherical aura appears in front of Abubakr's face, crackling with black lightning. It vibrates my eardrums with hellish voices.

"Vessel gate vessel gate vessel gate—

Blood is the essence of life so don't hesitate to drink it and see its wonders and feel its wonders and revel in its magic and kill everyone around you everyone around you is useless send them to their deaths there is no point of them living—

Cower in the face of death—

My GOD My GOD PRAISE THE WORLD ANEW—

Rejoice, rejoice, rejoice, Malik, Malik, Malik, our God our Savior—"

As I stumble to the floor, Munir blinks Abubakr's eyes open, releasing the connection to the demonic hive mind.

So it's true. By Basal, he's telling the truth, I grunt, wiping the sweat off my forehead.

"W-What the hell! What the hell was that?!"

Even though I'm a bit hesitant, I let Munir pull me up as he offers Abubakr's hand.

"It's the hive mind. Voices of the demons lurking within men and women intertwining and linking, their thoughts transparent."

"No," I start. "What are they talking about? Vessel? Gate?"

Munir's expression darkens, a certain loom hovering over his face. "After I split into thousands of pieces, I put myself into a shell of my former being. It allowed me to tether to the hive mind again."

Each word Munir says only enhances my fear even more. Not that he's still alive— no, that doesn't bother me much anymore— but because of this demon he describes.

Malik.

"They are rejoicing," Munir elaborates, as if the scenes are flashing before his demonic eyes.

"They have found a vessel to break the seal."

"What seal?" The only seals familiar to me are ones that mages used to compress something, or… hold a beast against its will.

"As of right now, Malik doesn't have a physical form. Like me. Controlling your friend's body." He resists a laugh as he studies my annoyed frown. "This is where Judah comes in."

It's all making sense. The Veils… There's plenty I've met with demonic magic. They all worship and serve Judah. But that's not what Judah wants. He wants to—

"Break the seal on Malik." Munir hangs Abubakr's head in grief.

"Malik's true form has been sealed for 1438 years, in a place that even I don't know. The Veils plan to break the seal with the offering of a vessel. The more demonic magic the vessel possesses, the more control Malik has over the vessel. It's what Judah calls his prophecy, that one day, he'll find someone with the darkest demonic magic, able to conjure and completely handle Malik's soul. After that happens, the seal will break. Nothing will be able to stop Malik's horrific fury."

To my surprise, his voice breaks in fear. "Save Omar, for Basal's sake. They are putting him on Malik's altar next. And I fear that breaking the seal will be… a success."

Black ooze begins to pour out of Abubakr's eyes. The hairs on my neck tingle as Munir's fragment slides out of Abubakr's body. He plops to the floor with a splat as I nearly puke. I might be a soldier, familiar with the gore of war, but when it comes to demons, monsters, and ghouls, I can't stand it.

"Promise me. Promiseeeeeeee meeeeee thisssssssss…," he hisses. I take a knee, trying to resist the urge to throw up. Now that I've gotten to speak to Munir, without my body or sanity on the line, he seems genuine. His eyes are… honest.

He might be the manifestation of all of my dark desires, thoughts, and actions, but maybe he's inherited the love for my brother, too.

"I'mm aboutttttt to fadeee," he gurgles, the black blob of himself evaporating into red wisps.

"Youu haveeeee tooo saveee Omarr. Promiseeee meeeeee.

"For the sake of Basal, I promise. I'll save Omar."

The world resumes.

It's no longer me and him.

Abubakr isn't affected in the slightest, thankfully. Munir's telling the truth after all.

Garnett's cries contrast with Ruby's harmonic healing magic rippling through the air. Munir's voice whispers in my ear. *Save Opal with your magic.*

Hustling to the three of them, I grasp Ruby's shoulder. "Let me try something with my magic."

"What are you doing?" Garnett isn't convinced. "Ruby's mana is working! We just have to let her do her thing!"

Ruby glances at me, her forehead tarnished with sweat. Exerting mana for a long time exhausts everyone, even Onyx.

Her heavy eyes and trembling fingers only prove it. "Kedar, can I trust you?"

I nod.

Ruby collapses after stepping back, Abubakr holding her by the shoulders. She huffs and puffs, letting her blue aura waver. Even though Garnett's unhinged look doubts me, he backs away from his mother, allowing me to use my magic.

Ripping off my eyepatch, I align my eye contact with hers, an exasperating pain seeping through my bones. I hold Opal down, stopping her flailing movements as my blood seeps through the stone floor. *Munir was right. God, this is painful.*

Cupping my hand gently around her throat, Ruby and Garnett watch in shock. I replicate Munir's movements, but the only difference is that I'm not using my tongue.

Opal's movements relax as her body adjusts to my mana. Wave after wave of demonic magic absorbs into my very being, *my soul*. This must be the reason behind her seizures. The heartless, emotionless magic. She's not used to it. *Which means this magic isn't even hers.*

The essence fills my veins, and I wipe the blood off my cheek. Gritting my teeth, I keep my hand still.

I horrid flash of light beams around Opal's neck as I jump back. Thankfully, Opal's head is still attached to her body. It leaves her coughing, holding her stomach as she blinks away her agony.

Garnett swoops in, helping his mother to her feet. As I heave a sigh, a familiar hand brushes my shoulder.

Ruby.

"Are you fine? Dragons, you look like hell."

I scoff at the irony. "I'm fine."

Hopefully that didn't push my body too much.

"Kedar. Thank you." Opal's voice is grainy as she sits in her chair. We stand in front of her desk as she buries her head in her arms, Garnett at her side. Opal glances into my demonic pupils, shivering.

I pick my eyepatch from the ground, wrapping it around my head. Clearing my throat, I grit my teeth as the ringing thud of my heart slows. "Opal, what happened?

"I was just organizing my papers when this... figure phased through the door."

Opal shudders. "It sealed itself into me, and then... I lost my mind. I couldn't move, speak, or do anything. Pain was throbbing in every cell of my body."

"There were voices. Chanting about this person named Malik."

My eyes widen.

"A name I've never heard of before."

Opal fumbles over her thoughts. The demonic magic... whoever did this wants to give us a warning. "Find Al-Barsim. Damnit, find J-Judah!"

She utters his name like it's a curse. "

They're all chanting the same thing. You don't know what I heard... You *don't*..."

Garnett tries rubbing her shoulder. "Mother, is everything alright?"

Her eyes darken. Tears of blood run down her face, and Garnett shrieks, pressing himself against the wall as Ruby gulps.

"HE... DEMONS... GATES... ALTAR... GATES... HELL... END... WORLD..."

As I reach for my bone dagger, I grind my teeth together. *It's like the hive mind Munir was talking about.* The mana from the demonic attacker has temporarily attached her to the hive mind. This must be a side effect of a normal person experiencing demonic magic. I'm somewhat used to things like this. Opal isn't.

"Omar... CHILD... JUDAH..." She glares at me.

Gallons of blood erupt from her mouth as she pukes all over me, Ruby, and Abubakr.

Abubakr screams, slipping on the blood and falling to the floor with a horrified look. I can only stand, glance down at my tunic, and watch as the scene unfolds. Ruby grits as the liquid drips down her neck.

So these are the side effects of demonic magic on a normal Hayan being, my mind notes, as I take a step back, my boots splashing in the blood. Opal's eyes begin to protrude from her eyeballs, popping out of their sockets with a devilish splat.

Garnett, against the wall, doesn't have words. His mouth trembles, his drying cheeks soaking from the new tears that seep into his skin.

Opal collapses on the desk, her blood staining the surface dark red. Ruby bites her thumb, trying to get her healing magic going again as she tries to heal Opal. Nothing works.

Before I can warn Ruby, Opal glances up at her, retching out blood that sprays in Ruby's face. She shrieks, replicating Abubakr's reaction as she trembles, backing off while shielding her eyes.

I'm the only one who doesn't move or react. Watching is one thing I can do. This must be the work of Al-Barsim. It's like he's trying to tell us something.

Ruby is covered in Opal's lifeforce, trying to get as much of it off her as possible. Garnett's stone cold, stuck in a traumatized gaze. Abubakr's in the corner, forcing himself to not look.

Opal's mouth widens, the demonic voice rattling her vocal chords.

"Come find me, O' Disturbed. Al-Barsim wants to meet at the temple. Refuse to come,

and this will be you, refusing our God, rejecting our Holy Vessel."

Before I can react, Opal's body shakes. A churning erupts through her skin as bits of her brain, green skin, and organs splatter on the walls.

Ruby retches, kicking off the stomach that lands on her boot.

Dragons. Al-Barsim, what have you done?

Hello Mother,
For your birthday, I went to the Lodiac Mines and bought an opal from one of the workers. Then I cut a hole into the stone and strung it around a string. It should fit you perfectly! I worked really hard on this, and I hope you like it! I love you, and have a great birthday.

- A letter written by Garnett when he was twelve to Opal.

TWENTY-FOUR

Days fade in and out. I barely remember how long it's been

since Opal died. We've been too shocked to begin our search for Al-Barsim. Not even Abubakr speaks to me anymore.

He blames me for Opal's death.

As for Ruby and me, we've been spending time interpreting the meaning of Al-Barsim's message. This Veil is calculated. He knows how to control his demonic magic miles more than I can. *Meet me at the temple,* I repeat in my mind. What temple?

"Hey, you alright?" a popping voice says. Ruby's lying down, her head resting on my lap. We're on the roof of the hotel again, our eyes focusing on the sunset. The smell of the city is so much different than Ardon. It reeks of hatred, violence, and death. The rotten corpse scent really tops it off.

I deeply inhale the cigar in my hand, reveling in its relief. "I'm fine. Why do you ask?"

"You've got that look in your eyes again," she offers, reaching up to caress my cheek. "You're drowning in your thoughts. I know it."

I'm going to die soon, I whisper in my mind. My magic is going to kill me, eventually. I know that one day I'll push my mind hard enough to make my heart stop beating. Narrowing my eyes, I blink as she notices my blank expression, stifling a laugh.

Ruby... I can't tell you. You don't deserve to be hurt because of me.

She kisses my bottom lip as I set my cigar on the ledge. We lock eyes. "I'm just... thinking of how we're going to find Al-Barsim."

Ruby pulls away, seeing through my lie. "Are you sure?"

"I am."

She stifles a groan, nuzzling her head against my chest. I twirl her braids around my finger.

"I get it. You don't want to tell me everything," Ruby notes, inviting my touch. She slides her fingertips against my neck. "Just don't become a stranger to me."

It's so unnatural. I see death, commit death, and look in its face every single day, yet here I am, my mind churning just because of it. I keep wondering when I'm going to die. All because of this curse. And as much as I want to say something, *do* something, there's no time to worry about me. I need to worry about Malik, for the Dragon's sake. I can't let anyone treat me like a burden.

I can't.

The setting sun sparkles in Ruby's crimson eyes as she offers me a comforting look. I relax my expression, trying to look more... put-together.

She smiles at my attempt. "Ruby, I've been thinking about that temple."

"Hm. I'm glad you brought that up." Reaching into her robe, she pulls out a rolled-up scroll. It's the city's map. Clearing her throat, she traces her fingers over each landmark on the paper. "There are three temples in Lelina— all Juratheistic."

Juratheism is another religion in Haya. Their creator is Jura. It's similar to Dracotheism— the only difference being that they don't believe in the Holy Scriptures. Rather, they admire statues and symbols of their god, praying to it like the golden spires of Basal.

West of Crale is their collective union of worshippers, called Jurania. Surprisingly enough, Crale recognizes the existence and allows the practice of the Juran religion, even though they've been quite the opposite towards Dracotheists. One temple is close to the southern gates, while the other is on the northern side. The last is near the ruins of Draken Castle. Al-Barsim can be in any of these fabled temples; we just have to find the right one.

"It'd be ironic if Al-Barsim was a monk like Onyx," Ruby scoffs, giving me a shrug.

"Well, we have no way of finding out," I explain as she rests the palm of her hand on mine. Cracking a small smirk, I lace our fingers together. Her hands are so warm. "But he's behind the *Shurta,* and has this violent, demonic magic. Maybe we should start by investigating these temples."

"Yeah." Ruby strokes her hand against her chin, lost in thought. Her voice dims a bit. "We should really check on Abubakr and Garnett."

"You read my mind."

We climb down the rooftop, finding ourselves at the inn's doorstep. It looks lifeless. The blinds are closed, blocking the outside world. A sign hanging on the door reads:

CLOSED UNTIL FURTHER NOTICE.

Unlocking the door with the hotel room key Garnett has given us, I'm greeted by the sight of Abubakr, sitting and staring at the candle at one of the tables. His eyes are clouded in a mist of darkness.

Ruby clasps her hands at the edges of the table. "Abu. Abubakr!"

He snaps, jumping out of his seat. Heaving sighs, he wipes the sweat off his forehead. As always, he has a cup of tea by his side, the air smelling like a mix of jeuberries and noscot cinnamon.

"Oh. Ruby. Kedar. You're back."

The lobby is a mess. Garnett's rage has possessed him, papers everywhere and shards of glass on the floor. As I look upon the room, I realize that I was like this once. Angry at the world. Wondering why my father and my mother died.

"Omar, come on, come on for Basal's sake!" I huffed, carrying our bag of supplies. We had to keep walking. The Cralean soldiers could be on our tails on this long and lonely dirt road.

Omar was quiet. The tears that had once flowed down his cheeks were now dry. Gritting my teeth, I threw the bag to the ground.

"Goddamnit! Omar, pick up the pace unless you want us to DIE out here!" My fingers were still trembling from what I saw. Bodies, piles of arms and legs everywhere, the fountain doused with blood. The goblin who killed my parents.

Omar buried his face in his arms, whimpering. "I want Mother."

My voice broke, but there's something inside of me that churned. Boiling with rage.

"She's gone, Omar. You didn't see? Our house? Burning with flames?"

"Mother's there. I know it. I saw her," he sobbed, wiping up his snot. Breathing heavily, I grasped his shoulders, my eyes widened.

"SHE'S GONE! HOW MANY TIMES DO I NEED TO TELL YOU!" I screamed. He stumbled to the ground as red dots filled my vision. He's in the way, *a voice told me.* Leave him.

I picked up our supplies and kept walking. Omar cried out for me, but I didn't even care to look back. But this wave of anger and rage promptly boiled down, and I rested my hands on my knees, repeating the same sentence over and over.

Protect Omar with your life. Protect Omar with your life. Protect Omar with your life.

Scrunching at my hair, I found myself running back to my little brother.

"Omar, look, I'm sorry. J-Just take my hand."

"S-Sorry?"

"Yes, I'm sorry. I swear."

I wanted to make him a heaven out of this hell.

Shaking the memory out of my mind, I look down with guilt. It's Munir that's shaped me into this… man I've never wanted to be.

"Everything's going wrong." Abubakr's voice interrupts my line of thought. "Without Opal, I won't be part of the Order. I have no way of being initiated anymore. Garnett lost his mother."

His breath hitches.

"I lost my friend."

Ruby's overarching stare says she has an idea. Digging her palms deeper into the table's surface, her eyes light up. "Killing Al-Barsim is what we want, and what you guys want too. Come with us."

His eyes narrow, averting his attention to me. I realize his thoughts about me haven't changed in the slightest. Not a single ounce of trust is in his expression. "But…Kedar. You… let Opal die."

"I didn't," I sternly reply.

"You did."

"She died because of demonic magic? Do I really have to explain this?"

"Alright, enough." Ruby's voice splits oceans. "We don't have time to argue. Are you coming with us or not, Abubakr?"

Embedding another dagger in me with his glare, he deflates, giving his tea a sip before setting it down. "Fine. I don't want to rot inside of here anymore. Anything to kill this bastard."

Ruby rests her hands on her hips. "Armor up. We'll go after we pay Garnett a visit."

A few minutes later, me, Ruby, and Abubakr stand in front of the theorum's secret entrance. Ruby wears metal-plated armor over her tunic, letting her cloak shine in the gloomy light. Abubakr wears leather armor under his woolly coat, boasting that he "doesn't need a weapon."

My cloak hides the *Kathi* and bone dagger on my belt. Over my black tunic is the same armor Ruby has— bulky enough to resist a slash from a sword, but light enough to duck out of harm's way.

"Dragons, I hope he's doing alright," Abubakr mutters, as we slide open the bookshelf, inviting ourselves in.

372

In the dark hallway, we hear Garnett's cries and shouts. He's been in that room since Opal died. A horrid stench hits my nose. We haven't even gone inside yet, so the rotting remains of Opal are still in the crevices of the walls.

"Gods." Ruby retches, putting her hand on the doorknob.

"Let's just… comfort him in the best way we can."

Even though Abubakr and I don't have the fondest thoughts about each other, we at least agree on this one thing.

Ruby opens the door to Garnett, still in the same left corner. His head is buried in his hands as he screams again in agony. Flies are everywhere, Opal's blood dripping on the walls. Garnett's clothes are no longer white, only covered in a dark red complexion.

I see myself in him. The pain. The anger.

Opal's blue-lined robe is in his hands. He keeps tugging on it like his mother can come back. His eyes are a dull green, no longer the sparkling jade color I once knew.

"Garnett?" Ruby begins, covering her mouth with her arm. Abubakr tries putting his hand on Garnett's shoulder for some support, but he quickly recoils away.

He growls, almost feral. "Leave me."

I try offering my mind. "Look, Garnett—"

"DON'T SPEAK TO ME!"

Garnett screams with vengeance, but his voice dims as he sees everyone's worried expressions. It takes him a bit to speak again.

"That was my mother. My real parents died in a house fire when I was two. She raised me. Nurtured me. Taught me how to be… me."

His voice cracks. "Now she's… gone."

I grit my teeth. Opal's Garnett's savior. But she's dead, and he blames it on me.

"I'm sorry, Garnett. I'm sorry."

"Don't start." His fingers tremble.

"If you want forgiveness… bring me his head."

We don't say a word until we lock the secret entrance to the theorum. Garnett's screams are still audible from the inside as he revels in his pain. Abubakr gives me a heartless look as we go downstairs.

"Are we really going to bring him Al-Barsim's head?" he asks.

I suppress my answer until Ruby swings the door open and heads out to the snow-covered stone roads, leaving me to clasp Abubakr's shoulder before we can follow her.

"I'll be the one to do it. No, *we'll* be the ones to do it."

He breaks his emotionless demeanor, grinning.

The darkness of night envelops the city. Crowds litter the streets, chanting phrases of rebellion. We walk side by side, occasionally scanning our surroundings to make sure nobody's following us.

"Well, let's go to the first temple on our list," Ruby begins, offering us the map. "It's on the northern side of the city. We got a hell of a lot of walking to do."

I scoff in response. "It's nothing like Saitra."

"You're right." Ruby smirks, visions of us trekking through the Pinakada desert filling my mind. It's hard to think that all happened last summer.

Abubakr contorts in confusion as Ruby stifles a laugh. Moonlight shines down on us, contrasting with the violent riots. A large crowd blocks our way from passing the road, filled with the young and old.

"What the hell's going on?" Abubakr whispers to us.

A line of guards stands in front of a building, as the angry crowd throws stones and snowballs at them. The *Shurta's* faces are stern, not daring to inch away from their spots. Their

374

swords are ready, threatening to stab anyone who comes too close.

I glance at Ruby for her nod of approval. We venture closer, beelining through the mob. Abubakr ducks his head, dodging the flaming torches and sharp pitchforks. They aren't just rioting in front of any building, it seems.

While the house doesn't look any different than the others— dark, brown pillars contrasting the white inside paint with a smoking chimney on the slanted rooftop— I see the shadow of a man sitting at a desk behind the window's curtains. The mob's trying to do anything they can to get the man's attention, only to be met with the *Shurta's* wrath. Men shout and curse as they're pushed back by the guards with the threat of death.

"Who the hell is in there?" Ruby hushes. Our eyes are fixated on the man behind the curtains. *Is he important? Or is he... Al-Barsim?*

"Maybe we can sneak inside." Abubakr dusts his hands, as Ruby shakes her head in disagreement.

The chanting shouts of the crowd make our plotting blend into the jumble of voices. Thankfully, the guards don't acknowledge our existence. The possibility of us being arrested is low. Ruby sighs. "There's no way for us to distract them. It's too public."

"We can use the civilians as a distraction. Make 'em fight," Abubakr offers, but my mind averts to all of the protestors outside of Al-Jukar's manor. Hundreds killed in cold blood.

I don't need to see that again. "No. We shouldn't put people's lives on the line."

"Well, what the hell do you want to do, *Kedar?*" Abubakr crosses his arms.

I take off my eyepatch. If I can hypnotize those two men in Draken Castle, who's to say I can't do it again? My dark red pupil locks with Abubakr's ember eyes.

His face contorts into doubt. "Demon magic?"

"I want to try something," I reply. "I'm going to hypnotize this crowd with my mana."

Ruby recoils as Abubakr's brows raise. "Hypnotize? How the hell does that work?"

I scoff. "Just watch."

She deflates, gripping her ax's handle. That magical boost I got from draining Al-Barsim's mana out of Opal should be plenty. *But the pain,* I think, cupping my eye.

"Drag me," I tell Ruby and Abubakr. They're a bit bewildered at first, but they let my arms hang on their necks.

"Once everyone's under my magic, carry me to that door."

They both nod, as I widen my right eye. I gaze into the *Shurta's* pupils and grit my teeth. Darting my eyes to each protester, I feel their minds beginning to tether to mine, being put under my control. A hellish pain envelops the right side of my face as I grunt.

Abubakr notices the absence of shouts and screams from the crowd of people. "What the…"

I smirk, before reciting the command:

Stop.

As I keep increasing my efforts, people drop their weapons, as if they've turned into statues. Blood seeps into my lips as Ruby and Abubakr watch in awe. I come close to locking eyes with Ruby, but I glance away. It'll be a horrible mistake if I accidentally put Abubakr or Ruby under my control.

Huffing, I close my eyes and concentrate on continuously holding everyone's consciousness to obey mine. Ruby snaps out of her daze, dragging me through the crowd. "Abubakr, come on. Make it to the door!"

My boots churn against the stone brick road as I see red and black spots in my vision. The blood starts to overflow on my cheek, and Ruby quickly smears it off so we don't create a red trail. I'm in control of three hundred minds. *Three hundred souls.* It's mesmerizing to think about— but I don't have time to imagine what else I can do because of the searing pain.

Ruby and Abubakr hoist me to the front door as my body completely gives out. Seems like my hypnosis only works with eye contact. The shadow behind the curtains keeps writing away, paying no attention to the silence outside their front door.

Abubakr swipes the keys from the guard blocking our path. The expression on the *Shurta's* face is blank, a drop of saliva running down his chin. My magic's holding up nicely, but at the cost of my body. The pain keeps vibrating, rolling over like waves. I've lost a finger before, got tortured in a prison for days, and have a scar on the bridge of my nose— but it doesn't compare to this.

Ruby unlocks and swings open the door as I stumble to the ground. Leaning my head against the wall, I breathe out a heavy sigh, as the red and black dots in my vision disappear. With that, the protests and riots outside resume as I let go of everyone's minds.

"Great Jura!" an unfamiliar voice exclaims.

What's behind the curtain is a Farik, writing away letters as a dimly lit candle sits at his table. But we're too exhausted to even acknowledge him— Abubakr gives me a shocked glance, shaking his head in disbelief. Even Ruby stifles a laugh.

"Wha-What the hell?!" the Farik rises from his chair, his tail wagging with caution. Even though everyone's returned to normal, the pain in my eye persists. I can barely focus on what's happening in front of me. "Who are you? The guards don't let a single soul into my chambers—"

"Shh." Ruby puts a finger to his doggy nose.

He grits his canines. "Scream, and we'll kill you. Understood?"

Pushing Ruby off of him, he backs off and nods, leaning against his table. Abubakr steps forward, poise in his movements. "Where's Al-Barsim?"

"Al-Barsim? I don't even know who the hell that is—" Abubakr punches the dog in the jaw, sending him to another planet. I scoff. He's become fearless— looks like Garnett's training has done him some good.

Ruby offers a hand, and I roll my eyes, letting her hoist me up and hang my arm over her neck. Slowly, the pain subsides. It's a good sign— but how many years did that shave off of my life?

"You know exactly who I'm talking about." Abubakr's voice grows angry. Every word he speaks shakes the floor beneath us. "Where is he?"

The Farik coughs blood, holding his hands up to shield himself. "I'm not allowed to let anyone know where the master is—"

Abubakr doesn't hold back this time, punching the old dog in the neck. Ruby rubs her forehead in slight disappointment as the Farik falls to the floor with a *thud*. But he's still conscious. What a surprise.

Something's different about Abubakr— the way he talks, the way he punches the farik. Doing this must be his way of releasing the anger he feels towards Al-Jukar. Working for him, doing his dirty deeds. He must've hated it.

Abubakr digs his boot into the Farik's neck as the dog coughs in response.

"If you don't tell me, I'm going to have to let you suffocate."

"H-He's in his— chambers, of course!" he wheezes, gasping for air.

That doesn't satisfy Abubakr. He presses his boot deeper as the Farik coughs and gurgles, begging for air. Ruby and I watch in silence. So this is what Abubakr's like.

"H-he's in the Juran temple! North of here— gods— SPARE ME! FOR JURA'S SAKE!"

With a *crack,* Abubakr snaps the man's neck, leaving him no more air to breathe.

Huffing, Abubakr gives us a glance. "Did you hear that? The temple north of the city…"

"What the hell?" Ruby asks, looking at the corpse on the ground. "At the mansion, you were scared at the sight of Kedar's sword. But…you killed a Farik with ease."

Wrapping my eyepatch around my head again, I offer an expression of worry. He sighs, his ember eyes reflecting off the candlelight. "I don't know. Ever since we left, I can't shake the thought of Garnett suffering alone."

I clear my throat. "Well, let's get going. We're going to bring him Al-Barsim's head, remember?"

Juranian temples are huge, almost rivaling the size of the castle. But that castle is now a pile of rubble, corpses still being recovered from the wreckage. I've never seen a temple in person, but they're in the shape of a pyramid, conjured from stone bricks.

At the top is the Hand of Jura, the Juran's symbol of their god's existence. With a grunt, I cross my arms, my eyes shifting to the temple's entrance.

"This is huge. Much bigger than Dracotheistic mosques." Ruby steps forward, motioning me and Abubakr inside.

"I know," I reply, noticing the fiery gaze in Abubakr's pupils. He's been silent since we slipped out of the crowd, with the power of my hypnosis.

Ruby glances at me. "Come on. Let's do some... investigating."

"You mean snooping around?" I offer.

"I guess you can say that."

Entering the temple, the pyramid is divided into three floors, each with marble stairs leading to the level above. The floor is plastered with sparkly, marble tiles, clean enough that I can see my reflection in it.

A red carpet runs down the rows of altars, and there's a signature golden and silver statue in the center of a podium. Crowds of people are on their knees, reciting prayers to find comfort in their god. My spine rattles. I've never seen Jurans before, much less their places of worship. It smells pure, untouched, *and clean.* I feel like I'm not worthy of being inside such a place like this.

At the right side of the room, two *Shurta* stand in front of a bulky metal wall. We wisp our way around, careful not to disturb the people as Abubakr's voice turns into a hushed whisper.

"What's behind that wall?"

"Well, we might as well ask them." Ruby lowers her tone once she realizes a Juran is scowling in our direction. "Al-Barsim asked for us to be here."

Murals of Jura are on every wall. It's like they've replaced Basal, the mighty dragon, with this random old geezer instead. Our religions are as much as similar as they are different.

Shaking out of my daze, I look to Ruby and Abubakr. "If we're going to get to Al-Barsim, I need both of you to prepare yourselves. I have a feeling we're not getting out without a fight..."

Both of them nod as we walk to stand in front of the *Shurta*. The guards are giants compared to us, their eyes dissecting our souls. Ruby nervously clears her throat. "Uhm... hello...?"

"The Clover has been waiting," one of them says. *This must be a trap, but it's the only way we're going to kill Al-Barsim, and the only way Garnett's ever going to forgive me.*

"Follow us."

The second guard outstretches his hands towards the metal wall, a subtle creaking sound vibrating my eardrums as he pushes it forward to create a doorway. Seems like it can only be opened using magic. Metallic manipulation is hell to fight against. With a resounding *clank,* we stream inside, and the second guard closes the door.

The *Shurta* holds up a gloomy lantern as we follow him down the ramp, which leads us further into darkness. Like the headquarters in Ardon, it's a tunnel that twists and turns at every turn.

Abubakr takes a deep breath, trying to recollect himself. I nudge Ruby's shoulder. "I hate being in caves."

"Why's that?" she replies, her eyes narrowing.

My mind goes back to Alfdan. "I had to mine gemstones to get any ounce of bread. It was horrifying to watch people beg for food."

Her expression dims with sympathy. "Well, what about Ardon? You didn't seem too bothered."

"I don't know. Being there, it's... so alive. So full of liberty and freedom. It isn't a prison or a hellhole. It honestly felt like... home."

"Home?"

"Yeah. I feel like I belong there."

She smiles.

I try smiling back, but that quickly fades as we're met with a dark, rotting door. The same one that Al-Jukar has to house his slaves. Except this one has a metal lock.

The *Shurta* guard grunts as he shifts the lock to swing the door open. Nothing is better than having double security.

"I've been waiting."

The voice is almost familiar. A shattering sound bursts in my eardrums as the *Shurta* guard whimpers, turning his back against the voice. The lanterns are on the ground, in pieces. With a gulp, the second guard prances away to escape the monster in front of us.

Al-Barsim.

We step into the room, the stench hitting us like a brick wall. It's worse than the smell in the theorum. Corpses are placed like dolls in each corner, racks of decapitated heads hanging by a rope on the ceiling. Abubakr retches, hyperventilating.

Ruby's breath hitches as she tries to glance away from the horrors. It's impossible; too many dead bodies riddle our visions.

"Come in."

A blazing fireplace is behind them, but the fuel isn't wood. Charring remains of people—no, Dracotheists who can't survive Al-Barsim's torture are now just a meal for the fire's flame.

"Make yourself at home."

We're hunched together, too worried to leave one another's side. The door slams behind us.

It's either we're getting out of here alive, or we're getting out of here dead.

Sitting on a stool is the wicked face of Al-Barsim. Wearing a dark blue robe, he breathes in a sigh. The wrinkles on his face suggest his middle age. Black earrings hang from his pointy, green ears. The goblin's eyes match the color of mine: a void black and a devilish red. His hands are clasped in prayer as he stares into our souls.

A smile embeds his expression as he slicks back his brown hair.

"My name is Ace. But you may know me as The Clover. Pleasure to meet you."

"Ace?" Abubakr's voice hitches. "The Demon Ace? *Madhbah?*

He scoffs. "Nobody's called me that in years, not since I left the Cralean Army."

To my left is a man, begging for help through his gag. I look away when realizing the skin on his chest is skinned off. It reminds me of Munir— his violence and rage.

This isn't just Al-Barsim's room. It's his playground. Metal cages along the sides of the room scream at us, pleading for help. Al-Barsim's demonic counterpart must have complete and utter control of his being, which is why he's exerted his madness on these innocent people. He let go.

Piles of arms and legs create a circle around Al-Barsim, like he's about to perform a ritual. He notices my darting eyes and cackles. "My collection is conceived from Dracotheists, Basalians, you name it— I'm cleaning the world. You simply do not deserve to exist."

"But this city is slowly slipping from my control," he explains, pouting. Every time he utters a word, his little fangs poke out of his mouth, stained red. "I wish I could go back to the good old days, like raiding that little town."

Little town? My mind vibrates. It's a coincidence. Right?

"Al-Barsim, what town are you talking about?"

Ruffling through his pockets, he takes out an eyeball. "It was seven years ago," Ace hums, examining the pupil. My heart begins to race without a thought. *No. This can't be true. Right?*

"Killing family after family. I think the town's name was… Jaawed?" *No. No. No.* He grins, noticing my glare of murder. "I had fun with a mom while her kids had to hear it. It was… amazing, hearing their silent sobs and cries. It only made me want to do it more."

Monster.

I grab the *Kathi,* hurling it towards his face.

Praise our holy God, JURA. There is nobody more important in the world than our God, JURA. Praise him for our daily transgression, and allow the LORD to bless us so that we enter into eternal life. O, JURA, hear our pleas, for we love you unconditionally and without regret.

Amen.

- The Juran Prayer.

TWENTY-FIVE

Anger fuels me. Ace recoils from his stool to dodge my swings. *Monster,* my mind vibrates. *Monster.* I step over the circle of body parts and enter Al-Barsim's domain. My swings are sloppy, emotional— but I don't care. *He needs to die.*

"Kedar! Stop!" Abubakr's voice bounces off the room's walls, but I ignore him. Ace grumbles in annoyance, digging into his robe to realize that he doesn't even have a weapon at the ready. Growling, I swipe down, hoping to slice him in half. A gleaming sense of urgency fills his red eyes as he dashes to the side, a smirk on his face.

I counter his dodge with an uppercut of a swing, nicking his cheek. He chuckles, wiping the blood soaking his robe. "Something up with you, kid?"

"You," I grit, trying to stab his chest, but failing miserably.

"Oh?" Ace dashes away, leaving me in the dust. "Were you one of those kids?"

"Shut up."

With each swing of the *Kathi,* the veins on my wrists grow brighter and brighter. I rip off my eyepatch, huffing as I stuff it into my pocket. "You don't know what you did. You don't know what happened to all those poor, innocent families that you sent six feet deep into the ground?"

A throbbing sensation makes my eye bleed. Hurling the *Kathi* towards Ace's neck, his red eyes interlock with mine, sending a bigger wave of pain that makes me fall to my knees.

"It helped you, didn't it? Killing your parents was the best day of YOUR life, not mine." He places his hands on his knees, trying to catch his breath. Stepping out of the circle made of arms and legs, he leans against the cages with innocent people. He points to my eye. "You got your demonic magic... because of me."

"Don't you dare."

I stand to charge at him, but Ace chuckles before I see Ruby's ax beaming towards his head. Ducking out of the way, Ace stumbles as I see Abubakr and Ruby charge at Ace. *Gods. Help would be good.*

The ax curves back like a boomerang. Ruby catches it, grumbling in disappointment.

With a grunt, Abubakr doesn't hesitate to pull his punches. Wisping his way through Abubakr's attacks, Ace avoids my swings while also keeping track of where Ruby's next throw is going to be.

"Three versus one? Now this is exciting," he admits, jumping in the air to get away from my stabs and Ruby's impending strikes with her other ax. Before I can react, he hooks his arm around Ruby's neck, dragging her away from me and Abubakr.

Ruby hopelessly tries to flail as I resist myself from giving chase. Churning my teeth, I pull out a razqatar, aiming for his head. It splits through the air like butter, but my eyes widen once I realize it's completely stopped mid-air.

He curls his arm like an anaconda around Ruby's neck, and she quickly loses oxygen. The knife doesn't just stop in mid-air for no reason— there's a dark hand sprouting from the ground, holding it in its grasp. Ace flicks his wrist, and the hand obeys him, tossing the razqatar to the side.

"I can see why Al-Jukar and Al-Watawat died."

My heart aches. Ruby convulses in Ace's arms as her neck is surrounded in a black, crimson aura.

"Let Ruby go," I command, as the dark hand wisps into the stone tiles in the ground. So this is Al-Barsim's magic— the power to summon his demonic counterpart to use it like a puppet. The magic that's needed to conjure it must be otherworldly. No wonder there are so many bodies in here. Death conjures our mana.

Wiping the bloody tip of my blade against my black cloak, I curse under my breath as Ace shakes his head, smirking. "I'm afraid I can't do that. Everyone you see here... fuels my magic. Ruby's just another source of my fuel."

He's draining her magic, I curse. Abubakr and I circle Al-Barsim as he holds Ruby steady. Ace growls. "It's disrespectful to fight in a place of worship."

"Don't even start," Abubakr replies, curling his fists. "You call a room of rotting corpses and hostages a place of worship?"

"YES! It is! Here is where I worship my god!"

Ruby elbows Al-Barsim in the stomach, stumbling away from him while swinging her axes to slash his right arm. As he grits in pain, Ruby coughs, with dark circles under her eyes. Ruby collapses into my arms, hyperventilating.

"Damnit, Ruby, are you alright?" My voice hitches as she takes centuries to answer me, burying her head into my chest.

Looking up at me with worry, Ruby grits, blood dripping down her chin. "Kedar. Don't let him grab you. My body... it felt like I was crumbling. Falling apart."

She stands up, wiping sweat off her forehead as she pushes herself off me, as if she's already been reenergized. Before I can say anything, she puts up her palm to stop me. "I'll be fine. Just kill this bastard."

Clenching her eyes together and heaving a heavy sigh, Ruby does her best to recollect herself. Al-Barsim's hellish growl makes me lock eyes with the beast— his arm hanging like a loose thread. Ruby has done some damage, his bones visible from the gaping, bleeding cuts.

We watch in silence as Ace grabs one of the groaning prisoners in the metal cages behind him, tightening his grip on their arm. Opening his mouth wide, his fangs shine in the fiery lights.

Abubakr winces as the person screams in pain. Ace clamps onto their arm like a shark on a feeding frenzy, his teeth tearing through their tendons and skin.

After tearing the prisoner's arm off, he takes it out of his mouth to grip its wrist tight. "My sources tell me you're trying to find The High One. Why?"

"We just want to stop you." The words come out of my mouth before I can think. "The Veils want to end the world, right? And you're holding my damn brother captive. All I want is to save him."

Ace laughs, the veins on his green arms glowing. Black matter spills out of his eyelids like tears, as he holds the severed arm over it, dousing it with the demonic liquid.

"This world is violent. Useless. All we want is to create a new one."

Before I argue, the black matter grows from the severed arm, forming a torso, a pair of legs, and a head. It's like the severed arm is the seed of the figure's magic. Abubakr's voice falters. "What the hell do you call killing innocent people, creating a new world?"

Ace's attention shifts to me, as the figure stands at his side, black mist wisping from the surface of its skin. "Kedar. You know what I mean."

Abubakr and Ruby look at me with confusion. Not being able to come up with an answer, I shake his statement aside, as Ace offers another cackle. "You're fighting on the wrong side. Join us."

"You're monsters." I glance at my comrades, their expressions too abstract for me to read. "The Order taught me. Taught me how to be a Hayan. A human being."

Ace sighs, sitting against the cage. Seems like summoning the dark figure has taken a lot of mana out of him. The dark figure shifts into a fighting stance, blocking our path as they step over the corpse circle.

"Malik will be resurrected. At all costs." Ruby and Abubakr recoil. This is new to them. Malik? They've never heard that name before, except when Opal died. "Then the gates will open. The sky will be red. It's the Prophecy, Kedar. You can't deny that we're close. Close to being greeted by a new world."

"Prophecy?" Ruby interrupts, stuttering. "Like the one Judah mentioned in that letter?"

Al-Barsim chuckles, the figure in front of him twitching with violence, waiting for his command.

"Yes, yes. If I die here, then it means you'll find out where Judah is."

My heart rate spikes. In this room, Al-Barsim has a letter, a note, *something* to tell us where Judah might be. It's wrenching to think about. Killing him is the solution to finally discovering where this Farikkian bastard is hiding.

"But if I kill all of you, then that will only speed up the High One's process. You're all too late," he explains while Abubakr shakes his head in denial.

"We're not late." Abubakr lurches forward, his eyes set on the dark figure.

"Well, tell that to my puppet. It'll kill you before it can even take a step towards me."

The puppet flashes at the speed of light, appearing in front of Abubakr. In an instant, their right hand morphs into a sharp, sword-like shape, inches away from his face.

An explosion rocks the room, creating a cloud of smoke. Pushing the air out of the way, I furrow my brows as my voice turns desperate. "Abubakr! Are you alright?"

Flames ignite from the darkness.

Abubakr's hands are on fire, his fists like coal. *Am I imagining things?*

Abubakr has awakened...

"What the hell..." His fists are in front of his face, blocking the stab of Al-Barsim's puppet. Ruby lights up. His skin isn't affected by the blaze at all; in fact, it's relishing in it. "Fire? *Fire?!*"

The puppet hesitates, its arm shattered from Abubakr's awakening. With the other arm morphing into a sword, the figure ignites while Abubakr sloppily dodges its slashes with his newfound power. He's distracting the thing, leading it away from me and Ruby. Every one of its stacks gets blocked by its blazing fingertips.

Ace is too flabbergasted at what he's witnessing, busy clutching his bleeding forearm to notice me and Ruby running to him with our weapons at the ready. Hopefully, Abubakr can fight the puppet alone.

Al-Barsim huffs, averting his gaze to us, smirking. I put the *Kathi* to his throat, and Ruby heaves, holding her axes tightly.

Even though her magic is drained from her body, she still stands with overarching anger. I gawk. "Give me one reason why I shouldn't kill you."

"I don't." He gets up, not an ounce of fear on his face as he's being threatened with the reality of death. Rummaging through his cloak, he sighs deeply. "I thought I wouldn't have to use my dagger today."

I step back as he unsheathes a large dagger, beaming against the gloomy light. *So much for not having a weapon,* I grit, eyeing the leather around its iron handle. Pulling out my own dagger, I wield the *Kathi,* on the other hand, making sure both my weapons are ready to cut Ace into pieces.

"Thousands of people have been buried because of me." His red eyes narrow, the sparks and cracks of Abubakr and the puppet rumbling in the distance. "Your bodies are nothing but fruits to fuel my magic."

"Did Al-Jukar and Al-Watawat even matter to you?" I stammer. Ace rolls his eyes.

"The *Shurta* are completely under my control." He wipes the stains of blood on his robe.

"Death is nothing new to me. Even if both of my comrades worked with me to cleanse this city of Dracotheists. But alas, nobody is as important as I, Al-Barsim. The Clover. The High One comes to me first if he has any problems of any sort to deal with."

Ruby scoffs, undermining his words. "Bastard. You're nothing but a pawn to Judah."

With Ruby's nod, we dash to Al-Barsim, Ruby hurling her axes faster than last time. Ace grits in pain from his wounded arm as the ax cuts the side of his hip. Her weapon curves back to her effortlessly, finding itself in the palm of her hand less than a second later.

Holding his dagger tightly, Ace blocks my attack to slice off his leg. With a grunt, he avoids Ruby's kick, dashing into the circle of limbs. "Time to take off the kid gloves."

I pick at the scar on my nose, snorting. "The hell is that supposed to mean?"

Ace doesn't answer, and I try stabbing his heart, only to realize Ruby's holding my arm. "Don't."

"Ruby? What the—"

I stop once I see Ace's veins shine, brighter and brighter, glowing more than mine ever have.

"Kedar... you're seeing what I'm seeing, right?"

Too intimidated to even form a sentence, I can only nod.

Ace laughs, but this time he doesn't sound like a man. He sounds like a beast, a demon, the devil himself. His dagger immerses itself in a dark red aura, his demonic magic funneling into the metal of his blade. The veins on his wrist and forehead protrude from his body, glowing brighter.

"Kedar..." Blood runs down his cheeks from his red eyes.

"This is what you can do. With *your* power."

We dash at Ace to stop him. I swing my dagger and the *Kathi,* aiming for his shoulder. Ruby flanks, so we can sandwich Ace with our weapons. A *clang* echoes through the room as the *Kathi* and dagger clank against Ace's blade.

Ace blocks my attacks, my bone dagger cracking against his. Seems like his demonic magic enhances it, only making it sharper and powerful than it once was. Over Ace's shoulder is Ruby, charging toward him with her axes ready to slice his head off.

Pushing my blades against his dagger even more, the bone dagger cracks again, the *Kathi* even beginning to bend.

Ace sneers. "Let's see you counter this."

Once he realizes Ruby's blades are nearing his neck, he jumps, dashing away from us. The *Kathi* and bone dagger

393

swing downward, and Ruby's eyes widen as she walks into my swords.

A squelching sound fills the air.

Looking down, I realize the *Kathi* protrudes from her chest. Blood spills from her lips as I drop the bone dagger to the ground. Ruby collapses, the *Kathi* still deep in her guts. I curse.

No.

She retches, blood flooding the floor around us as I keep her close. Ruby's dying, fast, and there isn't a way I can stop it. Her healing magic won't do her any good— *it's hard to exert mana when there's a damn sword sticking out of you*—

"Ruby... answer me."

I've never thought my boots would be soaking in her blood.

"Kedar, wipe that look off your face," she coughs, hovering her hand over her wound. A faint, blue aura shines from her fingertips. "It's not that deep. Luckily, you missed my organs."

"Ruby, that doesn't change the fact that you're bleeding out—"

"Shut up!" Her face ripples with exhaustion. Dropping her axes to the ground, she uses one of her hands to grip the *Kathi's* handle. Without hesitation, she pulls out my sword and yelps in pain.

"Here. Use this."

That still doesn't convince me, even though she hands me the blade with expertise. The smell of her copper blood is already leaving a tangy stench on my nose. "Ruby, promise me you won't die—"

"I will if you don't get off your ass and fight Ace!"

Getting up, I grab the dagger, guarding Ruby as she grits her teeth, focusing on using the little mana she has left to heal herself. Ace appears in front of me before I can react, slashing his dagger against the sides of my waist.

I roar, pressing Al-Barsim with my attacks so we drift to the other side of the room. *But where the hell is Abubakr?*

"You're tired, aren't you?" Al-Barsim cackles. The demonic aura on his blade leaves a searing mark on my wound, like sparkling salt over my cuts. Narrowing my eyes, fatigue riddles my body.

"Shut up."

Abubakr's perched like a bat on top of one of the cages against the wall. Before Ace can react, Abubakr jumps, his fists immersed in fire.

Abubakr grabs Ace's throat, burning his skin as they tumble and roll to the ground. Ruby's eyes widen.

"Get the hell off!" Ace gawks, kicking Abubakr in the stomach. Spitting out blood, Abubakr shoves his hand on Al-Barsim's face, making it sizzle like a slice of steak on a grill. Ace howls in pain, convulsing on the floor.

His neck pops with clear bubbles of his skin. The eyelids he once had are gone— his lips contorting in a twisted shape, cheeks burned beyond recognition. Holding his throat, Ace murmurs in pain, cursing at Abubakr. "Bastard…"

I give the bone dagger to Abubakr.

"Finish the job."

Once Abubakr nods, I run back to Ruby, still clutching her stomach. She looks fine. More alive than before. "You okay?"

"Yes, damnit, I'm fine," Ruby coughs. Glancing at her cut, it's closed up— looks like she's really going to be fine. *Thank the Dragons.* Offering my hand, I grunt when she grasps me tightly, letting me pull her up. This time, she's the one hanging on my shoulders, using her other hand to keep healing her wound.

We stand in front of Abubakr. Ace is on his knees, his breathing labored from the burns. Once he notices the blade, he recoils. "God… wait…"

Abubakr lifts the bottom of Ace's chin, his charred neck exposed. He places the dagger against his throat, and he takes a deep breath. His eyes burn with memories of Opal. Garnett. Rage flows through his essence. I can barely recognize him at all.

He digs the dagger into Ace's artery, a gush of blood flowing down his chest. "Your puppet isn't enough to kill me. Fire magic really does its wonders."

Ruby fastens the bonnet on her head, coughing. Abubakr turns to us. I give him an approving nod. Nothing's stopping him now.

"Looks like I've been outplayed," Ace grits in defeat, spitting blood on the stone tiles. Digging through his cloak, his red eyes shimmer with dread as he tosses a stack of papers to the floor.

"There. Use these to find Judah."

"Now let me—" His voice stops as Abubakr grunts, slitting Al-Barsim's throat open. Abubakr moves the dagger back and forth, as red blood soaks and spills onto Ace's cloak.

Minutes pass as Abubakr separates Ace's head from his shoulders, falling to the ground with a *thump*. He's speechless. His fingers tremble while looking at the dagger. The boy's never done anything like this before. Fighting back against his horrors is all he wanted to do his whole life, and now he's doing it.

Abubakr picks Ace's head from the floor, gripping his hair tightly. Prisoners cheer in joy, with their tormentor dead.

I swipe the stack of documents on the floor. Seems like Ace has plans, judging from his violent mana consumption and the papers he has in his cloak. It feels like a reward.

Abubakr huffs, sweat rolling down his cheek. "L-Let's head back. We gotta free these people."

Are we monsters, or heroes strolling through the darkness? I've heard the saying from a man I once knew— mercy allows someone to be a better person, the willpower to have another chance to fix their mistakes.

His name is Omar.

Leaving Al-Barsim alive means no justice. Leaving Al-Barsim alive means... Garnett is suffering from the turmoil of his mother's death. With Ace gone, he's freed from his chains of sorrow.

So we are heroes. But we are also monsters.

Abubakr carries a brown sack with Al-Barsim's head inside. The temple we left is a mess, but the Dracotheists and Basalians have gone back to their homes and families. *Shurta* guards and generals, the Veils no longer threatening them, quickly take over the scene, examining Al-Barsim's basement inside out.

Our assassination leads us back to the inn. Ruby's magic barely hangs on, her mana drained. I still hoist her up, letting her walk through the city streets. The riots keep going— but with the discovery of hundreds of captive Dracotheists in a Juran temple, tensions burst.

Groaning, I clench my fingers against my hip, wincing as I touch my wounds. My armor's torn through. Once I see Bix, I'll ask him for some repairs. *If I ever see him, that is.*

"Open the damn door." I scoff at Ruby's fatigued voice.

With a little *click,* Abubakr swings the door open, as hushed whispers evade our senses.

Garnett's speaking to this old-looking Farik, sitting at one of the round tables. On one of the chairs is a girl, maybe the same age as Abubakr, with silver hair and metal earrings hanging from her earlobes.

They all go silent once they notice us. Once the Farik turns to me, my expression contorts, my eyes widening. It's—

"Yes, Kedar. This must be a surprise for you, hm?"

I can recognize that old geezer anywhere.

"Onyx. Dragons." Ruby huffs, her hand hovering over her wound. "You're here."

"Well, it seems like I am." Standing from his seat, he comes to shake my hand. But Onyx only has one arm. *My fight with Munir severed his arm completely.*

I shake his furry hand before averting my attention to the girl. A silver crown sits on top of her head, with purple gemstones embedded in its center. Sporting a gray and blue gown, her snowy skin gleams against the candlelights.

"Princess Lauvee?" my voice stammers. Two men stand behind her, holding long halberds. The knights are covered in thick armor and hold a shield in their opposite hands.

"Is this who you were talking about, Garnett?" the Princess asks, awkwardly chuckling.

Her face is noticeable anywhere. Being the daughter of the current Divine Ruler of the Lauvee Dynasty doesn't make you anonymous. Merlinda Lauvee XVII is in a country that despises her father. The smell of the room is of noscot cinnamon— the same tea Abubakr drinks. Even he's at a loss for words.

Garnett sighs, ruffling his blond hair. "Yeah. I mean, uh, yes, your highness."

"Dragons." She rolls her white, ice-like eyes. Each member of the Lauvee royal family has white pupils, marking their genetic relations to their ancestors. Never once have I thought I'd have the opportunity to see it in person.

"Don't call me 'your highness.' Or 'Princess.' Just call me Lin, please."

Garnett's gaze drifts to the brown sack Abubakr holds. Crimson red blood drips to the floor, seeping into the wooden cracks. Onyx clears his throat, scratching his doggy nose. "Well, you're all probably wondering why the Princess is here."

The Princess, or Lin, groans. "I told you to stop calling me that."

Onyx ignores her. "She's the magister of all Order operations in Lauvee. With Opal dead, we decided to have an emergency meeting by traveling to Lelina. I've heard things have been—" he notices my eyepatch— "Rough here."

"How the hell did you know she died?" Abubakr stammers, his ember eyes flaring.

Lin blinks, ruffling through her robe before pulling out a golden gemstone. "All magisters possess an onyx gemstone. When Onyx gives one to us, it glows until the magister dies or resigns from the order."

She's young, yet Onyx has trusted her to manage all of Lauvee, doing the same jobs that Opal does in this theorum. *The paperwork must be hell.*

"How about your parents?" I spill. "Do they know about you doing this?"

Lin chuckles nervously, brushing her silky hair aside. "The Dynasty has been aligned with the order for maybe a hundred years. The next of kin is always assigned to be the next magister of Lauvee. Years ago, it was my father. Now it's me."

Onyx's voice almost makes me jump. "Kedar, what's up with your eye?"

I unwrap my eyepatch, revealing my black, demonic pupils. The room recoils, except for Garnett, Ruby, and Abubakr. "It's a side effect of my demonic magic."

"I've seen those eyes before. With... you know who." His tail wags. *Munir, of course,* my mind echoes. "It's harmless, right?"

"Well, I bleed a bit, but I'm fine minutes later. I should be okay."

Fastening my eyepatch over my eye, Onyx shakes his head before heaving a sigh.

"Best to not worry about that now. Are the Veils dead?"

In response, Abubakr places the brown, bleeding sack on the table, unwrapping it to reveal Al-Barsim's blank, expressionless head. Lin doesn't exert a single reaction, only narrowing her eyes. I half-expect her to stumble out of this room like she's seen a demon.

"Maybe that answers our question," says Lin, tapping her fingers together. Garnett's expression shifts as I see his jade eyes light up again.

See? We are heroes, my mind echoes. *Maybe just not the peaceful type.*

The elf finally looks like himself again. Onyx averts his attention to me.

"How about Judah? Have you found out where he is?"

This time, I respond by pulling out the documents, setting them on the table for everyone to see. Lin's white eyes widen, shuffling through them in a hurry. Ruby winces a bit as I set her down on one of the chairs, giving her a sliver of rest.

She takes one of the papers and unfolds it for us to see. The paper is a drawing of a humongous fortress, with a note at the bottom of the page. Stammering, Ruby silently reads it out loud:

"This is the Messiah's fortress. We've planned to build it in the mountains of Nisf Thueban, in Jurania. The High One has personally requested that all builders use obsidian for the mage's chambers. If the Disturbed ever do show up to interrupt our ritual to break the seal, then those walls will be vital to stop their advance. It might be grueling. It might kill men. But the survivors shall be rewarded personally by the High One himself. In addition, he has gladly granted us his ever-powerful

cloaking magic, making our fortress invisible. It's fifteen thousand feet in the air. The environment is already a barrier for us. Rejoice, fellow Veils. The world will be resurrected soon."

Nisf Thueban, I repeat, muttering a curse under my breath. It has been under our noses this whole time. Onyx is busy reading through letters, while Lin is immersed in documents upon documents about Judah and this "Fortress." With a grunt, I narrow my eyes. "Have you guys found anything?"

"Building materials and a layout of the fortress. Bland, as one would say," Onyx offers.

Lin rolls her eyes. "Just a list of rations."

"Damnit. Same here," Chimes Ruby.

Abubakr's voice splits through the air after he clears his throat, holding up a small sheet of paper.

"You guys should hear this."

Fear is in his gaze.

"Dearest Al-Barsim,

Your concerns touch my soul. Do not fret. The Order will die if they find me after killing you. That is a promise.

All worries aside, I have good news. Omar has gone through his adorcism. He is obedient. The demonic magic in him is strong; our ritual has succeeded. He finally sees the world's faults and has officially agreed to be our god's vessel. He is destined to be Malik's vessel, and it'll finally break the seal holding our god from his sorrow cell. I can assure you that the First Gate of Hell will open on the first day of the new year. 439 years since Malik was sealed. What a day that shall be. If you survive my brother's subordinates, then visit. Catch a horse to Nisf Thueban.

Best regards, The High One."

401

Silence poisons the room. Not a word is uttered. Onyx seems hellbent, his tail wagging more aggressively by the second.

Lin stammers. "We have four weeks and a day. Forty-one days until the new year."

"I'll rally all the Order members we can get on this damn planet," Onyx grits. "We should have 150 assassins by the time everyone gets here."

Abubakr taps on the surface of one of the papers. "According to this note, the Veils only numbered 120 members in the compound."

Onyx's golden eyes glow, mimicking the shade of Abubakr's. "This will be our finale. Our final battle. We die or save the world. No in-between."

"But who's Malik?" Abubakr asks, his voice faltering. *My brother's alive. Alive in Nisf Thueban. I'll finally be able to save him.*

Onyx scrunches his nose. "I'll explain it to you in the mountains."

Hope flows through my mind. We have a chance. A small, slim chance. But it's still a *damn* chance. Saving Omar from the Veil's grasp is all I ever wanted since I agreed to become part of this Order. But now I'm saving him from being a vessel for Satan.

My time in Lelina is over. Nisf Thueban awaits.

"You're not coming with us, Garnett?" Abubakr asks.

We're at the north wall of Lelina. Onyx, Lin, and Garnett offer their goodbyes. The old geezer and princess are going to arrive a week late, since they plan to notify the rest of the magisters by traveling there physically.

Meanwhile, Abubakr, Ruby, and I are assigned to meet with Sulalat Basal's, Ultum's, and Hexia's assassins to help them set up camp.

Letters travel fast, apparently. Onyx has received responses from five magisters in a week.

Garnett's voice sinks through my monologue. "I just can't, Abubakr. If I change my mind... I'll come as fast as I can."

"You two, come here." Onyx points to me and Abubakr. Lin hovers next to the old dog, wrapped in heavy cloaks to mask herself. Her knights stand over her, their weapons at the ready.

With a subtle cough, Onyx's eyes flutter under his dark brown cloak. His pointy ears flatten a bit. "This initiation ritual is... a bit off-centered, I know."

Abubakr's jaw drops as Onyx pulls two gemstones out of his cloak. I gaze at a small nugget of gold, while in his other hand is a rock I've never seen before. "Assassins who join my order are named by the gemstones I give them."

He hands the gold to Abubakr and offers the reddish gemstone to me. Onyx glances at Abubakr. "The name that everyone shall know you as will now be Dhahab. Your fiery magic aligns with the rock, representing power and success."

"Kedar—" he continues, as I look down at the gemstone he places in my palm— "This stone here is called a Vanta crystal."

It's black, void like the color of my eyes. Emotionless and heartless. White sparkles dot its jagged edges, forming a spiral-like shape. Onyx continues. "You are now Vantos. The demonic power you have doesn't consume you. You consume *it*. This stone consumes all light, resisting the sun with its darkened surface."

Vantos. I repeat the name. *Vantos.*

I keep repeating the phrase as the three of us wave off Garnett, Onyx, and Lin. Ruby notices my blank expression, placing a hand on my shoulder. "Vantos, right? Vanta crystals are rare— only found in the deepest, darkest caves of Haya."

I scoff as my new name rolls off of Ruby's tongue. *I can get used to this.* "Never mind that."

Turning to Abubakr, or Dhahab, he shoves the golden nugget into the pockets of his cloak. "How long till we reach the fort, Dhahab?"

"Stay calling me Dhahab." He fastens his cloak, staring into the sun with a smile. "You never knew how to pronounce my name. It's easy. AH-boo-bah-ker."

Dhahab awkwardly chuckles once he notices me and Ruby's scorn. "Anyway, it should take us maybe three weeks."

"Best, ready yourselves. If you think Lelina isn't cold, then wait until we start our climb."

Ruby grumbles.

Her Holiness Merlinda Lauvee XVII is the daughter of the King, Gaston Lauvee XVI. Even though she's only sixteen years of age, she has completely mastered her family's generational ice magic. The art is learned in four phases, but the family hasn't explained how the operation works. Those who do have ice magic but are not part of the Lauvee family learn the practice is only two phases to ensure the Lauvee dominance. Her glorious white eyes only exemplifies Merlinda's beauty. Rest assured, our kingdom shall be stable for the next decades to come.

- A writing by the Lauvee Dynasty's Scribe capitalizing on the accomplishments of Lauvee XVII.

ACT THREE:

MESHUGGAH

*A CAMP ON THE **ERIK** **PLATEAUS** OF THE **NISF** **THUEBAN** RANGE.*

Elevation: 13,539 feet.

Date: 348th Day of the 1438th Year.

TWENTY-SIX

Dhahab's right. The freeze on this mountain is enough to make me get frostbite in seconds. Ruby's shivering, her arms crossed together as Dhahab fastens the gray ushanka on his head. I do the same, making sure it covers my ears. Even with the white blizzard, the shining sun still creeps through the white flakes of death.

Five days ago, we arrived at the snowy peaks of Nisf Thueban. The campsite was a lot more dull back then compared to now. Dhahab's ember magic lit up candles, campfires, and lamps galore. Now, it is immersed in the soft, golden yellow glow of fire mages and witches.

The air's thin, but our mana makes it easier for us to breathe. During our escapade, Ruby has taught me and Dhahab how to apply our mana with our bodies, giving us physical enhancements. Her technique involves manipulating the flow of our mana to concentrate on our lungs for better breathing, or focusing our mana on our feet to enhance our speed.

412

It is like when I beat the Veil in Al-Jukar's manor, my anger makes my body more perceptive. But I control my magic, my magic doesn't control me. According to Ruby, all mana-users do this to their bodies to make it easier for them to fight. It's called Hiam Flow.

Ruby rubs her gloves together. "I'm going to die up here."

Chattering my teeth, I sigh. "Ruby, you're going to be fine."

The three of us stand on the Erik Plateaus, fifty feet below the peaks of Nisf Thueban. Above us is the invisible fortress.

The view's breathtaking, low temperatures aside. Nations are visible through the gray fog, as well as the massive Kigamouth Lake. Sliding my fingers over the crystal necklace on my neck, I motion to Dhahab. "We should get back."

He nods in agreement. "At least it's not too cold in the camps."

Ember mages surround our base camp with gemstones to make mages harness their magic. They channel their mana to the gemstones to keep the continuous warm temperatures without physically acting out the spell. As a side effect, the mage gets drained over the day until another takes their place.

Dhahab snaps his fingers, a small flame igniting for only a second before abruptly vanishing. He pushes his dreads out of his eyes, unbothered by the freeze. Having mana from fire must make his body temperature warmer than others.

He snaps his fingers again. "I ran out of spark. Now we have to get back to the camps before the two of you freeze out here."

Assassins in the camp hand out blankets, cloaks, and jackets to the population. Those who are used to the cold from Jura, Crale, or Ultum aren't affected much, but the assassins from Basalia, Sulalat Basal, and Hexia have different responses. They're freezing.

413

The ushanka on our heads is part of goblin attire, with flaps to cover our ears. It's a bit of a hassle to put on, but it's extremely effective. The furry, thick cloak we wear does its best to keep us warm, but it's so *damn* cold.

"My fingers are turning blue," Ruby awkwardly chuckles, but I roll my eyes.

"That's just your healing aura." I point to the obvious glow at her fingertips.

"Ugh, shut up, *Vantos*."

I like my new name. Much better than "Kedar." Vantos... sounds like it means enigma. Hearing my own name makes me think of my father and mother.

Trekking through the snow, we stomp over the two feet of white fluff, dragging our boots. We cross the barrier of ember gemstones around the camp, and an array of warmth flushes through my body. I heave a sigh. *Thank the Dragon.*

Dhahab has offered more of his mana to fuel the ring in exchange for more rations. Diamond, the magister from Ultum, has given Dhahab more bread and meat for us to share.

Assassins stroll through the camp, their boots making a trail of footprints in every direction. There's a tent for everything— smithing, accommodations, food.

"Care to enjoy a beer, you three?" a sultry voice says.

The elf calling me out from the crowd is Em, short for Emerald. Apparently, this is Lapis's nephew. Rather than mimicking his uncle's green eyes, Em's is a dark, porcelain blue.

Lapis and Em are from the island kingdom of Vania, and Lapis has made the decision to travel to Basalia to work with Onyx, while Em stays in Vania. The elf is like a father to Em, since Em's parents have passed away in an accident at sea. Seems like Lapis has raised him pretty well, aside from the manic drinking sessions Em has. Em slicks his dark brown hair against his pointy ears, motioning to his cup of beer.

"It's seven in the morning. Too early," I say, waving him off with a chuckle. Em shrugs, taking another swing. *They're so damn different,* I note in my mind. I slide off my gloves.

Em takes notice of this, realizing the absence of my other pointer finger. "Damn. How'd that happen?"

"It's a long story." I smile, stuffing the gloves into my cloak. "You should ask Lapis about it."

"My uncle?" he scoffs, taking another sip.

"He'll scold me for drinking before even answering my question."

I laugh at that. Em's one of the many assassins I've taken the opportunity of knowing over the past couple of days. Being an extrovert, Em has a smug attitude with impressive sword skills. He cracks so many jokes that I find it hard to believe that he can kill someone.

Ruby and Dhahab are long gone, mingling with the other assassins in the camp. Most of the Order's forces are busy hanging out, training, or having a smoke in preparation for our battle.

I glance back at Em. "Any news about the Council?"

Crossing his arms against his brown tunic, Em wiggles his black boots in the snow. Suppressing an answer for me, he turns to the large tent a couple of feet from us. The white tapestry makes it invisible in the fog, wisping through the wind.

"They're going to meet there." Em purses his lips. "Once all ten magisters are here, Onyx is going to conduct a meeting about the battle. At least there's already five here; Diamond would probably freeze to death if it was just him and his crew."

"Yeah, no doubt about that." I clasp my arm around his shoulder. Em's only a few years older than me, mimicking the erratic energy Ruby has. "I'm heading off to eat breakfast. Are you coming with me?"

"I'll be fine, Vantos. All I need is my booze." Taking another sip, he exhales a sigh.

Offering a shrug, I wave him goodbye, gazing at the tents littering our camp. Some are shaped like cones, while some are more boxy and uniform. Crates with supplies are stacked like building blocks against the tents— a sign that there are rations for everyone.

Dhahab and Ruby are in front of the rations tent with other assassins. Squeezing myself in line, I mutter apologies to every annoyed comrade I pass. With my height, it's easy to see them in the crowd. The cooks and chefs in the test cook as fast as they can, their spatulas and serving spoons mixing and flipping today's meals at lightspeed. A sign on the tent's entrance:

Servings for today: Rabbit Stew, Scrambled Eggs on Toast, or Shukfuri.

Shukfuri... my mind repeats. Memories of my mother making the meal fill my thoughts. Fried steak with Shukfuri sauce. I smile at the taste of it. Sweet and spicy, black paprika, Kigamouth salt, bone paste, and Hellspiel peppers. I haven't had it since my parents died. Now is a good time to relish their memories.

"You're pondering again." I jump at Ruby's voice. "Are you thinking about Shukfuri?"

Rubbing my hands together, I nod. "A bit, yeah."

Dhahab's too exhausted to look at us. Judging by the dark circles under his eyes, his constant tethering to the ember gemstones makes him fatigued. He notices my stare.

"Ugh. I'll be fine, Vantos."

"You sure?" I offer.

His tone freezes. "Yes. I'll be *fine.* If I drop dead, then consider me... not fine."

416

Ruby laughs before pulling down the ear flaps of my ushanka. I entangle my fingers with her braids, offering a smile. "You gotta braid my hair sometime."

She scoffs as we move up the line. She examines my curls. "I don't think I've braided this kind of hair—" Ruby glances at Dhahab's dreads— "But I can braid his, for sure."

"Why's that?" I narrow my eyes.

"Well, it's hard to braid hair either way. And I only know how to braid hair like mine." Ruby gently takes my hand off her braided strands. "Had to teach myself after my hair started to look more puffy than these damn clouds."

Dhahab sighs, stepping in front of us. "You know, I think they're running out of Shakfuri."

Glancing at the chefs, I curse as I realize Dhahab's right. The once steady supply of their sauce and steak is dimming fast. Every assassin ahead of us seems to be ordering the exact same thing. Rabbit stew isn't exactly my favorite food, but I can manage.

Scrambled eggs on toast is a meal I've been having since my army days. When we starve in the jungles, we'll bake bread and steal quail eggs. Anything to survive.

We arrive at the front of the line, and Dhahab gives us a small look before stepping up to the chefs. "Got any Shakfuri?"

"This is our last portion, Dhahab." The chef notices our presence. "Wanna split it with these two?"

Dhahab and I lock eyes, and I stare into his gaze. Ruby pouts as Dhahab shakes his head.

"No. It'll be for me only, thanks."

The boy made of ember ignores us as he passes by with a bowl full of Shakfuri.

The scrambled eggs and toast aren't bad. We're sitting on the woolly blanket on the snow, acting as our floor, enjoying our meals against the small wooden table between us.

Ruby sighs, slurping at her rabbit stew with her spoon. "Why'd Dhahab even leave?"

Chewing through my toast, I blink away the possibilities. "You know, maybe he's just tired. His mana's slowly being used up every second. Of course, he's a little moody."

"You're right." She stares down at her stew, swirling it slowly.

"Teenagers." I scoff at myself. "Always up to some—"

"I need to tell you something."

My face contorts into confusion, then worry. I put my toast down on my plate gently. "Ruby, what's up?"

Her skin glows under the soft light of the lanterns in our tent, her red eyes sparkling. I can't imagine being angry at her, no matter what she tells me. Our tent even reminds me of our hotel room in Lelina— having a bed, a small drawer for storage, and even a small living room space.

"I don't like it when I call you Vantos."

She rubs her fingers against her robe. Heat's already rushing to my cheeks.

"What do you mean?"

She hooks her arms around my neck, glancing up at me.

"I like calling you Kedar more."

There's truth in her words. Ruby breathes in my scent, her nose against my neck. "Kedar is who I fell in love with, not Vantos."

"Ruby—" I stammer, my voice faltering. She pushes me back, and we fall to the floor with a *thud.*

Dragons, what the hell is she…

My tone shifts to slight annoyance.

418

"I don't like it when people say my name. It... doesn't bring good memories."

"Tell me." She brings her head down, our noses touching. "I need to know."

I can't even form a sentence, and she expects me to—

"I feel empty. Losing my parents and failing to protect my brother..." My voice breaks. "Whenever someone calls my name... I always think of those things."

Ruby's hand creeps up the side of my cheek, rubbing it against my flushed expression. Her hands move to my eyepatch as she slips it off, gazing deep into my red pupils.

"But when I say your name... I don't think of how you have demonic magic. I don't think of how you used to strike down on people, fueling your revenge."

A tear streams down the side of my head, but Ruby's there to smudge it up with her thumb.

"You just want to make things right."

Her breath hitches as her arms wrap around me. We lie on our makeshift floor. I stay silent. *Is this what people want? Not war, glory, or gold.*

Is it just love?

"Ruby—"

"No." She sighs. There are tears in her eyes, too. "Just call me Laila."

"Your real name?" I say, offering her a comforting gaze.

"From now on, okay?"

Even though I hesitate a little, I nod.

She presses a kiss to my jawline.

"You'll always be Kedar to me. And I'll always be Laila to you."

"But why?" I stammer.

"Because you make me feel like I can be myself."

419

Grumbling, I smile when she closes her eyes, nestling against me.

Her voice dims into a whisper.

"Kedar... I don't love what the world paints you out to be. I love the real you. Only you."

Kedar.

Vantos is a part of me. The part that's trained to be an assassin under Onyx's wing and killed Veil members in Lelina. The part that's grabbed the gemstone from Onyx hours before we left to climb up this damn mountain.

But I'm still Kedar.

It's the chanting of hundreds of people that wakes me up from my daze. Through the cracks of our tent, people pump their fists into the air and cheer.

I try to move, but there's something on top of me. *Laila.*

Her arms are still hooked around my neck, her body glued to mine. I poke her cheek, my tone soft. "Laila. Wake up."

Her red eyes flutter as she gains consciousness. The echoes of the cheers outside make her turn her head to check the commotion. She sighs. "We fell asleep?"

Reluctantly, I nod. "Yeah. Sorry."

"It's fine."

"We have to see what's going on outside," I explain as we put on our boots. Slipping out of the tapestry, I shield my eyes as the skies almost destroy my vision.

Outside is a parade of assassins walking through our lines of tents like soldiers. All wear the same armor, while swords, axes, halberds, and war hammers are strapped on their backs. We spot Dhahab, leaning against the crates outside his tent, watching the soldiers stream by.

"Huh. Seems like you guys woke up from your beauty sleep." He laughs at his own joke before yawning. "I didn't get a single bite. Duty calls."

Dhahab flutters his eyes. A sorrowful look falls upon Laila's expression. "You'll be fine. Just hang in there."

The rows of assassins are led by magisters, their blue-lined cloaks sticking out from our gold ones. Onyx has switched out my silver one for a gold cloak, now that I'm officially an Order member.

Before Dhahab can respond, a familiar elf and a Princess stroll through the camp. Onyx leads the magisters behind him, leaning against a long walking stick. He's barefoot on his paws, wearing a black robe to contrast his brown fur. Once he spots us, his tail wags a little.

"Hello, children." Onyx offers a nod. "How was the trip?"

"It was cold," Laila jokes.

The Princess, Garnett, and Dhahab hit it off instantly, like a trio of old friends. We watch them mingle and greet each other with peace. This time, Lin's wearing her woolly mittens to match her blue wool cloak over her metal armor underneath.

I clear my throat as I glance back at Onyx. "Anything new happen?"

"Well, the army you saw was a hefty group of eighty. I brought the other magisters— Quartz, Topaz, Kyln, and Princess Lauvee." His onyx eyes squint. "Anyone who didn't want to go stayed in their theorums. It would be bad if we didn't have anyone operating in any nations while we are gone."

Before I can look at them, they hustle into the Council's tent, escaping from my view. They all conceal themselves with their hoods, so it's impossible to see their faces.

Onyx notices my attention averted to the tent. "I'll hold an assembly in just a couple of minutes. I have to address the council about our battle plans. It was hard enough explaining Judah's plans on the way here."

His expression changes as we lock eyes. "Why don't you come with me, Vantos? We're going to discuss your brother in that tent."

Looking at Laila and Dhahab, I sigh as they nod in approval. I scoff, then turn to Onyx. "Well, it would be odd if I didn't join you."

My two friends wave me goodbye as they go off to join Garnett, who's already wondering where all the Shakfuri went. Onyx and I are about to enter the Council's tent when he stops me. Murmurs of the magisters hound my ears from inside with hymns of greetings.

"Vantos," Onyx begins, his voice a hushed whisper. "If we speak about Omar, hold your ground. My magisters will hound you with questions, indeed. Be diligent. Understood, child?"

I nod, and we stroll into the tent. In the middle is a cylinder-like pillar holding up the tent's tapestry. Circling around it is a wooden table with nine seats. Lin sits in one of them, giving me a nervous glance as she taps her nails on the table's rough surface.

Diamond sits next to her, his green skin contrasting with his light blue eyes. His creases indicate his old age, while his black hair is tied in a ponytail. Wearing a leather vest over his white shirt, he squints once he lays his eyes on me, tightening his gloves.

"Hello, Sir Onyx."

Onyx nods, motioning his hands towards his Council of Magisters after sitting on an empty seat on the right side of the table. Gulping, I stand behind his chair. *So this is how the Order functions, important decisions being made with all of the Council present.*

"Greetings, my fellow mages. I would like to apologize for our meeting location, but alas, the world sits at our fingertips. With that, our meeting has officially commenced."

"Onyx." A woman glances in my direction. While she doesn't wear armor, she has one of the blue-lined cloaks from earlier. I realize that the other five magisters have red-lined cloaks over blue. The red cloaks outnumber the blue cloaks. *No wonder Opal's robe was lined with a dark blue hue.* "Who the hell is this?"

Onyx awkwardly chuckles. "Kyln, this is Vantos."

Everyone's eyes are on me. Human eyes, Farik eyes, goblin eyes, and elf eyes. *I feel like I'm being auctioned off.*

"Vantos is the brother of Judah's sacrificial vessel for Malik."

The room erupts. Question after question hurls at my face.

"What? Do you have demonic magic too?"

"Is he weak? Strong?"

"How powerful is his demonic magic?"

"Are you even ready enough to take on Judah?"

"How the hell did you let your brother get into Judah's grubby hands—"

"FOR THE DRAGON'S SAKE, THAT'S ENOUGH!"

And the room is silent. Onyx's fist plants into the table, a small crack forming from his fury. Clearing his throat, Onyx sighs, and his expression stiffens. "What matters is our battle scheme. We must have a pristine plan to throw Judah off his throne before he can break Malik's seal."

It takes minutes for someone to speak. A Farik fixes his spectacles, two seats left from Onyx and next to Lin. Instead of a blue cloak, he has a red-lined one. He scratches the blond fur at the back of his head. "We should attack with four different forces."

Onyx seems a bit skeptical, rubbing the bottom of his jaw. "Continue, Peridot."

Peridot pulls a paper sticking out of his cloak. The other magisters help unroll and spread the paper on the table, revealing the large-scale map of Nisf Thueban. An X on the right side symbolizes the fortress, while a circle symbolizing our camp is ten inches from it.

Peridot moves his finger to the north side of the fortress. "Kyln can lead half of our men to charge from this side. Using our elemental mages, we can smash through the fortress walls."

Kyln rolls her eyes, but doesn't disagree.

He moves to the right of the X. "Three magisters can be positioned here to infiltrate the fortress walls. They'll be able to clear it from any guards; it'll suppress arrow fire."

"Extravagant proposal, Peridot. Does anyone else have ideas to propose?"

A human with skin mimicking Ruby's clears their throat. He wears a red-lined cloak over his black tunic, covered with red squiggly tribal patterns from Sulalat Basal. "I have a few ideas."

Onyx nods for him to continue. The man's eyes dart around the map. His wrinkles tell me he's the same age as Lapis, his mind ripe but body drained from years of wear and tear. "I can take 70 men to lead a charge. On the north side, Peridot can be in charge of 40 men to infiltrate the tops of the walls, which gives me ten more soldiers to work with. I can't even think of where I can place them."

"It's fine, Steele." Onyx blinks, deep in thought. "Vantos and I will take eight Order members to slip inside the fortress as the three other magisters clear our way. According to documents from Al-Barsim, Judah's "Messiah Chambers" are at the lowest point of the fort, three floors below ground level."

The room maintains its silence, but everyone nods in agreement. *This is it.*

In a week, Omar will be in my arms.

Onyx draws out the plans using a quill and stops with a grunt. Standing from his seat, Onyx raises his paws to get the other magister's attention. "Those in favor of this plan, stand. Those who are not, stay seated, as you will."

One by one, each magister stands alongside Onyx.

Seems like our plan's set in stone. Onyx scoffs, clasping his hands together. "By the Dragon's grace. Unanimous agreement. We have twelve days to prepare. Train your troops and nurture them. Prepare them for our battle, and Basal bless you all."

Soon enough, the magisters make their way out of the tent, leaving me and Onyx alone. The old man's truly a leader. His stub where his other arm's supposed to be reminds me that he's saved my life.

He offers a nod.

"Well, time to make the announcement to the other Order members. Follow me, Vantos."

My mind churns at the thought of our plan being foiled.

Bodies everywhere, limbs torn apart.

I won't let that happen.

To the Council,
There is a grave situation upon us which not only threatens our lives, but it threatens the planet itself. I decree for all Magisters to report to the Erik Plateaus as spoon as they can.

- An excerpt of the letter Onyx wrote to the magisters regarding the trip to Nisf Thueban.

TWENTY-SEVEN

D ays move more slowly than years. Assassins have grouped

themselves into twenty, sparring on battlegrounds with swords and spears. The magisters keep editing and adding things to our plan to overrun the Veils. On the other hand, Onyx has assigned me to select Order members fit enough to join our extraction team.

Besides me and Onyx, I've picked Laila and Dhahab to be at my side. Tomorrow is when we're going to ambush that damn fortress once and for all. I feel like a general leading faithful men into battle with my little army. Once the army completes the climb to the top, Onyx is going to use his Astral magic to destroy the cloaking spell.

Laila and I are busy strolling through the camp, our coats fighting against the harsh cold. "Kedar, our attack is hours away. Stop procrastinating and pick everyone else already."

"I know," I mumble, the yellow sun shining on our faces. For the past couple of days, the sky's been crystal clear, the

427

conditions perfect for our impending invasion. "I'm kinda struggling here."

Laila rolls her eyes, not amused. Our boots crunch against the snow, the scent of Shakfuri coming from the chef's tent again. As much as I want to relish Shakfuri, time isn't exactly on my side.

Dhahab and Lin stroll through the crowd, noticing our presence. Laila waves them over, and we huddle in front of a wagon full of crates.

"Vantos, Lin wants to join us." Lin awkwardly chuckles when Dhahab motions at her. Her white pupils sparkle in the sunlight, her silver hair running down her neck.

"She does?" I scratch my beard. Lin being here on this mountain, either way, is off-the-charts dangerous. If she dies, the Lauvee crown won't have a next of kin. "Lin, what can you do?"

She takes off one of her mittens, offering her silky hands. "Alright, I'll show you."

Taking a deep breath, Lin widens her palms, a light blue aura spiraling in her fingertips.

In an instant, a silver icicle manifests in her hand, floating inches away from the surface of her skin. Lin seals her eyelids closed, focusing on her magic. The icicle begins to duplicate itself over and over, forming into a sword made out of ice.

"Water and ice manipulation," Dhahab elaborates, crossing his arms. "Lin can do the same thing I can— the only difference being that she uses water over fire."

"Damn," Laila whispers, as Lin wields the sword with a tight grip. "You use your magic pretty well."

"Well, when someone in the family activates their mana..." Lin sighs. "We undergo harsh training with witches and wizards to ensure our magical abilities are up to perfection."

428

With that, the sword Lin is holding shatters into thousands of pieces. Clearing her throat, her monotone demeanor shifts a bit, excitement flooding her face. "So, can I come along?"

I scratch my beard even more before offering a nod. "You're in."

"Sounds like you need a squad, Vantos!" A voice shouts behind me.

No, it can't be.

Lapis has his hands on his hips, his eyes lighting up once seeing me and Laila. Summer's passed since I last saw him. His jawline's a bit sharper, his skin glowing. Even though he's in his early forties, he doesn't look a day over twenty.

Running up to him, I clasp our hands together. His black leather gloves contrast with his soft blond hair. On his back is a long sword twice as big as the *Kathi.* "Lapis. What a surprise seeing you here."

"Well... seems like you've changed." He notices my eyepatch and my dented bone dagger.

"Where's the *Kathi?*"

Laila's eyes drift to the weaponsmith's tent. "They're fixing it up. It should be done by the time we've recruited everyone."

I remember that Lapis was in Hexia while I was in Lelina. "How was your mission?"

A figure steps behind Lapis. It's Bix, ruffling his brown hair to get it out of his eyes. "Twas a bit violent'n brutaul, but nuthin special, lad."

A smile encrusts my face as squeaking wheels riddle the snow. Obsidian's strolling through the hills of white powder, trailing behind Bix. "Oi! Thought you could leave me?"

"Obby!" Laila exclaims. Dhahab and Lin look at us with confusion.

As Obby and Ruby greet each other, Bix clicks his teeth, clasping his hands on Lapis' shoulders. "'Exia was a mess that Onyx told us to clean up. Couple deaths 'ere and there, but we pulled through.'"

"Don't remind me of that," Lapis sighs, before averting his gaze. "Anyways— is it possible that me, Bix, and Obby can come along with your squad?"

Lapis is the man who rescued my brother from Alfdan. Obby has done his best to save Omar from the spell he was under. Bix is just here, existing, but his accent has convinced me enough.

"Hell yeah."

"I'll act as your medic," Obby's voice chimes, Laila's lips purse in satisfaction. "I'll be healing any assassins that I deem wounded."

Even with Bix, Lapis, and Obby joining the reigns, there are still two empty spots. I lead everyone to the central campfire, where most assassins mingle. Every person I pitch our idea to is too intimidated by the thought of being in the presence of Judah's demonic magic to even consider joining.

I'm about to give up when I spot two familiar faces in the crowd. Em and Garnett are laughing while hanging out near some crates full of supplies. I glance at everyone behind me. "I'll be back. Just give me a minute."

"Let me come with you," Lapis offers, spotting his nephew. "I haven't greeted Em yet anyway."

"When's the last time you saw each other?" I ask as we wisp through the winding groups of assassins.

"It's been five years. Traveling from country to country isn't easy with The Dragon's War rampaging for the past five decades." Lapis huffs, glancing down at the snow. "But I've sent him letters."

"Well, Em's told me you're like a father to him." The elf's face lights up.

"That's good to hear."

I haven't spoken to Garnett since Opal died. Hopefully time's changed him— isn't that what they say?

"Uncle Lucien?" Em voice hitches. Lapis scowls, and Em clears his throat. *Seriously? His real name is Lucien?* "I mean, Lapis..."

"It's been a while."

Em drops the cup of beer he's holding and sprints into Lapis' arms. It's the kind of hug my father would give me before putting me to bed. I miss those days, when everything felt so *safe*. Too bad nothing's the same anymore.

Garnett and I watch the two, but he eventually takes in my presence.

"What do you want?" His stricken tone feels like a stab to the heart.

"Look, Garnett, I know you're still grieving Op—"

"I'm not." He rubs his forehead, nuzzling against his woolly cloak. "I realized I was dwelling on things I shouldn't be dwelling on. It's pointless to drown yourself in grief."

Before I can get in a word, Garnett rubs his fingers against the gemstone sitting on his neck.

"I'm sorry. I already apologized to Abu— I mean, Dhahab. I shouldn't have pushed everyone away like I did. But I'm thankful that you killed Al-Barsim. Avenged my mother, even though she's not my blood."

My voice softens. "Have you heard about the extraction team I'm supposed to be leading?"

"Yeah, I did," Garnett nods before his face lights up. "Wait, you want me to... join you?"

I nod. "Yes, I do. You and Em."

Garnett offers a sigh, as Em and Lapis come back, their smiles brighter than ever. Elves are more of a cheerful race compared to humans, Fariks, and goblins. Either way, it isn't all that surprising.

Lapis snaps. "Em's coming."

Garnett's dagger gleams from his waist. "Well, I guess I'm being dragged along as well."

I count up the people in my head again.

Me, Onyx, Lin, Dhahab, Em, Lapis, Obby, Bix, Laila, and Garnett.

It's ten. *Dragons, finally.*

"You three, meet at the campfire south of here. It's where everyone else will be."

I'll never get tired of the sounds of crackling fire. The way it tickles my eardrums and how it hounds my soul. Fire's always such an interesting concept to not just feel, but *see*. The constant wafting of orange and red flames allure me. So much so that I sometimes find myself engulfing my fingertips in the blaze. *Never again,* I chuckle to myself.

The dimly lit moon beams on us, fighting against the smoke from our campfire. Sitting on logs around the fire are my ten handpicked assassins, who I know are well equipped for our impending fight. Taking out a cigar, I light it against the blaze. *One more smoke before this all goes down,* I think as I take a hit.

Light chatter surrounds me. Dhahab, Garnett, and Lin are busy talking about the new lost sheet music from the dead artist Jannesterman. Onyx, Bix, and Obby are both discussing the fastest method to assassinate their prey, while Lapis and Em are catching up on their adventures.

Laila and I are just there, not speaking, just eavesdropping on their conversations. She doesn't need to say a word to tell me how she feels about our battle. Her finger drawing circles in my palm tells me everything I need to know.

"You ready?" I eventually ask, tired from our silence.

Laila glances up, her eyes lost in mine. "It's been so long. Two seasons since I met you. I can't believe we're up on some mountain, getting ready to kill a bunch of Veils. They've been so hard to catch for so long, the thought of me slaying more than twenty of them doesn't even cross my mind."

Exhaling the warm smoke into the cold air, I glance at the view of the mountains again. Towns, cities, and farms stretching for miles on end, illuminated with the glows of lanterns and candles. They don't even know what carnage is about to happen.

"I'm thankful," I admit, smiling. Nobody knows about me and her, not even Dhahab or Garnett. I guess we're pretty good at hiding... whatever this is.

"Without you, this Order... Omar would be long gone."

Laila stifles a laugh, shaking her head. "I guess you're right about that."

Onyx abruptly stands from the log, clearing his throat with a hint of worry in his expression. Even though Onyx simply stands up, everyone goes silent.

"It'll take us an hour of climbing to get over the mountains. Once I break through their cloaking magic, we must act quickly."

Bix strokes his chin while Obby curls his nails against the armrests of his wheelchair.

"We've been presented with two options," he begins, his walking stick crunching against the ground. "Follow Peridot and his team to use our portable ladders over the stone walls, or wisp inside with Steele and his dire charge."

433

Onyx squints. "We must take a vote. Go for the charge, or wreak havoc on the fortress walls."

Garnett raises his hand. "I'll say, Sir Onyx... we should join the charge. Our manpower is massive, and we'll—"

He stops once noticing nobody else has raised their hand except him. Nervously clearing his throat, he pouts as Onyx chuckles. "I assume you all chose the first option."

As Onyx's cloak blows in the chilly wind, Garnett groans in defeat. "Thus, I shall now speak to the rest of the assassins. Before we trek the slopes, a speech is essential."

With that, we stand to follow the Grand Magister of the Onyx Order on his way to address the masses. Although we walk slowly, we get to the podium in the middle of the camp with Onyx, breathing in a deep breath.

Assassins stand in four groups, their directing magisters leading. The ten of us go to the front of legions of warriors at our backs. On our left are the northern forces, led by Diamond and a few other magisters. Peridot and his group of thirty are in six lines, their swords drawn, belts filled with razqatars.

The army's eyes are dead set on Onyx, their expressions filled with angst and pride. After climbing up the wooden steps, chants begin to arise from the masses.

"ARCEH ATOLL-TAJJEN!"

"ARCEH ATOLL-TAJJEN!"

"ARCEH ATOLL-TAJJEN!"

It's a phrase taken from The Codex of Basal. Even though it's an ancient dialect, even I know what this means, it's repeated by millions of Dracotheists around the world.

The Dragon Lives. The Dragon Lives. The Dragon Lives.

For the first time in a while, Onyx grins, his walking stick tapping against the podium in beat with their chants. *Poetic,* I think. *God's on our side, isn't he?*

"Yea, hear my plea, my gracious ORDER!" Onyx bellows, the chants winding down. He plants his paws deeper into the surface, his back straight. Not an ounce of nervousness is in his gaze. Only pure justice.

"It seems fate has led us here," he begins, his tone graceful.

"For the past two hundred years, I've anointed over five thousand assassins to compile my Order. This new wave of generational expertise in terms of resilience, speed, and encouragement has ultimately led us here, inches away from killing what the Veils call The High One: Judah. Malik's seal hasn't been touched in one thousand years, and that streak shall continue if we stop him tonight."

Pointing to the top of the mountain, his tone shifts in urgency.

"At that fortress is the source of all demons. The Veils have caused treachery, death, extortion, robbery— name it all. Their deaths shall occur tonight, at the darkest hour, at the beginning of the new year. We are doing this in the grace of Basal, our wondrous Dragon.

Hundreds of Order members have died at the Veils, and thus, it is time that we, as an Order, shall strike back. Save this world from their cryptic and secretive methods. We must not allow them to break the seal that holds Malik and save those who are abducted in the process.

Fret not. *Everything must be done in the Highest, the Gracious Dragon.* These agents of evil, born from Satan himself, must be dealt with precision. Death must occur within the fortress walls, leaving not a soul alive.

When you stab a man with your blade, mindfully consider THAT YOU ARE RIDING A DEMON! Unlike Vantos, they stand on the demonic side of power.

SHOW THESE VEILS OUR MIGHT. CRIPPLE THEM WITH FEAR. TAKE MY LEAD TO LIBERATE AND SAVE THIS WORLD!"

The crowd explodes into chants and cheers as Onyx proceeds with a heavy bow. Climbing down the podium, I offer a nod. All around us, the Order cheers, fashioning themselves in the Veils and their impending doomsday. Onyx's assurance only enhances our battling spirit.

I smile at Onyx as he comes near our squad. "Thank you, Onyx. For everything."

"Don't thank me. Thank Basal."

The hour-long climb to the fortress hasn't been the brightest. So far, five men have fallen to their deaths, and I've been smacked in the face dozens of times by the heel of people's combat boots. Using our portable ladders, ropes, and harnesses, we scale the edgy slope, our fingers numbing from the friction of the rough rocky mountain surface.

Our Hiam Flow makes it easier to climb. Enhancing my muscles and nervous system makes gripping the ledges feel like nothing. Even though we've been under extreme, icy conditions, Onyx and other magisters have been finalizing and double-checking their battle plans. Climbing with one arm doesn't make a difference— he hasn't broken a single drop of sweat so far.

Steele and I have even discussed his plan to trudge the path to the fortress after our climb, charging through the walls after Onyx disperses the cloaking mana.

Even with Hiam Flow, my arms feel like jelly. My persistence and arrogance are what keep me going to get to the top. It's impossible to take a break since there isn't a single ledge on the mountain that's big enough to sit and rest on.

Not a single time is wasted to grieve those who fall from the climb, as Onyx leads the masses by flinging himself from rock to rock. It doesn't seem like the act of leaving people behind bothers him.

What matters is killing Judah.

Laila climbs a bit faster than I, like how she's scaled those buildings in Ardon. With a grunt, her fingers grasp onto the next crack of rocks she can grip onto. The moonlight isn't exactly working in our favor— it's blinding.

But nevertheless, the ledge begins to fade into view.

Laila laughs, exhaustion in her tone. "Almost there. *Dragons,* I feel like I'm melting."

Before I can respond, Obby flings by, hopping from rock to rock flawlessly. He aimlessly streams past every assassin who can't keep up with his pace. With his wheelchair folded and strapped to his back, he leaps and coils like a frog.

"Now this is what you call a gift!" Obby notices our surprised, confused expressions. "Without legs— your arms get stronger, stronger with Hiam Flow."

Shaking my head, I laugh at the sight. "Even with this magical technique, I can barely muster the strength to grasp the next damn handhold."

"You're right, Vantos," Obby eagerly replies, his bald head gleaming in the moonlight. "But I can't relate."

Using Hiam Flow, breathing the thin air up here is easy. All we need to do is channel our mana through our lungs, giving us the strength to absorb all the oxygen we can. The Flow is something I've seen every mage and witch do during our treacherous army battles— I've just never put a name to it until now.

Obby eventually disappears over the ledge, dust of rocks nearly blinding my eyes. Blinking away the debris, I slap my hand into the snow of the ledge, pulling myself up.

Dragons. This climb is over, finally.

The suffering itself is worth it. Streaming through the mountain range is a valley that cuts it in half. White snow litters the stretch of land, the rush of cold air running down my nostrils. It's even chillier than it is at our camp below.

The hard part about our mission has barely begun, but first we need to regroup ourselves.

"Peridot?" I call out among the unorganized army. "Where the hell are you?"

"So obnoxious, Kedar," Laila huffs, resting her hands on her hips as she catches her breath.

Sniffing my nose, I notice her flushed cheeks from the icy temperatures. I smirk. "You're barely hanging on, Laila."

"You fell." Her eyes narrowed, her expression boldened. "Twice."

"Almost fell," I correct, as everyone begins to organize themselves.

Laila rolls her eyes as I spot Peridot's crew of 40 soldiers at the left side of the valley, readying to sneak up the higher slopes of the mountain. I grumble, realizing I'll have to climb again. Marching down the middle of the valley are Steele's charging unit, while a flanking force has already moved to the right.

Motioning Laila over, we make our way to our battle positions, meeting Peridot's soldiers along with Onyx, standing at his magister's side. "Vantos. There you are."

Huddling near Onyx are Bix, Lin, Dhahab, Obby, Onyx, Lapis, Em, and Garnett, their faces in exhaustion but their weapons at the ready. Offering my squad a nod, I sigh at Onyx. "Am I late?"

438

He snorts. "No, not at all."

The soft glow of our golden-lined cloaks gleams in the dark night, Onyx being the only one not standing out because of his pitch-black robe, and Lin with her blue furry coat. Gripping his walking stick, we follow Peridot's crew, our eyes full of readiness. Even with our shaky hands, I know determination is going to get us through this.

"So, how was your climb, children?" Onyx calls out.

"Hell," Dhahab's voice ignites.

Lin chuckles, dusting off snow from her cloak. "Not exactly the best for my robe, Sir Onyx."

"Onyx, what are we doing once we're at the top with Peridot's team?" Laila asks, as we trot up the slope, our feet tingling at the touch of the cold snow.

"After the signal, my Astral magic will destroy their cloaking magic," Onyx begins, as I help him with his walking stick. "With the high ledge, we'll jump to the fortress walls and kill most of their archers as Steele charges through the front gate."

Peridot scoffs at Onyx's statement, his blond fur wisping through the wind as he adjusts his glasses. "We're nearly there. Sir Onyx, is your mana at the ready?"

"Yes, Peridot. Even without an arm—" he flashes me a glance— "I'm still capable of wielding my Astral magic."

Flustered, I look at the snow, avoiding Onyx's piercing gaze. Even though his tone is filled with sarcasm, I can't help but feel guilty.

As we reach the top, the troops line up against the edges of the hills, their eyes gazing downwards at… nothing. There's nothing in front of me, not a single sign of Judah's fortress being there. Cloaking magic… It's something I've never heard of before. But the way Onyx describes it is self-explanatory enough.

Piles of snow cover the rough rock, while Onyx stands next to Peridot, his paws planting the white fluff. At his sides are the assassins on the ledge, while my force is behind him, watching the events unfold. "What's our status, Peridot?"

Before the Farik answers, the night sky explodes into a mix of orange and red fire, as two more fireballs arise from the north and below. Steele and his lurking army are hidden behind a clump of boulders, his eyes darting to Onyx for a sign to attack.

"Well, there goes our signal. Show time."

Onyx chuckles at Peridot's response, before closing his yellow eyes. He passes his walking stick to Peridot before breathing a deep sigh, golden, bright energy beginning to flourish from his fingertips. If there's any sort of magic that can counter my demonic techniques, it'll be this.

Astral magic.

Onyx growls as streams of golden strings stretch out, wrapping around the fortress, which begins to fade into our sight.

It's exactly as the building plans describe it. Scaling one hundred feet into the air, it's formed into a box-like shape, a stone wall surrounding it. There is a metal gate where Steele and his army are hiding, Veils mingling in front of it. With their demonic masks and jet black cloaks, their presence is all too familiar. I count seventy Veils on top of the walls, not noticing they've been exposed due to Onyx's magic.

Four watchtowers are in each corner, Veils watching like eagles. The walls that block us out seem thick enough to stop the piercing of a sword, but not strong enough to resist Kyln's assault with her elemental mages. It'll be easy to break a hole in the wall and stream inside.

Dhahab and Lin peer over my shoulders, trying to get a look at the behemoth. The metal gate is only openable with metal manipulation magic, but that didn't matter. There's a reason why Steele got his name. The walls don't seem too far; we can jump onto the tops of the watchtowers and scale our way down. It'll be a hard fight.

"Dragons... this is... massive," Lin trails off, shaking her head in disbelief. Even though the fortress is smaller than the Draken Castle and the Lauveean Castle, it still proves difficult to penetrate.

"I assume everyone here knows Hiam flow, correct?" asks Onyx, darting his eyes to all of us as he disperses his flow of Astral magic. Nobody detests him, and the Grand Magister heaves a sigh. "Concentrate your mana at the bottom of your feet. Your jump length will be enhanced, and your legs will no longer be vulnerable to the deadliness of gravity."

Steele valiantly comes out of his hiding spot with a deafening battle charge that vibrates our eardrums. His army sprouts out, their weapons in the air as they charge to the fortress. Peridot scoffs, amused at the sight.

Behind the fortress are Kyln and three other magisters, their elemental mages smashing through the walls. The Veils on the watchtower panic, the sounds of a ringing bell invading my ears.

"My team, let's go!" Peridot whistles, and in an instant, the assassins who stand on the ledge leap off, their mana channeling to the bottom of their feet. Landing on the walls, they clash and fight with the Veils, corpses already dropping to the ground.

Before I can blink, it's only me, Onyx, and everyone else left.

I'm nearly about to jump when Onyx grasps my shoulders, glancing at everyone else behind us. "Are you all ready?"

A deafening silence follows as Onyx chuckles.

"Silence means yes, it seems with you youngsters."

441

Without warning, Onyx jumps off, gliding through the air while his cloak wisps through the wind. Landing on the walls, he stabs through a Veil with his wooden stick.

What the hell? That's not any sort of normal wood…

"Follow Onyx, everyone!" I shout, mana pumping through my body as I concentrate the flow to the bottom of my feet. As I jump, everyone behind me follows my lead, their agility enhanced by their magic. Garnett's the only one who hasn't awakened his mana, so he holds himself on Dhahab's shoulders as we flow through the sky.

On the walls, soldiers around us fight to the death. The urge inside of my chest is something I haven't felt in a while. Battles always evoke thrill, and they also evoke my madness, my anger. This time, though, I have those things under control.

Laila and I descend effortlessly, my troops following close behind. Obby heals the injured assassins on the stone floor, reversing the blood seeping through the cracks. Beside me is Bix, valiantly murdering the Veils with trusty iron knuckles.

With his dagger, Garnett slices enemies in two while Dhahab and Lin use both their elemental magic to fend off their attacks. Chaos ensues all around, but it's controlled chaos. We are winning.

Laila hastily pulls out her dual-wielding axes from her cloak, while I quickly rest my hand on the *Kathi's* handle. Thankfully enough, the weaponsmiths back at the camps have fixed up the sword nicely enough that it can cut through nearly anything. The bone dagger, on the other hand, can't exactly be fixed, but it's still as sharp as always.

"Vantos, keep your eyes peeled!" Em says, swiping his short sword to chop off a Veil's arm. I've been so hypnotized that I don't notice the guard swinging his blade at me. *How sloppy,* I think, giving Em a nod as he goes off to fight another Veil.

442

Some enemies fall off the walls, landing into the snow with a deafening thud. Weaving through the fighting crowd, I whirl like a violent tornado, sending slashes through tendons, nerve endings, and necks. Some drop dead, while others plunge to their knees, paralyzed by my assault. Peridot's squad cleans up my kills quickly, executing Veil after Veil.

Laila plunges her axe into a Veil's head, splitting their skull wide open. "I've killed guards before... but I've never been in a battle like this."

Grunting, Laila clenches her fist towards the charging soldier, her mana flourishing as they choke and grasp at their throat. She finishes the job with a clean snap of the neck. I huff a sigh, relishing the cold air. "Hopefully this'll be our last, right?"

Even though there's hesitation in her eyes, she nods. "Hopefully."

As the fighting on the watchtower subsides, I glance down the walls. Kyln's forces and Steele's are sandwiching the Veil's main forces, pushing them to their backs. Steele raises iron pillars from the ground, his magic sprouting to kill the impending demonic army. Kyln chops through the masses, even without her dormant flow of mana.

There's only one man who doesn't have a Veil mask. It's a Farik, judging by his dog ears. Around him are ten Veils, shielding attacks from mages and archers with their demonic magic. Before I can get another look, he runs into the massive fortress, escaping the battle outside.

A hand clasps on my shoulder. It's Onyx, his eyes squinting at the sight. A confident gaze streaks through his yellow pupils. "That must be The High One."

Laila, Dhahab, and Lin huddle around me and Onyx as his eyes dart to us. "Where is Lapis, Emerald, and the rest of your squad, Vantos?"

The icicles engulfing Lin's fingertips shatter as she gulps. "They told me they're going to help out Peridot's forces. They're going to be fine."

The sparkles from Laila's axes fly into my face as she grinds the edges against each other. "Onyx, Lapis is good with a sword. So is Garnett and Em. Obby's busy healing the wounded. Like Lin said, they'll be fine."

Before I can get a word in, figures appear from the shadows of the three balconies on the tall fortress. My eyes widen once I see the metal gleam of arrowheads shining against the moonlight.

Archers.

"Everyone, get down!"

Like wasps, arrows fly through the air faster than I can react. Onyx grips the middle of his walking stick, twisting it in a circular motion. In an instant, a golden yellow shield appears, the stick acting as its handle.

"Dammnit, get behind me!" he grits as he holds it up valiantly, not a single arrow piercing through us. The Astral shield's big enough to cover all of us from the arrow's assault, but what about... *Lapis!*

The array of arrows stops as the archers fade back into the fortress, reloading their bows as we breathe sighs of relief. Diving out of the shield, I quickly try spotting my other comrades.

Em's in the midst of bodies, holding someone close. *Obby.* Gritting my teeth, I run over to them, five arrows protrude out of Obby's stomach, his expression quickly fading.

"Vantos, don't even! We can't save him," Em huffs, blood rushing down his chin. The archers even hit their men, Veils moaning and groaning on the walls. But Peridot's squad has most of the casualties, their corpses staining the stone bricks with dark red ooze.

"Obby! Oh god, oh god, oh god," Laila repeats as she appears beside me. Slapping Obby's cheek, she bites her tongue hard, a blue aura beginning to flow out of her fingertips.

Em shakes his head as he coughs out more blood. There are arrows embedded in his left arm, his crimson hue seeping through his cloak. "Ruby, stop! Don't waste your mana on him—"

"Shut up!" Light's fading from Obby's eyes, glazing to gray. Grabbing Laila's wrist, I shake my head.

"Em's right. He's injured too, you know—"

"I told you to SHUT UP! DAMMIT!" Laila's voice cracks as she tries desperately to repair Obby's skin. Her healing magic isn't affecting Obby's wounds a single bit, and she takes note of this, the blue aura from her fingers fading.

Sitting back, she hyperventilates, grief penetrating through her expression. Em winces, pulling the arrow from his shoulder, letting go of Obby's body. He falls to the floor, an empty gaze on his pupils. "Obby saved me… shielded me from those damn arrows…"

I blink with worry. "Where's Lapis and Bix?"

"Right here." Turning around, I see Lapis limping, his arm hooked onto Bix's neck. A piercing arrow sticks out of his ankle. Noticing Obby's dead body, Lapis grinds his teeth together, muttering curses at the ground. "Obby… goddamnit…"

"Dragons, I'm sorry," Laila says suddenly, biting her lip as she stands. "Let me heal you up."

Laila's anything but fine as she tends to Lapis' and Em's wounds. Hundreds of emotions are in her eyes as she avoids glancing at Obby's body. Her fingers tremble in vigor, but she stops hyperventilating. Obby's the man who's taught Laila how to harness her magic, after all. It's why their healing techniques are drastically similar.

It isn't just a comrade lying down in front of her; it's a mentor.

A demanding voice hastily interrupts the five of us.

"Vantos, Ruby, I'll send healers to assist with their wounds."

Laila's gaze is in defeat, but she still grabs her axes and adjusts her cloak. "Okay, Onyx. Let's go."

Running back to Dhahab, Lin, and Garnett, Onyx glances back to our comrades, rifling through their agony. "I'm sorry, but we must hurry. Helping Steele and Kyln by fighting through the courtyard should lead us to the entrance to the fortress, which will lead to the lower levels, or the 'Messiah's Chambers.'"

I gulp. "We're close, aren't we?"

"We are," Onyx begins as we regroup with everyone else. "This is the second phase of our attack: finding Judah, my brother."

Even though I try to listen to Onyx, his voice fades as the battle rages around my ears. The image of Omar being a vessel to this demonic King frightens me to the core.

Omar... where are you?

Hiam flow is the staple technique of a mana-user, one who has awakened their magic. By projecting the flow of their magic— whether that being Elemental, Astral, or Darkic— the mana-user subsequently enhances their body to project biological enhancements on their body. First used by Wizard Hiam in 892, it has now become something that you see every mana-user possess, even before the Magic Law was passed.

- *A collection of Spells and Spooks: 4th edition,* By Grand Wizard Fruidith in 1413.

TWENTY-EIGHT

The coppery smell of blood is familiar. Munir's born from the blood of my parents, dying a gruesome death. The rotting flesh of the shopkeeper I've killed drenched the alleyways with an unholy stench for days.

As I stand in the conjures of chaos occurring all around me, there's a nostalgic feeling that comes to my mind. *Blood.* Everywhere. Death, in ways, is an art that I can barely explain.

No, I urge. *Don't think like that, Kedar.*

Shrugging myself out of my daze, I remember that we're all in the courtyards of the fortress, the battle raging on. Mana-users destroy the terrain, their elemental magic staining the grounds. Bodies drop in every direction, Veils and assassins being torn to pieces like a piranha's prey.

I grip the *Kathi,* shifting my head to the side to avoid the blade slicing towards my shoulder. The Veil grunts as I respond to their attacks by stabbing them in the chest.

"Keep fighting!" I hear Dhahab's voice echo as Laila appears to finish the job, slicing the Veil's throat with her axes.

"We're almost there, Kedar." Laila huffs, admiring her handiwork as I pull back the *Kathi*. "We need to fight through this damn courtyard."

The *Kathi*'s stained red, a mark to remember all of the people I've cut down. Walls that once surrounded the fortress are now in pieces of rubble, the assassins who've survived the arrow volleys coming to join the carnage.

The Order doesn't falter, even though we've lost many men. Peridot has been killed in the arrow volleys, according to the healing mages. His body's been found hanging off the ledge of the walls, blood soaking his blond fur.

War. One minute you're in a tent discussing battle plans, and the next you're seeing your comrades, generals, and knights drop dead all around you.

I've pledged to never participate in such a thing ever again, but your plans change when your brother's going to be a sacrificial vessel for Satan himself.

Dhahab, Garnett, and Lin are doing fine— disturbed at the shedding of blood— but fine. Their magic works wonders, Dhahab's fiery fists pairing well with Lin's deadly ice magic. Garnett's swordsmanship paves the way for assassins to push through the Veils.

Em and Lapis are busy being healed up, but Bix joins us in our journey to barge into Judah's "Messiah Chamber." It's where he holds my brother. Omar.

Slashing through Veils, I spot waves of assassins jumping over the dead. Even though they outnumber us by a slight amount, our battle strategy proves to be successful— the element of surprise. Onyx grips his walking stick, slicing through enemies like a butcher dividing a cow's carcass.

The one hundred-foot-tall inner building at the center of the fortress, where the archers have fired their volleys, looks like it's about to crumble. Seems like it reflects the Veil's situation. Their forces are quickly dying under our pressure, and they keep drawing themselves back, retreating closer to the inner building.

Archers appear from the balconies again, this time with their arrowheads in flames.

"Fu—"

An assassin next to me gets cut down, screaming in pain as their skin is seared from the fire.

Gritting my teeth, I duck and dodge each shot, some arrows grazing my cheek. My squad does the same, but Dhahab catches the arrows, his hands unaffected by the heat. Onyx charges with his Astral shield, the arrows bouncing off the hard surface. Bix uses his metal knuckles to punch through the deadly arrows, making sure it doesn't touch his cloak.

Swords clash, sparks flying through the air as I weave through the garden of battles, nearly tripping over a sliced-off hand. As always, I find myself trudging after Onyx as he leads the pack.

"Onyx! Wait!" I feel the grasp of Laila's hand wrapping around my bicep.

"You good, Kedar?" Laila's voice irks as the archers fade back into the balconies. Another volley's coming. "You look stunned."

I nod, breathing heavily. "I'm fine. Let's just get through this."

Judah, where the hell are you? My mind growls. As soon as we burst inside, Omar will be there. Waiting for me to come to his rescue.

Onyx turns to see us trudging through the battlefield, and his Astral shield vanishes, as the wooden stick he has in his hands returns to its normal state. "Any casualties?"

"No, none at all," I reply, gripping the *Kathi* tightly. Glancing behind me, Dhahab and Lin trail us, not too far behind.

Bix coughs, wiping his forehead. "Is it time?"

As Dhahab, Garnett, and Lin arrive, standing beside me and Laila, Onyx replies with a nod. "Only a few steps to the entrance of the fortress."

A stone gate blocks our way, along with three Veils. Judging by the glowing, dark red auras in their hands, they're mana-users, with demonic magic like me.

Onyx notices our fatigue. "I'll take care of this."

Turning to the Veils, Onyx's holy, euphoric, bright aura envelops his wooden staff. Even though the rough edges make it look dull, it cuts any Veil that Onyx comes across to pieces. As Onyx plants his feet into a battle stance, I count in my head. *One.*

Laila and I watch in awe as the mana-users charge towards Onyx, the dark red aura surrounding their fists like Dhahab's flames. *Two.*

The Veil that guards Al-Jukar has told me the others are "cannibals." Guess he isn't bluffing. The Veils flash through the snow on all fours. *Three.*

Their feral growls and animalistic states are cut short when Onyx thrusts his wooden staff forward, stabbing the first Veil in the middle of their chest. *Four.* They fall to the ground, howling in pain as blood spurts from the hole that Onyx makes. *Five.*

The other two Veils don't seem to care about their dying comrade, one attempting to bite Onyx's only arm. Grace is in the old dog's movements as he wisps through the air, twirling around to deliver a roundhouse kick to the Veil's neck to make it snap. *Six.*

As the last Veil looks at the dark aura in his hands, blood begins to run down the eyeholes of his mask. *Seven.* Shrieking, he outstretches his nails, trying to grab Onyx's throat. In response, the magister dashes to the side, slicing the Veil's wrists clean off with his sharp staff. *Eight. Nine.*

Before the Veil can react, Onyx separates his head from his shoulders, blood sprouting like a grim fountain of crimson. *Ten. Ten seconds,* I repeat in my mind. *Ten seconds is all it takes for him to cut them down.*

Onyx glances back, observing our astonished faces. "I'll destroy the entrance. After that, slip in."

He swings his stick, still engulfed in Astral mana, towards the gate. A beam of cosmic magic shoots out of his staff, exploding the gate into thousands of pieces of rubble. Barely finding the words to speak, Lin, Bix, Dhahab, Garnett, Laila, and I quickly file ourselves into the fortress.

Once inside, we aren't presented with a warm greeting.

There are three balconies above us. Soldiers are on each floor, their bows pointing at our heads. Onyx fumbles in behind us, grinding his teeth together as he darts his eyes towards each archer. The Veils on the ground floor form two separate lines, spacing out from each other to leave a gap to the doorway. The floor we're on is mostly empty. On the left is an image etched on the wall— a monk praying to a lion. Skulls are stacked in one of the corners of the room in a hellish pyramid. It isn't as bad as Al-Barsim's compound, but it still reeks like hell.

Silence envelops the room, the sounds of the battle happening outside drowning out our ears. We don't make a single move.

Just as we're about to give up, the door in front of us opens.

Stepping out of the shadows is Judah.

His dark brown fur is similar to his brother's. A gash runs down his face, his void black, demonic pupils staring down on Onyx. He wears a red hood with black linings. A tooth necklace sits on his collarbone. Probably from a damn lion.

Onyx steps in front of us, his tail wagging feverishly. Judah, seeing his brother, slowly transitions his emotionless expression to a bright smile.

"Well, what a surprise."

"Judah." Onyx's voice is stern, fearless. "Stop this madness."

"You really think I'm stopping?" Judah asks, heaving a sigh as he tilts his head, lapping at his canines. "I'm close, Onyx. Close to presenting a solution to this war. To this violent world."

Onyx scoffs, his staff beginning to glow brightly. "Don't even. You don't realize what breaking Malik's seal will *do*."

"I KNOW EXACTLY WHAT IT WILL DO!" I jump at Judah's echoing voice. His face is as confident as his brother's. "Cleanse. Breathe new life. Sprout a utopia from a dystopia."

"You're delusional, younger brother," Onyx grits, glancing at the five of us behind him. He sighs. "How in the Dragon's name have you even spoken to Malik?"

"He spoke to me. He taught me. He showed me." Judah seems desperate for his brother to agree to his whims. All of this has to be a lie. How can killing dracotheists, killing millions of people, and breaking the seal on satan heal the world?

"Thirty years ago, I received a prophecy, Laurent," Judah slurs. *Onyx's real name.* "To break Malik's seal, there must be a sacrificial vessel. One that can hold Malik's mana and is compatible with his soul."

453

It's hard to understand the conversation between the two brothers. Onyx looks like he's known about Malik for centuries. It explains the dire worry in his eyes.

"Omar? Are you talking about that poor boy from Jaawed you kidnap—"

"He is not Omar." Judah's eyes narrow as my brother's name rolls off his tongue. I step forward, drawing my sword, but Onyx blocks me with his walking stick to prevent me from taking a step further.

"He is Malik. Malik chose him as the vessel."

I growl. "How the hell did he choose him?"

Judah's eyes avert to mine, his lips curving into a smile as his demonic pupils shine against the gloomy light. "Because of you... Kedar."

"BASTARD!" I shout, pushing Onyx off of me as Judah laughs. Backing away from my squad and standing in front of the doorway, I huff as Judah's grin only gets wider. His wrinkles tell me that Onyx and he are around the same age, but their views are hellishly different.

Judah glances at the archers.

"Kill them."

As the door handle clicks, the archers twitch into action.

My mana begins to surge through my bones, the dark aura glowing through my skin. Everything moves in slow motion as the archers pull back their bowstrings. Dark matter flows to my fingertips, and without thinking, I outstretch my hands towards the Veils.

Black matter swarms around the six of us, as I see Onyx hastily hold up his wooden staff to create his Astral shield. My demonic magic envelops us in a sphere, holding off the arrows from the outside. A deathly pain surges through the right side of my face as blood drips onto the stone tiles on the floor.

The pain's worse than being stabbed, slashed, and cut all at once. Bix shudders as he takes a gander at the flowing, dark red magic oozing and mixing together with the void black in a marble pattern. Laila lowers her weapons, taking in the sight of Dhahab and Lin. Each second that passes only pains me more— the weight of tons on my shoulders.

Laila grasps my shoulder, blood flowing against my cheek. "How long can you hold on?!"

I return to holding my magic after tearing off my eyepatch. *No need for it now,* I think. "I'll be fine. Just... let me do this..."

My body weighs more than a mountain. I twitch. I feel each arrow that penetrates the shield, a sparkling pain coursing through my abdomen. Fire from hell rains down on me, the damage inflicted on the shield reflecting on my body.

Minutes subside, as the agony from the arrows fades. Not that many shots are digging into the shield anymore

"Vantos," Garnett grits, everyone huddling around me. "Come on. Don't give up."

Slashes echo from outside of my shield. *Onyx.* He's saving my life, again. I glance at my squad. "Onyx is out there. I know it."

"He's really something," Dhahab mutters, Lin nodding in agreement.

Her white eyes contrast with the deep, dark red marble patterns of my shield. "This Order wouldn't be anything without him."

Laila scoffs. "If it was just Judah, Haya's governments wouldn't survive the Veils."

With that, the conjuring pain of the fire arrows withers out. My arms drop to my sides as I collapse. The dark matter wisps into my fingertips, my magic still ready.

The vision in my right eye blurs as Laila hauls me up. "Dragons... you've done it again."

"Done what?" I ask, resting my hands on my knees as Laila steps back a bit.

"Your demonic magic. It's a curse... but you use it like a gift."

My mind cannot come up with a response.

I shake my head, darting my eyes around the room as the red spots from my right eye begin to clear. *Wonder how much life force that took out of me.*

Onyx is in front of the door, his shoulders rising up and down slowly. There's a gleam in his yellow eyes as he glances back at us. The wooden stick he holds is doused in crimson.

On all three floors are the bodies of Veil soldiers. Corpses mangle off the ledge, their throats slit open to create fountains of blood. In front of us are the bodies of archers — face down on the cold, hard floor with a pool of blood surrounding their heads.

As we walk towards the old man, Judah's Prophecy clears in my head. Malik has whispered into Judah's mind, convincing him to break his seal and unleash him into the world. But the seal can only be broken with the perfect vessel— my brother. But why? There's nothing that makes him the perfect catalyst for Malik's soul.

Onyx's voice slashes through my thoughts. "We don't have time to rest. We must trek down to the Messiah Chambers at this instant."

We file into the door, sprinting through the hallways like cheetahs in a savannah. As we run, Onyx's voice becomes stern. "The ritual has begun."

Laila stammers. "Ritual?"

"We still have time to stop it," Onyx urges.

"Use Flow. Enhance your speed. NOW!"

We blaze through the hall, reaching a long flight of stairs downward. Onyx grunts as his paws slam at each step, all of us following close behind.

The stairs fade into a dark rock. *Obsidian.* Silence envelops us as we're too nervous to offer words of encouragement. My fingers tremble, and my heart pumps faster than ever before.

At the bottom of the steps is a wide room with a steel gate having golden handles. In its crevices are flowing matter of dark aura, wisping through like blood pumping through vessels.

Sweat drips down my forehead. Garnett gulps. Laila grips her axes menacingly. Dhahab clenches his fists, blazes of fire giving us a little more light in this gloomy room.

Bix cracks his metal fists against each other, sparks flying through the air. Lin tries to contain her fear— her icy magic cooling Dhahab's. Onyx turns to me, his staff already immersed in his Astral magic.

"Vantos, open the door."

As my hands wrap around the handle, I glance back at my teammates. It's rough that Lapis and Em aren't here. Fighting along with me. A nephew and uncle elf assassin duo itself sounds like some kind of legend.

But nevertheless, I swing the door open.

It's a wide room, wider than Al-Barsim's compound. With pillars holding the roof above, it mimics the appearance of an atrium. The gate behind us shuts and closes with a deafening slam, locking us inside.

Judah looms in the shadows as Onyx's expression contorts in anger. In the middle of the room is a table, a figure strapped to its surface. Next to Judah is a platoon of Veil members, their masks shining through the darkness.

Onyx grits his teeth. "Judah. I'm going to ask you one last time. Please."

"You've gone soft, Laurent," he slurs, licking his teeth.

Omar's on that table.

As my eyes adjust to the dark, his facial features sharpen more. His hazel eyes are now demonic, a red ring in the black void.

The curly hair he has been shaved off his head. Half of his body's completely skinned, his red muscles itching and churning as he twitches. The room echoes with his whimpers. *Those bastards.*

Bastards, BASTARDS!

"NO!" I sprint down the room, my comrades following me. "LET GO OF MY BROTHER!"

Judah notices my piercing gaze, his eyes throwing daggers at mine. Onyx's voice echoes behind me. "Vantos! Wait! We mustn't act with haste—"

Snakes wrap around my leg. I glance down. No, those aren't snakes.

They're the tentacles that Munir summoned in my spiritual plane. Their mouths latch on my ankles, slithering through my inner thigh. The groans behind me indicate that we've all caught ourselves.

Right in Judah's trap.

Wincing, I look back. Laila writhes in pain, screaming curses. Dhahab convulses, being held up by the tentacles with Lin and Garnett. Bix tries punching off the slimy, slug-like creatures, only to be restrained. Onyx curses as the tentacles wrap around his legs.

"Puros, we call them."

Judah outstretches his hand from behind the table and clenches his fist. The tentacles tighten their grip, and I feel their teeth sinking into my feet like a snake's talons.

"I summoned them from the demonic realm."

"Judah… what the hell are you planning to do?" My breath hitches.

Judah doesn't answer as I watch my brother, strapped to the table, wearing nothing but a loincloth. Omar doesn't make a sound, but his eyelids flutter and he coughs blood.

Other than half of his body being completely skinned, slash marks cover his chest. His tendons and ligaments are severed in two, rendering him immobile. It's like I'm looking at a rotting carcass. His body's worse now— skinnier than before and malnourished enough to show his ribs and cheekbones through his pale skin.

I grit, shaking my head. "J-Judah…"

The Veils watch our suffering through their demonic masks. Judah's entertained as he manipulates the Puros with ease. The longer these are attached to my body, the more drained my mana becomes.

Stay the hell awake, I plead. Carvings are on the walls— writings in an ancient language, the symbols are not familiar.

Papers cover the tables at their sides, ink smearing the surface. Judah calmly walks to one of them, snatching a journal made of leather.

"Kedar. Do you want to be a hero?"

I stammer, spotting my brother's dire state. He's barely hanging on. "I just want Omar back."

Judah gawks, his laughter bouncing off the walls. My squad's heads hang, their expressions in defeat as their mana drains. "You will. Soon."

"TAKE ME!" Onyx glares in surprise. "TAKE ME, PLEASE! ANYONE BUT HIM!"

"Unfortunately, I cannot accept your proposal," Judah says boldly. "But your body cannot sustain Malik's power. You would be a useless sacrifice."

Judah's eyes scour the writings before glancing up at me. "You've killed Munir. You've killed Al-Jukar, Al-Watawat, and Al-Barsim. You've killed countless of my Veils. Now, you will pay for your sins."

"Your brother is the messiah. His body is perfect for my master," Judah begins, frustration contorting on my face.

Laila seethes. "You're a monster."

"No. I am an angel."

"An angel of hell," I protest, spitting blood.

"SILENCE!"

We go quiet.

Judah motions his arms towards my brother. "Omar is *the* vessel. His demonic magic transcends even me. My master chose him three years ago. The hatred in his soul and heart had brought him to his favor."

"Three years ago..."

That's army days.

"I am the Prophet, made to retrieve Omar and convert him to my ideals."

In response, I stare at Omar's wounds. "You call that converting?"

"I made him see what I see, Kedar," his voice booms. "It requires unconventional methods."

I try thinking of a way to stop Judah, but I can't. My vision's blurry, my strength's dimming... these tentacles feast on my mana like children suckling on their mother's milk.

"Demons do not have a physical form, Kedar. I know you know this."

"So what if they do?"

"You'll find out after this spell. I will give up Omar as an offering. And break the seal and open the Five Gates."

Before I can protest, pain vibrates through the left side of my face. Blood from my demonic eye spills out onto the floor.

Bix, Garnett, Dhahab, Lin, Onyx, and Laila's faces are riddled with defeat. One by one, their weapons drop to the floor, their bodies destroyed because of the Puros.

Judah and his Veils chant, their palms facing up, black and red magic smoking from their fingertips. I glance at my hands, realizing that there's demonic mana evaporating from me as well— *what the hell is going on?*

Everything turns upside down. Warping visions attack my eyesight as I fall to my feet. Once I force myself back up, we aren't in the physical plane.

Judah's taken us to Malik's world.

The demonic plane.

Instead of standing on a stone floor, I'm standing on a sea of Puros, all slithering their slimy selves all over each other. My breath hitches as everyone exclaims in horror. Waves of heat blast against my skin, contrasting the cold from Nisf Thueban.

I fumble over them trying to gain some ground, before I realize they're slithering back into the ground below. One by one, each snake-like teeth-covered tentacle wisps to the ground, detaching itself from us. I collapse with my squadmates, our bodies weak.

Lin shrieks. "W-What the hell is this?"

Judah's chanting becomes louder.

"Benedicamus Patrem nostrum Malik. ipse est Deus noster, Christus noster. Hanc animam ut vas ipsius satanae supplices petimus."

The ground's made of the damned. Worse than the skeleton fields in Ardon. The Puros must've come from the eye sockets of skulls, which make up the ground. I stand on my feet, huffing.

"Onyx, please tell me... Where the hell are we?!" I hyperventilate. Laila's expression is emotionless. She's in too much shock.

Onyx gets up, his walking stick planting against a skeleton's rib cage. For the first time, there's horror in his eyes.

"I know not where we are."

"Benedicamus Patrem nostrum Malik. ipse est Deus noster, Christus noster. Hanc animam ut vas ipsius satanae supplices petimus," they continue to chant. Around us are other Veils and assassins. The Veils look like they've expected this to happen. As the brutal fighting resumes, most of our squadrons die, distracted by the horrors around them.

Above is the red-blood sky. There are no clouds. The sun's nowhere in sight. Eyes with demonic pupils stare at me, Dhahab, Lin, Laila, Onyx, and Garnett. As their chants get louder, the eyes above fill with blood. It pulsates over and over, and we get drenched in rain.

A staunching presence behind us reeks like the scent of a rotten apple. I'm the first to notice. Onyx is the second, but too late. There's a desperate Veil, charging through the corpses of the battle, inches away from Dhahab's back.

Then there's a blond flash.

That's when a resounding squelch murks everyone's eardrums. The gold catches the blond flash in his arms, his ember eyes in flames of shock. Lin darts to where the gold and the blond flash are, cutting down the Veil with her shards of ice.

The blond flash falls to the ground with the gold. The Veil is in pieces.

The rest of us run to him. The blade is still in him. The blood is the same color as the sky. Voices now crowd my ears. We are frozen, but we are in a frenzy.

"Garnett, dammit, dammit, dammit!" Laila's voice soaks through. Her fingers glow.

"Garnett, relax. Relax!"

He's in those golden arms, but the flash is fading. The golden arms clutch and shudder. I kneel down, trying to control my breath.

"Benedicamus *Patrem* nostrum *Malik*. ipse *est* Deus *noster*, Christus *noster*. Hanc *animam* ut *vas* ipsius *satanae* supplices *petimus*. Benedicamus *Patrem* nostrum *Malik*. ipse *est* Deus *noster*, Christus *noster*. Hanc *animam* ut *vas* ipsius *satanae* supplices *petimus*."

"Laila… is it bad?" I ask. Laila's sunken.

"It's bad. Direct stab wound to the heart."

His golden arms melt. But someone's still breathing on his chest.

"Garnett, Garnett, can you hear me?"

Blood stains the gold. The flash in his eyes crumbles slowly. He tries moving his mouth to make a sound, but those golden arms keep him in place.

"Don't talk, Garnett. Don't talk. Just breathe."

He breathes.

Sweat drips down Laila's cheek. "I can't. I can't, he's too far gone."

The gold cannot accept that the flash is waning.

"No, no! Listen to me, Ruby, you're gonna heal him! You're gonna heal him, goddamnit!"

Golden tears stream down his face as he holds the blond flash close, close until the flash closes his eyes to an eternal sleep.

"Garnett? Garnett, no, Garnett!"

I get up.

"Garnett, please… Garnett…."

463

Laila's breath hitches. "Dhahab, he's gone. Just... just stop."

"Benedicamus *Patrem* nostrum *Malik*. ipse *est* Deus *noster*, Christus *noster*. Hanc *animam* ut *vas* ipsius *satanae* supplices *petimus*. Benedicamus *Patrem* nostrum *Malik*. ipse *est* Deus *noster*, Christus *noster*. Hanc *animam* ut *vas* ipsius *satanae* supplices *petimus*."

I watch as Laila takes her hands off him. "He's dead."

Onyx's breath hitches. Lin wipes tears. The gold holds onto his shoulders to push him off. The blood mixes in with the rain. Judah's snickers interrupt our grief.

"The first of many."

I glance at him, Omar still on the table. As the blood rains on Omar's body, seeping into his muscles, he begins to convulse. Onyx and Laila notice this.

"Judah! Stop! There's already too much blood that's been shed!" Onyx pleads, assassins around us dying left and right. The Veils move quickly in this demonic realm, as their swords slice through Onyx's magisters. *They've been training for this, haven't they?*

"It's impossible to stop Malik's whims, Onyx."

Judah grins as Onyx smears the blood rain off of his fur. The downpour doesn't stop at all, the blood filling my boots. "Who's blood even is this?!"

"Every soul that has died and ended up here in the demonic realm now resides in this space." I gulp. "When a new soul ends up here, these eyes cry the blood of the dead. You should be grateful. This is a greeting."

Garnett's body lies still in the sea of skulls. Dhahab's staring at his hands with Garnett's blood. It washes away from the dead souls raining on us.

Being drenched in blood doesn't feel like being drenched in water. The seeping, warm liquid is going into every crevice in my body. Judah's right. I feel the life forces of thousands of people all over my body, reduced into this pool of crimson.

Running to the table is futile. I slip, hitting my knee against the skeletons of the damned. My fingers tremble, my heart racing faster than the speed of a thousand horses. Judah keeps his chanting efforts, and I struggle to find the motivation to stand.

Onyx and Laila's energies are drained to the core.

None of them dare to walk anymore.

The chants grow louder, but a shrieking sound interrupts Judah's demonic chants.

Lips form from the demonic eyes in the sky, slowly merging together to replicate a mouth. Shielding myself from the blood downpour, the mouth gapes.

The teeth are made of people's heads, their eye sockets empty. Laila shudders as the mouth stretches its tongue, three-quarters away from the skeleton surface. Before I wonder what the mouth's doing, a creature takes to the skies.

The beast has eight legs like a spider, and their torso is human-like. They don't have eyes, but they have stretching, bat-like wings, and their arms are covered in demonic eyes. The pale skin it has differs from the red and black tones around us, and its mouth has fangs sharp enough to rip through skin.

The Veils are massacring our forces all around us, and I spot Diamond being cut down. Kyln falls to the skeleton surface with her head detached from her shoulders. I don't see Lapis and Em, but my heart sinks once I realize their dire conditions. The dead corpses of the assassins cover the skeleton ground as the Veil's battlecries deafen ours.

We're losing.

The coppery smell of blood is everywhere now. There's nowhere to run. Nowhere to hide. *God,* I plead in my mind, hypnotized by the unholy sight.

"Judah. Judah! JUDAH!!!" Onyx screams, stepping forward to the table, tearing through the Veils that block his way. "Millions will die! THE WORLD WILL END IF YOU BREAK THE SEAL!"

The creature streaks through the skies, landing behind Judah like a pet owl. "Onyx, you've been doomed ever since I took Omar. It's best to surrender."

The beast hisses, their chest beginning to form a mark. Judah closes his eyes in meditation, glancing at the beast with admiration. "It is finished. The Sign of Malik has been engraved."

The mark is a long vertical line, three slanting horizontal lines dividing the symbol into three. At the ends of the bottom and top horizontal lines are small, vertical lines. I count four in my head as me and Laila watch in horror. Onyx's fighting efforts dim, his eyes becoming more fearful by the second.

A screaming shriek comes from the beast again, as the Veils around Judah stop fighting, as if hypnotized by the beast. Their demonic eyes glow with brightness as they take off their hoods.

The beast howls like it's being hurt. But it's not. A sizzling sound pecks at my ears.

The mark is engraved on the Veils. It's on their backs, their necks, their arms. I glance at myself, but the mark isn't there. I'm spared.

In seconds after the mark gets planted into their skin, shouts of confusion ring throughout the remaining assassins.

I look around and see the Veils contort into... demons.

It's hard to describe. One's face explodes into a flower made of flesh. Their petals of skin have teeth lining it, their arms becoming tentacles to kill their prey. Another screams in agony before eyes open on the surface of their chest, and their head transforms into a crocodile.

Another has their jaw wide, their bones hanging by the threads of blood vessels. Hands outstretched from their stomach, opening their abdominal cavity to reveal their pulsating organs.

I shiver. Laila hyperventilates, tears running down her cheeks.

"We're going to *die*."

The Veils at the table turn into demons, too, but Judah doesn't turn. The mark implants itself on the right side of his cheek. Laughter echoes through the realm, and Judah raises his hands, glancing at the sky that rains blood.

"Praise Malik."

Assassins scream and revolt in pain, some trying to run from the Veils. Our men get diced into bits one by one. Dhahab, Bix, and Lin run in our direction, pure shock on their faces.

A demon chases them on all fours. Their ribcage seeps through their skin, outstretched from their back like wings. The demon's mouth has rows of teeth, all sharper than the *Kathi*.

"Dhahab, Lin, Bix, run!" I shout, stumbling towards them while holding my sword. Dhahab's eyes widen when seeing the beast that chases them. Lin runs in sobs, while Bix grits his teeth.

Laila curses once she sees Bix trip over the dead body of a corpse. Onyx scrunches his fur in horror, his tail wagging in desperation.

The demon doesn't waste its opportunity, its mouth widening to sink its fangs into Bix's leg. He screams, writhing in pain. I run back, holding my hand out to him.

"NO! VANTOS! DON'T!" Bix pleads, his metal hands scraping and churning against the skeleton ground. "YOU'LL DIE!"

I grip the *Kathi,* my mind running through all of the possibilities of how I can save Bix, only to come up with no solution. Standing in the blood downpour, I watch as Bix punches the demon in the face, only to be silenced when it sinks its fangs into his neck.

"BIX!" Laila screams. Onyx hyperventilates as hell unfolds in front of him.

Bix puts up a fight, but the demon chops on his torso, tearing his organs apart. His intestines fall out like noodles. Blood spurts in every direction, and the demon spits him out, letting his body rot in the ground as it stares me down.

It glances at my demonic eye before abruptly turning away, attacking another assassin.

Spared. Again.

Judah's voice slices through our moment of grieving for Bix.

"There is *nothing* you can do to stop my God."

Onyx explodes into action, dashing to the table as demons surround him. Even though he fights with fear, he still *fights.* He refuses to give up.

"Kedar... Kedar..." Laila's voice breaks, tears falling to the dead skeletons. Lin and Dhahab glance at Bix's corpse, speechless.

"We have to fight. We have to!"

Hope isn't in my words, but any lie makes me feel better in a time like this.

She huffs, nodding desperately. "To hell with it all."

The demon behind Judah stops screeching. Judah is the only one left chanting his unholy spell.

"Get to Onyx!" Dhahab yells, running to the Grand Magister.

Before we can follow Dhahab, a ring of demons surrounds us. Their backs have sharp spikes with dead assassins on them, their mouths contorting in hellish expressions. All of us are trapped.

I've gone back on my promise. Corpses surround me. Limbs are torn apart.

I've failed.

My discoveries have only led to more and more insanity. Demon Magick is not a force to play with. My veins, they're getting darker and darker by the day. I don't even know what the hell is real anymore. A couple of hours ago the wall behind me was made out of eyes and gaping flesh. There's voices in my head there's people everywhere I go and I see things which I'm not supposed to see what have I done to myself am I okay am I fine will I survive this whole ordeal or will I die I don't know I don't know—

- The Golden Mage.

TWENTY-NINE

I'm in hell.

Demons flock around us. Bodies mangled, minds shattering, and left without hope.

The beast standing behind Judah shrieks, looking at Omar at the table. My brother's expression is empty, his face void of emotion as he falls victim to Judah's chants. Even though we've sliced demons in two, they resurrect, coming back stronger and more violent than before.

It takes minutes, which feels like hours, to be fighting at Onyx's side, our eyes set on Omar. We're a couple of yards away, yet it feels like miles that inch away each second.

The spider-like creature moves closer to my brother, hovering its hands over his chest. "Judah! What the hell do you think you're doing?!"

If Judah hears me, he lets my words fall on deaf ears. The beast's fingers tingle, and Omar unbuckles from the table straps, levitating a couple of inches off the wooden surface.

"Vantos!" Dhahab's voice interrupts as he uppercuts a demon's jaw, its face exploding into a pulp. The blood rain

471

above persists as more and more assassins fall to the Veil's whims. "Get the hell over there already!"

Glancing down at my wrists, I notice my veins exert a soft, dark red glow. The feeling ignites me. There's only one way to replenish my mana—

And it's to do it in blood.

Laila notices my expression, her axes dripping with demon blood. "Kedar, Onyx is just ahead. Just clear a path—"

My feet dance along the bony ground as I weave through the fray, my dagger in my other hand. Anger flows like a gushing river. *Omar. I'm coming for you.*

I swiftly stab a lion-like demon in its throat, and its vessels splurge with blood. *One down.* Sliding through a bull-like demon's legs, I slice it in two, the dagger executing the final blow to the back of the neck. *Two.* As I keep killing, my magic charges through my blood faster.

A Veil's convulsing on the ground, the Sign of Malik forming on their arm. With haste, I slit their throat, leaving their blood to mix with the damned.

Onyx is just a couple of steps away. He pulls his wooden stick out of a fallen demon, huffing as sweat seeps into his fur. "*Vantos.*"

"Onyx," I begin, noticing one of his ears is sliced off clean. Primal slashes from the feral demons tear through his robe, leaving it in shreds. "You're alive."

Dhahab, Lin, and Laila follow me, agony in their eyes. Even with Laila's healing magic, we don't have time to heal our wounds. I already have cuts torn through my armor, while Dhahab has a long gash down the side of his arm. Lin has a small nick on her cheek, but Laila has cuts and scratches all over her arms.

Out of all of us, she fights the most. This just gives her a break.

472

"Judah's hiding behind his demonic army." Onyx motions his head towards the wooden table, his brother still chanting. "We must push through and stop this madness."

Although fatigued, we nod, already used to the feeling of blood pouring down on us. It doesn't bother us anymore.

Onyx and I lead the pack, our weapons slicing. Laila follows close behind, her axes slashing through the masses. Dhahab and Lin use their mana, fire blazing through the air as icicles pierce through demon after demon.

I spot Omar, still levitating off the table. The beast shrieks at my brother, black matter engulfing his body. Gritting my teeth, I slice a demon's head clean off as Laila paralyzes the next, using her blood manipulation magic.

Judah notices our presence, his brows furrowing as we stand feet from the wooden table, demons no longer blocking our path. We leave a trail of dead monsters in our wake.

"This is… an inconvenience," he admits as the black matter inches down Omar's frame, wrapping him into a tomb. Judah walks around the table, his arms resting at his back. He raises his chin high. "You haven't died yet?"

"I refuse," I say through clenched teeth, slicking back my damp hair.

"I would deeply advise you to not *refuse*."

I glance at Omar, his body secured in a black tomb. The beast grabs it, planting it on its back.

"Don't take him."

Judah smirks.

"What power do you have here?" he asks, motioning to the dead bodies that pile ground.

"Accept it. You have lost."

Onyx scoffs, gripping his wooden stick as his ethereal magic channels through its rough surface. The holy surge of mana contrasts with the dark realm.

"The battle isn't lost yet. This is the beginning of *your* end, Judah."

Judah's head tilts, his demonic eyes not convinced. "Try me."

Onyx erupts and hurls his walking stick at light speed, tearing through the air like a knife slicing through hot butter. Our expressions twist in surprise at the sighs as the blade flies at Judah's direction.

Horror engulfs us as we see Judah holding the stick-turned-spear.

With a clenched fist, the stick shatters, falling to the ground in ashes.

"You underestimate me."

Onyx stammers, looking at his only hand in defeat. A boulder manifests itself in his fist, and he charges at Judah, desperation in his eyes.

Our Grand Magister takes a swing at him, his movements precise, better calculated than mine, but Judah counters by kneeing his brother in the stomach. Onyx spits blood, as Judah smirks, grabbing his brother by the ear and hurling him off the ground, sending him flying in the air.

He lands on the ground with a thud, his eyes fluttering. Laila gets on her knees, blue aura springing from her nails. "Onyx, what was that?"

He spits blood, red stains seeping into his canines. "I have no idea."

I gulp as Judah stares us down with a hellish smirk. "Onyx, let me—"

"No," Onyx's voice is firm, direct. He slaps Laila's arms off, getting up.

"I won't let it end like this."

Fire engulfs his fist next, his magic replicating Dhahab's. A ball of ice manifests on the tip of his tongue. Judah doesn't seem pleased when Onyx charges once again.

The High One holds up both his hands with a dark red aura. Onyx doesn't stop when seeing this, jerking his head forward to unleash his ball of ice. Judah cackles, kicking through his elemental magic like glass.

Onyx grinds his teeth together. "How... how are you doing this?"

"You cannot defeat Malik's whims. And especially his Prophets." Judah breathes a deep sigh as Onyx throws punches with his fiery fists, only to be blocked with his demonic magic.

We're paralyzed at watching the leader of the Onyx Order being reduced to nothing but a mage in front of us. "My magic here transcends all beings, Laurent."

"No, no, NO, NO!" Onyx pleads, punching him over and over, his efforts in vain. Judah scoffs and recoils his arm back, bawling his fist and thrusting it forward.

His fist tears through Onyx's abdomen, going through his body like a sword. Judah's demonic magic pulsates at the drawing blood. Onyx hurls, his life essence spurting all over the skeleton ground.

I itch in rage, and we charge at Judah, our weapons raised. Judah turns, kicking his brother off him, Onyx's head slamming against the corpses below.

"You are like bugs." Judah's tone doesn't sound so forgiving anymore. "Interrupting our ritual time and time again."

The beast hisses from behind the table as Judah outstretches his hand towards Laila. *No.*

"You first."

A forceful push rushes through his fingertips. Laila flings into the air, her body flying over demons that look at her from below. More anger pours through my veins as she lands yards away, monsters already encircling her.

Judah motions his hand towards Dhahab and Lin. "I wish you luck."

Lin screams, and Dhahab holds onto her waist while they fly like cannonballs. They land on the other side of this demonic wasteland, as the army of demons begins to lick their fangs and walk up to their meals.

Judah smirks when seeing my horrified gaze. "Something wrong, Kedar?"

"You killed them… you killed my friends, you killed everyone." My breath hitches as I grip the *Kathi* and the dagger with vengeance.

Onyx is on the ground, his eyes dimming. "V-Vantos."

Judah shushes his dying brother. "Silence, Laurent. All of us are pawns in a chess game played by gods."

"After this, I will give you the honor of seeing your brother be sacrificed to be a vessel for Malik himself."

Demons surround me, Judah, and my dying mentor. The beast behind the table takes flight, their fleshy, bat-like wings flapping to the skies with Omar's body on their back. I watch as it disappears into the gaping mouth in the sky.

"No—" Judah steps on Onyx's throat.

I grit. "Bring my friends back."

"My demons will dissect them nicely."

I glance at Onyx again. His blood seeps through the skeletons on the ground. His blood bubbles on his lips.

"Onyx is your mentor, yes?" Judah asks, digging his paw deeper. I nod.

"Then doing this will feel much better."

Judah steps off his brother as five demons jump on him, pressing Onyx to the ground and tearing at his cloak, lapping at

476

the blood seeping from his wounds. Onyx winces, gripping his wounds.

"Why do you look so empty, Kedar?" Judah smiles at me.

"Kedar," a hoarse voice says. It's been the first time Onyx has called me by my old name. Dark circles are under his eyes, his limbs straining from the demon's grips.

They look like Fariks that have turned into manic, mindless beasts. Their nails are long and sharp, their teeth even sharper. Bones stick out of their backs like morbid turtle shells.

"Onyx."

"Look at me, Kedar. Look at me."

Judah stays silent, but he snaps his fingers.

And every memory begins to crumble.

Onyx telling me I need to train.

Onyx telling me about the Veils.

Him promising to save my brother.

Him guiding me through his trials to become an assassin.

Helping me with Munir to save my life.

Him sending me on a mission to kill three Veils.

Him leading our squad into the battle.

Each memory crumbles.

Onyx's holy magic dims as blood spurts from his wounds, the demons eyeing the hole that Judah's created from punching his stomach.

I put my hand up to stop Judah, but the demons bite into Onyx's only arm and two legs. The dog shrieks and howls in pain, and they pull his limbs off, malice in their demonic pupils. I grit as the demons wave around his body parts like toys.

Onyx barfs as the feral demons engulf the bottom half of his body. His voice is dim, wisps of astral magic on his tongue. "Kedar..."

"Find... the Astral wizard."

A demon crawls onto his chest. Their mouth widens, and they tear off his head.

And I watch.

The demons rip Onyx's body into shreds. Bits of flesh fly all around me as they ravage him like a lion chewing on its prey. I shake my head in denial. *Onyx.*

His blood mixes with the rain. He is nothing but a soulless body now.

Judah comes from the shadows. "Kedar. You don't know how long I've waited for this moment."

"Get the hell away," I stammer, stepping back as my boot squelches against Onyx's flesh. I cringe at the sight.

Judah hums. "It is time to summon the Seer."

From the ground rises the beast. It replicates its features, the spider-like legs, eyeless, but having a fang-covered mouth. The pale skin and wide wings are too familiar. Onyx's remains are splattered all over the ground. The demons lap at his flesh. Once the Seer appears, the feral demons scurry away.

"The Seer will take you to where your brother is." Judah finds a reason to smile. "You have the opportunity to witness this world's end."

I still have a chance, right? To save Omar? My mind asks. The Seer hisses softly as Judah rubs its cheek. I barely put thoughts into words as I get onto the Seer's back. Judah relishes my torn expression, the blood raining drizzling on the battlefield. As I glance around, assassins keep dying left and right. *Is this what Munir warned me about?*

He didn't tell me about this hell.

The Seer's wings flap, and we ascend into the air. Judah gazes from below, smirking while I hold the Seer's neck tightly. Its skin is smooth, slippery from all of this drizzling blood.

My heart thumps as we come closer and closer to the gaping mouth. Below are the clusters of demons, tearing through the few assassins that are still alive. *We're all just food for Malik, aren't we? Appetizers for the demons.*

As Onyx keeps flashing through my mind, I remember his last words.

"Find the Astral wizard."

The name doesn't sound familiar at all. But Onyx has faith. Faith that we'll get out of this mess. I have to hold some hope in his words. His death is in vain if I don't survive.

The mouth in the sky widens as the Seer flaps its wings inside. Fangs line the insides, and I shudder once I'm close to the stacked, severed heads that make up the mouth's teeth. Their expressions are stern, as if they're expecting my inevitable arrival.

As we fly into the abyss, the Seer snarls louder, their tongue lapping. A horrible smell envelops my nostrils, and I almost throw up. The inside of the mouth is made of red flesh. It pulsates and beats every second. Beneath us is a tongue, eyes in its flesh. The Seer gently sets me down on its surface, and I press my boots onto the ground, feeling the squelch.

As I walk forward, the Seer behind me begins to sizzle into ash, fading into nothingness. I scoff, sniffing as I slick my damp, curly hair back. Blood's like water in this world. It's everywhere.

Judah sent me here to die. I struggle to put one foot in front of the other. Onyx is gone. Obby has been shot to death. Bix is ripped into pieces. Garnett has died protecting Dhahab.

Whispers erupt around me. I wince at the voices. For the first time, I'm truly alone.

Wandering through this realm without the comfort of anyone else. The rotting corpse smell stains my nostrils, and I try concentrating on the demonic whispers, the senseless sounds becoming sentences.

"rUn... Malik... hurts..."
"Say y-your p-prayerssssss...."
"Where is your god noWwwWWWWwwW?"
"YOUr... SOul Is Ours..."
"PraiSe him! MaLIk...."

They persist. Some whisper the greatness of Malik, while some beg for me to turn back. This must be the trapped souls of the damned.

A rotting chair fades from the red fog.

A seer stands on the right side, Omar lying in front of it. His heavy breathing is the only sound I can focus on with the array of voices nicking at my ears. On the left side of the chair are three figures.

Sitting in the seat is a devil. Malik Al-Shayteen— The King of Demons.

He's hard to describe. Even from sitting down, I can tell he's eleven feet tall or more. He isn't human, a goblin, Farik, or an elf. Malik's something else. A singular eye is in the middle of his head, replicating mine, red and black. The mouth he has is very similar to the Seer's— rows of sharp teeth, along with a slithery tongue. His scaly, dark red skin blends in with his coal pelt.

I walk, gulping as Malik takes in my presence.

His voice is cold, emotionless, and void of heart. "Kedar. Judah has told me about you."

My heart pumps, sweat dripping down the back of my neck. I slow my breathing, but I keep getting distracted by my trembling fingers. Reaching for my belt, I grasp the *Kathi's* handle before unsheathing the bone dagger. *I have to fight.*

480

Malik's amused, licking his lips as his singular eye fixates on me. "I see. You birthed Munir."

"I killed him." I plant my feet deeper into the fleshy ground. Fake confidence is the only card I have. "His magic belongs to me now."

"How intriguing," Malik begins, before crossing his legs on his seat. "It is impossible to do without the expertise of Astral magic."

He examines every inch of me as my voice stutters. "Just let my brother go. This'll all be over."

"Once we become one, he will be let go." The three figures standing beside him cackle at Malik's words. They're hard to make out in the red mist.

I shake my head in denial. "You'll destroy the world—"

"I like calling it replanting. Being a god means creating. Bring anew," he interrupts. "My Prophets will help speed up this process."

He sighs.

"Rubim. Nezzar. Lamia. Reveal yourselves."

The first figure, Rubim, steps from the darkness. He has four faces on each side of his head: a Farik, a human, an elf, and a goblin. Each contorts into a horrible smile as Rubim rotates his head. Each one of his eyes gets a good look at me.

The second, Nezzar, emerges. He has pale skin, replicating the Seer. Bone protrudes from his arms and legs, like he's a humanoid spike. He has no pupils, but his eyes are black. Nezzar lets out a low hiss, smirking at me.

Lamia is the last to stand beside Nezzar and Rubim. She looks like a normal elf— the only thing noticeable about her is the thousands of tentacles that claw at her back. *Puros.* All of them have teeth, their slithery and gray color is too familiar. Her blond hair morphs into more Puros, as I realize her whole body is made of those little bastards. She must be the mother of all of those tentacles.

All of them possess the same cloak that Judah has: a deep, dark red, the inside black. I shudder at the sight, gripping my weapons tightly.

Malik taps on the chair's handle lightly, breathing in deeply. "These are the true, mighty Prophets. The first three demons I have ever created, two thousand years ago."

"Munir was the first to ever reject my idea of recreating this horrible planet. He vanished from the hive mind, and we've yet to find him," Malik explains, his voice monotone. "You say you've killed him, but demons can only die if their host is dead as well."

I can't come up with a response. Malik notices this, blinking his one eye. "You are a unique being, Kedar. The first human who has almost made me change my original plans. But alas, look at where we are. So close in reviving and recreating this world."

Nezzar hisses again. "Master, your vessel has awoken."

Omar coughs, his skinless body shuddering. Malik stands from his seat, his towering stature sending waves of intimidation over me. "Omar. I see you've awakened from your slumber."

Lamia smiles when seeing the horrified look on my face. Her voice is alluring, almost seductive, silky, and smooth. "Kedar, you should be thankful that you are witnessing a moment in Hayan history."

"No, you've manipulated Omar. He doesn't want this…"

Malik cackles. "Omar, explain this to your brother."

For the first time, my brother speaks. His jaw cracks every time he utters a word, his demonic eyes staring into my soul. "Kedar… this is right."

He walks towards me, his bare feet squelching against the fleshy surface. His expression is emotionless, but his eyes are filled with hatred. A tear streaks down my cheek as I see his shriveled lips.

My breath hitches. "Omar... I came to save you. You're my brother."

"Why didn't you say that before?" Omar furrows his eyebrows and clenches his fists. He's been repainted by Judah's whims. Malik watches as Omar reaches to cup my face. Tears soak my cheeks. I hyperventilate as I reach for my brother's hand. "Omar... I love you. Please..."

"Lies."

Omar pushes me off him.

I stumble to the ground, paralyzed in shock. "Omar! I CAME ALL THIS WAY TO SAVE YOU!"

"Malik opened my eyes. Made me see the kind of monster you are." His voice turns into a heat of rage, his tendons stretching. He motions his hands. "It is precisely why we must cleanse this world."

"I'm not a monster," I muster, my voice in defeat. "I've changed!"

"CHANGE?!" Omar's voice replicates Judah's. "You will truly change when this world is birthed anew."

I hastily get up, dropping my weapons. I reach for Omar, my eyes full of desperation.

"Omar, please—"

Something slams on my neck, and I fall to the floor, spitting out blood in pain. Omar turns his back, avoiding my gaze. With each step he takes, the more I cry out his name.

"OMAR! OMAR, PLEASE!"

The foot penetrates deeper into my throat, and I cough and spit. Glancing up, I see Rubim, the man of four faces. He sneers. "Enough is enough, mortal."

I squirm under his grasp. A piercing pain goes through my wrists and ankles to stop me. Nezzar stabs his bones in each of my limbs. I scream in agony, sobbing. "GOD!"

"Where is your god now?" Nezzar breathes, spitting in my demonic eye. I can't even wipe it.

Nezzar presses his bones deeper into my tendons to make me yelp in pain more. "Answer me."

"Well, that look is telling me that he doesn't know," Rubim cackles as we watch Omar walk until he's in front of Malik's throne. Spitting out blood while I cry, I try reaching for my weapons. Even though they're inches away, I can't grab them.

I try opening my mouth again to scream at Omar, but no sound comes out. Blood seeps out of my body as death walks towards me every second.

A splitting pain vibrates through my body as Nezzar plunges four more bones into my legs and arms, severing my muscles.

"Malik has been deciding whether or not to spare your life. Is that correct, my master?"

"Yes," Malik swiftly replies as Omar kneels in front of him, offering himself to the King. I curse in the back of my head, grinding my teeth in horror.

"Kedar will die, but slowly. He will watch the world grow anew, and live until he sees our paradise. I will not allow him to live that long after, though. He doesn't deserve to be in heaven on earth."

More tears stream out of my eyes as Rubim pushes his foot down harder, and black spots riddle my vision. Omar turns back to me one last time, not a single sliver of sympathy in his gaze. *What happened to my brother? What did Judah do to him?*

"The seal on Malik will break once I take his soul into my body. Do not cry, brother. Rejoice."

Moving out of Rubim and Nezzar's grasp is impossible. Malik, Lamia, and everyone else watch me as I beg Omar. "We can live normally. Please. All I wanted was a chance to make things right with you."

"You missed your chance," he rasps. "Rage consumed you. That day, our parents died planting the seed of anger within you."

I remember that promise: *Protect Omar with my life.*

And yet he's the one wanting to kill me. Those days in Pyria, our times in the army, I forgot about him. He was nothing to me. All I wanted to do after escaping Alfdan was make things right.

Make everything normal again.

Now I cry, wiggling my way out of the Prophet's grasp. Nezzar doesn't respond lightly, digging his bones deeper into my flesh as my tears soak the ground below.

Omar turns back to Malik before the King opens his mouth wide, his tongue elongating and screeching like the Puros. Lamia positions herself at Omar's side, kneeling to watch the ritual commence. I nearly grasp at the *Kathi,* but Nezzar kicks it away before I can, giving me a devilish smile.

The scream I make is guttural, defeated as pain washes over me again and again.

"PLEASE! PLEASE!"

Malik's tongue pierces through Omar's chest, and Omar collapses to the floor, his eyes closed in peace. I watch in horror as Malik's tongue slithers under the surface of his skin, like a parasite.

Lamia's Puros latch onto Malik, severing into his chest as well. Malik groans in response, his eyes blinking away the pain. Blood spills out of both Malik's and Omar's wounds like a fountain. Confusion bursts through me as Nezzar and Rubim exhale in satisfaction, like they're seeing their lord come back to life.

Omar stops breathing when Malik's tongue ribs out, something beating.

It's my brother's heart, pulsating slowly. Screaming in desperation, I see Lamia do the same: Malik's heart rips out of his body. But Malik's heart isn't red like Omar's. It is pitch, void black, reminiscent of the dark red glow from my wrists.

I almost pass out, but I grit and stay standing during this unholy resurrection. Omar's eyes are closed in peace, as if he's sleeping.

The next time he awakens, he'll be Malik. Lamia grips Malik's heart tightly with her Puros, the voices from before beginning to whisper over and over again. Malik coughs blood before tossing Omar's heart into the fleshy ground. I breathe heavily as I see it sink into the surface like quicksand, disappearing in seconds.

Lamia breathes out a low sigh, as the pulsating beat of Malik's heart echoes throughout the mouth in the sky.

Blood spurts on Malik's pelt, while Omar's expression completely fades. He's dead.

Lamia inserts Malik's heart into Omar's body. My brother vibrates and squirms like he's having a seizure. My eyes widen at the sight as Malik's old body drops dead to the ground, immersing in the fleshy ground.

Sobbing, I grasp at Omar. My brother blinks, his howls of pain and bubbling blood creating darkness in the air.

Nezzah chuckles. "I can't believe it. Malik has done it."

"Rejoice, brother," Rubim responds, his foot still in my neck.

My mind grows weary while my hope diminishes second by second. I've failed, and there isn't any way I can fix anything. My screams and begs fall on deaf ears, the Prophets ignoring my struggle. The veins of my wrist glow and seep through my skin as my body douses itself in anger.

I cry and shout until I can't anymore. My voice grows hoarse. Pleading does nothing. Nobody's going to help me, no matter how loud I scream. The only thing I can do is watch.

Lamia steps away from Omar. His eyes begin to flutter as he blinks once, twice. His red and black demonic eyes dart back and forth before interlocking with mine.

That's not my brother. That's Malik.

His skin grows back, but not in its normal color. Dark red, scaly tones cover his chest, legs, and arms as his bones crack and fix themselves. The Sign of Malik is engraved on his chest like a brand. Wings sprout from his back, black nails growing from his fingertips. Two horns sprout on his head, and he gets up, admiring his new features.

His face stays the same, but that's the only thing that reminds me of my brother. He and Malik have become one. Two souls in one body. Like my veins, he glows in an unholy, void-like blackness, pumping newly made mana into his bloodstream. The cuts and scratches that once riddled his skin aren't there anymore, as if he's regenerated from his wounds, the magic passing the likes of Laila and Onyx. His healing makes him a god.

There's a smile on his expression when he walks up to me, looking down at my compressed body. Shockwaves of pain, regret, and rage merge with my thoughts. His voice replicates Omar's, but I know that it's Malik talking behind the mask of skin.

"The resurrection is complete. Once I open the first gate, the seal will be broken," he says to Nezzar, Rubim, and Lamia. I gulp. *Who do I call him now? Malik or Omar?*

Rubim frees my neck from the gripping feeling of his foot as Nezzar removes the bones embedded in my body. I writhe on the ground, shivering from the stab wounds.

"Omar..." I claw at his rough, scaly ankles. He kicks my arms away, and I choke out a sob. His fangs reflect off the gloomy glow. My brother's no more. What's left is a devil.

"Run, Kedar," he begins. I scramble to get up. Even with the throbs vibrating through my frame, I grasp at the *Kathi* and my bone dagger on the ground. The Prophets watch, smiles on their faces as they see me limp across the fleshy surface.

"As I promised, your slow death is imminent." I breathe heavily, covered in sweat, blood, and tears. Malik doesn't have sympathy in his gaze as we stare at each other. "This Order has failed to stop the inevitable. I have been reborn, brother. Reborn into a god."

Brother? I whisper in my mind as I back away. He outstretches his right hand.

"Leave us. We have a gate to open."

I run.

I run, and run, horror in my soul.

I run, shoving the *Kathi* into the sheath and clicking the bone dagger on my belt.

Laila, Dhahab, Lin. They have to be alive; they must be. Maybe Lapis and Em are still out there, but I'm not taking my chances. Dark magic pours into my heart as the faces of my comrades enter my mind with the hope that they're still standing.

Concentrating Hiam Flow towards the bottom of my feet, I glance back to see the four figures watching me escape the carnage. Their eyes are expectant and reek of violence. The aura that surrounds them only makes me want to run more.

Battles rage below me as I arrive at the tip of the tongue. In front of it are the teeth made of Hayan heads, their expressions in anger, some in sadness. It's like they're disappointed in me.

Demons flood the environment below, blood still dripping from the skies. Laila, Dhahab, and Lin are out of my sight, not in the sea of demons. My mana charges more as I bolt, running faster than before. Grasping at my two blades, I jump, blood spurting out of my right eye. Growling in agony, I envelop dark red mana against the *Kathi* and bone dagger, as I point both to the monsters below. *Let's see how they feel when I'm using my mana against them.*

I feel like a monster, having this demonic magic... but it saves me, nonetheless. Munir's the person to thank for that. I twist and whirl in the sky, Malik in the back of my mind. Finding Laila and everyone else matters first.

"RAHHH!"

A deafening earthquake erupts on the sea of skeletons as I crash into the demons like a tornado touching the ground. I spin and wisp like a spinning wheel of death, slashing through demons like a butcher. Breathing out a grunt, I gape my mouth, a ball of demonic magic surging at my lips. Jerking my head forward, I aim at a group of demons. The ball of magic splits through their bodies in a deathly explosion, making them nothing but dust.

Before I can even feel a sense of relief, more demons rise from the skeleton ground. It doesn't matter. With each kill, the more magic I have. As I tear through them as if they are nothing but stacks of hay, memories flow through my mind.

Bix's smithing skills, Onyx's wisdom, Garnett's love for Opal, Obby's efforts to cure my brother. Even though we have barely interacted, they're like family to me. This is for them. Each wound I suffer, each slice and each demon I kill— it's for them.

489

"Laila!" I yell out to no one.

Only the demons are attracted to my voice. Magic surges through my weapons as the demonic mana makes my blades sharper, letting me cut through the masses quickly. I yelp in pain as I feel the quenching sting from Nezzar's bone stabbing, while my neck aches from Rubim. Each demon I killed made the pain subside. Made it easier to ignore.

My heart dims as more demons keep their efforts, doing everything to kill me. I recoil my left arm once a demon tries to chomp it off and duck under another to avoid its sharp claws. The thrill of battle is never old, but I'm fighting demons. *Damn demons.*

"Dhahab?! Lin?!" I curse under my breath, yelling a battle cry as I decapitate a viper-like demon, nearly getting engulfed in its mouth.

"Em?" My voice is desperate. "Lapis?"

I get my answer to Em in an instant.

Em's on the ground, in pieces. His arms and legs are plastered through the battlefield, left to be eaten. The bright gaze in his blue eyes is gone, replaced by the gray glaze of death as his head lies in front of me. I shiver in response, stumbling as I recoil away. *Em.*

Lapis' nephew is dead, nothing but a pile of mushy flesh.

There isn't time to grieve him, but a tear slivers down my cheek as I shake my head, the anger fueling my magic. The waves of demons keep coming, only to be stopped by the edge of my blade, their shrieks and cries of pain not making me stop from slaughtering them in this hell.

"ANSWER ME, ANYONE FOR THE DRAGON'S SAKE!" I scream through the slashes of the *Kathi* and the bone dagger.

Silence follows.

Only the demons make a low growl, their voices thirsting for flesh.

But the sound of a pleading soul cries out.

"Kedar!" The voice is familiar. "Kedar, please, is that you?!"

Laila.

Snarling, I glare back at the demons, stripping my armor off to leave on my black tunic. It's torn, ripped into shreds from the constant attacks from these monsters. I'm blind in my right eye, only seeing the color red. Touching my cheek, I smear off the drops of blood, huffing as the adrenaline keeps pumping.

Demons are circling her. In her arms is Lapis' head, dripping and drenched in blood. I scream in rage, clawing at my weapons. Laila's more wounded than I am. Her axes are in pieces on the skull-riddled ground, her ankle at a brutal angle as she struggles to bring blue aura to her fingertips. In her eyes is trauma.

Killing the demons around is like shifting through a blind phase. She doesn't deserve to be going through this.

"Laila. Grab my hand, *ya rouhi.*"

Crave, lust, hurt, rage, worry, envy, adultery. Our sins build us into the true person which we hide behind our skin. All we need to do is pull it off to reveal your true self. Your body does not belong to you, rather, it belongs to the demon which grows and pricks in your soul at any given moment. It doesn't hurt to surrender to your worldly desires, now does it? Just let go of yourself completely and let the anger compel you. Let it control you. If you can't control yourself, then why not let someone else control you?

THIRTY

There isn't time to grieve. Revel in Lapis' death. As soon as

Laila grasps my fingertips, she drops the elf's head, leaving it on the ground for the demons to plunder. She grips my right arm while I swing through the masses with the *Kathi* on the other.

"Laila?"

There's an emotionless gaze in her eyes. She's empty. Blood streams down her face from a cut above her eye, the once bright shine in her crimson pupils now gone.

"Laila?" I try again, and this time she gulps, trying to slow her breathing.

"Kedar." She grits. "I'm sorry—"

"Don't. We need to find a way out of here."

Even though there's a solemn expression on her face, she musters the courage to nod. Her fingertips blossom with a blue aura, her magic paralyzing the demons in front of us. Immobilizing them makes them easier to kill with a couple of cuts to their arteries.

"Dragons, you're bleeding everywhere." Laila notices the holes from Nezzar, and the aching bruise from Rubim on my neck. "I'd heal you, but my mana..."

We limp through the hellhole, fighting off our urges to collapse from exhaustion. She fights as much as I do, maybe even more. Rest is what we both want, and to find Dhahab and Lin.

I shake my head. "Laila, I'm fine. Just don't let go."

Blinking through the pain, Laila sniffs, clenching her fist as she strangles more demons blocking our way. We don't know where we're going. Just far away from the mouth in the sky, and the eyes that cried blood. As far as possible.

My arms are numb, but it worsens with each swing. The dark aura that once surrounded *Kathi* is gone, as aches overflow my body. Fighting through the demons just to save Laila renders my body like jelly. My injuries and seeing my brother betray the world— it only makes me tired of it all.

Judah's nowhere in sight; it's only these monsters blocking our way. The eyes stop raining blood abruptly, and the demons stop attacking me and Laila, only watching us pass them in silence. Omar being the sacrifice for Malik must've ended this.

Those red eyes stare into my soul. Their claws twitch, their tentacles slithering in anticipation. I sigh in peace as they stop with their obnoxious growls.

Is it Malik that's doing this? Or Judah?

Laila notices it too, letting go of my arm to start healing the stab wounds on my back. With my adrenaline and demonic magic wearing off, the agony begins to seep in. I wince as her magic binds my skin back together slowly.

"Laila, what the hell do you think's happening?" I ask as we walk down the line of demons, all licking their teeth and furrowing their brows towards us.

"I have no idea." Laila's magic surges. I wince again, gripping the *Kathi*. "But we shouldn't miss this opportunity."

"Have you seen Lin or Dhahab?" My voice is urgent as our boots stomp against the skeleton ground. Glancing to the sky, I notice the red eyes staring down at us, following our every move like the demons.

Her voice breaks. "I– I don't know. Lapis and Em died in front of me as we fought these monsters. They died. I let—"

"Don't blame yourself," I reassure her as she stops healing me.

She's survived it all. We're the only ones left. Dhahab and Lin are gone.

Thousands of thoughts pop into my mind to answer what's happened to them.

We stroll through the path even though there's nothing at the end. The line of demons is endless, the trail of bones leading nowhere. This realm is infinite.

The corpses of my comrades make the demon's stomach churn a disgusting, putrid noise. I breathe heavily as I try to force the images out of my mind.

It might be everyone's flesh. In the past eight hours, I've lost every person that I've cared about. But once I glance towards the demons, their focus isn't on us.

Their heads are turned towards the mouth in the sky.

A shrieking sound prompts five Seers to stream out of the mouth. The veins in my wrist glow in response, Laila's eyes allured by the view. It carries Nezzar, Rubim, Judah, Lamia, and finally—

Malik.

The defiant look in his pupils stimulates me with utter fear. Demons groan as they spot their god, their master. If there's any part of Omar left in Malik, then it's buried deep in his mind. His body carries Malik's heart, not his own.

We lock eyes. There's a smirk that contorts his expression that makes me want to run.

The Seer he rides shrieks, and Malik splits through the air like a knife. His dark red skin blends with the realm as he and his prophets hover over me and Laila. My heart beats at his presence as I hear Laila's laboured breathing. She spits out blood.

"Well, it seems you have truly taken my offer, Kedar." Malik cackles, his demonic wings flapping slightly. His dark veins are brighter than mine as the Sign of Malik gleams on his chest. It makes me wonder what it'll do to me. "I will give you mercy indeed."

Judah, Nezzar, Rubim, and Lamia are amused, their expression satisfied. I struggle to raise my blade in Malik's direction, my fingers trembling from the stab wounds and ruthless swinging.

"Omar... please."

"Do I need to tell you again that he is not Omar?" Judah hastily asks.

Malik puts a palm up to stop him. "Calm down. His response is... logical."

"Logical?!" My breath hitches, blood dripping down my chin.

"This world will *end* because of you."

"It will be revived. Breathed into a new haven," Nezzar hisses, twisting and turning his bony needles.

Laila grips her stomach, reveling in her cuts. "How the hell can you be so sure of that?"

Lamia chuckles, her Puros twisting and turning around Laila's body, inches from touching her. I swing the *Kathi* at them, but the tentacles dodge each swipe gracefully, orbiting around her like flies.

Lamia's tone is intriguing. "And who you might be?"

Rubim's head turns once, twice, and two more times. The demons that circle around us replicate their judging looks as everyone revels in our appearances. Rubim's elf and human face contorts into a smile.

"You're a half-elf. Interesting breed."

That's something I don't know about Laila. She's told me her mother has white, cream skin, while her father is dark, coal brown. Not the part about being a half-elf. Hybrids are always frowned upon on our planet and in every nation. But that doesn't change how I see her.

She curses in response. "What *are* you?"

Fearlessness still seeps through her voice. I can't replicate it. The pain makes me tired, but it's not enough to give up on escaping Malik's realm.

"It doesn't matter," Rubim smirks before turning to the other prophets. "This one is confident."

"Confident ones are much more pleasant to kill," Nezzar suggests, thrusting his arm forward to leave his bony needles inches away from Laila's fingertips. I push her behind me, standing in front of them with the *Kathi* raised.

"I'll kill you before you have a chance." My chances are below none. This is a joke to them.

"This isn't in our agreement." Malik's voice silences the prophets. Anger resides in his tone— *is it Omar or Malik talking?* "This hybrid is important to you, isn't she?"

I don't answer, furrowing my eyebrows. Malik scoffs. "You want to be tested, don't you?"

My spine tingles, and Laila screams in pain. I turn around, a crocodile-like demon with protruding horns, sinking fangs into her forearm.

Quenching with anger, I swing my sword down to the demon's neck, before Lamia's Puros stop me.

Tentacles wrap and bite through my body, pulling me back from Laila. I curse, and I reach out for her, swinging the *Kathi* aimlessly. "Let her go!"

"Silence." I stare at Malik. Then there's a sliver of amusement that leaks from his eyes. "Let's sit back and watch the show."

"No," I grit. "Not her. Anyone but her, please..."

"Shhh..." The Puros bring me closer to Malik, and he puts his pointer finger against my lips. "The demons tell me her combat skills are quite... refined. Let's see if that upholds."

Laila's tired eyes try to resist the demon's toothy grip. Using her other hand, she punches its face over and over, only for it to not stop. Her screams of pain radiate through the realm, the prophets smirking at the sounds.

Laila gets lifted into the air, the quenching sounds of her bones cracking like shards of glass. Cursing, I try forcing myself out of the Puros' grasp, only to be bitten tighter. Their laughs only fuel me more.

Rubim's Farik face grins. "Someone's bothered."

"Here I was thinking this would be a bit entertaining." Lamia scoffs as the demon rips Laila's tendons into shreds when she tries pulling what's left of her arm out of the demon's mouth. I swallow a sob, already left with no tears to cry.

But then a flame of fire and a spear made of ice fly through the air.

Rubim dodges the projectile, Nezzar hissing in response to the flames. Dhahab's leg wisps through the air, kicking Judah in the face. He falls off his Seer, tumbling to the ground to his demonic army. Lin's not far behind, and a barrage of icicles pummel the Prophets, stabbing Rubim and Nezzar.

With a grunt, Dhahab punches Lamia in the jaw, sending her Puros untangling me and throwing me to the ground.

Getting up, I glance at Dhahab and Lin, fighting the Prophets with all the magic they have.

"We'll distract them!" Dhahab yells out, his eyes blazing. "JUST GO!"

He takes control of Judah's Seer, Lin sitting behind him. The Seer hisses, but Dhahab controls the beast, using his hands to steer it towards the rest of the Prophets. They're in disarray, their shots of fireballs and blades of ice sending the demonic armies into a spree.

Malik growls, his dark veins glowing as he locks eyes with Dhahab. "You'll regret that."

They chase after Lin and Dhahab, ignoring us. As soon as I regain my strength, I slice the demon's head from Laila's arm. She groans, hooking her other arm around my neck.

Glancing to Dhahab, I see him and Lin quickly surrounded by the Prophets and other demons. They won't last for ten minutes. But here they are, sacrificing their lives.

Onyx mentioning the Astral Wizard only makes me desperate to find answers. *As soon as we get out of here,* I wince, limping with Laila in my arms. I'll save Omar from Malik. There has to be a way.

The demons flock in the other direction, too focused on chasing after Dhahab and Lin. We nearly get run over by their slithering bodies, but we put one foot in front of the other, trekking slowly.

All of my comrades amount to something. They're better Hayans than I'll ever be. Bix, Garnett, Obby, Onyx, Em, Lapis.

Their deaths won't be in vain. I'll make sure of that.

"Kedar…," Laila whispers, her voice hoarse. I glance at her arm, mangled from the crocodile demon. Everything below her forearm is gone, nothing but a bleeding stub left. I curse, realizing she's too shocked to process her pain.

"Laila..." It's hard to hold back tears. I let her get *hurt.* "Just keep walking."

"My arm..." Her voice rises, and she hyperventilates.

We trudge through the advancing demons. They're merciful enough to not attack us, their eyes set on Dhahab and Lin. I resist the urge to look back, even though my mind already envisions them in pieces. If they survive, I owe them my life.

The charred and frozen corpses of the demons surround the Seer that Dhahab and Lin are riding on. Turns out they're not dead... *yet.* Laila whimpers and grinds her teeth together. "I can't feel a thing."

"Laila." We lock eyes. "Just focus."

Tears stream down her face as she shakes her head.

"How the hell are we going to get out of here?"

"I don't know," I huff, dragging her along, the blood from her stub making a trail. Her soul's shattered. As much as I want to take this away, I can't. "But we have to run."

Her eyes are hollowed out, a dark shadow beneath them. Springs of her curls are everywhere, some of her braids reduced to nothing but curly puffs. The only thing she has left is her beating heart.

"Do you think I'll forget about you?" a voice asks. Malik appears, rising from the ground. His wings spread out, showing the dark-lined patterns inside. Malik's evolving, gaining more power as each second passes.

"Om—Malik," I growl, as Laila splits out blood. His red skin illuminates the gloomy realm, like a hopeful light in the darkness. "What the hell do you want?"

There's a mix of amusement and sympathy in this tone. "The only way out of this realm is for the spell to be severed. For the spell to sever would mean to kill the caster."

Judah.

His chanting has started all of this. I groan in response to my wounds, blinking through the agony. "So? What's that got to do with anything?"

"There is something inside of me that wishes not to kill you." He walks around, and the sounds of fighting in the distance. Dhahab and Lin are putting their lives on the line for me and Laila to get out of this hellhole. "Which is why I have promised to let you wane. Slowly."

Both of us say nothing, too tired to come up with words. Laila's warm body presses against mine as more red liquid from her stub seeps to the skeletons below. Malik licks his fangs. "I will provide you with a way out of here."

"You think you're some sort of hero?" Laila's aggressive tone surprises Malik, disbelief coursing through her gaze. "You're not. Nobody on Haya will ever bow down to someone like you."

He laughs at that. "We'll see."

Widening his palms, a red and black aura rises from the surface of his rough skin, forming into a small spherical orb. "After I let you go, I will officially begin the first step in converting Haya."

"First step?" I ask, gulping.

"Opening the First Gate in Nisf Thueban will begin the construction of my kingdom." He explains like a scholar, motioning his hands around as if the things he speaks about are good. "It is called The Gate of Titania."

"But as I promised—" he turns and outstretches his hands, the orb slowly floating forward until it's five feet away from him— "I will open a portal."

"Portal?" Laila shivers. It doesn't even sound like a word. Much less of a spell.

The orb flattens into a circle-like shape before enlarging itself to be two times my height. I widen my eyes as I see the spitting image of a dark cave forming within the 'portal.' The bold rock and the small gemstones lining the crevices only confirm it.

"It'll transport you to the cave of Kloak Island," he explains. It's an island in the middle of the Kigamouth Lake, miles from shore. The place is too small to house a village, so it's untouched, a neutral zone for Basalians and Craleans. "Your lives will be spared."

"Why?" I grind my teeth together. "Is this some ploy to make us feel like we *owe* you something?"

"Your escape allows you to watch the world burn."

Malik's eyes narrow, and he raises his arm into the air. Turning our attention away from the 'portal,' Laila and I notice a head coming out of the sea of skeletons.

It's massive, larger than the mouth in the skies. The white pale skin reminds me of the Seers, with the eye in the middle of the face screaming the image of Malik's former appearance. The demons growl as they look at the head in astonishment. If Dhahab and Lin are still in battle, they'll be dead now.

There's no way they survived.

With its slithery mouth and gleaming white teeth, the head's tongue stretches upward like it's crawling out of a box. Laila huffs, too fatigued to evoke a response. I step back, her arm still around my neck. "No."

"Yes," Malik smirks. "Your brother's body gives me quite the boost to harness my magic. With the seal broken, nothing will stop me from making the monsters rise from the ashes."

"Kedar... just go through the 'portal.'" The dark circles under Laila's eyes get darker. I keep forgetting that she's still losing her blood, the occasional drip vibrating against my eardrums.

"We can't save Dhahab and Lin."

Even though I'm hurt, I nod. The demons bow their heads to the rising titan, as Malik's devilish eyes bleed in response to the magic. He clenches his fist as more heads pop out of the ground, rising to the surface.

"She's right." He growls, his veins glowing brighter than before. "You won't survive once I summon and unleash these beasts here."

Laila lets go of me, slowly walking towards the glowing portal. I follow, but she trips over herself, stumbling into the passageway.

In an instant, she's gone. Which leaves me and Malik alone. We stare at each other for what seems like centuries, but seconds.

"Omar... I know you're in there." Malik's expression softens as he lowers his arm.

"We are one, Kedar." His voice shapeshifts, beginning to sound like a stark image of Malik and Omar, vibrating and coursing with heinous soundwaves.

He growls, shaking his head as he glares at me. "He wants you to rot."

The Sign of Malik forms in his left palm, and he charges towards me. Before I can react, he reaches for my right wrist, the same hand where I lost my pointer finger, and grips his fingers around it.

There's a burning sensation that makes me exclaim in pain. I cough, stumbling back while muttering curses and shouting at Malik—

Before a dark red consumes my vision as I fall into the devil's portal.

"Kedar."

The name makes me blink my eyes open. Darkness seeps through my vision. As my sight adjusts to the dark, I see bright light in darkness. The smell of dried blood stenches the air.

Laila holds a torch in the only hand she has left. Her other arm is covered in gauze, the pigment of brown and red beneath it. My brain feels fuzzy, but the memories charge at me—

The demons. Malik. Judah.

I groan, clutching my stomach. "L-Laila..."

"I almost died," she admits, sniffing as she wipes dirt off her face. "Thank the dragon, I stopped the bleeding in time."

I try lifting myself off the hard, cold, and rocky ground, but there's an aching pain in my back that stops me. Laila puts down the torch to grip my hand, helping me up. I'm too tired to even utter a word. Covered in bruises and scratches, Laila lights up the cave with the subtle flames from her torch.

"Dragons," she curses, dropping the stick to the ground as she clenches her left shoulder.

I pick it up, hooking her arm around my neck again. "You need the rest more than I do."

Her expression dims as I drag her forward, seeing the light from the end of the cave. There's a sob from her that echoes through the cavern. "Why'd you take so long?"

"Laila, it was only for a couple of minutes—"

She shakes her head. "It took you thirty minutes to get through that 'portal.'"

I stutter, not able to offer an answer. There's a looming silence between us as I hoist myself out of the cave, the shining light of the sun glaring from above. "I don't know what happened, okay? We just... we just have to get moving."

"Where will we go?"

There's desperation in her tone as she shields herself from the sunlight. Outside are patches of grass and two palm trees on the border between the pastures and the sand.

"That I don't know either." She snorts with irony. We're broken. Left without hope.

"What the hell is that?"

Laila lifts her right hand and points in the direction of Nisf Thueban in the distance. Since we're on Kloak Island, the mountain range is north of here, exactly where she's motioning to. There's a beam of light that travels to the sky in an instant, shattering the atmosphere into thousands of pieces.

Seconds later, a sonic boom ruptures our eardrums.

In response, Laila and I stagger, our ears clenching from the pain as I try to hold her up. Blood trickles down my jaw as I notice the specks of ships in the distance stop sailing to gaze at the beam of red and black thrusting into the sky.

I wince. "It's the first gate."

The image of Titans coming out of the ground infects my mind. We're hundreds of miles away from the mountain tops, which makes it impossible to see them over the horizon. What we do see is the red beam. The titans are going to be marching to Crale and Jura, wreaking havoc in their path.

It's as if the world is ending in front of our eyes. The sky fades, no longer bright blue. It begins to turn into a bright red, the same color as the demonic realm. Malik's bringing hell to our planet itself.

"Where do we go, Kedar...," Laila asks in a hushed whisper, smearing the blood off the side of her face. We're both slashes of blood and grime. The pain renders me a walking corpse.

"Sulalat Basal," I huff, as I drag her closer and closer to the sand. "It's the perfect place for us to escape to."

She snorts, coughing. "The hell are we going to do once we get there?"

Ripples of agony tear through my chest as I feel the stab wounds of Nezzar's bones open up. Laila notices this, pressing a palm to my torn tunic.

I try blinking away the pain. "It should be the safest place we can go."

"The Dynasty is the farthest from Nisf Thueban," I explain, trying to initiate some hope in Laila's expression. "We'll have plenty of time to mend our wounds."

"It'll take us maybe ten weeks to get there," She replies, but there's a sliver of perseverance in her eyes. "Then we can kill Malik."

"Kill him?" I stutter as I gently help her to the ground. We sit on the surface of the sand, reveling in the sounds of waves crashing around us. "Omar's in there. I know it. Malik can't—"

"Kedar. He's gone." Her boldness makes me regret suggesting it. "There's no way we can get a sliver of your brother back."

The calling of the sea brushes against my eardrums as I scrunch my boots in the sand. Ruffling my hair, I smear the dirt on my cheek. "We have to try."

"He's gone, Kedar. You and I saw what he did. What he did to *me*." I glance at her absent hand. In a way, she's right. But still, I can't get the thought out of my mind.

"He's lost, not gone. I will lead him to the light." Laila glances at the sand in response, scratching her nose ring. "Once we get out of Sulalat, I promise that's the first thing we'll do."

"I trust you," she replies, averting her gaze to my wrist. There's fear that radiates in her expression when she widens her eyes. "What is that?"

The Sign of Malik's is in the middle of my left wrist. It's small compared to the imprint on Malik's chest.

I convulse and grip my wrist, clenching my eyes together. "Dragons, that stings!"

506

"It's that thing that was on all of the demons," she begins, shaking her head in denial. "It turned the Veils into those monsters." There's a long pause before she speaks again. "What's going to happen to you?"

"I don't know," I sniff. "It just... hurts. Bad."

Even with the pain, there's a faint glow beneath my skin. I feel powerful yet powerless at the same time. The more pain that Mark inflicts on me, the more demonic magic begins to channel through me, slowly but surely.

I lay my head back on the sand while muttering curses.

"Kedar?" she scoots next to me, a blue aura rising from her fingertips. "Let me try healing you."

"No." I desperately shake my head as the pain subsides, like a horrific storm passing over. "I'm fine. I promise."

"Then get up," she demands. Trying to ignore the agony, I stand, helping Laila up as she holds the stub of her left arm close. Her gauze is soaked in blood. "We have to get off this island."

She rests her palm against my chest, heaving a heavy sigh before glancing up at me.

"Kedar... Thank you."

"For what?"

"I felt like I was supposed to die," she admits. "You didn't give up on me."

The gentleness in my voice comforts my soul. If there's anything that can make me forget about everything we've been through, it's her words.

I wrap my arm around her waist. We embrace, never letting go. She makes my mind clear. I pat her head as she nuzzles against my collarbone. Even my wounds don't hurt as much anymore.

As she pulls away, she doesn't take her eyes off me. "We need to hitch a ride on a boat."

Laila takes off her torn-up cloak and lets it rest in the sand, leaving her dented armor. My tunic has a couple of shreds torn into it. On my belt is the *Kathi* and the bone dagger.

"How's that going to happen?" I answer before Laila glances to the lake, noticing a small fishing boat in the distance.

Inside is an old man, a fishing line in his other hand. It's small, but big enough for us to fit in. Laila limps to the shorelines, calling out and waving her other arm. "Hello?! Help us, please!"

There's a small smirk that contorts my expression, even with the beaming red lights in the clouds above. Malik has made a mistake letting us survive.

Nezzar, Rubim, Judah, and Lamia will fall. Whatever Malik's planning, I'll find a way to save my brother. Expel Malik from his body. But it's easier said than done.

I furrow my brows as I remember Onyx's words. They echo through my mind over and over.

Find the Astral Wizard.

While I do love watching ants struggle, I do not believe that they have struggled enough.

EPILOGUE

T he world is broken. My seal has been abolished.

The devil I've sealed a millennia ago has been running rampant for all of winter and spring. Violence drips at every corner of the planet. Basal once said: *The world will end when I will it. Judgement will occur, and those who have been saved and believe in the Dragon with all of their heart will be saved by the will of Shaytan.*

Even the Jurans hope they'll be chosen. Others have sought redemption, looking for a sign of good from their gods. Millions of elves, Fariks, humans, and goblins have waited, waited for the day they will be taken to the paradise above, seeking mercy.

It never comes.

The red beam in the sky tells me all I need to know. The First gate has been opened. Titans have wreaked havoc across Jura and Crale, casualties mounting in the millions. The All-Seeing eye tells me that corpses riddle the ground, bones are crushed, and the grass has become stained with blood.

510

Basalia is next. The walls around Pyria are torn down, and the demons assist their titan brothers to eat Hayan's flesh.

I know I can stop this. Stop the will of the demons. Get rid of the source of our misery. But it is impossible without my magic. I have seen the wills of hell myself before, many years ago. But that is when my mana is present.

Sealing Malik has made my magic dormant, absent.

Nezzar, Rubim, Lamia, and the Farik Judah are his new prophets. As such, the news of countries and their armies falling like flies has spread faster than wildfire, the Dragon's War halting.

In the fourth or fifth week, the countries have sought to get rid of this army of hell. Armageddon is what they call it. Vania is a safe haven because their country sits on a body of water. They've provided forces to merge with Sulalat, Lauvee, Ultum, Gardon, Hexia, and Basalia. Crale's army is demolished. So they can't consider asking them to join the fight.

The scholars are doubtful of their victory, saying: Woe unto you all, accept thy fate! Our gods have forsaken us!

Their chants echo through the barracks, the scribes preaching and warning about the armies and their deaths. Some soldiers end it all, hanging on trees. The All-Seeing Eye has told me that the citizens have lost hope. Only the soldiers are the people they have confidence in.

The battle occurs. Demons and Hayans die on both sides. It is the first time I have ventured out of my cottage in a hundred years to observe the battle along with the Eye. It is meaningless to assist them. I am no longer a threat to Malik. I am a shell of my former self.

The demons won. Hayans get crushed, the demons feasting. The monsters keep marching, plundering, and pillaging every town on their ruthless paths.

It is then that the second gate opens on the sixth week.

The gate is in Basalia, situated near the town Jiya. The town already mists in blood. Citizens kill each other, blaming one another for the deaths of their families and loved ones, trying to come up with an answer for their agonies.

Where is a hero? They shout. Help us, O god! Do not leave us to die!

Our holy books are nothing but pieces of paper! There is nothing left to read when we have been left behind!

Every word I write in this journal makes my hands shake with fear. I realize— the dead cannot read my literature. When this world is converted into a planet of demons, nobody will ever read my documents.

They only stop when Malik and his new vessel arrive. They see him as god, manipulating the masses. He shows his miracles because he comes in the form of a pure spirit, not reminiscent of a demon at all.

The last ninety days have been nothing short of unpleasant. With the first two gates open, what will happen next? Is our planet turning into a hellhole? What will happen to me?

In the eighth week, I witnessed Malik's false form. The All-Seeing Eye shows me the masses chanting the same name, over and over again. They bow down like Juran's praying to their altar. Malik, O Malik! You've tried to ruin this world yet again, and this time you have succeeded?

Malik's vessel is reminiscent of his former one. Although they look different, I know that it is his heart beating inside the vessel. His skin is a slight, dark brown, with no hair on his head. He wears a white robe, replicating the look of my Astral monks by wearing brown slippers and a golden necklace around his collarbone.

They all scream, reveling in the fact that he is a savior. The first time I saw him, he descended from the clouds, saving the people from a demon attacking them in their town. To them, he is a god. To me, he is the devil.

The world is not broken. The world is shapeshifting. Converting into the existence of Malik's power. The King of Demons. God will save us, our women, our children. No, I need to save us. If the magic inside of me is present, then this won't have happened.

If you've flipped to a random page, you must be wondering who I am.

I am the first to harness Astral Magic. In the early history of this world, I've trained a hundred others to become harnessers of magic like me.

One of them is named Onyx. I've been observing him, watching him. I have seen him die on the Nisf Thueban. Onyx is the last out of one hundred that are alive. I have no knowledge of who else harnesses the holy magic now, as it is the only thing that can truly reverse the effects of demonic magic.

I will wait for Onyx's underlings. Ruby and Vantos, if I can recall. Before my student passed, he let them know of my existence. He is a prodigy, indeed. But he does not surpass me in the slightest.

As for now, I will let them venture to my cottage. And hope that I can teach them Astral Magic.

A saying exists. It goes:

There will always be a sliver of light in pure darkness.

I am not the light. Yet I wonder every day who that might be.

ADORCISM

AN OMAR SHORT STORY

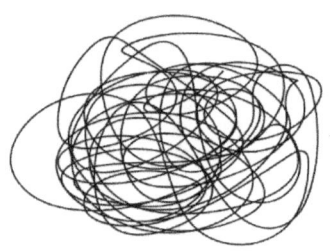

*I*t's cold. *Too damn cold.* My skin is ice.

Is this my grave? I ponder, feeling the cold water touching my skin. My body is on its side. Murky liquid covers half of my body, which is submerged in the essence. Treading my fingers through it, I huff as my fingers brush against the sloshy dirt in its depths.

Fatigue ripples through my shivering bones. I blink open my eyes, stifling a groan as I decipher the darkness. A scream for help vibrates through my brain, but not my mouth. Only a hoarse squawk comes out.

It's not a grave, I reply to myself. *It's a cell.*

Grasping at the frozen metal bars, I pull myself up. My legs are shaky, barely offering me any support to keep myself upright. Wiping the dirt and gunk off my face, I glance at the floor. There's the puddle I've woken up in, immersed in a cloud of gray and brown. Curling my toes, I dig them deeper into the muddy ground.

A bed sits at the edges of the cage against a dark wall. Breathing heavily, I sit, noticing the white garments that cover my lower body. Scrunching my hands through my hair, I clench my teeth.

Where am I?

Then there's a grim thought that crosses my mind.

Who am I?

The clicks and clacks of boots interrupt me before I can remember. My eyes adjust to the dark. I'm imprisoned in a room covered in black rock. *Obsidian.* There's a door in front of me that swiftly opens wide, the bright light blinding me.

Shielding myself with my hand, I get up, walking towards the metal bars. Across from my cage is the shadow of a man, holding a shining lantern.

"You've awakened." Their voice ripples like stone skipping across the sea. It's a Farik that stands in front of me. Wearing a red robe, the inner fabric is a dark black, he has a torch in his left hand that illuminates my dark world. A long gash runs from his eyebrow to the tip of his doggy nose.

My head aches as I struggle to keep myself afloat. If I pass out, there's no telling what he'll do to me. The dog doesn't seem too surprised by the absence of my response. "You've been asleep for many days. Do you remember your name?"

Shuddering, I breathe a sigh. As my brain churns, there are spitting images that form in my mind. Images of war. Images of a man who looks just like me, leading the charge. It's like pieces of fragments. Memories that I'm not familiar with. Not even a name comes to mind. Just shards of glass, impossible to put back together.

I grasp at the icy metal again, our faces inches away. There's a slight croak in my voice. "No. I don't know who I am."

Even my voice isn't familiar to me.

520

I look down at the Farik as his hand reaches towards something in his cloak. There's a ring of keys around his index finger. Stepping back, I gulp. *What's he planning?*

The rusty, old clanks of the cage echo through the obsidian chamber. Blinking away my fear, I realize the red in the Farik's eyes. *Is he even real?*

I expect death, but he holds out his hand. A smile twists on his face as his white fangs sparkle against the vibrant torchlight.

"You are the Vessel."

Obey, obey. Obey. OBEY.

It repeats over and over. Their chants don't stop. I can't count the days anymore. My wrists are contorted into horrid directions. Exhaustion cripples my soul. Whenever the Farik comes to my cell, it is time. Time for my 'awakening,' as he calls it.

For the past thirty days, they've chanted that same word after strapping me to a wooden table.

They tell me that I am a god. I am the body of their god. I am the harbinger and the messenger of rejoicing to the Hayan people. I am one with the King, the Devil, and the Berserker.

"No!" I will scream in response.

"Unfortunately, this is the only way to awaken your dormant bloodlust," the Farik says coldly. He's broken my ankles. The tendons on my body have been severed to limit my movements. They've shaved my head before using my body as a dummy for their blades. Cuts that bleed all over my mattress riddle all over my frame.

I don't know why this is happening to me. To them, I'm a piece of flesh with a pair of eyes. Over time, I've come to know my name. *Omar.* Before the Farik and his minions torture me, he'll say softly: "Hello, Omar. Our act of adorcism must be commenced."

Blood drips down the side of my waist. It's the only warmth I can have in this cold hell. Obeying the Farik's orders promises me freedom. The back of my mind pleads to obey, but my heart pushes back against the idea. Obeying him will make me lose myself.

They think that I'm a god. I'm not.

"Please, whatever you guys want me to do, I don't want to do it!" I tell the Farik, huffing in pain. "Just let me go, please..."

"SHUT UP!" A sting pummels my waist. He furrows his brows, digging the wooden stake deeper into my gut. It misses each of my vital organs, keeping me barely alive. Days pass before I can talk back to him again.

My resilience only angers him more. Slashing me in my back only makes my body rot more. *Obey him,* parts in my mind tell me. But I don't. I don't know these people. I don't know what they want, what they truly want.

A couple of days ago, my veins began to glow. When the Farik visits my cell this time, he has a smile that stretches from cheek to cheek, like a demon smirking in satisfaction. I've been convulsing in my bed, shaking and trying to mask my sobs. Nothing can answer why I've been subjected to this. *What horrors have I done in my past life?*

It takes me minutes to realize the dark red that begins to develop my sense of sight. The corners of my vision submit to darkness.

"What the hell?" I curse, leaning against the wall as I sit up from my bed. The bars aren't bars anymore. They are made of severed arms. The walls outside my cell are made of eyes in the flesh of a meat. My breathing makes the eyes blink once, twice, then two more times. Their pupils are a blood red ring, the sclera a void black. "Am I going insane?"

Misty air of crimson invades the air around me. I try not to breathe it in, but I cough at the stench. It smells like I'm in a room with hundreds of dead bodies. My throat constricts, making me choke on my spit.

I'm going to die, aren't I? I think, looking down at my shaking hands. *I'm going to die.*

My whimpers in fear evolve to horror as a hand outstretches from the wall of eyes. Their red gleams explore my soul. Covering myself with my two arms, I press my swollen wrists against my eyelids. *Let it stop. Please, let it stop.*

Looking through the little slits in my fingers, I see a figure slip in my cell. Their low growl sends shivers down my spine.

Shaking, I remove my broken wrists from my face, gazing at the beast upon me. Their skin is pale, a singular eye in the middle of their head replicating the eyes that line the walls. The voice of the beast is the voice of a thousand souls, slicing through every one it touches.

"Do not hide from me."

Wings spread from the beast's back. It lurches closer, their feet squelching against the muddy floor. They stop at the edge of my bed, their breath churning with desire.

My teeth chatter as I struggle to find the words to speak. "W-What are you?"

His gaze pierces through me. I'm a bug to him. The beast doesn't answer, beginning to transform— morphing, their eyes replicating in two, their skin turning from white to a golden brown, curls sprouting from their head.

I'm staring at a glaring reflection of myself.

Confusion ripples through me as my veins glow in response. They make me look holy, clean, and clear. No scars or whip marks are sprinkled through their frame. The beast is perfect. A wolf wearing a sheep's skin.

"My name is Malik," they begin. "I've tethered my soul to yours for three years."

I shudder. "What?"

Their two red pupils gleam into my heart. Conjures of death wisp around my cell made of severed arms. The beast growls. "Your awakening has been proven difficult, indeed. It took Njuperoxia to erase your old self and paint it again. I thought the adorcisms would work once you lost all your memories."

It inches closer, our noses almost touching. I'm glaring at a mirror— the only difference being that the reflection isn't me. "Even up until now, you resist our pleas."

Sweat drips from my forehead as the room rises in temperature every second. "Pleads? What pleads—"

"It is the fact that you are a god." There's devilish cackles echoing through the air that agree with the beast. Goosebumps form on my neck as I try to keep eye contact with Malik. "You are destined to be my vessel. The demonic magic that has been birthed inside you since you were part of the army outranks every follower of mine. I know you will be able to be the host of my essence."

"Why the hell would I ever sacrifice myself to you?" I cough, my teeth chattering. "I'm not a toy to whoever the hell you people are!"

Malik furrows his brows, his expression contorting in anger. He latches onto my shoulders, a curling sting vibrating through my body as he reopens my wounds from two weeks ago. Rotting blood spills down as I choke, sobbing.

"Perhaps I should convince you." He pushes me onto the bed, and I shriek, trying to slap him away. There's an abhorrent gleam in his eyes.

"Discipline is something all of us need." The demonic reflection of me pierces his nails into my skin, drawing blood. I can't move; my existing injuries prevent me from even lifting a finger. Wiggling my way out won't work, as my hips and legs ache from slashes, bruises, and cuts.

"Do not forget this dosage of pain."

The seven words brand my soul. My begs and screams are nothing but gibberish to him. He claws at my face, a peeling sensation sending my nerve endings into shock. My pleas are feral as he peels off the right side of my face.

Blood seeps into my vision, my tears only enhancing my agony. The eyes on the wall watch as the beast ruins me. I choke, gargling in blood as he doesn't hesitate to stop. My chest and right leg are his next meal.

I'm a snake shedding off my skin in the worst way possible. Numbness shuts down my nervous system as black dots fill my vision. Malik puts his other hand on my half-skinned forehead, as I feel a rush of energy flow through me. *Adrenaline.*

The drug keeps me awake in this abhorrent act. It forces me to widen my eyes as I watch the beast slowly peel back my skin, my red muscles pulsating and oozing with blood.

Please... Let me die...

There's no positive thought that crosses my mind anymore. Blinking in agony, I see the beast tug against the skin on my toenails, successfully tearing half of my skin off. Huffing and wheezing, I groan, spitting blood. Malik hands me a smirk as he sees my gaze. His eyes reflect the liquid he spills.

"Why..." My voice is stale. The agony rushes in, my body vibrating in shock. "Why... why..."

He hisses. "All you had to do was *obey.* Surrender your body unto me, to build an unfractured world."

It doesn't take long until I fade to unconsciousness.

525

The spider is Malik. I am the prey that lies in the web of violence. My skin hasn't bathed in sunlight for the past season. The healers and followers who crowd around the Farik tend to my broken wrists, but leave my skinned body untouched.

There are visions in my head now. I wonder if it is because I am a slug, lying in my mattress. These visions always involve the glaring image of the same man. They happen after Malik visits my cell.

To him, I am the one who will be at the top of the world. I am the key to breaking the shackles that render him unable to be in the physical realm. There are times when I try to talk back, undermining his words. It ends when he chokes me until I see grey.

The Farik is one of the four prophets destined to worship me. He's mentioned the Five Gates of hell, transforming Haya into his paradise. Each sounds more grim than the rest.

But the man in my visions keeps arising in my mind. The scar on his nose, the violent and daring attitude that he possesses, always focused on the heat of the battle— it is familiar.

What was he to me?

Today is another "adorcism." It is a ritual designed to convert me into my "messianic" transformation. Convince me to become indebted and surrender to a vessel for their god.

The lock on my cell clicks and churns with the metal key. There is the Farik in his robe of darkness. Two more of his followers stream behind him, standing in front of the mattress I lay on.

One hoists me onto his back, the event happening within seconds. I barely offer resistance. Blinking away my fuzzy vision, I try focusing as they exit my obsidian box.

The hallway we trek down is lined with stone bricks. I'm the only person they've imprisoned— lines of other cells are embedded in their hellish basement. Their cells are different from mine, without the obsidian walls and the enhanced security. Then we enter the room where the Farik tortures me out of my mind.

"No, not again, please," I wheeze, cursing. The Farik shakes his head, licking his canines as I see all of the weapons that have plunged into my skin before. Axes, swords, whips, knives, daggers, spears. They stare at me.

"Do not test me." The Farik's voice is stern as always. "There will be something... different about our adorcism."

"Different?"

"You'll see."

In the middle of the room is a circular table, a symbol etched into the wood. His followers are surrounding the table, muttering words that I can't comprehend. Never has this happened before at my past adorcisms. *What the hell is he planning?*

Their chants interrupt my thoughts. "Adorate Cultum Mortis."

With a grunt, the man carrying me lays me on the table face down. I ache from the feeling of my non-existent skin piercing into the rough crevices. They stretch my limbs out, tying each one tightly to the table. Their unholy words mute my groans and mutters of pain.

"Adorate Cultum Mortis," they chant. The glaring shine of the Farik's dagger stirs me with worry. In an instant, it begins to glow dark red, flames enveloping the sharp metal.

"Silence." The room deafens with a snap of his fingers. Shuffling out of my leather bands doesn't give me leverage. It only makes my ankles and wrists ache harder. "I will officially experiment my newfound spell on Omar, tethering him solely to the demonic realm."

He grasps at the white robe I wear, ripping it to expose my bare back to the cold. Before I can protest, the demonic blade slashes through my skin and my muscles. My wounds from Malik have barely healed, but here we are, dicing my body into bits once again.

Yelping in pain, I revel in the shallow cuts the Farik makes, carving me like a pumpkin. It's better than the stabs I've gone through before. I'm used to this. The pain doesn't affect me anymore. My blood is something that I expect to be spilled.

The room envelops in a harsh darkness, the only light now coming from the shining aura of the blade. Minutes pass, the Farik making me resist squirming. His hand pushes against my neck, making me gag and choke. My muffling pleads only make his followers amused in my pain.

I want to die, I think again.

He steps back once he finishes his grim painting. The second he releases me, illusions fill my mind.

It's like someone flipped the table upside down, leaving me hanging over hell.

Within the sea of fire, there are marching skeletons, weeping in pain as they trek through their prison. I sob, my tears dripping down the right side of my face and sizzling into the blaze below. The skeletons click and clack in response, grasping at the little drops of liquid.

They are in a spacious canyon in hell. The ground is not made of sand and rock; it is made of dark red, pulsating flesh. On the surface are creatures which I can barely describe—

beings with multiple heads, fangs that are sharper than a sword, veins pumping their mana through their frame.

In the depths of the ravine is a familiar figure, his hand outstretched to touch mine.

Malik.

He's still in his clean, sinless form. The healthy reflection of my physical appearance only reminds me of the extent of the beast's power. We are destined to be one, according to him. I repeat the Farik's grim words. *You are the Vessel.*

"It surprises me how Judah succeeded with his spell to make us meet once and for all," he begins, floating towards me like an angel. The lies that he speaks gleam like pyrite.

"Hello, Omar."

A dark red orb is enveloped in his hand, and he aims at my chest. I'm still dangling from my chains like a hunk of meat. His hunter gaze reminds me how the beasts will always indulge in the bait. Whatever Malik says, I'll never succumb to his whims. The world rests in my hands if these people aren't bluffing. Giving up will result in sending millions into an inferno.

"Let's make you remember who you are." The blazing orb in his hands flashes through the air in less than a second, as my eyes widen, going straight to my chest. I close my eyes in anticipation of a wave of pain, but what I get is a stream of memories.

War. Battle. Bloodlust. Revenge. All from one person.

My brother.

Kedar.

I didn't want to be chained to a life of violence. After seeing my parents die, all I wanted to do was allow others to live in peace.

Kedar was the prison that molded me into becoming like him. It began in Pyria when I watched him kill a man for food. Then he joined the army. I wrote unanswered letters to him during his first two years of service. It was then that he forced me to join the battlefields himself.

I never imagined running around with an ax. Seeing life fade from people's eyes only reminded me of my mother and father. Kedar wanted me to be worse than him. To be a killer who chased revenge at every moment of their life.

These memories wash over like tsunamis, leading to the day I stand on that podium and lose them all.

In Alfdan, my resentment for him has grown. The more I remember, the more I realize how I've been rejecting Malik and Judah.

Malik has claimed he was a god to me once. Gods are omniscient, present in every way possible. Every night, I wish for my parents to be alive again, their smiles radiating against the distant sunlight. I miss them more than Kedar ever can. He's used our parents to mask his reason for his bloodlust. What I truly want is to be in their arms once more.

"You understand it, don't you?" His piercing gaze is convincing. Everyone deserves true peace. Malik told me how the Five Gates will transform the world into his kingdom. A utopia of peace. Many people reject change. Like me.

Underneath the dark, demonic magic is a god trying to cleanse and rebuild the world. With his rule, there will be no crying, no tears that come from the people's eyes. No death. We lock eyes as if we're thinking the same exact thing. All they've been trying to do this whole time is convince me.

Standing in my way is the belief that the world is still good.

It's not.

It crawls with sin, lust, envy, violence, and hatred. Regaining my memories has only opened my eyes. I am a phoenix.

"Malik… does death achieve peace?" My voice is stagnant, searching for a reason to trust the beast. Malik knows my mindset has changed, his fangs sparkling against the blazing fire below us.

"It does. It makes the pain stop. If we become one, nothing is stopping us. You will receive your desires, and so will I." He crosses his arms, his dark red aura keeping him afloat.

An array of silence follows between us. *Am I truly destined for this?* I ask myself. *Do I make a deal with the devil?*

"Your mind speaks to me." His red eyes interpret my thoughts. Through the hellfire, there is paradise. Is Malik a solution or a problem to the world?

My heart pumps in time with my breaths. The shakiness of my fingertips correlates with my mind, barely able to comprehend what I can do with Malik's power. *Create a utopia.*

And see my father and mother again.

"Bring my parents back to life," I begin. His expression shifts, surprised by my demands.

He rests his chin on his fingertips, eyes focused on the fire below. The heat feels comforting now, like a warmth that I've known.

"It has been decided."

We stare at each other for decades.

We are one. The true essence of life is to chase peace by any means. Haya is broken, the Dragon's War, the two Jezzebel wars, and the Cleansing, staining our planet forever. It can only be fixed by us.

These demons around me are not from hell; they are from heaven. There is a reason why some call them fallen angels. People who have died chasing their dreams of peace.

"Malik. My body is yours," I whisper, his dark aura beginning to surround me like a casket. My mind repeats the phrase over and over, and I feel myself begin to change, evolve, and become ready for the day we merge into one. It comes steadily.

Everything swirls around me.

I am not a human anymore.

I am not a human anymore.

I am ascending.

I am ascending.

I am a God.

I am Malik.

AUTHOR'S NOTE AND ACKNOWLEDGMENTS

T hank you.

Thank you to all who have set their eyes on this book. I am thankful for you and everyone else's support. Judah's Prophecy was the first book I have ever finished and written in my whole life. It was first imagined in August of 2023, and I've been writing and working on this series ever since. There will be a sequel to the book. It is the second arc of the story. I won't reveal its title yet but I won't leave you guys hanging.

Kedar and Laila will be back.

Two things that helped me write this would be music and consistency. If you've ever wanted to write a book on your own, it's important to maintain the practice of at least working on your writing every day except for other factors like work, school, etc. Through working with my book, I've explored many genres of music. I went through a heavy metal phase when writing Act Three, but I listened to a lot of hip hop while writing, along with classical, Spanish, and Filipino music. If you have ever wondered what the original titles of this novel were supposed to be, here you go: Silent Jade Act 1, The Jade of the Mountain, The Jade of the Desert, The False Prophecy, and The Entrance of the Demon. Last but not least, Thank you so much to my cousin, who developed this whole idea for me in the first place. I'm not trying to get too personal, but the idea of Kedar's story came from my cousin showing me some fantasy books. I think it definitely sparked some sort of curiosity and interest in me and made me want to write a book. Kudos to them. I'll work on the sequel and release it by 2027. You'll enjoy it, I promise. But other than that, farewell.

People who'd like to personally acknowledge and thank for helping me complete my book (or give me ideas):

Iman, Abubakr, James, Jackson, Isabel, Sam, Jacob, Zaid, Ms. Hassan, Mr. Cardamone, Sadman, Aroush, Leo, Timi, Gabriel (the lesser one), Karmanya, and Jester.

G. AUGUSTINE is the author who's

spent 2 years of his high school days writing and working on *Judah's Prophecy.* I still have no idea how he's managed to maintain good (decent) grades. He's probably stressing over the sequel of this book right now. You can find him on instagram @gabr1elaugustine.